ONE MINUTE IT MATTERED WHO AND WHAT THEY WERE. THE NEXT IT DIDN'T.

The next instant was about nothing but chemistry, wanting, and gripping, starving needs that had yearned for this connection for far too long. The moment where Destiny demanded obedience.

Kestra's fingers slid into the crisp, curling hair at Noah's collar. She couldn't help herself. She had dreamed of him as often as he had dreamed of her. Whether she would admit to her needs or not, she craved the reality of him. The feel of his thick hair curling between and around her fingers was rich realism. Her opposite hand skimmed fast and hot over his clothing in search of far more carnal sensations. Kestra shaped him with her fingers and palm, down his chest, over his ribs, and around to his back, a thorough exploration of the musculature of his flank.

The Demon King responded.

Noah

The Nightwalkers

Jacquelyn Frank

ZEBRA BOOKS
KENSINGTON PUBLISHING CORP.
www.kensingtonbooks.com

ZEBRA BOOKS are published by

Kensington Publishing Corp.
850 Third Avenue
New York, NY 10022

All Kensington titles, imprints, and distributed lines are available at special quantity discounts for bulk purchases for sales promotion, premiums, fund-raising, educational, or institutional use.

Special book excerpts or customized printings can also be created to fit specific needs. For details, write or phone the office of the Kensington Special Sales Manager: Attn. Special Sales Department. Kensington Publishing Corp., 850 Third Avenue, New York, NY 10022. Phone: 1-800-221-2647.

ISBN-13: 978-0-8217-8069-5
ISBN-10: 0-8217-8069-7

First Printing: September 2008
10 9 8 7 6 5 4 3 2 1

Printed in the United States of America

Prologue

"Whosoever wishes to know the fate of Demonkind must consult these prophecies . . .

". . . as magic once more threatens the time, as the peace of the Demon yaws toward insanity . . .

"We must enforce ourselves more strictly as the time approaches. In the age of the rebellion of the Earth and Sky, when Fire and Water break like havoc upon all the lands, the Eldest of the old will return, will take his mate, and the first child of the element of Space will be born, playmate to the first child of Time, born to the Enforcers . . ."

—Excerpts from
The Lost Demon Prophecy

"Kes . . . what are you doing?"

"I thought I'd wash my hair," came the whispered, tart reply over the slightly static connection. "What do you *think* I'm doing?"

Jim chuckled softly under his breath before reaching to tap the mike of his wireless earpiece, just to annoy her with the noise. Then he clarified, "I meant I wanted to know which room you're in."

"The Billiard Room," she said dryly, "with an unusually heavy candlestick in one hand." She paused and Jim heard her grunt softly over the open line. He leaned forward a little in his chair to peer at his computer monitor. "I'm in the machine room. Where else would I be?"

"Okay. I was just wondering."

There was another brief pause, full of soft static.

"Incidentally, why do you ask?" she queried at last.

"Oh, no reason. It's just that I have this huge red blob on my infrared screen that looks suspiciously like a security guard heading in your direction," he informed her, snapping his gum in her ear over the mike.

Kestra cursed through her teeth, glanced around with sharp, seeking eyes, and turned her face upward almost out of innate instinct. After a quick calculation in her head, she scuttled rapidly across the vastness of the equipment room and headed straight for one of the air-conditioning turbines. With a running start, she stepped up onto the rim of the large machinery and launched her lithe, dark figure straight up into the air.

There was a clang as her hands just barely made the catch onto a pair of sturdy pipes that ran across the high ceiling. She immediately began to swing herself until she was able to get enough momentum to hook her feet over the piping. Without a single further sound, she wriggled herself up into the darkness of the tight plumbing. She sprawled over it, lying across it as if it were a casual cotton hammock instead of a series of conduits that ran both hot and cold against the press of her flesh. Once secured in the shadows of the one direction nine out of ten rent-a-cops invariably failed to look in, all she could do was wait. She covered the earpiece on her ear with her hand, not wanting to risk any chance of Jim or random static giving away her location.

She didn't have long to wait before the guard made his appearance. Kes rolled her eyes shut for a moment, thinking that Jim had cut his half-assed warning pretty damn close.

The guard had no reason to hide his progress, so she could hear his footsteps from the moment he entered the stairwell just outside the door leading into the room. The door clanged open, recoiling off its backstop as the guard released the metal handle that he'd opened it with. In spite of all this noise, Kestra made very certain her breathing never went above a barely audible whisper of sound.

The guard clomped across the concrete floor, walking the straight path between the rows of turbines on one side, and water heaters on the other. He flicked on a Maglite and swept it back and forth over the dark shadows surrounding him. Kestra closed her eyes briefly, praying to whatever part of the universe it was that protected people like her. Then she watched the approaching man carefully for any signs that he took note of the tiny green lights on the undersides of half the gas heaters, which were guaranteed to be out of place.

He didn't. He made it to the far wall, turned, and retraced his steps. He passed within a foot of her both times, but of course did not look up. He barreled out of the basement door with a noisy bang, his clomping footsteps echoing away up the stairwell.

Kestra exhaled a half breath of relief. After she was reasonably sure the guard was far enough away and had no intention of immediately returning, she leveraged herself out of her makeshift hidey-hole. She laid her forearms along two narrow pipes and, using them like a pair of parallel bars, swung her legs down. She released, allowing the momentum to somersault her over just once, then lofted into a perfect landing on the dusty warehouse floor.

Resisting the habit of taking a gymnast's bow, she swiped at the sweat dotting her forehead, smearing the dust and silt from the exteriors of the pipes across it, and turned her attention to her communications system and her smart-ass partner.

"Thanks for the warning, James," she said with low heat.

"You're welcome." He tried to sound bratty, but she could tell he was relieved to hear from her.

"James, I thought you said there was no one on the premises," she hissed.

Jim winced, knowing that he was definitely going to be in

a huge amount of trouble for being wrong about that. "There's not supposed to be. The guy's off schedule. I'll let you know when he moves on to the next building."

"Not good enough. I want him out of my perimeter completely."

"Well, what am I supposed to do? Kidnap him?"

"There's an idea," she retorted, kneeling down in front of the turbine that had just helped her escape the guard's notice. She shrugged out of her backpack and withdrew her last two square packets.

Kestra left the backpack behind and scurried low across the floor to the next gas heater. She rolled gently onto her back and reached beneath the unit. There was the distinct clang of metal on metal as the strong magnet on the back of the packet stuck to the underbelly of the furnace. She flicked the switch on the front and waited while the lights went from yellow to green.

"The point is," she continued as she rolled out from beneath the unit and moved cautiously to the next one, "that I specifically said no civilians in the kill zone. It was your job to see to it that's what I got. That is why I spent a month timing this operation just right."

"It's not my fault the guy changed his routine, Kestra."

"Make it your fault, James," she bit back as she hesitated next to the last furnace. "Make it your responsibility. You have twenty minutes to get him out of the kill zone. I don't care *how* you do it, just do it! And there better not be anyone else."

"There isn't. You and the guard are the only two heat sources in the entire warehouse row, save a rat or two." There was a distinct pause. "Do you have any suggestions on how I can protect your civilian without getting arrested?"

Kestra thought about that for a moment, using the time it took to attach the last device to the last heater in order to mull over the situation.

"How long does it normally take for him to round off the row and start on the docks?"

"There are three buildings in the row. You're the first on

the round. If he follows form, it'll take well over an hour. And if he rounds onto the docks, he's going to spot you. I don't care how sneaky you are, Kes, you don't want him wandering your escape route."

"Damn." Kestra slid out from beneath the furnace and stood up. She dusted off her backside with more violence than necessary and marched toward her backpack.

Then she stopped and cocked her head to the side, her incredibly light eyes brightening just a little more as she thought of a possible solution.

"Oh, James?"

"Yeah, Kes?"

"Do any of the buildings *opposite* those in this row have an alarm system?"

"All of them. Take your pick."

"And are they part of our rent-a-cop's minimum-wage jurisdiction?"

"Why, *yes*, they *are*!" Jim gasped comically, knowing she was already done formulating her plan.

"Now, call me crazy, but if you were a security guard and one of the alarms in one of your buildings went off, you'd run like hell to check it out, wouldn't you?"

"Oh, you're definitely crazy," Jim agreed with a chuckle. "And you're also right. But how do you plan to set off an alarm and not get caught? Don't we usually do that the opposite way, where you *don't* set off the alarm? Do you even know how to set one off?"

"How hard can it be?"

"And not get caught," he reminded her.

"Mmm."

"And blow up the row . . . ?" Jim added.

"Yup."

"And not get caught," he reiterated most importantly.

"Uh-huh."

* * *

Almost exactly twenty minutes later, Kestra dropped from the dock into the rear of the speedboat docked there. She whipped off the tie line and punched the ignition button. The motor roared to life; the only sound possibly louder was the blare of the alarm in the distance.

Kestra aimed the boat directly out of the harbor and toward the open ocean. She glanced down at the cabin when James stuck his head out of the hatch.

"You forgot to blow up the warehouses," he said dryly.

"Yeah, I know."

The row of warehouses blew up.

Chapter 1

The Miserable Princess
A Demon Fairy Tale

Once upon a time, fairly long ago, there lived a Princess. This Princess was in need of a husband, or so her father thought. She had a responsibility to wed an upstanding male who might one day become King of all their people. She had a responsibility to have children who would become strong and powerful members of their society. That was what Princesses were supposed to do during that time very long ago.

However, this particular Princess, though she was kind and good-hearted, did not like to be responsible, she did not like being told what to do, and, most of all, she did not want a husband.

One day, the Princess, who was named Sarah, was forced to attend a competition between the males of her father's people. She did not wish to go, but her father had told her that if she did not, he would choose a husband for her and she would have to be satisfied with his taste. He would hear no arguments, for he had lost his patience with his headstrong daughter.

So the Princess went to the royal booth and sat in her chair and frowned at everyone. She had to be there, but she did not have to pretend to be happy. Her father had said nothing about being happy or nice to anyone.

Princess Sarah looked around at the field of competitors with bored, cornflower blue eyes. She feebly brushed back her long, golden curls as she sighed. This was the third such competition her father had arranged. The Princess knew he hoped that somewhere on that field there would be a Demon who would finally catch her eye. There was no real reason why her eye should not be pleased, because Demon males were as wondrously handsome as Demon females were breathtakingly beautiful. Certainly they were all well mannered, elegant, and highly educated after so many decades of immortal life.

The Princess, however, was only 110 years old. She thought she was far too young to think about tying herself down to a husband who would probably want babies and obedience. Male Demons were notorious for their arrogance and their need of total control of all things they felt they had a right to control. The Princess did not need another person telling her what to do all the time. She wanted to choose in her own time, when she felt right and ready, and when she found a male who looked upon her as an equal, rather than a worker who required orchestration.

Sarah shuddered at her own thoughts.

In spite of their high-handedness, males of her race were far better than the human mortals when it came to the matter of marriage. The idea of being treated like property, a man's chattel he could use and dispose of in the fashion of his own choosing, was a nightmare.

As for Ephraim, the aforementioned King of the Demons, she knew that he held high hopes that she would be one of the rare and lucky Demons who became part of the Imprinting.

The Imprinting was the meshing of the hearts, minds, and souls of a male and a female who were compatible with each other to a point beyond perfection. It was reputed to be a connection that transcended the complexities and intensities of mere love. It was an engagement of power that her father hoped would one day coalesce in her womb and produce the powerful potential of a future King of all Demons.

"Noah, what on earth are you reading to her?" Isabella asked in a curious whisper.

She had just entered her daughter's bedroom, taking in the sight of her two-year-old, who was draped lazily across the current Demon King's lap. Leah was lying on her back in the cradle of Noah's biceps and forearm, with her arms splayed wide, wrists hanging limply as she snored softly and drooled against his silk-covered chest.

The King looked up at his Enforcer, the female counterpart of a pair, and smiled in a way that was both bashful and charming. He winked one gray-green eye at her, his darkly patrician features softened by his mischief.

"It is just a fairy tale," he explained in a hushed voice, folding closed the small book in his hands before setting it onto the floor by his knee.

He reached for the sleeping child in his lap, touching gentle fingertips to her limp form. At that careful caress, Isabella's daughter slowly began to turn from her flesh-and-blood form into the soft, localized cohesion of a cloud of smoke. The young mother held her breath as Noah manipulated the little cloud into her railed bed and, with practiced ease, returned her to her natural weight and form.

Isabella had seen Noah make similar transformations

dozens of times, including to herself. He was a master of the element of Fire, and she did trust him implicitly. She knew from experience that it was very much a harmless trick, taking only the minimum of his awesome skills and power to perform.

As a mother, though, a mother who had until three years ago been all too human and as ignorant of the existence of these elemental beings as most humans were, she couldn't help the concern that fluttered in her stomach as she understood that her child was being manipulated on molecular levels. She laughed at herself mentally for her silly anxieties a moment later. Noah was powerful and well practiced, the basest of requirements the Demon race expected from their elected King. Everything about him broadcast the natural fate he had been born to. He had been crafted out of a mighty lineage of Demon genetics, forged and tempered, having the awesome patience, wisdom, and education required of a great leader.

Even sitting as he was, there was no mistaking the grandeur of his height, nor the sculpture of a physique just as artistically molded as his mind was. He was not a warrior by nature, but neither did he remain on the sidelines in a soft, padded throne while others went into the fray for him. Isabella had fought by his side and she knew how strong he was, how cunning, and, above all, how merciless he could be when he faced an enemy that threatened the things he held dearest to his heart.

However, she felt she knew him better this way, cuddled up with her daughter in his role as a foster uncle who had probably spent as much time with the darling little girl as her own biological parents. Bella had barely given birth when it became very clear that Noah and Leah were going to be inseparable in their adoration for each other. He showered the child with love, attention, and blatant favoritism. All of this in spite of the fact that he had more nieces and nephews of his own blood than Isabella could count.

Bella didn't look too closely at the great fortune of this adulation the King had for her child. As with anything, there were hidden layers to it all, most of it redirected emotions from a man who sat in a position of power, and that kind of enormous sovereignty could be all too lonely. All Bella could see at the moment was that Leah looked diminutive in Noah's embrace, somehow no longer seeming to be growing too fast and too darn independent, as she had been complaining to her child's father just the night before.

Leah was truly in no more danger from the King's power than she was when her Earth Demon father separated the child from gravity and sent her squealing and giggling into the air with barely a backhanded thought as they played. Isabella realized that she was still prone to the occasional human foible of fear, a knee-jerk reaction that was habit more than anything. However, she was always able to overcome her trepidations quickly. All she had to do was think of her Demon husband's highly moral nature, his powerful sense of justice, and the fact that this intense compass also guided many of the Demons in high positions in their society, a category Noah defined even as he fell into it. He made a point of setting the example he intended all others to follow.

"Well, your fairy tale is apparently a great success," Isabella whispered, reaching down for the book with clear curiosity.

Noah turned suddenly, grabbing her wrist and deftly removing the journal from her hold.

"Thanks," he said, tucking the book protectively into a pocket on the inside of his jacket.

Isabella frowned slightly, rubbing her wrist where he'd grabbed her a little too enthusiastically, clearly having forgotten his own strength. It was nothing to her, really. After all, she wasn't human any longer. Well, mostly not. She was a hybrid of ancient Druid and modern human genetics, and since she'd developed significant strength with her other freshman abilities, she'd barely even bruise from the King's rough handling. Still, if she'd been wholly human, that grip would have broken her wrist clean through, and it wasn't like Noah to be so unthinking.

"Time for me to get going," Noah said, gaining his feet quickly and reaching to plant a fast kiss on her still cheek.

With a twist, the Fire Demon morphed into a column of smoke. The column collapsed and scattered across the floor, scudding in all directions for cracks and crevices leading to the outside of the manor.

He was gone barely a second before a storm of dust swept violently into the room, surrounding Isabella's tiny figure. It snapped suddenly into the shape of her husband, his arms already wrapped tight around her and her wrist coming under immediate inspection.

"What the hell is the matter with him?" Jacob barked, his displeasure over the King's rough, thoughtless handling of his bride all too clear in his tone and expression.

Since Isabella had become his Imprinted mate those three short years ago, Jacob had found himself with little tolerance for other men touching her, never mind causing her even the smallest of harm. His possessive temperament was part of the nature of their particular Imprinting.

Until Bella had arrived and threaded herself deeply into the tapestry of Jacob's soul and of his existence, the Imprinting had been so rare that it had only ever been talked about in Demon fairy tales, like the one Noah had been reading to Leah. For the male Enforcer, the intensity of knowing what a rare treasure it was they shared made him irrationally overprotective at times. Still, he was better now than he had been at the start of their relationship. Of course, facing his wife's exasperation and frustration after each excessive incident had played its part.

"I don't know," Isabella murmured in reply to what had been intended as a rhetorical question. "Jacob," she said suddenly, turning in his arms and wrapping anxious fingers around the loose fabric of his burgundy shirt where it was tucked tightly against his lean waist. "I'm afraid." She laid her dark head on his chest, burying her pretty face against his shirt until she could feel his warmth pulsing against her cheek. "I'm afraid that someday soon our friendship with Noah is going to be tested in the worst possible way."

Jacob frowned even more darkly, his entire countenance a dark storm of intense, overcast emotion. Troubled clouds scudded over his heart as well.

He didn't pretend to misunderstand her. He was the Enforcer. He had been so for over four centuries, elected by the King himself to keep Demon law in strict alignment. Every time the Hallowed moons of Samhain or Beltane neared and passed, any Demon who was without an Imprinted mate could be tempted into straying toward the frail humans or other vulnerable races. These innocent, unsuspecting creatures were not likely to survive the passion of a Demon trying to satisfy dark, clawing hungers that were as primal as the need for food, water, and breath.

The intensity of the effect only grew worse with each passing year. Each Hallowed moon that progressed saw those who, no matter how strong and how self-disciplined they were, slipped back into the more ruthless, animalistic nature that Demon ancestors had long ago been born to. When this type of chaos blossomed, it was the duty of an Enforcer to see that it did not turn toward innocents, and if it did, to severely punish the offender.

Bella and Jacob were the only Enforcers. That meant insane behaviors would always end in a confrontation with one or both of them, a confrontation that the temporarily insane Demons always lost as the lucid, organized Enforcers tracked and trapped them.

Then there was the terrible punishment to follow. This duty rested solely in Jacob's hands. Isabella had not developed the stalwart, armored heart that was required to mete that punishment out, and he hoped she never would. It was a responsibility he took on gladly because he would rather her heart stay sweet and unburdened. Punishment for a Demon was an unspeakable thing, and the humiliation of it tended to stigmatize the one who suffered it for a long period of time afterward.

In the end it meant that neither of them could pretend not to see the indications of a Demon who was pressing at the edges of sanity, their sense of civilization and moral sagacity rubbed raw with the growing phase of the moon. It was little details, ones that made an aura vibrate with high-strung tension, or the occurrence of aberrant behaviors that were ever so slight but that warned them that the Demon in question was struggling with his own volatile nature. These were the sparks that indicated a fuse was lit and growing ever closer to a deadly moment of explosion.

Apparently Isabella was seeing those signs in the Demon King. If he were going to be honest, Jacob would have to agree, although the very idea of it made his stomach churn. If they were forced to battle so respected and powerful a man, so beloved a friend . . .

Isabella looked up at him with sad, understanding eyes. She was his spiritual mate, and as such had telepathic access to all of his thoughts, but even if she hadn't been able to hear his wishes, she would know what Jacob was praying for.

That Noah would find his destined mate as soon as possible.

It was the only thing that would prevent the inevitable juncture of confrontation the King and his Enforcers were heading toward. Destiny, whom all Demons revered for both Her diligent forward motion as well as Her capricious sense of humor and irony, intended the Imprinting to be the Demon race's salvation. Jacob would never fear the potential of his own madness during the Hallowed moons again. That potential had been whisked away when Bella and the Demon prophecy about Druids like her had fallen into his lap. That was when they had all learned that it was possible to find soul mates in the Druids lying dormant and hidden in human society. It promised to rescue an ancient species trembling on the brink of madness.

It also had the potential to diminish the need for the Enforcers. One day, home and hearth would take up more of their time than hunting and being harbingers of punishment. However, there had been very few matches in the past three years, which certainly didn't make up for centuries of the nearly absolute absence of the Imprinting. Bella and Jacob's relationship was a small drop of fortune in the vast bucket of turmoil that the Demons swam in each Hallowed season.

Jacob bent over his petite wife and pressed gentle lips to the inside of her slightly damaged wrist. As a Druid, she would heal quickly enough from the injury to allow her to forget it by morning; as her Imprinted mate, Jacob felt even the slightest of her pains far too keenly to ever forget them that easily. And though he knew she saw his thoughts clearly, he sought to soothe her troubled heart.

"I think you fret overmuch," he chided her gently, smiling when she absently curled her fingertips over the contours of his cheek in reflex to his kiss. "Noah is tense, I agree, but you can clearly see he understands what needs to be done to divert himself. He has survived six and a half centuries of Hallowed moons without ever stepping out of line. Noah hardly needs a little snippet like you, hardly three decades old, trying to mother him."

Her violet eyes widened at the insult, her mouth opening slightly before she recovered, her gaze lighting with understanding.

"You are trying to get my back up on purpose so I won't worry," she countered. Dark lashes fell to shadow her gaze and she leaned into him to press her cheek over the beat of his heart. "I love you for that," she said, sighing deeply and softly.

Jacob's hand came to the black curtain of her hair, stroking it top to bottom, knowing the caress soothed and contented her. She relaxed against him, making a small sound of pleasure. "We both see the straining at Noah's spirit, little flower," he told her with infinite gentleness, "but we will trade our friendship with the King away if we spend it watching and waiting for him to self-destruct."

Isabella nodded gravely once and then reached for her husband's mouth with her own parting lips as she buried comforting fingers into the charcoal-and-chocolate hair sweeping over the nape of his strong neck.

"You are right," she sighed, kissing him tenderly again. "You are absolutely right."

* * *

The scent was sweet, like spun sugar that flew in threads through the air of a successful carnival. The innocence of it belied the overwhelmingly mature sensation of heat and pure animal hunger that washed over him. It was a craving he knew, and yet had never known its equal in depth. He was blinded by it, clenched tight as if his entire body were a single flexed muscle of awareness and anticipation.

She had fought him every step of the way. She always did. Sometimes he thought she did it just to vex him, but mostly he could sense her hostility was all a part of a power struggle she felt she needed to win, whatever the cost. He suspected she was too young a creature to be so jaded, yet it rang true in the antagonism with which his arrival was always greeted. This was the one thing he could be certain of, if nothing else besides her cotton candy scent and long, pristine white hair.

But she was meant for him, chosen by Destiny whether she wanted to be or not. All of this emotional static of resistance was eventually pushed aside as she was overwhelmed with other feelings that spoke to her soul, bypassing her learned behaviors and well-enforced mental barriers. He ruthlessly used this to his advantage, countermanding her enthusiasm for jockeying for power until she was made to realize that the Imprinting was a force which neither of them could ever hope to do battle against.

His fingers and hands curved around firm, feminine flesh that was of a supernatural texture. She felt like the petals of a flower, but so much silkier, so very much more vital. She exceeded the simplistic adjective "soft" in hundreds of ways. Yet there was no mistaking the strength beneath her silken skin. What would she do, he wondered, to make herself so strong? What would she look like when his sensual and emotional war on her forced the inevitable surrender?

He craved answers to all of this as he heard her breath, close and frustrated, rolling thick and slow over his nerves and skin like a mist-laden Louisiana breeze in high summer. He felt her hair, a heavy mass of white-water silk that poured haphazardly over his too-hot skin in such a way that he felt bound by the tangle of it.

Hard as he tried, powerful as he could be, he could not see her face. He tried to ask her name, but was speechless. The paralysis of his vocal cords extended at times to every extremity. He could feel, but not touch. Then he could touch, but only hear her response. He could look and not truly see. There was nothing but the gleaming white blond of that endless hair. He gritted his teeth with unfathomable frustration, fighting the mystical binding that held his dominant will a prisoner.

All he wanted in the world was to see her face.

Noah woke with a jerk and a staggering intake of breath. He sat up with the sudden violence of the freedom of reality, his long, strong fingers entwining around covers that were already tangled around his bare hips and legs. As he tried to feed himself with sharp intakes of oxygen, sweat skied down the aristocratic slope of his nose, beading and dripping off it, accompanying those skimming nearly every other surface on his skin. His dark hair was drenched. The pattering sound of the droplets coming off slightly curled ends and dropping onto stiff sheets was identical to that of rain on a rooftop.

As he gathered his bearings, the Demon King brought the sheet up to his face to swipe at the moisture that nearly blinded him. That was when he realized the fabric was scorched stiff, as if someone had left an iron on it for too long.

And that, in spite of its burnt state, it still carried the scent of sweetly spun sugar.

Chapter 2

Corrine looked up when she heard the polite knock on the front door of the home she shared with her husband, Kane. Her russet brows drew together and she tilted her head. She put aside the book she had been reading, uncrossed her long, slim legs, and stood up slowly.

It was unusual for the people she associated with to bother with such a commonplace courtesy as knocking. The Demon society her husband came from didn't have the same sense of privacy that humans did. Considering that her husband's friends and family were just about the only people she associated with nowadays, the knock was more than just perplexing.

It was worrisome.

There was danger that came under such guises. Things that seemed terribly ordinary, yet were out of the ordinary, sometimes heralded equally unique hazards.

The Demons were currently, as they had been upon occasion in the past, at odds with a sect of misguided humans who hunted them using deadly force and black magics. These humans had taken it upon themselves to rid the world of all the

Nightwalker races. Vampire, Lycanthrope, Demon, and Shadowdweller . . . they would probably even hunt down the gentle, delicate Mistrals as well if they only knew about them. All that seemed to matter to these types was that these races had power that they did not.

They feared.

And fear always led to prejudiced actions. Being formerly human herself, Corrine understood very well the cruel, brutal things human beings tended to do when faced with things of great differences that they didn't understand. To make the situation far worse, about two years ago a very powerful Demon female named Ruth had taken leave of her morals and senses and had joined ranks with these self-appointed butchers. She had provided them with information that had led to the increased vulnerability of the Demon race. Ruth had held nothing back, especially since the death of her beloved daughter, which she blamed on Noah and those highest in power.

Corrine shuddered with the chill that crossed her soul as she recalled the attack on her own sister Isabella, which had almost killed her and the unborn child she had carried at the time. Corrine herself had fallen victim to these forces once already, snatched from under her very own roof. Coupled with some of the gruesome reports Kane had discussed with her, it was clear that no one would be truly safe until Ruth and her companions were all neutralized.

Ruth's revenges had too often begun with a simple knock on the door. Kane was constantly warning her to think carefully before she moved anywhere outside the circle of his protection. Now, though he was always close to her in spirit and could always use his power as a Mind Demon to teleport to her side in a heartbeat should she need him, she still felt enormous trepidation when she realized she was pretty much alone and facing the unknown.

"Corrine?"

The faint call sent a wash of relief through her, forcing an involuntary sigh to escape her. She moved hurriedly toward the door after hearing the familiarity in the voice coming from the other side. She yanked open the portal, smiling when the promise of the voice was fulfilled with the handsome visage of the Demon King. Her welcoming expression warred with the urge to scold him for giving her such a clear case of the heebie-jeebies.

Noah smiled at the slender redhead, noting that, as usual, she was mostly composed of a riot of abundant coils of hair. She was taller than her sister Isabella, more willowy and leggier than his little Enforcer's decidedly compact and curvaceous figure. In fact, if it were not for their attitudes and Bronx accents, Noah felt there would be nothing to suggest they were at all related.

Noah did take note of the relief on her face, however, and felt the kinetic energy of her residual fear like a tepid breeze. It was then that he realized he had given her a scare, and he kicked himself for not giving his actions more thought.

"I am sorry," he said softly to her, reaching for the hand that gripped the door frame, taking it warmly between both of his after prying it free. "Did I frighten you?"

"Scared the daylights out of me, is more like it," she declared, her Bronx enunciation heavier than usual due to her ruffled calm. "Since when do Demons knock?"

"Since Druids who are part human with very human foibles started joining our ranks," he rejoined, chuckling under his breath as he placed a soothing, chivalrous kiss on the back of the hand he cradled. "I am trying to set an appropriate example."

"Your efforts are appreciated," Corrine commended him, blowing a coil of her hair off her face with exasperation, "but next time, warn me before you make attempts at non-Demon behaviors. I had visions of pissed-off magic-users about to bounce me into the ground. Or worse."

She finally relinquished her fear, stepping into his offer of peaceful affection, hugging him with warm, familiar welcome. He put soothing energy and tenderness into the embrace, pushing it into her until he sensed her heartbeat slowing down from its frightened flutter. He had come to seek solace, to free himself of a torture that had gone on too long already. He hadn't come to thoughtlessly frighten her to death.

"You are looking well," he said, almost at the same time she was thinking that he wasn't looking quite like himself.

Even under the worst duress and circumstances, Noah would always look as powerful as he was. As a Demon of Fire, his energy resources were virtually unlimited. He could borrow from the energy or life force of anything that lived or sparked in order to revitalize himself. Corrine suspected that, were it not for the lethargic compulsion of the sun that all Demons fell under, Noah would not even need to sleep to replenish used resources of the day.

But it was no secret to Corrine, or anyone else who had even the slightest familiarity with the Demon King's usual easygoing nature, that Noah looked more than a little tense around his edges.

"So," Corrine said, this time infinitely more relaxed as she did so, "what brings you to our little corner of the world?"

"Oh, just visiting," the King said lightly, linking his hands behind his back as she stepped back to allow him access into her home. "Kane is not here," he noted.

"No. He's visiting Jacob at the moment."

She watched the King's smile automatically grow wider at the mention of her brother-in-law's name. Corrine thought, with no little amusement, that the King's fondness for Jacob was obvious. Unlike humans, Demons weren't constricted by the confusing rituals that preceded the revelation of one person's feelings for another. In fact, it was safe to say that they wore their hearts on their sleeves, embroidered in wild red, with indicator signs flashing in neon that said point-blank the value one person had within the heart of another.

It was one of those things in their complex culture that she'd come to appreciate and enjoy. Still, Corrine was amused by the way Noah made his favoritism for Jacob so evident. But she understood that Noah and Jacob had a very special sort of friendship, one that could only be formed between two men of outstanding and distinct power.

However, she was puzzled as to why Noah had dropped by her home. Though her sister and brother-in-law were extremely close to Noah, his affection didn't naturally extend just by familial association. To say she and Kane were special friends with the King would have been an exaggeration. Oh, they were as welcome and loved by Noah as any other member of Demon society, but it was rare for the monarch to single them out without there being a purpose behind it.

So Corrine watched him with no little curiosity as he wandered into their comfortable home and looked it over with interest. He'd been there once before, though not in a circumstance that would have allowed him to take much note of the décor or the warm, feminine trinkets that Corrine had added to it. Still, you didn't rush a King to reveal his business, and for the moment Corrine was content to simply visit with him and let him come to it in his own time.

"Why are you not visiting your sister while Kane visits with Jacob?" the King asked conversationally, his rich accent a denser, older version of her husband's. Noah was more than a half millennium older than Kane was. Kane's verbal affectations had come from being raised around the inflected English—Jacob's inflected English, to be exact. Like Jacob's, Noah's elegantly distorted English had come from the Ancient Demon language itself, learned long before English had fallen from his tongue.

"I see her often enough," she assured him, leaning casually into the archway that led into the living area Noah was inspecting with singular fascination. "I'm actually taking a day off from watching my rather rambunctious niece. Leah is going through the Demon/Druid version of the terrible twos, and believe me when I tell you, I deserve some time to myself. Especially with Samhain not too far around the corner. Once your Enforcers get busy Enforcing, I'll be babysitting quite a bit."

"Indeed," Noah agreed, his tone a little more grave, whether he was aware of it or not. "And I believe Leah is a Demon. Although she is part human and part Druid when you see her lineage in her parents, their children . . . that is, any children born of Demons and Druids can only be one or the other. It is why the races were able to remain separate for generation upon generation. Of course, we cannot know for sure until she comes into power as a Demon does or remains dormant as a Druid does . . . but the Prophecy speaks of Leah as a new breed of Demon—" Noah cut himself off, drawing even more of Corrine's curiosity as he fidgeted with a small statuette in a manner that was very much out of character for the unflappable King. "Your sister will be busy these next nights. I had wondered who she would entrust Leah's care to, considering that Demons can never be fully trusted around Samhain and—"

He broke off again, wrestling with intense private thoughts. Of course Corrine was quite familiar with the drawbacks that came with Demon holy days like Samhain and the phases of the moon around them. Just as she was familiar with the benefits of them.

It had been a full Samhain moon that had brought her and Kane together, giving her a blissful new life filled with passion and love. However, it had come very close to completely destroying her in the process. Corrine could appreciate Noah's trepidation. Also, the King wasn't married, or mated as the Demons called it, and that made it all the harder for him. Corrine hadn't noticed any signs of Noah losing control, but it wasn't exactly her area of expertise. What she *could* see was his disturbance of the moment.

Noah's restraint was legendary and unparalleled, and his nature was consistently serene. It was only ruffled when his family came under threat. Even a threat to his society as a whole couldn't disturb him to the depth that a threat to those dear to him could. So to see him disturbed in any way incited concern as well as curiosity.

Despite the soft warning in the back of her mind, Corrine threw patience and protocol aside with a sigh. "Noah, is there something I can help you with?"

Noah looked up from his distant study of the figurine, his jade eyes with their clouds of gray meeting hers in that way that only someone of royalty or great position seemed able to manage. Noah wasn't a cruel or overtly strict monarch, but he was a man used to the privileges that came with his position, a position he'd earned the hard way. Demons selected their royal leader on merit alone, not entirely because of lineage or fortune of birth.

"Come on," she coaxed the King gently, advancing into the room and purposely putting the warmth of her body into the influence of his personal space. It was a trick she'd learned from Kane. The best way to soothe the sometimes volatile temper of a Fire Demon, he'd told her, was to bring the warmth of her energy and its good intentions so close to them that it had a soothing effect. "I'm aware you care for me and Kane as much as anyone else, but you're not in the habit of dropping in just to shoot the breeze. You love my sister like that, not me."

Noah looked down at his feet and chuckled softly, a short sound followed by a rueful shake of his head. "You shame me," he said quietly. "I never realized I played favorites so obviously."

"Frankly, I prefer to be ill-favored," she teased him with a pretty, flirtatious smile. "When you love someone, Noah, you elevate them to remarkable status in your circle of advisers or in your army of defenders. By all means, Noah, love my sister and leave *me* the hell alone!"

Finally, Noah truly laughed. He threw back his head, the reddish highlights within the ebony fall of gently curling hair gleaming sharply in the muted gaslight that lit the room. The sound of his laughter was infectious, and it made Corrine laugh with him. It also eased her to hear it, to see him relieving himself of the seriousness of whatever it was that was on his mind.

"You know something, you may have just thwarted your own effort, Corrine. Until now, I do not think I have truly appreciated the warmth of spirit and heart that runs through your family. I have credited one sister, while overlooking the other. For that, I beg your forgiveness." He gave her a smart, cordial bow, and she stepped back from him with a chuckle.

"Damn it, if you make me a Council member or something, Kane is going to freak out," she joked.

"Sorry. Only Elders are allowed on the Great Council."

"Then explain my sister!" she demanded, reminding him that Isabella was barely thirty years old, not the requisite minimum of three hundred.

"Well, that is different. She is an Enforcer."

"Yes, yes." Corrine waved that off the way only an older sister could wave off a younger sister's accomplishments. "Don't make me accuse you of trying to change the subject again, Noah."

"Perish the thought," he assured her, his eyes turning serious again only a heartbeat after his words had. This time, she allowed him the pair of minutes he took to order his heavy thoughts. "I have struggled with myself for quite some time about the matter of seeking you out, Corrine," he began at last. The King paced away from her briefly, and then turned to look at her. Corrine watched as he rubbed his hands together, as if warding off a chill. The concept of a Fire Demon catching chill was preposterous. She bit her lip, held her tongue, and somehow managed not to overstep herself. "Since we found you and Isabella, we have only been able to find three other Druids. Can you tell me why? What do you think is the cause?"

The question was pretty much out of left field, but if Noah was headed in the direction she suspected he was, it perhaps wasn't so off topic.

"I have only a theory," she responded willingly. "No one knew Druids still existed. Every Demon thought Druids had been annihilated in the war a millennium ago." Corrine knew he was familiar with the history, so she kept it brief. "But when Jacob met Bella, and the night Kane touched me for the first time, triggering the birth of our dormant Druidic DNA, we all learned differently."

"A hard lesson," Noah observed.

"Yes," she agreed. She tilted her head down with a half smile on the corner of her lips, the expression seeming more ironic than amused. "As you know, once a Druid's genetics are triggered, they must remain within relatively close proximity of that Demon who will become their perfect Imprinted mate. Since Kane and I were separated right after our first contact, I was deprived of his key energy and suffered for it.

"With Bella, power acquisition was nearly instantaneous. With me, because of the energy starvation that Gideon likens to brain damage, it took a year or so before we even knew that my key talent was the ability to quest for the hidden Druid hybrids destined to be perfect mates for the Demons fate designed specifically for them." She gave him a wry little smile. "So the first part of my answer is centered on the setbacks I suffered when I first became Druid, since there really is no other way to determine the unique Druidic dormancy that's hidden amongst millions of humans."

Corrine exhaled a deep sigh.

"The rest of the blame, however, lies at Demon doors," she said. "I'm at full power now, Noah. I have been for the better part of a year. I've made no secret of what my main Druidic ability is. Still, I have to wait for your Demons to voluntarily come to me in search of their mates." She flicked a frustrated glance over him as he stood there as the ultimate representation of his people. "They've been inexplicably recalcitrant. Why only three other Druids, you ask? Because there's only been three Demons who have come to request my help. I can't chase Demons down and force them to let me seek their mates. I need them open and willing in order to aid me in the success of my search. And those three Demons who did come to me? They reeked of the mental and physical desperation of Beltane and Samhain.

"I'm convinced that they came to me only as a last-ditch effort at avoiding doing something rash that would attract the punishment of the Enforcers." She exhaled a short, bitter-sounding laugh. "I suppose I'm looked on as the lesser of the two evils. Better to be saddled with a Druid mate than to find the Enforcers bearing down on you." She shook her head. "I don't understand it! In human culture, we spend our lifetime seeking and longing for the perfect soul mate, most of us never knowing anything close to it. We're left hurting and jaded as we fail over and over again. But here your people have a guaranteed path, through me, to finding that very thing, and they approach it like complex dental work or a plague! Maybe you can explain that to me, Noah, because I know I don't understand it.

"Am I wrong when I say you were all raised on fairy-tale stories of the glories of an Imprinting?" She realized she'd struck a chord when the King no longer met her eyes and shifted his weight uncomfortably. "If I were suddenly told that stories like Cinderella and Sleeping Beauty were absolutely true and all I had to do was knock on a certain door to find my Prince Charming, I would fall all over myself to do it." Then she smiled and blushed, memories of waking for the first time to find herself tethered to a perfect man scudding through her mind. She recalled the undeniable craving for unity with Kane. "I'd never heard of the Imprinting," it provoked her to say passionately. "It wasn't part of *my* folklore. Yet now I accept it in my life with enormous pleasure and gratitude. Why is it your people can't?"

The King didn't respond immediately to the sharp scrutiny in the question. Instead, he looked directly at her at last and reached to touch two fingers to her chin, making her turn her eyes directly up to his. She looked into the smoke and jade swirls of emotion as he studied her for a long, silent moment. Corrine somehow managed to remain still and relaxed under that unnervingly penetrating gaze. She had no idea what he was looking for, nor how he was searching for it, but she suspected it was important that he find it before answering.

"You let me lead myself quite neatly into your little trap, did you not?" he accused softly, but without any real malice.

Corrine didn't pretend at ignorance.

"Noah, you're their King and you're unmated. If you won't come to me when you so clearly long to, so clearly *need* to, why would any of your subjects do otherwise?"

"Have I been that obvious?" he asked, his tone tight with his tortured feelings on the topic, his hand reflexively tightening around her jaw.

"I would have to say . . . only since your Warrior Captain married the Lycanthrope Queen. He was the last highly positioned bachelor you kept close to you. First Jacob; then Gideon and your sister; and then when Elijah fell in love with Siena, it wasn't long before you started grumping around the castle."

"Damn it," Noah cursed softly, releasing his hold on her roughly. He paced away from her, running an agitated hand through his hair.

Corrine was abruptly aware of her husband's telepathic presence flaring to alertness in her thoughts. He was protesting the way Noah was treating her, but she pushed him firmly away, scolding him to mind his own business, that her discussion with Noah was a private one. Kane backed off with impressive immediacy, respecting her desire to respect his King.

"You have to understand," Noah said at last as he stared out of a nearby window, "it has been a very long time since the Imprinting has become an issue any of us have had to give any true thought to. For centuries it has been as rare as . . . as . . ."

"A snowball in hell?" she offered.

This time Noah wasn't inclined to laugh or let himself be eased by her humor. His fingers curled into a fist that he pressed against the window frame. "Hell." He laughed mirthlessly. "The human concept of hell has always amused me, especially considering the fact that 'demons' are reputed to be its main occupants. I am forced to admit that there is some truth to that imagery today, Corrine. I fall asleep every day at sunrise, but I get no rest. This is because I visit my own personal hell, where agonizing beauty, pleasure, and a gluttony of satisfying emotions lie always just out of sight and reach. I dream of her. Every time I close my eyes, I dream of this woman you are meant to find for me. I have dreamed of her every single day for six months straight."

Corrine winced visibly as he imparted this information with such clear pain. She'd had no idea that it had come to this awful form of torture. To suffer the elusive dream of your perfect mate for half a year must indeed be akin to hell for a species who felt as deeply and powerfully as Noah's did.

"Why wouldn't you come to me sooner?" she finally asked him, knowing beyond any shadow of doubt that this was what had finally brought him there.

"Because I am a King, little Druid. You come from a culture where that no longer means as much as it does to us, but surely you have gotten a better idea of it as you have lived with Kane."

"I have. Enough to know that not one Demon under your rule expects you to remain single and alone for the sake of your reign." Corrine braced her feet apart and settled her hands on her hips. "In fact, every Demon I know would scoff at that notion. Don't blame this on your people, Noah. I may not be an expert on your society, but I do know that nothing would please them more than to see you give your heart into the hands of your Imprinted mate. So let's skip the bullshit and come to the real point of why you've lain in bed, day after endless day, torturing yourself rather than coming and asking me for help."

"Damn you, woman," he barked, banging the window frame so hard with his fist that the glass rattled. "Has your husband taught you nothing of how you should speak to someone in my position?"

"Oh, kiss my ass," Corrine blustered as her famous familial temper got the better of her. "If you're just going to spout the cloud cover of protocol and all that high-handed crap, then I would prefer you not waste my time!" She stepped closer to him, in spite of the fact that his temper had caused the air around him to heat up considerably. "If you were any kind of a monarch you would jump at the chance to set a good example for your suffering people. And they *are* suffering, Noah. The longer they remain unmated, the more likely it is they will cave to their instincts and find themselves breaking laws and putting innocents in danger. You're a remarkable leader and scholar. Where is your intelligence when it comes to this? Kane tells me you've hunted for centuries to find the cure for the suffering that overcomes your people on the Hallowed nights. Well, it's here, Noah," she said vehemently, thrusting her fingers against her breastbone. "It's inside me! Come to *me*. Make *them* come to me!"

"Corrine . . ."

"What? What excuse is it now?" she barked.

"No excuse," he assured her quietly. "Just confession. Confession of the one truth behind all of the questions you ask with such righteous merit."

"Which is?" she prompted.

"Fear," he responded with a sigh. "Pure and simple fear."

"*Fear?*" Corrine gaped at him for a beat. "What in God's name could you possibly fear from the Imprinting? Noah, are you blind? Haven't you seen the scope of the new love surrounding you these past three years?"

"Yes, yes," he said with impatience as he turned to look at

her at last. "I have eyes and sense. I see you all, revolving around me like little planets, deep in your own little worlds made up in the space between your locked gazes and impassioned bodies. I watch until I am black-sighted with jealousy, Corrine!"

"Noah, please . . . forgive me," she begged earnestly, her pretty brow furrowed in confusion. "I don't understand. I truly want to understand, but I don't. What is it you fear? Why be jealous when I can give you our joy for yourself? You are so brilliant, but I see no logic here!"

"I am afraid . . ." He hesitated, the phraseology unfamiliar and bitter to his taste. "I am afraid I am too late."

"Noah . . ."

"She has suffered. She has been through some great pain and I was not there to spare her," he confessed quickly. "I do not know what it was, or even if she suffers still, because her emotions are always so volatile. I am afraid of bringing her to me, of thrusting her into this existence. Being my Queen is not an easy life, Corrine. She will be in danger—especially in light of recent events. She will become a target. Yes, she will be accepted by most, but those who do not accept can be brutal with their opinions, as you no doubt know from your sister's experiences. I ask you, how can I, in good conscience, bring an already tortured soul into my world for my own selfish needs, knowing all of this?"

"Noah," Corrine said with soft surprise. "Noah, you will bring her here so you can love her. There is no hardship in the world that can't be made better with the type of love the Imprinting can bring! You said yourself, you don't know if she is still suffering. Would you leave her there, will you let it continue, knowing you can stop it?"

Noah made a distressed sound and his eyes darkened to gray. The thought was unconscionable, and it tore through him like thousands of sharp, shredding tines. In a single sentence Corrine changed his misguided ideas of nobility to horrified realization. He was suddenly overwhelmed with the feeling that he had wasted time. Now he realized that time was a black enemy and he was in a deadly race with it.

"Tell me how," he demanded. "Corrine, help me."

* * *

The Miserable Princess
A Demon Fairy Tale
Cont'd . . .

As nice as love stories about the Imprinting sounded, Sarah was very practical for a Princess. She knew her father was looking for a miracle, just as she knew she was the one who would end up going mad from his desperation to fix the odds more in royal favor. At the moment, that meant propping her up prettily in her throne, displaying her like a frilly trophy to be won. It was like being set afloat on a raft in a sea of greedy piranhas, and Sarah was not stupid enough to dangle a single welcoming toe into the water, lest she get chewed up and spit out into a form nothing like herself. So Sarah set her mind to the task of being so cold and so disinterested that no one would dare approach her.

Just then the Enforcer walked onto the playing field.

An immediate chill rippled outward from the place where he entered the arena, both through the participants and the crowd in the stands above. It was clearly visible as it shuddered through them all, every adult and child, the murmur that buzzed loudly all around her. The hostility and, yes, outright hatred everyone felt for this powerful man who enforced the King's laws and extracted harsh, mortifying punishment for those who broke them was palatable.

Sarah shivered in spite of herself as she watched the Enforcer cross into the playing field, seemingly oblivious of the stir of emotions he was creating all around him. If she were going to be honest, she would have to admit that when she put fear and prejudice aside, she was still left intimidated by his prowess alone. Had he been a simple warrior, he would surely have made a glorious name for himself in battle, as well as prize competitions like this one. But his battles were fought against his own people.

He was the one true villain in the picture laid before her. The villain condoned by the King.

His name was Ariel, far too angelic a name for one who even looked the villainous part. He was bearded and mustached, though both were trimmed close with an almost single-minded perfection. Rough dark brows slashed above his eyes, and his hair was barely long enough to make the queue it was tied into at his nape. His hair was dark as pitch, but the sleek, silky shine of it was fastidious, showing off an almost navy tint of highlights in the too-bright moonlight.

Just then, thick, sooty lashes parted and revealed the icy blue eyes that so easily terrified everyone who faced off with the Enforcer. They were as glass, frigid and sparkling like shaved ice.

And they were looking directly at Sarah.

The Princess felt another chill blow over her, shuddering down her skin until she was covered in goose bumps. Her childish behaviors were forgotten in an instant and she straightened imperiously into the figure of a woman of her station. She could not tell clearly if that was a smile he was taunting her with, his whiskers in the way, but there was cold amusement in his eyes.

He boldly advanced to the stairs leading up to her viewing box, oblivious of the startled scramble of powerful Demons making haste to create a path for him, as well as adding a few steps more to ensure safe distance. Princess Sarah was afraid, too, her heartbeat wild and her palms becoming damp with it. But she clutched her moist hands around the arms of her throne and forced herself to smile at him, just to prove to him he couldn't intimidate her, even though she had never been as close to him before as she was apparently going to be in just another minute. . . .

* * *

At first, all she could hear was the low, steady thrum of a heartbeat.

She lifted her cheek, felt the coolness that crossed it as she left a pillow of perfect warmth. The heartbeat became distant as she raised her head farther and blinked her eyes for clarity.

The next thing she was aware of was that haunting, sense-numbing smell. Every single time she closed her eyes it was there. The scent had temperature, if it was possible. Heated, but not overtly so. It was mellow on some levels, like gentle musk and flirting masculinity. On other echelons it was headier. Rich and smoky.

Yes, that was it.

Smoke. Softly burnt cedar, smoldering maple, and the sweet tang of apple wood.

It was his *scent.*

It was the same scent that had wrapped around her time after insane time for endless months. It haunted her constantly, sometimes in frustrating, imposing ways, and other times in a darkly passionate manner that made her crawl with frustration within her own skin.

He didn't like it when she moved away from him, and it always showed in the possessive sweep of his hands as they threaded into the straight fall of her hair. She knew by instinct alone that her hair fascinated him. He was always touching it, holding her prisoner by it, drawing it to the rub of his lips.

She was too tired to battle him. After six months of this blissful, exasperating torture at his persistent hands and stubborn nature, she had become too addicted to the way he could eventually bend her to his pleasure and her own. Before he had come, she had prided her-

self for her control of her own body. Gymnastics, martial arts, and marathon runs were her measuring stick, all of which she had excelled in at one point or another in her lifetime.

But it all went to hell in a speedy little handbasket the moment his fingertips touched her skin and his breath whispered against her ear. He spoke, she knew, but speech was wiped away into unintelligible whispers and hot clouds of increasingly excited breath.

She didn't mind so much, though. She couldn't see the features of his face, so she could tell herself that it was purely imagination and therefore safe to indulge in.

Then she would remember that her imagination had been fixated on this mysterious man as well as his alluring scent and feel without fail, every single time, and she would feel the quickening of her heart as she acknowledged on a very distant level that this was all more than just a dream. This was the thought that always panicked her into struggling with him, trying to fight him even though she knew how futile it was. He never had to force her to his will; he could do it well enough with the sweet skill of his touch alone, with the sweeping seal of his lips and mouth as he slowly devoured her resistance along with her kisses.

Kestra ripped out of sleep with a growl of annoyance, forcing herself awake just so she could make the audible sound of protest and denial. She lay in the dampness of sheets misted with perspiration, breathing hard and feeling her chest ache with the violent pounding of her heart. She pressed a palm to her rib cage.

"Damn you!" she cursed up to the ceiling, though she was unsure if she was cursing the dream man, God, or herself. No matter who it was, they were playing massive head games with her when she was asleep and at her most vulnerable. It was exhausting her, wreaking havoc with her concentration, strength, and equilibrium, all of which were her primary tools in her work. When James started noticing she was off her stride, then she truly knew she was in trouble. She needed sleep, but sleep brought *him*. When she tried to stay awake, she always failed miserably, falling irresistibly into unconsciousness and subsequently his unending thrall over her.

Kestra slid out of bed, walking her hot, damp body through the cold room. She paced in her thin, plaid boxers, rolled at the waist to better fit her trim hips, and white ribbed tank top, trying to shake off the kinetic restlessness these dreams always left behind.

She needed to get laid.

That was the only thing she could come up with at this point. It had to be the reason why she indulged in these highly erotic fantasies in her sleep, only to wake up more unsatisfied than ever. James would have laughed at the idea of her latest solution. He knew her well enough to know that blowing things up was her best form of release, not sex. But she'd just torched an entire dock of warehouses that previous night, and yet here she was again, dreaming the dreams of the deeply, deeply sexually deficient.

"I can't take this anymore," she muttered to the cold, empty room. "Something has got to change, and it better damn well do it soon!"

Chapter 3

"Kane, you're supposed to be making yourself scarce," Corrine called from a distant upstairs bedroom.

"What does it matter where I am?" Kane asked stubbornly, switching instantly from voice to thought as he pressed his point. *I am always with you anyway. I see what you see and feel what you feel.*

"You're also a Demon of the Mind, more capable than others of distancing yourself from this Imprinted link of ours." She stopped shouting when she appeared at the head of the stairs, looking down at him where he leaned back against the enormous banister, arms folded firmly over his athletic chest. "We've discussed this as much as I'm going to discuss it. Noah will be here very soon and I want you long gone by the time he arrives."

"Noah isn't himself," Kane countered, "and I'm not at all happy with the way he treated you the last time he was here. I don't think I've ever felt you that angry before."

"That's because," she said as she began her descent, "the subject has been a sore spot for me for a very long time now. It wasn't the way I'd have approached it with him had I been prepared. Coming out of the blue like that, it pinched my temper before I could prepare a more diplomatic approach." She reached the bottom of the stairs, releasing the excess material of the caftan she wore so loosely before leaning her warmth into him comfortingly. "The end result is satisfactory enough. I finally have the opportunity I've waited for since this power of mine first came to light. Don't you see, Kane? Once I do this for Noah, once I find the female Druid who is destined to be his, others will finally come willingly to my door."

"And I know how important that is to you," Kane agreed softly, reaching up to cradle his wife's face between gentle, reverent fingers.

"So very important," she said with quiet vehemence. "I've been little better than useless to your people these past three years. I've just as much destiny awaiting me as any of you do, and I've longed to fulfill it."

"I know," he murmured, leaning to touch his mouth to hers. "I know how frustrating it's been for you. But won't you at least let me—"

"No, Kane. Please," she begged as she reached to brush back the errant curl of hair that fell crookedly over his forehead. "Respect my wishes in this."

"You know," he sighed, closing his eyes as she added a kiss to her coaxing plea and touch, "I'm powerless when it comes to you."

"It has nothing to do with me. It has to do with giving your respect to Noah's need for privacy and maintenance of pride. If the tables were turned, knowing the process I must go through with him to find his mate, would you want an audience? Would you want someone watching as you revealed the parts of yourself that feel the way you do for me?"

"I've never made a secret of my love or need for you, Corrine."

"But imagine, for a moment, if you had to show the world the loss of control, the pure drive of lust that first led you to try and capture me, even in spite of the law and the fact that your own brother would be forced to punish you should you get caught?" Corrine brushed soft lips and a softer whisper over his ear. "Remember that feeling, Kane, that you felt the moment Jacob did catch you? The shame attached to hunting down an innocent human while under the influence of the full Hallowed moon? Remember what you felt before you learned that it was okay for you to love me?"

"Sometimes," he sighed quietly, "I forget what life was like without you." He smiled against her lips as she tried to heal that injuring thought with her lush little mouth. "But I'll never be able to leave you if you keep kissing me."

"Mmm," she agreed, her lips rubbing enticingly over his.

The pressure of Kane's mouth suddenly disappeared, along with the support of the rest of his body, leaving her to stumble against the banister he had vacated as she waved frantically at the sulfuric cloud of smoke his sudden teleportation had left behind. She coughed just as a second cloud of smoke skidded into the foyer from beneath and around the cracks of the front door.

This cloud coalesced with a sharp twist into first a column, then the tall, sturdy figure of the Demon King. Corrine instantly hid her waving hands behind her back, smiling at Noah with hopes he would be a little too preoccupied to realize her husband had sensed his arrival with barely enough time to retreat.

"Good evening, Noah."

"Good evening, Corrine. Did you rest well?"

"Very well. Are you ready?"

"As ready as I may ever be," he assured her.

Corrine reached to take his hand and led him deeper into the house. She'd long ago set aside a room for this purpose, and though it had gotten very little use searching for Druids, she used it often in meditative practice. Noah followed with unusual silence and a forced serenity, but he couldn't help but admire the sanctum Corrine led him to.

It was draped in dark fabric, with no lights save the multitude of candles she had lit on every surface and in every corner. Each stick of light was settled on glass, filling the room with refracted prisms that changed and danced along every surface. The floor was covered with pillows, all shining with satin and velveteen colors.

The candles gave off a variety of scents, from simple to exotic, but he was also aware that small metal dishes of herbs had been set to smoke. They infused the room with a haze and a spiced scent as rich and pure as the Earth itself.

"Before we begin . . ."

He turned to look at her. "Yes?" he asked.

"You said you have dreamed of her."

"Yes."

"Is there anything specific you can remember that you think might help you to go back to her and what you already have sensed about her?" She smiled softly when he gave her a perplexed look. "You're not the first to dream of your mate, Noah. In my limited experiences so far, the people I'm questing for have always had a singular memory, a trigger that instantly brings them to that place beyond the waking state where they have met their soul mate. Simon, for instance, always heard music when he dreamed of Tirana. "Fortune, Empress of the World," to be exact. Not what I would call romantic, but that's not for me to judge."

"For what purpose must you know this?" the King asked, coldness lacing his tone.

"Noah, if you close yourself off on a simple detail like this, we won't make any progress. We'll just be wasting our time. Please," she said, softening her intent as she touched his arm and leaned closer to his personal warmth. "Trust me. I'll never reveal what happens here to anyone. Kane has even made remarkable effort to distance himself from me for this. You know we'd never dream of betraying you."

"No," he decided, "you would not. And I do know that. I meant no insult."

"Come on, I can tell there is something that makes you think of this woman."

"It will sound . . ."

"A little strange? Yes. I know. Three others before you have said that very same thing."

Noah laughed at that, shaking his head ruefully. "I should have known this would not be a bland experience. Very well." He cleared his throat and flicked stormy green-gray eyes up to meet her gaze. "Sugar," he said at last. "Spun sugar, to be exact."

"Cotton candy?" she clarified.

"Yes. That is the modern name for it."

"Okay," she said simply. "The taste of cotton candy it is."

"No. Not the taste. The scent." He sighed with frustration when she lifted a brow. "Have you never been close by while someone spun sugar? It is a scent in three dimensions. You smell the strands that fly away into the air, but you taste it, too, and you feel the sweet stickiness against your skin." Noah suddenly stopped his impassioned description, flushing uncharacteristically when he realized he had followed a tangent that was far more intimate and revealing than he would have wished to share under any other circumstances.

"I understand," Corrine said gently, taking his arm and leading him into the center of the room.

She kneeled down on one side of a large, curved dish with twigs and coal arranged within the center. She indicated that he should sit on the opposite side and he did so, settling into the comfort of the pillows. The haze of herbs and incense quickly cocooned the Demon King with a soothing influence.

"Light this," she instructed softly, touching the edge of the metal bowl with a single finger. She inhaled and exhaled deeply, closing her eyes as he performed the elementary task of concentrating on the bowl and letting the carefully arranged items within burst into flame.

Noah felt the energy in the room shift sharply, sweeping

around him with soothing pressure, forcing him to relax further. For the Druid who was only rudimentarily familiar with her power, it was a massive accomplishment to manipulate the Fire Demon's energy without his permission. If she hadn't drawn him so suddenly into this focused, calming state, he might have had the knee-jerk reaction to resist.

Corrine had been practicing time and again for just such a moment. She'd felt weakness and powerlessness when she should have felt just the opposite upon meeting her Demon mate. She had spent the three years since then fighting tooth and nail to make up for that. She'd been her own best form of a Druidic occupational therapist, always pushing herself, always wanting and reaching for what she felt she'd been cheated out of early on by a cruel twist of fate.

Now she absently waved a hand at the door she had left open, sending it swinging shut with a muffled click. It would have astounded the King, had he been paying attention. Instead, his eyes were fixed on the soothing familiarity of the flame he'd created. He had always been able to find comfort in the heart of a flame. Corrine had known this. Everyone who had seen him sit for endless hours contemplating the eternal flames that burned in the fireplace of the Great Hall of his castle knew this.

"Let's begin," she said at last.

Kestra wasn't even aware she had fallen back to sleep until strong hands caught her around the waist and pulled her sharply forward against a wall of solid flesh. He reached for her hair, skimming his fingers through it as if he owned all rights to do so. She tried to see him, but there was nothing. He was there, but brushed into a swirl of colors just beyond definition. She reached up in spite of herself and tried to bring his features into dimension with the touch of her hand.

She gasped when she realized she could feel the shadow of coarse whiskers against her fingertips. The shocking realness of the sensation started her heart racing as she jerked her hand away. Lunging back against his entrapping hands, she might as well have not been moving at all.

"Tell me who you are . . ."

Kestra froze at the sound of his voice, deep and rich with an exotic accent, something from one of the oldest of European cultures. She had traveled through enough of them to know one when she heard one, although she couldn't place the precise origin of his inflections. She was aware of how much it seemed to suit him, the new detail falling perfectly into the mental construct that she'd been putting together slowly over the past six months.

Neither of them had ever spoken a complete word in all the months of these persistent, obsessive dreams, these ceaseless nightmares and the haunting captain who starred in them as he steered them. She felt terrified and fascinated all at once at the unexpected development.

The dimness cleared slightly and he drew her closer, as if she weren't resisting at all, his hands beneath her ribs and his fingers pressing more firmly into her skin as he counteracted her opposing strength.

"Why are you doing this?" she demanded as she struggled against the violent impulses desperately riding her, telling her to hurt him in order to escape the force of his will. It wouldn't be fair to harm him when he'd never been abusive with her. His most offensive act had been to make her succumb to the cravings of her own body, an act she had to admit was a reward as much as it was a torture. Still, she hated how easily he could sway and manipulate her.

"Because you *refuse to leave* me *alone," he responded, tension strung like overtaut piano wire through*

his words, just as it was strung through the solid bundles of muscle he held her against.

"Let go of me and I will gladly leave you alone," she hissed through her teeth. "It's your only choice. I'd just as soon tap dance on nitroglycerin than tell you anything about me!"

He laughed. It was a perplexing, utterly galling chuckle that made her face flame with fury. She despised it when she wasn't taken seriously, laughed off as if she were some kind of joke.

"Tell me where you are," he growled under a quiet, intense breath. "I must find that sharp tongue or die trying."

Suddenly his fingers were sliding over her face. She jolted back, but no sooner had she jerked away than they danced over the sweep of her neck and spine, followed by the eerily close cascade of his hot breath. He had a way, a way only possible in dreams, of surrounding her like that. With sensation and unexpected contrasts. Contrasts that chased across her every nerve ending and dogged her resistance with single-minded sensual warfare.

"No . . . I won't let you do this to me again!"

"True," he said, his tone suddenly soft. His fingers stilled, his breath pooling into a heated cloud against the curve of her neck between her throat and shoulder. She felt vibration twanging through his entire body. It broadcast how much restraint he was using. Her memory of earlier, more unrestrained dreams filled in the blank information. "It does make it all the harder," he said at last.

Kestra swallowed noisily, turning her head aside as her eyes burned with inexplicable emotion. He had just voiced the very feelings and frustrations she'd expressed to herself earlier. Of course he would. He was a construct of her mind. Her waking thoughts were following her into her dream.

But hadn't she read somewhere, once, that the minute you realized you were dreaming, the dream lost its impact? That you tended to awaken shortly after? If so, why was she waiting around? Was she waiting for his accursed touch, so like magic and sparkling starlight as it played over her rigid, reluctant body? Was she wishing him into existence just so she could feel? Feel in ways she was so incapable of in her waking hours?

"No, Kikilia,*" he murmured softly against her brow. "This time, it can be different. Tell me who you are, and I can show you what you are capable of when you are awake. Tell me your name, and I will find you and end this mutual torture once and for all."*

The request made her want to laugh in his face at first, but that was quickly followed by a prickling rush of chilling terror. There was not much in the world that frightened her, but his proposal struck that rare, eerie nerve of panic. It was so numbing that it took all her concentrated effort to utter the single word:

"Never."

"She must tell you, Noah. Make her tell you," Corrine urged, her panting breath falling against his cheek as she whispered in his ear. "I have brought you as close as I can for now. You must make her tell you, Noah."

Kestra was aware of something changing in his intent and emotion. He was suddenly impatient, the feeling sweeping away all softness and coaxing sensuality.

"Why do you resist me so? Every night you fight until you are too weak to deny what you must acknowledge. It is a pain you do not need to suffer."

"If only I would be more feminine, soft, and compliant, perhaps? I'm no lady? Well, you're right. I don't

behave myself, I don't talk softly, and I am not gracious. Six months of this manipulation and you still don't know a damn thing about me. I would think I'd dream up someone smarter for myself."

Again, that frustrating chuckle, as if the ruder and cruder she was, the more she delighted him. He was driving her mad!

"I have been clever enough to find my way around your quills so far, little porcupine," he said, his voice low and dangerous all of a sudden. "It happens every night. Somehow, I know it will hurt you to remind you of that, but it is still the truth of the matter."

It did hurt. It stung like lemon juice in a razor's cut. Kestra growled with frustration until her head fell back and she was screaming. She resented that part of herself that succumbed to his seductions. So what if it were just a dream? She should be able to dictate what constituted an enjoyable dream!

And because she resented it, she hated him.

"Very well," she hissed hoarsely. "Kestra. Kestra Irons. Now come and find me, you son of a bitch. Meet me in the real world and find out how far all this Euro-trash charm of yours will really go. I swear, if I ever set eyes on you in my waking world you will be centuries of sorry!"

She reached wide, swinging to slap him across the face. But the slap altered in the last minute and was actually a closed-fisted pop, square across his jaw.

Before this night, everything had always been so dreamy and ethereal, so compellingly sweet and soft. The punch was unbelievably satisfying, and unexpectedly painful. She reared back, swearing harshly as her bruised knuckles stung as if they were on fire.

She heard him curse, too. Then he spat. She felt him glaring at her through the blurry existence, so she was shocked when he laughed softly.

"Nasty little thing," he accused her.

Suddenly she was given a real lesson in how strong her phantom adversary was. He grabbed her by both arms, jerking her clear off her feet. He found her unwilling mouth with ridiculous precision. She was shocked to realize her fantasy even went so far as to provide the tang of his blood as he took his kiss with possessiveness and a headstrong determination. Had he truly been real, it would have had the potential to brand her, the power to mark her as his.

Only his.

Suddenly the scent of strung sugar spun away, as if sucked out of the room by a vortex, and Noah opened his eyes with the shock. He found himself staring into wide green eyes, separated by a wending coil of cinnamon-colored hair. Hair he felt against his lips, trapped by his mouth and hers.

Noah choked, thrust Corrine away in horrified shock, and swiped the back of his hand across his mouth as he looked frantically around the sanctum for any hint of her jealous husband's arrival.

"Noah, it's okay," she said quickly, soothingly. "It happens. When I take on the spirit of the Druid you seek, it is a complete possession, as far as your soul is concerned."

"Corrine . . ."

"Noah, listen to me. It is just a side effect of the process. It was never me in this room with you. Not unless I pulled myself aside. I am a medium. A channel. I bring the message only. I take no part in how it is delivered or"—she smiled soothingly as she reached to touch his bloodied lip—"or received."

She turned over her hand, shaking out her fingers, one of which was surely off-center from normal.

"Corrine," Noah said, his horrified tone reflecting his expression with perfection, "you broke your finger!"

"Actually, Kestra did when she borrowed me to pop you

one. And I don't think it stops at a finger," she confessed, gingerly touching the bones on the back of her hand, which had already begun to swell. "Noah, has she always been so hot tempered? So angry?"

"Let us just say," he admitted, "that this was one of her more impressive nights. What we lack in words, she often makes up for in body language."

"You should have warned me she would be so . . ."

"Intractable?" Noah gave her a crooked little grin. "I tend to look on it as one of her charms. It has grown on me."

"The difference is she doesn't think you're really going to show up at her doorstep one day. You know otherwise. Maybe you should discuss the matter with Magdelegna first. Your sister seems to have a knack with unwilling people."

"Perhaps."

It was not lost on Corrine that the Demon King was going to, in great part, relish this particular expedition into dangerous waters.

There's something about these Demon men, she mused.

The more you fought them, the more it seemed to encourage them. Intellectually even more than physically. But Corrine couldn't help but feel a little trepidation. For a short while, she'd become a part of this Kestra. There was something not entirely copacetic about her. However, Corrine didn't have enough information to quite place her finger on it. Hopefully, when they worked on their next and final session the following week, after they were rested from this night's exertions, she would better be able to make sense of the matter.

"Come," the King said abruptly, taking the Druid by her uninjured hand and rising to help her to her feet. "We should get you to a medic."

"Is it true you don't take contracts on people?"

Kestra turned slightly from her study of a lovely oil painting, looking over her shoulder to examine the dapper man who sat behind her in a double-breasted silk suit, wiping a handkerchief repeatedly between his hands.

Sweaty palms, she mused.

"I'm a businesswoman, Mr. Sands, not a murderer." Kestra finally turned from her perusal of the expensive piece of artwork, tossing her long white braid back over her shoulder with habitual emphasis. "And I'm not here to discuss options on future endeavors. We do that on my terms, at a place and time I choose." She smiled softly, walking with practiced grace across the thick carpet covering the penthouse's floor. "We're here to fulfill payment. Nothing more, nothing less."

She laughed cordially when he did, coming to stand on the opposite side of the coffee table that sat before him. She looked quite refined in her simple silk dress with single-roped pearls around her throat. But as she braced her legs apart and cocked one hip ever so slightly, Sands could see the tight pull of well-honed muscle flexing up her calves and thighs. There was no mistaking what lay beneath the feminine glamour.

"Well, Ms. Irons, that's what you're here for, after all," he agreed affably.

Sands leaned forward to place a small box on the glass coffee table, using two fingers to slide it across to her. She waited until he sat back again before she reached down with a single fingertip to lift the cover of the box, revealing the money within it. She closed it immediately.

"You don't count?" Sands asked.

She glanced up at him from beneath lashes as white as her hair, her almost translucent blue eyes training on him.

"Do I need to?"

"Of course not."

"Why not?" she asked casually.

Sands laughed. "Are you kidding? Anyone who would try to cheat you would have to be insane."

"And that's why I never have to count," she rejoined, picking up the box and tucking it into her purse. She shouldered the leather accessory with ease, as if all it had within it was a comb and lipstick, not nearly a quarter million dollars in cash.

"We'll be calling you again," Sands said cordially.

"I would imagine so."

Sands stood up, wiped his palm on his kerchief, and extended the hand to her. Kestra merely smiled politely and kept both her hands on her purse strap.

Jim had always accused her of having a sixth sense so uncanny that it gave him the willies. The shiver that suddenly walked up her spine, resting with a sharp tingle at the base of her hairline as it was doing right now, had never failed to alert her that something wasn't quite right. She preferred to think of it as her subconscious putting together telltale clues that her conscious mind didn't take direct note of.

She lowered her thick white lashes until they all but obscured the blue diamond irises of her eyes. She glanced around the room yet again, as she had been doing since stepping into the unknown territory. This time she caught the slightest shadow of movement in the hallway behind Sands's back.

She sighed, long and regretfully, flicking open her icy eyes so she could give him a cold glare. "Whatever you're planning," she hissed chillingly, "let me warn you it isn't a good idea."

Then, without waiting for a reply, she swung out with her now heavily weighted purse and clocked Sands upside his head. He hadn't expected to be the one taken by surprise, so he fell like a dead tree in a winter forest.

Kestra popped out of her heels and made a mad dash across the room. Heading for the door would be a mistake, leaving her too open if the person in the hallway was armed, so she dove over the breakfast bar and into the kitchen where she would be out of his or her line of sight. Unfortunately, it put her far from the only exit from the penthouse.

She reached into her bag for her gun, dropping everything else as she cupped it in her hands and laid her finger over the trigger. All the clues to trouble were now in the forefront of her mind, making her curse herself for missing them at the outset. Sands's sweaty palms. His question about whether she would kill for money. He'd been nervous and feeling her out about how dangerous she might be. What he'd failed to take into account was that she didn't consider self-defense murder, and she wasn't above taking the life of anyone who threatened to do the same to her.

She glanced toward Sands as she eased into the kitchen entrance. He was bleeding heavily into the formerly pristine carpet, still out cold near her abandoned shoes. Her mind turned to the question of how many others were possibly hiding in the enormous suite. She didn't usually meet for payment in a private place, and now she recalled why that was a very good rule to adhere to. Also, she'd dismissed Jim from his usual duty of monitoring her safety from a nearby vehicle.

It wasn't the time for self-recriminations, however, so she put her bad choices aside and concentrated on getting out of the situation alive and preferably unwounded.

In reality, she was screwed, and she knew it.

A reality that set in a second later as the wall near her head exploded. She yelped as drywall was flung everywhere and in rapid succession as someone shot through it from the opposite side. All she could do was drop down to the floor as the wall shattered above her, raining plaster and, after a bullet struck a pipe fitting, water down onto her. She had no choice but to get out of range, crawling back into the living room area quickly.

She barely had both knees on the carpeting before a huge hand grabbed her by her braid and jerked her hard to her feet.

As was often the case in these situations, she never had a chance to figure out why she was being targeted.

She felt the burn of a hot gun muzzle against her temple just before she was shot through the head.

Chapter 4

One Week Later

The next week, Corrine opened the door after a very gentle tapping called her attention to it. She peeked cautiously around the door, her mouth opening into a surprised O when she saw Noah. Draped slackly over the Demon King's chest and shoulder was Corrine's decidedly comatose niece.

"What do you do, suck the energy out of her?" Corrine accused in a heated whisper. "I can never get her to sleep like that!"

"I hope she will not interfere," Noah whispered back over the raven dark curls that were such a clear combination of both her parents' traits. "I got roped into emergency babysitting."

"Because I had to turn them down." Corrine giggled. "Don't you ever say no to them?"

"Why would I want to?" he asked with a shrug of the shoulder that wasn't occupied by Leah's head.

"Good point. It should be okay, seeing as how she's asleep. Let's tuck her in. I take it you haven't been able to find Kestra through physical searching yet?"

"No, not yet. Besides her name, her hair color, and the fact that she spoke what I think was American English, there is not much else to go on."

"Well, we'll take care of that tonight."

"Corrine?"

"Yes?"

The Demon King hesitated as she turned back to look at him expectantly.

"I have not dreamed of her in almost a week."

"Noah," she chided softly, moving to cover his hand warmly where it rested on her niece's back. "Stop worrying. The closer you get to her, the less you'll need to dream of her for contact."

"Are you sure? It feels . . . I feel like everything about me has suddenly gone vacant. The dreams were driving me mad, but suddenly I find myself wishing I had never complained about that."

"Relax. Put the baby on the couch and come to my sanctum. Let's start the ritual and put your mind at ease."

They were having difficulty this time when, in Corrine's limited practice before then, it should have been easier. The seeking Druid was sweating from the heat of all the flame around her, not to mention the heat Noah was giving off due to his deep concentration. As he focused singularly on the search for Kestra, it took away from the sense he used to regulate such power overflows. Tonight, the as-yet unborn Druid named Kestra seemed farther than mere miles could measure as they meditated and pushed out with their combined power to locate her. Corrine was driven by her fear of failure. She couldn't be unsuccessful for the first time with, of all people, the Demon King.

True, whoever Kestra was, she had great potential for enormous power. There was little question. Even Corrine's experience, slight as it was, had shown her that power attracted power. It was genetics that linked Demon and Druid, when it came down to it, and it was only reasonable that a powerful man like Noah would mesh with an equally suitable partner, one of unfathomable scope of talent, once his real touch "switched" her Druidic abilities on.

Remembering how Kestra had fought with enormous strength of will and fear-driven determination, Corrine was positive that it was the Druid herself who was shunting them away. Though she might not have conscious control over her latent powers, her subconscious might well be tapping in to them in a classic "fight or flight" push. It was clear from the last encounter that Kestra was very wary of Noah. It didn't matter that she didn't know his name or face. The untried Druid still must be feeling the fact that Noah was more than a dream, right down to the core of every feminine instinct she possessed. If not, why would she have been so hostile and defensive?

Corrine had avoided touching Noah this time, knowing how uncomfortable he had been when he'd found himself kissing another Demon's mate. It was an affront to his deeply embedded sense of honor, no matter how much she explained to him that it wasn't she who had been on the receiving end of the kiss, for all her physicality in the exchange. Her soul had remained untouched. If it hadn't, Kane would never have stood for it. Neither would she. But now she was afraid that these foibles and acts of decorum were interfering with what they needed to do to succeed. And because she refused to fail at anything ever again when it came to her Druidic abilities, she pushed protocol and permission aside and reached for Noah.

He started violently when her hands, chilled and damp in spite of the heat all around them, cradled the contours of his face. His eyes opened as hers did, and she leaned over the fire between them so that their foreheads touched and her eyes bored deeply into his.

Suddenly the scent of spun sugar exploded into the air, drowning out every herb and tendril of smoke. That central focus of scent lasted for a moment, then whorled around to include others. Scents of the place where she was at that very moment. And that was what they wanted. They wanted to know where to find her. Noah was desperate to find her. Corrine was desperate to give him this wish.

"Unc No."

Corrine and Noah started as the little voice came out of nowhere and everywhere at once. Their heads snapped to look at the doorway, where Leah still clung to the impossible achievement of turning the doorknob to have access to her aunt Corrine and her "unc No."

The disruption of their concentration burst into the room like a supernova, a tangible blast of energy that spewed fire and the scent of cotton candy. Corrine screamed, throwing up her hands as flame blasted in her direction.

The flame passed harmlessly through her and Noah both, but hot on its heated heels came the sensation of being torn apart at the molecular level. There was a spectacular rending, tearing through them with agonizing, contorting pain.

And then . . .

Silence and darkness.

The wail of a child penetrated Noah's mind, triggering the autonomic response to draw a breath. He gasped, coughed violently, and struggled to rapidly stagger to his feet. His eyes were burning. From what, he couldn't fathom. He instinctively reached toward the cry of the Enforcers' child, dragging Leah to himself as his balance failed and he fell back down to a single knee. Blindly, he ran hands over the warm little body of his charge, all the while forcing himself to breathe in a semblance of a regular rhythm. He felt Leah's pajamas were intact, as were her hair and lashes, both of which would've been damaged if the inexplicable flames he'd seen billowing into the room had singed or burned her.

He was grateful to realize she was more frightened than

anything else, and he cuddled her closely, shushing and swaying with her as he tried to rub clarity into his burning eyes. He was impervious to fire, so he couldn't understand why he felt as if he'd been burned. He would never have thought that the ritual to find his mate would in any way be capable of causing harm to anyone. It was inconceivable. He was still struggling with denial and unanswered questions as he groped into the smears of light and dark in search of Corrine.

"Hush, Leah, you're safe," he rasped soothingly to the child, somehow managing to sound far more convincing than he felt. Suddenly his hand hit silky soft curls, his fingers weaving into the red strands that came into focus as he leaned closer to them. Everything seemed so loud, hurting his ears. Everything smelled so harsh and tasted so bitter. But it all seemed to calm down just a little when he finally touched the cool, clammy skin of Corrine's face.

He heard her cough, and she jerked beneath his touch.

"It is all right," he reassured her as she rasped and gagged for breath. He blindly pulled her against him, instinctively bringing both females into the circle of his safeguard. He might be sightless and disoriented, but he'd be damned if he was going to let either one of them move a millimeter away from his protection.

Noah turned his face to the right when he abruptly realized something very important.

Sunlight.

There was no mistaking the sensation of sunlight. Especially after being taxed by whatever ordeal it was that they had just been churned through, there could be no other cause for the unmistakable lethargy that meant pure sunlight was shining down on them.

"It is dusk," he argued out loud. "It is night!"

Corrine went rigid against him as she realized why he was in conflict over that point.

"We're still indoors," she said with a whisper, her hands brushing over the floor beneath her knees. She recognized by touch bits of the things belonging to her sanctum, until she swept her fingers to the left toward Noah and touched carpeting that was unmistakably deep with pile.

The floor to the sanctum beneath the pillows was only bare, polished wood.

Noah couldn't remain on his knees a moment longer. He hauled both of his charges up with him as he gained his feet, bracing his legs apart. He closed his eyes to discontinue the reflexive need to visually identify his surroundings. He took a deep, cleansing breath and reached for the power that centered everything that he was. It cast out of him like a net, a wholly different sensory network that blanketed the entire area. He sensed the pure energy of the sunlight, the life forces of a few animals and a dense population of humans.

Kane and Corrine lived in solitude, their closest neighbors all Demons themselves for the most part, and even they were a good mile away. At first it felt no different than anything else he had always sensed with ease and an almost careless ability, but the information Noah's power was giving to him made no sense. It felt as though he were standing on the edge of a city. A human city.

That was the moment his vision finally decided to cooperate and join his other senses. He hadn't even realized he'd opened his eyes until they focused on something in front of him.

A room, large and expansive, carpeted from wall to windows. Windows that looked down on an enormous metropolis. It only took him a moment to recognize enough buildings to identify it as Chicago.

And yet . . .

When he turned his head to the right, he was still in Corrine's particularly designed sanctum. He focused down at his feet, trying to make sense of the trick of his eyes.

There, as if spliced together, was the line where two drastically different floors met and fused, polished oak and halves of pillows meeting up with plush carpets and pristine barrenness. He stood between this unlikely meshing of rooms, a foot on either side, holding Corrine to his right fully in the room he knew, and Leah on his left, fully in the room that was foreign to him.

For a moment, it felt as if he'd been frozen still in the middle of one of his sister's teleportations. When a Mind Demon teleported someone else from one point to another, those two points appeared to squeeze together, making it seem as if you could step from the origination to the destination instantaneously. However, Noah knew this wasn't the case. When the two places of a teleport met, it was in a queer distortion of shapes and sounds and visuals. Nothing was clearly definable until you stepped fully in one direction or another, and the effect of the transport washed away a moment later.

So how had these two places connected in this Escher-like fashion? Modern metropolis suite looking down on a city from on high, and peaceful country setting in rural England?

He didn't have time to contemplate it any further. The sound of voices slowly faded in around him, echoing everywhere, disjointed as he looked for the people they should have been coming from. Instinctively, the Demon King stepped toward the side of the split that he knew best, the one without apparent variables that could threaten their safety. As he did so, the foreign room seemed to flicker with a strange pattern of sunlight. He glanced toward the expansive windows. He drew in a sharp breath as he realized the clouds and the weather were changing, as well as the position of the sun.

More specifically, it all seemed to be running backward, from west to east across the sky. It only took twenty seconds for it to stop at a point that seemed to be shortly after dawn. As the light faded out to that warm half-light of a bright, promising sun and the remnants of the very last touches of a rose and violet dawn, the voices came closer and people suddenly took their positions in the room.

A woman and a man, one seated on a couch, the other standing almost a hand's reach away from Noah as she gazed appreciatively at a painting hanging on the wall. Since the painting was partially cut off by the spliced nature of the joined rooms, Noah came to understand that this effect was only being seen by those who had apparently caused it.

Which, of course, meant nothing when the woman spoke clearly for the first time, and a whole new recognition set in.

Noah's breath caught as she stepped back, turning away from her appraisal of the painting, giving him the full picture of her tall, athletic figure, the curves and shape of which he knew purely by heart, and the saucy swing of a pristine white braid of hair.

She crossed the room with refined movement, a well-practiced gait that had clearly been learned, covering up the more natural slink of her body as he watched the line of her spine and hips. Noah barely heard her conversation with the man whose nervous energy was grating over his senses. He was too astounded, realizing he was actually looking on the fully focused face and figure of the woman he had dreamed of so incessantly.

"Whoa."

Corrine whispered the word in a mixture of fear and a truly felt sense of accomplishment. She reached out to touch the invisible barrier that marked the change of locations, but Noah stopped her with a firm hand on her wrist. It hadn't seemed dangerous when he'd straddled both sides of this strange connection from that world to this, but what if the other room suddenly disappeared, and Corrine's curious hand along with it?

Noah didn't have time to worry about that. Out of his peripheral vision, he saw Kestra swing out with her purse, clocking her companion hard in the head with it. Corrine gasped as she saw it, too, and together they watched as the blonde made an inexplicable dash across the room and flew over a counter and into the kitchen. A short while later, an all-too-distinct series of bangs went off. Noah didn't even have time to react. A second man had appeared from the hallway a short turn away, just in time to meet up with Kestra as she lurched back out of the kitchen on her hands and knees.

He grabbed Noah's mate by her braid and promptly shot her in the head.

"No!" the Demon King bellowed in shock and the sudden collision of despair as the next few seconds played out in a horrific display of blood and undeniable loss of life.

He lurched forward, unthinking of those he guarded.

But it was too late.

That strange distortion of sight suddenly overwhelmed the Demon King once more. Everything faded and twisted, and that rending sensation of being picked apart one cell at a time bolted through him. In all the times he'd adjusted his form on a molecular level, he had never experienced such agony and such a lack of control. He tried to breathe, but had no lungs with which to do so. Not in that moment.

The next instant he could, and the deep reflexive breath that followed carried the overwhelming scent of burning herbs and candles. He lost track of those he held for a moment, but soon was aware of all three of them crashing down hard onto the velvety pillows that covered the floor of Corrine's sanctum.

Corrine was coughing harshly, and then he felt her grasping at the sleeve of his shirt, clearly just as blind as he was once more.

"What the hell just happened?" she managed to say hoarsely.

That told Noah that this was far from the response Corrine had been expecting, though he'd already assumed as much. He finally found Leah, cradling her close to his chest again as her little body was racked with coughing. He rubbed violently at his eyes, trying to force himself to see. It did little good, so he was compelled to take a seat, with Leah on his lap and Corrine leaning heavily against him, and wait his eyesight out.

Just then a sharp distortion of air blew into them, followed by the unmistakable odor of sulfur and smoke that cut through the aroma of burning herbs.

"Kane!" Corrine cried out her husband's name, recognizing his arrival even though she couldn't see him.

"Corr! Noah! What the hell happened?"

Noah felt Corrine's presence and warmth being drawn away from him. He blinked in the direction of her energy signature and the copper red of her hair suddenly came into blurry focus. He immediately turned his attention to Leah, continuing to blink away the weakness of his eyes as he tried to examine the child for injury.

"Kane, are they injured?" he demanded of the younger Demon.

"No," Kane assured him as he kneeled to inspect Leah. "Covered in soot, but otherwise no worse for the wear. Are you okay?"

Noah had no idea how he could possibly answer that question. Relieved of his urgent worry over Leah and Corrine, the full implication of what had happened, of what he had just witnessed, weighed on him with a sudden and bright devastation he could remember feeling only at the worst moments in his long life. And yet this was somehow much keener. It sliced through flesh and bone and straight into the depths of his soul.

He let Kane draw Leah from his hold, and then stumbled through the blur of pillows and candlelight until he could touch a wall. He pressed his fingers into the lush velvet covering the wood paneling. The thick pile crushed beneath the onslaught of his clenching fist.

"Noah."

He felt Corrine's hands on his back, her empathy all too apparent in the tenderness of her touch. Noah couldn't bear the comfort. He didn't want to be comforted. He shrugged her off hard enough to make her stumble backward away from him.

"She is dead," he said, his voice far rougher with emotion than he would have liked. He ran cold fingers down his soiled face, focusing straight ahead until the detail of the fabric before him came into clarity. The truth of his words was devastating to him, and on so many levels. He laughed mirthlessly at the capricious nature of fate. "Now I know why I have not dreamed of her in a week. Those dreams are . . ." He swallowed hard, trying to tamp down emotion far too violent to express in front of gentle friends. "They were a connection that needed both sides to be completed. And now I just stood here and let it happen again!" He turned sharply to look down at the redheaded Druid. "You were right. I was so stupid. I wasted six months. If I had come to you when this started, she would have been safe under my protection when she needed me most!"

Corrine closed her eyes, fighting back her sympathetic tears. "I don't understand any of this myself, Noah. You can't be sure—"

"I am damn sure, Corr. Did you look out the windows? The sky went from noon to dawn, moving time backward to the moment this thing occurred. Backward to what I am guessing was a week ago, to the day I ceased to dream of her. And do not tell me there was nothing I could do to change it. I felt that carpet beneath my foot! I could have—I should have *done* something! I could smell the difference between this room and that one. I felt the energy of an entire city beyond it. For that moment, that place in time was as real as this place is right now."

The monarch finally took a good look at the tall redhead who, in spite of a layer of grime, seemed to emanate power. She had done a potent and amazing thing, a feat beyond all expectations of her abilities, and the aftermath showed in overbright green eyes and an aura that glowed like a Christmas tree.

"Consider," he said, this time more gently. "How would Kane suffer if Isabella had found you too late, Corrine? I have a right to grieve this loss!" The declaration promptly ended any discussion. The room vibrated with pain and tension, the silent noise punctuated with the occasional cough of Corrine's niece.

"Yuck," the child declared. She licked her hand and rubbed it on her clothes in an attempt to clean the soiled palm. Leah was fastidious about cleanliness, though clearly not as much so about germs.

Wordlessly, Noah crossed to Kane and plucked his charge out of her blood uncle's hands, carrying her across the room. He held the child to his chest with one massive hand, and she instantly hooked her small, skinny legs around his waist, her head dropping onto his shoulder with contentment and the security that her uncle Noah would help her. The way he held her, however, grabbed at Corrine's heart. Leah was hooked around him as if she were some sort of bulletproof vest, protecting his all-too-vulnerable heart.

Kane moved to hold his distraught wife when her thoughts and emotions impacted against him like a train wreck. He followed her gaze, which was affixed on the door to the room as if Noah were standing on its threshold instead of having already passed through it.

"Shh, sweetness," he soothed softly, leaning to kiss a dirt-streaked cheek sympathetically. "You'll see. He'll be fine in time. Like any death, this will be grieved and then it will be put aside."

"I wish I could believe that," Corrine whispered to him on a fast, nervous breath. "The last time someone learned of the death of her potential Druid mate, she went mad."

"Mary? *Ruth* drove Mary mad, Corrine. From the minute that child was born she was spoiled, sheltered, and held much further above her station by Ruth than was warranted. The mother was to blame for her daughter's actions because of her carelessness in Mary's upbringing. That can never happen to Noah. Noah comes from an upbringing that defies explanation and a place I couldn't even begin to put in plain words for you." Kane shook his head when he felt her puzzled expression. "Not a physical place. A metaphysical one. Noah was born with something none of the rest of us could ever lay claim to. It's why he, above all others, is King."

"That's why he, above all others, deserved a complementary Queen," Corrine replied.

Noah knew on some level that the child he was now watching play contentedly before his hearth was responsible for what had happened.

The Prophecy had been clear and unmistakable. The Enforcers would give life to the child who would be the very first of his or her kind to have the power to manipulate the element of Time. Though she was only a little over two years old, Leah clearly had shown the first evidence of her ability, an astounding event even had it been a well-known element like Water or Wind. Even his remarkable power had not come to him at such a young age.

Of course, she had no idea what she had done or the significance of the part she had played. Suddenly certain things began to make sense to him. He spent enormous amounts of time with this special child. Though she'd had no conscious control of what she was doing, somehow Leah had formed that conduit through time for him. Perhaps it was simply a child's desire to please that had triggered the subconscious ability. Leah loved her uncle Noah with incredible devotion. She strived to do things that would please him. Combine this with the power of his and Corrine's wills, their need to be successful in their hunt, and it had made the perfect catalyst for a child with an untried power who wanted nothing more but to give him what he wanted. What he needed.

And for a terrible moment, Noah wanted to use her for exactly that reason. The King was a scholar, so he knew full well the implications of altering time, and a person's presence in time. However, he couldn't bring himself to care for that long second of self-indulgent thought.

Noah stood up abruptly, pacing over the playing toddler in order to lean close against the mantel. Normally the proximity to such intense heat would comfort him, but this time it did not.

He wanted to burn. Oh yes, he was impervious to any and every form of flame or molten fire that the natural world could offer up, but this wasn't what he meant. In his dreams, *she* had made him burn. Kestra Irons. He laughed with the dry irony of her last name. The metal iron was toxic to Demonkind. It burned on contact. Just like Kestra.

The fire of passion was no stranger to him; he manipulated it well and with arrogant skill, and he had more than one lover in his history who would attest to that with a longing sigh of remembrance. This thing with the woman who had pervaded his sleeping world was out of reach of all of that. It was transient and lacking cohesion, and yet somehow all the more real. Now made unreal and inescapably out of reach for all the rest of time as he knew it.

Unless . . .

Noah shivered. He was unused to selfish thought. He was a man who lived every moment of his existence with the well-being of so many others as his first priority. Family. When not family, Council. When not family or Council, the multitude of his subjects. If none of them, then the races of others with which they associated. That was the essence of a good monarch. Everyone else must come first, especially those you loved best.

In that moment, all he wanted was to put himself first.

Whatever the cost.

No matter who had to pay.

Isabella entered the King's castle without even bothering to knock. It wasn't so much that she had developed altered manners from living in Demon society as it was that, to Noah, privacy was an alien, if not impossible, concept. Dozens of people moved in and out of his home throughout the night, and he expected it to be so.

Since Noah still had Bella's daughter in his care, she had even more cause to march in unannounced. She rounded the wall of the foyer, entering the Great Hall and heading automatically for the enormous fireplace that Leah was constantly in front of, whatever the season, whenever she stayed with him. Her steps hitched when the Turkish rug, so well worn from years of children playing upon it, lay as abandoned as the toys scattered over it.

She wasn't worried, just surprised. She crossed her arms over her middle, her fingers drumming thoughtfully in the curve of her waist for a moment. She was a hunter, like her husband, and all she need do was quiet her thoughts and concentrate on her target. She would find them wherever they were in the enormous house without having to shout or search rooms. Filtering through scent and residual patterns of warmth, she was able to sort out which belonged to her daughter and her liege.

To her continuing surprise, it led out of Noah's home entirely. This perplexed her because it was nearing dawn. The dawn and the sunlight were things best avoided for those of the Nightwalker races, aside from the incredibly powerful Elders. And while that description fit Noah, her daughter was a very different matter. Though a Demon and Druid mixed child was a unique creature, there was no guarantee that her mother's blasé human immunity to the sun would be an inherited trait. For Demon children, the sun could make them very weak and ill. It even had the potential to kill vulnerable children not yet in their power. They would fall asleep and simply never wake up. Isabella and Jacob had never had a desire to test their child's tolerance to sunlight. They would wait until she was older before trying such tricks.

It was unusually irresponsible for Noah to take the little girl elsewhere when daylight was so near, especially because Isabella or Jacob always came and collected her exactly one hour before the dawn. Still, the young mother didn't worry or panic. Leah was with Noah, after all. The King would rather die than expose her to harm. He was probably already on his way home and just running a little late.

So Isabella turned to flop down into the seat nearest the

fire, sighing contentedly as she stretched out a body quite weary from a long night's work. The closer it got to Samhain and the full moon, the more she and Jacob were forced to hunt down Demons who lost control of their logic and normal temperaments. After a night like the one they had just had, she was always very tired and more than happy to go to bed.

She wouldn't have to worry about another out-of-control Demon until dusk the next day.

Corrine lay down in bed gratefully, feeling exhausted mentally and emotionally, both of which manifested in her body as weary muscles and achy bones. Kane was already in bed, anticipating the coming dawn that left him so lethargic. She had showered off the soot and soil of the night's exertions, so she brushed her still-damp hair out into a fan of dark coils, back over her pillow, with a single sweep of her arm. With choreography of thought that came so easily to telepathically connected partners, Kane turned toward her and drew her warm curves tightly against the cradle of his body.

"Sleep," he murmured gently. "The coming night will provide ample time for you to obsessively worry."

"I know. I just can't escape the feeling that we shouldn't let Noah deal with this alone," she whispered back to him.

"I agree. But day is come and he will sleep like the rest of us. We'll attend him first thing in the evening."

"Thank you," she said, hugging the arms wrapped around her.

"I haven't done anything," he chuckled, rubbing his cheek against hers.

"Go to sleep. I'll tell you why you're so wonderful in the evening."

Corrine punctuated this with a yawn, closed her eyes, and quickly fell asleep, still smiling at her husband.

Chapter 5

Something disturbed Corrine in her sleep just enough to make her brow furrow. She turned her head restlessly, but was suddenly halted as an abrupt hand on her mouth stilled her movement and pushed her head back into the pillow with a heavy weight.

Despite the depth of her sleep, Corrine's eyes flew open wide. She panicked for all of a moment, but then realized she recognized the man who was leaning over her in the slightly brightened room. She exhaled with relief as she looked up into Noah's gray-green eyes.

Her relief was short-lived. As she looked up at the King, Corrine was overwhelmed with the very powerful intuition that something wasn't right. First of all, Noah would never approach her in such a rude manner. No matter how badly he might need her help, he simply would not ever wake her behind her husband's back. Or, in this case, leave him sleeping beside her in ignorance. Corrine's heart began to beat a rapid cadence as the King leaned farther over her, boring his gaze into hers so deeply that she felt as if he were strip-mining her thoughts with angry clarity.

"If you attempt to wake him, I will be forced to drain his energy even more than I already have," Noah whispered to her, his gentleness of voice and manner giving her a terrible chill because it was so clearly in opposition to his actions. "If I do that, it will leave him quite weak and vulnerable to the day. He is young yet, Corrine, and I do not know what that would do to him."

Corrine flicked a wide, frightened gaze from Noah to her defenseless husband. She couldn't control the panic in her thoughts, so she closed her eyes and briefly prayed that Noah's manipulations and the lethargy of the day were enough to keep Kane from picking up on her alarm. The connection that had grown between them was now so strong that there was very little guarantee of that. For the first time she wished she were still at that weaker level of telepathy that had made it so hard for them to communicate mentally early on. She had no idea why Noah was leaning over her, threatening her and her husband in the bright light of day, but instinct screamed at her that it wasn't quite Noah who was looking down on her.

She opened her eyes once more, giving a single, distinct nod. It would be senseless to fight him. Not only because she had no power with which to do so, but because even if she did, he could easily overcome her.

How she longed for her sister's ability to siphon away power in that moment. Oh, she had a version of this herself; every Druid did. However, in their human/Druid hybrid way it tended to be limited only to their Imprinted partner. It was part of the balance that helped soothe the Demon soul and control a Demon's power in its less controllable moments. As with Bella, the trick was to turn it off. It was this ability, as well as the emotional weaving of souls, that kept a Demon safe from madness. It was another reason why an Imprinted partner was even more precious to a Demon than diamonds.

Noah was dragging her out of bed with a painful hand around her arm when that thought and all its implications sank into Corrine's awareness. It was nearing Samhain, the moon becoming fuller every moment, the pressure of its influence weighing down heavily on even the most powerful and moral of Demons. The realization altered her entire perception about what was happening; however, she couldn't protest in any fashion. Noah's grip was like iron, holding her to his body and forcing her into silence. The Demon King was hot against her back, completely at odds with the few degrees cooler that normal Demon body temperature was compared to humans. His bare fingers scalded her lips and cheeks like tea that was a little too hot. He marched her out of the room and closed the door behind them. Only when he shoved her toward the stairs did he finally release her.

Corrine didn't even look back at him. She lowered her head and obeyed his obvious command in silence. She preceded him down the stairs as she tried to force herself to think. If she attempted to wake Kane, Noah would instantly recognize his shift in energy. She wasn't even sure she could rouse her husband so far into daylight hours and after he had been manipulated by Noah's powers. Noah was right. Kane was too young to have even the dregs of a hope of coming up against the King's powers. Corrine was even more disadvantaged.

When they reached the first floor, she realized with increasing dread that she wasn't Noah's sole focus. Leah, who was curled up asleep on the couch and sucking her thumb enthusiastically, was also involved. Corrine was frightened and baffled as she rushed over to her niece. She gathered the babe to her breast protectively and searched her quickly for damage.

"What the hell is the matter with you?" she cried out, glaring at the Demon King with the infamous temper that ran through the blood of her family. Noah smiled, and somehow that chilled Corrine more than his anger would have. He moved over to her and Leah, leaning forward slightly to meet her wide, green eyes.

"Your sister and her husband will be here soon. Even my talents are not enough to mislead their chase for very long."

That was his answer. There was only one thing that would make him avoid the Enforcers, and he had confirmed what Corrine had already been coming to understand.

Noah had succumbed to the madness of the Samhain moon.

Corrine felt a stab in her heart, realizing that she had partially caused that. The understanding that his destined mate was dead, and in a violent manner that could have been avoided had he only acted sooner, would make for a powerful catalyst toward a surrender to the Hallowed moon. She and Kane had made a grave mistake letting him go off alone in grief.

"Noah, whatever you're thinking of doing, you have to know that it will bring you into conflict with those you love! You will force Jacob and Isabella to—"

"They can try. However, I doubt they will be too eager to do so with their daughter and you, Corrine, in the line of fire. Now stop stalling and get into the back room. The longer you take, the more you increase the chance of them actually taking part in that confrontation you so dread."

Silently, painfully, she tore her gaze from his and obeyed him. The implications of the situation she found herself in were almost too excruciating to bear. She hadn't done many searches for mates thus far, but she had never once entertained the idea that there could be negative consequences. If she had taken a moment to worry about it, she would have understood that an incident like this could very well keep Demons away in droves. Even more so than they already were.

She was occupied with this thought when she was harshly shoved into the room she used for meditation, the one that had seen such tragic revelation only a few hours ago. She fell onto her knees in the mess of soiled pillows and tumbled herbs that Kane had coaxed her into waiting to clean up the next night. The room still smelled heavily of burnt herbs, the char of fire, and even the traces of that moment of time in Chicago.

"Wake the child," Noah commanded frigidly, righting a

few candles and lighting them and the remnants of herbs in the brazier with a simple thought.

"Impossible. Not at this hour of the day."

"I will help you," he said, again gracing her with that disturbing smile.

Sure enough, Leah stirred in her arms with a cranky protest and a whine. Corrine hushed her as she apprehensively watched Noah manipulate the surroundings of a place she held sacred.

"Noah, please, what do you expect me to do? I don't even know what I did the first time!"

"Just do what you always do," he said serenely. "It was Leah who brought me to her. You merely gave her a path."

Corrine realized the truth in one heart-stopping breath. *Of course!* She knew the prophecy of Leah's birth as well as anyone. Why hadn't she realized this earlier? The incident had happened the moment her niece had intruded on their ritual. And now Noah clearly hoped to reproduce the effect. But to what end?

"I will not let her die, Corrine."

"Oh my God, you want to bring her into the present," Corrine gasped, the realization horrifying her. "You want to try to save her and bring her here! My God, Noah, do you have any idea what the ramifications of playing with fate can be? You and your Demons revere Destiny. It's your religion! And you don't even know if it's possible to—"

"I know that if I can do this, it will save her life," he interrupted her coldly, "and that is all that matters to me."

Of course it would be that simple to someone in his state of mind. Isabella had once told her that no one could reason with a Demon in the throes of a Hallowed compulsion, save maybe the Enforcers. Their presence alone tended to have a powerful quelling effect. However, Corrine was beginning to doubt that the mere act of the Enforcers materializing before him would have much of an effect on Noah. He knew what he wanted, and clearly he was willing to do anything to get it done. Even things that, when he came back to his own ordered senses, would devastate him.

Tears filled the young Druid's eyes as she thought about that. The only thing she could be grateful for was that Leah was far too young to understand what was going on and would probably not think twice about treating her uncle Noah the way she always had. Corrine knew that even if this all stopped that very moment, she wasn't capable of doing the same.

"Noah, you can't be sure you can do this. You could be risking all of our lives for a life that ended a week ago. Please! Please don't—"

She choked on her next word when the King's hand closed like a brutal vise around the back of her neck. He gathered her hair in his fist and jerked her head back so she could see his eyes. Cold and gray and lifeless, they radiated the distance of his rational mind.

"I suggest you start focusing on your task."

Jacob materialized out of a cloud of dust seconds after his wife. She was already several feet in front of him, reaching out with every known sense for any trace of their child.

"I don't understand," she bit out with helpless frustration. "This is the second time we've taken the wrong path, Jacob."

"What I do not understand is why Noah would take off with Leah in the first place. Perhaps it was against his will? I cannot imagine how that would be possible, but the confusion of energy we keep encountering . . ."

"It is as if we are being purposely misled." His wife completed his thought for him, drawing her bottom lip between her nibbling teeth. She shivered violently, wrapping her arms around herself as if trying to give herself comfort. "I should have known something was wrong when the castle was empty. Instead, I waited for an hour, wasting precious time thinking that any minute Noah was going to materialize with our baby in his hands."

Jacob stepped up to his distraught mate quickly, drawing her into a comforting embrace. He fought the urge to get wrapped up in her emotions, knowing all too well that one of them had to keep their head. He would wait until he found Noah before he did anything rash. The truth of the matter was that he had an inexplicable urge to throttle the monarch, whether this was something he could have prevented or not.

Even so, he tried not to follow the specific line of thoughts ghosting ominously in the back of his mind. If he contemplated the worst, it would make Bella even more upset. It was near impossible to keep thoughts away from one who was as intimate with his mind as he was, but he would damn well try for her sake. Still, he was all too aware that this year's Samhain moon was unusually potent, the very reason they had been forced to have someone babysit their child from dusk to dawn night after night in the first place. Combine that with the fact that Noah's behavior had been somewhat erratic lately, and it made for a frightening recipe.

Still, no one had ever heard of a Demon harming a child while in the throes of Hallowed madness.

"There's always a first time for everything," Isabella whispered softly.

Jacob cursed under his breath. He hadn't meant to fully entertain his thoughts. "It could be that he left Leah somewhere else and what we are following is Noah playing whatever tricks he feels are necessary to delay us while he engages in whatever mayhem. I do not believe for a second that Noah would harm Leah."

"Why now? It's daylight. How can he be expending this amount of energy? What would drive him so hard against his own sense of right and wrong when the moon is not even out?"

"It is out, love. The moon is always out. It never goes away. It is not like the sun, which is blocked from our sight and senses by the whole of the Earth on a daily cyclical basis. When the moon comes into phase, it remains in that phase day and night. And I think we both know that Noah is far too powerful and efficient at his skills to have to worry about replenishing every iota of energy he expends, whatever the time of day."

"And so . . ." she prompted.

"And so I say you quit playing this game of merry-go-round and go to the most reasonable place you think Noah would leave Leah if he were dropping her into someone else's care. Borrow enough of my power to get you there and let me know what you find. Meanwhile, I am going to make sense of this trick of trails and hunt down our monarch before he does something he will sorely regret."

"Okay," she agreed. She quickly kissed his mouth. She closed her eyes, but didn't take the time to enjoy the intimacy of the touch. She focused inside herself where she kept her ability to siphon Nightwalker power. She didn't hesitate to tear an enormous chunk for herself out of Jacob's power. He would replenish quickly once she was out of range, using the resources of the Earth around him. Her borrowed resources, however, were limited to what she stole and the amount of time she could maintain a grip on them. It had taken her quite a bit of practice to engage in even the most rudimentary form of this skill; this one was a little more on the monumental side.

As she fled in a frantic cloud of dust, Jacob exhaled and sat down hard on the ground. In his sudden physical weakness, he could only watch her go. But it wasn't long after that before he got up and began to unravel the web of deceit his liege lord had woven for him.

"You don't count?" Sands asked.

Kestra glanced up at him from beneath lashes as white as her hair, her almost translucent blue eyes training on him.

"Do I need to?"

"Of course not."

"Why not?" she asked casually.

Sands laughed. “Are you kidding? Anyone who would try to cheat you would have to be insane.”

“And there’s the reason why I never have to count,” she rejoined, picking up the box and tucking it into her purse. She shouldered the leather accessory with ease, as if all it had within it was a comb and lipstick, not nearly a quarter million dollars in cash.

“We’ll be calling you again,” Sands said cordially.

“I would imagine so.”

Sands stood up, wiped his palm on his kerchief, and extended the hand to her. Kestra merely smiled politely and kept both her hands on her purse strap. Handkerchief or not, she wasn’t about to get slimed, and she wasn’t going to give him the opportunity to grab her by her hand.

The thought gave her pause. That was when she realized something wasn’t quite right. The shiver that suddenly walked up her spine, resting with a sharp tingle at the base of her hairline as it was doing right now, had never failed to alert her that something bad was about to happen to her.

She lowered her thick white lashes until they all but obscured the blue diamond irises of her eyes. She glanced around the room yet again, as she had been doing since stepping into the unknown territory. This time she caught the slightest shadow of movement in the hallway behind Sands’s back.

She sighed, long and regretfully, flicking open her icy eyes so she could give him a cold glare. “Whatever you are planning,” she hissed chillingly, “let me warn you it’s not a good idea.”

Then, without waiting for a reply, she swung out with her heavily weighted purse and clocked him upside his head. Kestra popped out of her heels and made a mad dash across the room. Heading for the door would be a mistake, leaving her too open if the person in the hallway was armed, so she dove over the breakfast bar and into the kitchen where she would be out of his or her line of sight. Unfortunately, it put her far from the only apparent exit from the penthouse.

She reached into her bag for her gun, dropping everything else as she cupped it in her hands and laid her finger over the trigger. All the clues to trouble were now in the forefront of her mind, making her curse herself for missing them at the outset. She glanced toward Sands as she eased into the kitchen entrance. He was out cold and bleeding heavily into the formerly pristine carpet, near her abandoned shoes. The question on her mind was how many others might be hiding in the enormous suite.

She was screwed, and she knew it. A second later the wall near her head exploded. She yelped as drywall was flung everywhere and in rapid succession as someone shot through it from the opposite side. All she could do was drop down to the floor as the wall shattered above her, raining plaster and water down onto her. As the path of holes being blown into the wall started to descend toward her prone body, she had no choice but to get out of range as quickly as possible. She scrabbled against the Italian tile, her stocking feet sliding without purchase as she pulled forward on her hands. She grabbed the carpet, her fingers of her left hand gaining purchase on the thick fibers of the pile. She barely had both knees on the carpeting before a huge hand grabbed her by her thick blond braid and jerked her hard to her feet.

She felt the burn of a hot gun muzzle against her temple.

There was the slap of flesh meeting flesh a second before the gun fired near her ear. Kestra dropped to the floor, but miraculously found herself with her head intact. Her ear was ringing painfully, but her attacker had missed. She looked up quickly and saw why.

A tall, black-haired man with the build of a roughneck had the gunman by the arm and did exactly what she would have done had she been given the chance. He broke it clean in half. He grabbed the screaming thug by the back of his collar, slamming him face-first into the near wall so hard that Kestra could easily imagine the snap of one or two more bones, even though she would be lucky if she could hear herself sneeze at that point.

But there was nothing wrong with her eyesight.

She watched as her assailant was dropped at the other man's feet without even a hint of care or concern for his life, an attitude of contempt she was very much inclined to share. Then she saw a second male, no doubt the one who had been playing turkey shoot with her through the wall, run around the bend of the back hallway.

"Look out!" Her warning was apparently unnecessary. So was the bead she drew with her suddenly remembered weapon. The newcomer left his first victim behind him as he stepped into the path of the second. It was as if he couldn't care less that these men were armed. James accused her of having a death wish sometimes; this man who was in the process of saving her life was that term personified, apparently. He was also incredibly fast. One second a gun was brought up in his face; the next he had hold of the other man's arm, wrenched it almost completely around, and moved to strike him in the face with a speed that was unreal for someone his size. She knew an expert fighter when she saw one, but this was out of the scope of even her experience. There was no trading of blows, just him eliminating threats with perfunctory ease.

He turned as the second gunman fell, and her eyes went wide at the imposing sight he made, sturdy legs braced apart, hands half curled into fists, green-gray eyes lit high with the fever of the fight. All of this while dressed in a wardrobe she could only identify as being antiquated. With skintight breeches and a loose, billowing shirt of silk tucked in at his lean waist, he looked like he had stepped off an old pirate ship. Right down to his highly polished boots and the brief ponytail held back by a simple black strip of leather or something like it.

"Come with me."

He held a hand down to her as she stared at him.

"As if!" she exclaimed, getting quickly to her feet and backing away from him. "Thanks for the help, but I am *so* out of here." She raised her weapon, eyeing him so he would take the threat seriously. She barely completed her next step back before he wrapped fingers like steel around her left upper arm, disarming her with embarrassing speed and ease, turning her to him and stepping close enough that they bumped bodies.

"Come willingly or not, it is your choice, but you *are* coming."

For a single suspended instant, Kestra felt the fit of their tense bodies as they stood close enough to exchange heat. Her heartbeat fluttered as she was overwhelmed with the feeling that she knew him somehow. Somehow, his fit and warmth and even his commandeering attitude were instantly recognizable to her. Recognizable, but not identifiable.

"I choose not to come," she snapped at him.

She moved with lithe, determined speed, breaking his hold on her arm swiftly as she recoiled to strike him. He barely ducked fast enough to miss getting clocked in the nose by her palm. She unleashed herself on him with rapid violence, landing half the strikes she intended to, clearly learning as she went how best to feint and orchestrate his responses. But Kestra fought with her emotions in this instance, probably without even knowing why. Her true advantage was that he refused to strike back at her.

He had been human.

But Noah was not human, and he was not very full of patience at the moment, either. *Ungrateful thing that she is*, he thought with an inner chuckle. Kestra was suddenly faced with nothing but air. Then she felt an arm wrapping around her from behind. He jerked her clean off her feet and up into his body, pressing her back and bottom tightly to the contours of rock-hard muscle beneath the delicate fabrics he wore. Kestra gasped when his free arm crossed over her breasts, trapping her beneath flat, open palms of his powerful hands.

"Good night, *Kikilia*," he whispered on a hot breath into her ear.

Kestra opened her mouth to lambaste him, but the next

thing she knew her body was draining of energy so rapidly she was suddenly terrified there wouldn't be enough left for her to draw her next, much-needed breath. She fell down into the will of his embrace, blackness overwhelming her.

Isabella coalesced with a sharp snap in Corrine's living room. It made no sense to her that Corrine would take Leah without sending Kane to them with a quick pop-in-o-matic message telling them so. Even if it had been terribly close to dawn, Corrine would have known she'd be mad with worry and would have found a way to reassure her that her daughter was safe in her care. Then again, Kane was limited to teleporting to places he had been to or seen before. With the two Enforcers running around like they had been, getting a locus on them would have been impossible for Kane.

Bella rubbed her hands together anxiously as she oriented herself to her surroundings. Right away her hunting senses flared to life, alerting her to the presence of not only her daughter, but her sister and the elusive Demon King. Instantly on the heels of that was the aura of something else . . . something powerful and distorted . . . and a blanketing underlayer of fear that was so potent, the little Druid could practically taste it.

Everything she sensed went directly into her husband's awareness, but she ignored his shouting voice of warning in her head as she ran across the room to Corrine's meditation quarters. She threw herself at the door, which burst open with the momentum of her weight.

The room was swirling with eerie, alien energy, a fog of smoke, and a crackling web of lightning that ran along the ceiling. The rush of air the opening door sent into the room pushed the center of the cloud of smoke back in an angry swirl. The wild billows and curls parted with abrupt violence, revealing the imposing figure of the Demon King standing within.

In his arms he held the limp form of a human woman.

Isabella gasped with shock, no matter how much Jacob's thoughts had warned her she might encounter something exactly like this.

"Bella!"

Isabella turned at the sound of her sister's voice, instantly making out Corrine's huddled figure and the fact that her daughter was clutched desperately in her arms.

"Be careful! He's gone mad!"

Isabella snapped her attention back to Noah. She instinctively braced her feet as she took note of his abrupt advance on her, the unconscious human woman still clutched in his powerful arms.

"Noah," she addressed him quickly and softly, "what are you doing?"

"Making things right," he answered as if it would explain everything. "She is mine."

"That may very well be," she said hurriedly, purposely putting herself in his path when he made the move to go around her.

He could have altered form in a blink, but he knew as well as she did what that would force her to do. If there was truly one person in all Demon society who could bring this to a quick end, it was Bella. But there was a price to pay when she snatched someone's power, so if she could avoid it, she would. She had taken of the King's power once already, with disastrous consequences that had nearly cost several lives, including her own. It wasn't something she wanted to repeat, especially with her vulnerable family in such close proximity.

"Noah," she continued, her voice pitched with calmness and gentleness. "If she is your destined mate no one will keep you from her. However, this isn't the way to bring the woman into our world. It isn't our way or the way of your laws."

Bella glanced down at the woman in question, taking a better look at her. Her head hung limply back over the King's left arm, a braid of pure white hair swinging in the smoky air. She was pale, clearly drained of most of her vital energy, a condition Isabella was familiar with enough to know who had initiated it. Since Noah had committed his crimes in Corrine's presence with apparent purpose, it was very likely that this woman *was* his intended mate. However, she could also be an innocent on the wrong end of the King's misdirected and volatile emotions. Either way, Noah was in no state to be in charge of the fate of a vulnerable human female.

"She looks weak," Isabella noted softly. "Let me help."

"Stand back, Enforcer. You will not take her from me."

"I didn't say I would," she agreed quickly. "But if you force us into an altercation, Noah, it could harm everyone in this room. Leah, Corrine . . . and this female as well. You're so powerful that I'd have to dampen your power with every ounce of my strength. There would be little room for finesse, Noah. The young woman you hold couldn't stand such a drain on her energy."

"As you say, Leah is in this room. Can so young a child bear the brunt of her mother's power?" he countered coldly.

"Perhaps not. But I can guarantee that you will not survive her father's wrath if anything happens to her or any of his family."

Noah looked up over the tiny Druid who blocked his path, to meet the black gaze of his male Enforcer. He realized then that Isabella had been stalling him while awaiting her husband's arrival.

Finally, the monarch visibly hesitated. One Enforcer; perhaps he could get away with the advantage in such a battle. However, the matched set was something else entirely.

It was this moment of hesitation that always heralded a turn in the dynamics of an enforcement situation. Jacob was quite familiar with it after all these centuries. The hesitation was no doubt as selfishly motivated as anything else the King had done in these past few hours, but it was also the first step toward logical reasoning. If he realized how futile his situation was, he would be on the path of recognizing the other flaws in his uncontrolled behavior.

Jacob put a hand on his wife's waist, nudging her gently in the direction of their child. As Bella hurried to inspect and protect her sister and her baby, Jacob squared off with his longtime friend.

He observed every detail of Noah's body language for a quick second, everything from the solid brace of his feet to the death grip he had on the blond woman hanging so limply in his arms. She would sport some serious bruises come the evening, but Jacob was determined to see that was the worst of the damage. It worried him that her breath came so shallow and that she was so deeply unconscious, but his senses, as sharp as all of nature, told him Noah hadn't had the time to put any other marks or damage on her.

"I will not allow anyone to take her from me. I no longer care what sacrifices have to be made, I will make them to keep her. Do you understand me?"

Jacob understood perfectly. In that moment, the King would go through every single living being in that room—in their very society—to keep his prize. Jacob knew the feeling well. Even he had once threatened Noah when he'd been forced away from Bella after their first intense encounter. It had torn at his soul and his sanity in a way that he didn't think he could ever truly bear again. Not without becoming pure animal and instinct, pretty much exactly like the Demon before him.

"I understand. But the only way you can truly keep her is to obey the law and its protocols. You realize that, do you not?"

Noah hesitated again, taking a moment to shift the weight of his burden a little higher against his chest. Jacob watched the King's eyes close briefly, his face turning closer to the woman's, the sound of his breath loud in the room full of people holding theirs.

"Very well."

Jacob and Isabella both cautiously exhaled. Corrine was less able to control her emotions, bursting into tears and falling against her sister in relief. Bella had no choice but to push her away. Her husband's command was ringing in her head and she rose straightaway to obey. She approached Noah carefully, swiping damp palms down the thighs of her jeans.

"Let me have her, Noah," she beckoned with a half smile and all the feminine coaxing she could muster. If Jacob had reached for Noah's possession, there was no telling what volatile reaction it could spark. To this day, Jacob himself had difficulties with other men touching or intending to touch Isabella. Therefore, he was highly sensitive to who should make the necessary move of retrieving the King's would-be mate.

The unconscious woman was nearly six inches taller and thirty pounds heavier than the petite Enforcer, but Bella was far stronger than she looked. Jacob watched her work her soft, soothing magic on the Demon King, her hand reaching to cover his warmly where it gripped his captive's shoulder.

"She . . . she is drained," he warned her, clearly reluctant to release her to anyone.

"I know. I see that. She will come around soon enough," she assured him.

"Only I can reverse it. I can feed her energy in general, but she is to be my one true mate. It is my energy she will crave as she becomes Druid. She must stay close to me."

Bella glanced at Corrine when she caught her nod of agreement out of the corner of her eye.

"Then she will stay close to you. Only, let me carry her. You . . ." Bella hesitated for a long, painful second that reflected a fear only her husband was fully aware of. She spoke before he could stop her. "You have frightened Leah. Go and comfort her. You know she always stops crying for you."

Isabella knew her husband was flushed with mistrust and barely repressed outrage at the idea of Noah touching their child after he had behaved so badly and with so little regard for her safety, especially because neither of them was at all certain Noah's episode was past him. However, Isabella knew that Noah would never relinquish the woman without redirection.

He finally acquiesced after a long moment, hoisting his burden into Bella's arms with a tenderness that belied all of his actions of the past minutes.

"Don't worry," Bella whispered to him. Noah nodded, drawing away slowly. He paused for several beats before turning toward Leah. What he ended up facing was the expressions of fright that neither of the females huddled together could have repressed even if they'd had all the time in the world to prepare for it.

It was this evidence of the cruelty of his actions that finally and truly hit home. Noah exhaled sharply with shock and breathless pain as true awareness battered him from all sides. He was surrounded by a roomful of loved ones he had betrayed. He had been running on borrowed strength and power for several hours, burning it off as fast as he could replenish it in his maddened momentum. When the insanity abandoned him, so, too, did his strength, and just as suddenly. Noah stumbled forward onto his knees, only the brace of his hand preventing him from falling facedown onto the debris-scattered floor.

With a child's fickleness of memory and emotion, Leah scrambled out of her aunt's arms and hurried to help her uncle. Her little hands cupped his face for a moment, and then she hugged his head and made the soft, soothing sounds her mother and aunt used to comfort her when she was hurt or upset.

It completely undid the Demon King. He blindly gathered the little girl in his arms, sobbing once with incredible pain into her neck before completely giving in to his emotions in front of them all.

Chapter 6

The Miserable Princess
A Demon Fairy Tale
Cont'd . . .

Sarah could hear the collective whisper that shifted like a wave throughout the viewing stands as the Enforcer came to stand before her. She looked up, feeling small and vulnerable in the wake of his tall, imposing figure. He was crafted out of muscle and sinew as a sculpture was shaped from marble. The calluses on his hands were visible, as was the scar that ran down the side of his left temple. Sarah's father had told her that he had been stabbed there once, with an iron blade. When she thought of how that must have felt, the metal that was so deadly to Demons burning like acid through skin and bone, she wondered how his sight in his left eye had been preserved. He was lucky that all he had suffered was a scar.

"Good evening, Sarah," he greeted her, his deep voice surprisingly soft.

"Enforcer," she said in return, nodding in her very best royal manner.

"Ariel," he corrected, an amused grin playing over his lips and sparkling in his eyes.

Sarah shrugged, telling him it did not matter to her one way or another.

"So be it," Ariel said softly. "I thought you should know that I intend to win this competition, and I will demand you for my prize."

Sarah gasped in shock and flushed with outrage.

"How dare you speak to me this way!"

"Adjust, Kikilia," he said with determined ease, "for soon you will be in my house, tending my hearth, and you will no longer be a Princess."

"I would rather be dipped in boiling oil than become mate to the Enforcer," she retorted, the acid in her voice meant to burn viciously. She thought he had incredible nerve to even think such a thing. No self-respecting Princess would give up her father's house and her title to live with the stigma of being the wife of the man who humiliated and punished his own kind. Granted, somebody had to do it, and her father respected him very much, but she was not about to become the wife of one such as he, no matter what he said to the contrary.

Ariel chuckled at her reply, but she did not understand what was so funny.

"Do you wish to give me a favor, my lady? Then all will know of your regard for me as I wear it onto the battlefield," he said.

She gasped, horrified at his sheer gall.

"Never!"

"Very well. It will not matter one way or another. Before dawn, you will belong to me."

Ariel reached out to her quickly, taking the liberty of stroking her fair hair and purposely running a fin-

ger down the length of neck hidden beneath it. She huffed, but not entirely in outrage. His touch burst like fire over her skin, soon moving to burn through her entire body. As he turned and walked away, Sarah was left numb and speechless with the riot of sensation and reaction that rushed through her body. Skin and breath, heart and blood, all of it. All of it. It was as if a brilliant candle had been lit inside her and, given another moment, would send yellow bursts of light out of every pore of her skin.

Sarah suddenly understood what raw panic and terror truly were. As a Princess, she had never needed to be afraid of anything. She had lived a very protected life and had always been safe from even the most rudimentary of fears.

Now, however, she was learning a rapid lesson in all those frightening emotions. The Enforcer had touched her, and now her entire body was raging with trapped light and sizzling energy. There was one and only one condition capable of moving such a violent emotional reaction through a body with no apparent cause or reason.

The Imprinting.

It meant that she was destined to be exactly what he wanted her to be. His mate. His partner throughout all the centuries of her life.

And there was nothing she could ever do to change it.

Except one thing. She could not deny him her body, nor the need she would have ever after to live close to him, but she did have the power within her to reject him in her heart. She could choose to refuse him even the smallest amount of love. If she denied him that, he would not truly conquer her.

Sarah's heart began to pound at the possibilities of defying one so powerful and deadly. That was when she decided that she should at least try to run away. Hiding could not hurt. So what if he was the best tracker amongst them, the ability the divine right of all Enforcers? She was a Demon of the Body. She had quite a few tricks at her disposal as well.

She would trick him first, and then she would run and hide. Nothing was going to make her do this terrible thing. No one was going to make her love so unlovable a male.

* * *

Syreena stood in the empty window casement, her slim hands braced on the cold, flat stone. The Romanian early winter breeze swept over the jagged mountain and chilled lakes before churning harshly up the walls of the towering edifice that had come to be her home, reaching her exposed position at last. The biting chill and powerful press of it blasted through the casement and into her body, snapping the heavy satin of her loose gown back until it was plastered against her like a white, shining skin, the excess fabric whipping behind her body as if it were a standard of truce.

When a man's hand slid into the curve of her waist, the contrary warmth of it gave her goose bumps that flushed up her belly and breasts. She turned to look down at him with a smile that was full of delight and mischief. She reached down with a stone-cold hand to stroke her fingers across his face.

Then she leapt out of the window.

Damien, Prince of the Vampires and husband to the high-diving woman, stepped up into the window she had abandoned and quickly leaned over to watch what would become of his wife.

She laid her arms back along her body as she rushed headlong toward the jagged rocks at the base of his family holdings. Her loose gown whipped and billowed, the fabric sheeting back until it slipped entirely free of her lithe body, buffeting into a swatch of swirling white as it continued on to the stones below.

Syreena, however, would not be joining it. In a flash, she went from the form of a beautiful human woman to the swift dip and reel of a small peregrine falcon. She did this just in time to avoid the sharp rocks below. And though she was famous for her "on the fly" Lycanthropy, she still had the power to take her husband's breath away with the trick, after making him hold it in a fearful moment of doubt. It wasn't that Damien doubted the skills of his clearly talented wife. She was the most skillful Lycanthrope alive. It was because he still had moments where he imagined he couldn't be so lucky as to be the first and only Vampire in his society for eons to know what true and lasting love really was. He was the only Vampire alive who was married, and to an outsider no less. He had broken a great deal of ground, and more than one long-standing law, in order to take her as his bride.

That had been a little over nine months ago, and a great deal had happened since they had gone public with their relationship. The results had been mixed. Some good, some bad. It was the bad things that drove his wife to jump out of windows in the highest towers of the castle.

He didn't have to tax himself to figure out what had happened that had her turning to her ability to fly as the falcon for release and escape. He was Prince of the coldest, most troublemaking race of Nightwalkers alive. And while their respect, civility, and Vampire law kept them in line for the most part, Damien's marriage to Syreena had given a few of the more unruly members of his society an excuse to start trouble. This trouble had taken all kinds of forms, but it was the most recent that had gotten under Syreena's skin.

Damien watched as she reeled toward the lake, flying like a quick brown and black kite, lofting from one shelf of air to another with a skill that always impressed him. The Vampire wasn't as assured of his shape-changing abilities as his wife was. He changed and became a large, glossy black raven while still safely seated on the windowsill. He'd only had the ability to become the raven for the last year. While he had flown all of his life in the shape of a man, a skill every Vampire had after a certain age, it wasn't until he had fed off his bride that he was able to become the raven. Now, as he flew after her, it was clear what the months since then had done for his skill. Still, he preferred to be cautious as he practiced. It would be silly to end a millennium-long lifetime with an awkward splat on the rocks below. It would be a rather ignominious end to the longest-reigning and most powerful Prince in Vampire history.

Damien chased down his wife with determination. She had given herself away, and he was fixated on hearing her troubled thoughts. Before she had wed him, she had been a Princess in her own right, heir to the Lycanthrope throne and counselor to the current Queen, her sister Siena. So she was no stranger to political machinations and the sometimes undesirable results that churned forth from them. But that didn't make it any easier for her to bear them. Not when they touched her so personally.

Syreena was diving toward the glassy surface of one of the mountain lakes. That was when Damien knew she was aware of him following her. She would make her next change on purpose, knowing full well how much he hated the bracing cold of winter water. That, more than the breakneck dive of earlier, could be successful at dissuading him from following.

She morphed from bird to dolphin about five feet above the water as she dove toward it. She cut the water cleanly, only a ripple from the break of her tail fins giving away her entrance point. Damien didn't follow. He lighted on a rock and changed back to his masculine form, crossing his long legs casually and resting a hand on his thigh as he waited for her to surface.

It wasn't that he couldn't swim. It was just that a Vampire's body temperature remained warm only as long as the blood from his last feed remained so. He had no circulation to speak of, so he steadily lost heat over time, becoming colder to the touch the further he got from his last feeding. If he followed his wife into the water, it would suck the heat out of him in an instant, and he wouldn't be allowed to so much as touch her or kiss her until he fed again and warmed his icy flesh. A delay like that would impede his desire to comfort her when she finally stopped her torrid escape.

The subject of his thoughts surfaced in the middle of the lake, this time in the shape of herself. At least above the water. Below, he had no doubt that she resembled a mermaid instead of a human, with a fin, not legs, keeping her buoyant. In all this changing, there was only one form she hadn't taken as yet that was available in her repertoire: the winged woman she liked to call the harpy. This gave her a total of five forms, two more than a normal Lycanthrope. She was a mutation, a unique creature amongst her people. Amongst all Nightwalkers. But extra forms or not, Damien would have known that anyway.

At last, Syreena began to swim toward him.

The decision now made to go to him, she did so with all speed, the strong fin below the water propelling her swiftly. She made the transition from water to land as smoothly as she had made all her others, tossing back her dark hair as it dripped sparkling water into the air around her. He uncrossed his legs, opening his arms to her, and she slid into his embrace as she knelt before the rock that made up his makeshift seat.

Damien sighed in tandem with her as she accepted his strong comfort. He placed a gentle line of kisses across her forehead and down to her ear, where he spoke softly to her. "If it will make you feel better, I can send Jasmine to Noah instead of going myself."

She released a breath that gave her away, reflecting how much she would prefer that. "But you said, as a matter of protocol and respect, you should bring this bad news to him yourself. And I hate to say so, but I agree it might be the better choice. Jasmine can be—well, she's your counselor, not one of your diplomats. Even she would agree there is a good reason for that."

Damien chuckled at the politely worded assessment of Jasmine's frequently volatile temperament. "True, but through everything she has been perfectly loyal to me. She would never upset my carefully cultivated relations with Noah and the Demon people. She knows how important peace among the Nightwalker clans is going to be for everyone's future." He paused thoughtfully for a moment. "Come to think of it, Jasmine could also stay there until some of this is resolved. Between her and Horatio, they would be best able to sense a threat of this nature."

"Mmm, and he is her brother. They should have a chance to visit."

"And I get to stay here with you."

"Now, that is definitely a bonus," she laughed. "Of course, Jasmine being hundreds of miles away skulking in someone else's hallways is a special benefit."

"You are very naughty," he scolded. "I would think you two would have resolved your issues by now. It has been almost a year."

"Yes, well . . ." She smiled briefly before she leaned in to kiss him, taking his flavor onto her tongue hungrily for a long moment before releasing him and licking her damp lips. His hands slid over her chilled back, her bare skin cool but still somehow warmer than his in some places.

"It is settled, then," he murmured softly against her mouth as he readied to kiss her once again. "Jasmine will go in my stead to warn Noah. We will stay here with Stephan and try to resolve the situation on our end. Perhaps all of this will be over quickly and come to nothing. Meanwhile, I will be home with my wife, keeping her warm and comfortable, and . . ."

"And taking advantage of her heat cycle so we can try to

get pregnant," she finished for him with relief. "Damien, I have waited so long to begin a family. If you left during my heat, I don't think I could bear the loneliness and knowing that every day you are gone will be an opportunity wasted. We have talked of nothing else for the past three months, ever since we decided we were ready for it . . . and that it would be the best thing we could do to bring our disparate backgrounds together. Perhaps, if you have an heir with me, the Vampires will stop all this infighting and will finally begin to accept the choice you made in me."

"Sweetheart, we have talked about this," he scolded her gently, running a broad, graceful hand down the length of her wet hair. "We will do this for us, and for us alone. As with our wedding, it is their duty to adapt to us. Those who do not adapt, those who think to fight me—let them come if they dare."

"Damien," she breathed nervously, sweeping her fingers into his hair and holding him in place for her mouth and its desperate kiss.

He knew her fears too well for words. Even without his telepathy, he had come to know her nearly better than he knew himself. She was more emotional than she normally would be, more fearful as her mating cycle rapidly approached and more of their impending future was put up for scrutiny.

Syreena had two mating cycles every year. Spring and fall, close to the full moon at Beltane and the one at Samhain. These short weeks every year were the only time she could conceive, no matter how frequently they made love at any other time. Last spring had been an experience unlike anything Damien had encountered in his long lifetime of dealing with women. She had been aggressive and insatiable. She had taunted him and teased him and used him to exhaustion almost every minute of the day from the beginning to the end of the cycle.

They hadn't truly decided whether or not they were ready for children before last spring's cycle had struck her, but once it had hit, they hadn't even been able to make an effort at caution or control.

In spite of their recklessness, however, Syreena hadn't conceived.

She had been devastated. It should have been impossible for her to fail to conceive. She'd never heard of a heat cycle not producing a child automatically, in the absence of actions or chemistry to prevent it. So her automatic assumptions began to fall into two categories: first, that something was wrong with her; second, and perhaps the worst of all, that a Vampire and a Lycanthrope couldn't conceive a child. Though there were hints in ancient writings that it was possible, there was no known written or living proof of it. Still, it was illogical for her to blame herself. The Vampire conception rate was notoriously low to begin with.

Regardless, if he was forced to leave her alone for the next cycle in order to take care of business at the Demon court, she would suffer a great deal, and very likely would be impossible to live with. If he thought the atmosphere in his home was hostile now . . . after three weeks with Syreena on a hormonal bender, in amongst a gathering of Vampires who disapproved of her to start with, there would be a lot of ramifications to deal with.

Neither could they leave together. Stephan and Jasmine could capably protect their holdings, but with the current civil unrest, it would be unwise for both of them to leave the homeland castle unattended. The more he thought on it, the more sending Jasmine seemed like the best solution for everyone. Of course, it would no doubt look like Damien was catering to his bride, an act that many of his species would look on as a weakness.

But Damien didn't care about appearances in this particular situation. He could never leave Syreena to cope with such a painful struggle when his mere presence could prevent it. Apparently she didn't realize that, or else she wouldn't have climbed the tower after hearing him discuss traveling to Noah's court. He would maintain patience, however. She was learning, just as he was, and it did no good for either of them to lose their tolerance for the other's misunderstandings.

For the present, she was catching a good case of the shivers and would be better off inside the citadel walls. He swept her up into his embrace easily just as his feet lifted from the ground. He flew them up to the very same window she had dived from earlier, leading her inside so she could warm up and rest with him as the dawn made its imminent approach.

When the Demon King entered the Council chamber a short time later, a hush fell over the Elders gathered about the triangular table. Noah stood for a moment, assessing the energy of the room. Gossip among Demons, he noted, was one of the fastest-flying creatures in all the world. He had no doubt that everyone around him was at least partially aware of what had so recently transpired.

He didn't hold still long, determined not to be read as reluctant to face his peers. He moved to the large chair at one of the three points of the table that marked its highest-ranking members. The other two points were occupied by his sister's husband, Gideon, who was the only Ancient of their kind, and Jacob, the Enforcer, who reached to cover the small hand of his wife seated next to him.

"I have called this Council meeting with one purpose only," he said directly, his deep voice filling the stone room and ringing back to him from the vaulted ceiling. "It is time we altered Demon law, Councillors, to suit the vast changes our society has undergone since the first Druid was discovered and accepted into our culture." He did not look at Isabella as he referred to her, the act too hard for him in that glaring moment. He would face that reckoning later, when there were not so many witnesses. "I have watched the centuries fall by just as many of you have, and we all know too well the price we pay every Samhain and Beltane because it is stamped on our genes that it be so.

"I have glorified myself in the past as a scholar dedicated to finding a solution to the cruel pressures we endure during those Hallowed moons." Noah paused to lay a hand on the smooth wooden surface of the Council table, leaning forward so he could meet all the attention focused on him. "Many of us have cried out with suffrage, cried foul when the Enforcer put us to the screws, and simply cried because sometimes the agony is just too much for a soul to bear." The Demon King straightened as the slap of his hand on the table resounded in the room.

"I tell you now I feel nothing but shame toward myself, toward us all, for enjoying the role of the victim too well. We have had three years in which to initiate changes and have barely made efforts to do so. If you think it is my recent transgression that makes me say this, you would be right. But even before that incident, the Druid Corrine had begun to open my eyes to our indolence.

"It comes to this: We have the means to put an end to this tragedy, and I am determined to make it the law to do so. As it stands now, the Enforcers are a necessary evil and they are vilified for representing the possibility of what we might become. That begins to end this very moment." Noah heard Isabella make a surprised sound, the squeak catching in her throat, and his mouth turned up at one corner as he looked directly at her. "The law is as I speak it now. Every unmated member of Demon society who is of Elder age will utilize Corrine's skills to find the Druid mate that is to be Imprinted upon them. Only this will cure our culture of its madness, and so it will be done. In the future I will expand the law to include adults. Of course, all are free to do so at any time or age if they wish it. The only reason I do not make it universally mandatory is because I do not wish to overtax our

Druid, who will hereby be referred to as our Matchmaker. It takes much effort, I realize now, to be a living divining rod."

He paused to take a slow, calming breath.

"I once said that Isabella would be the first note in the call to save us from ourselves. I realize now that, as she is the note, her sister is the symphony. It is the responsibility of every member of this Council to set an example by being among the first to approach the Matchmaker in this matter."

The silence broke at last, nearly the entire table erupting in protest both large and small.

"Noah, you cannot do this," the Body Demon Peter protested, his chair scraping back loudly as he jumped up. "You have no right to command us to do something that should be a personal freedom for every living creature in the world. No intellectual being should be forced to find a mate!"

"*Every* being is forced to find a mate," Noah countered sharply, the bite of his retort like a slap in the face. "You have never crossed that maddening line, Peter, so you do not know what I mean. Let me assure you that every creature of the world is stamped with the drive to find perfection in companionship. It is encoded in every fiber of our beings. It is because we have taken the unnatural course of solitude that Demons are being forced by nature, by these Hallowed moons and their madness, to follow our internal compass toward our intended partners no matter what the cost.

"Believe me, Peter, you do not want to pay the price I have paid. I walked this world so desensitized to the needs of my soul and my body that I failed my most perfect Destiny and dispatched my mate to her death. I refuse to see that happen to another of us. I am ruler of this race, and I *will* force this dictate upon you. And as with any law, those who do not obey will face my Enforcers. I will press the matter with severe ramifications that will far outweigh the penalty that already exists. A punishment I must now suffer that will add to a pain that if I could share it—" He broke off, swallowing visibly but refusing to break contact with the dozen pairs of eyes watching him with bated breath. "I could pardon myself from this if I wished, but what kind of leader would I be if I did not expect myself to follow the laws I set down for all others?"

"Noah, no one here expects you to suffer the humiliation of—"

"Please," the King cut in, his voice hoarse and pained. "Those of you here who call themselves my friends will not tempt me any further on this matter. Jacob and Isabella will see I am justly served for my transgression. To be quite frank, no one deserves the right more than they do. This meeting is adjourned."

There was no more argument and, mercifully, not even a sound of debate or speculation. Noah turned from the table and crossed back to the door. He halted before going through it to turn slightly back to those behind him.

"Bella, Jacob . . . you will attend me."

The King closed his eyes when, after a moment's pause, he heard the sound of two chairs pushing back across the marble floor. He finally crossed the threshold, refusing himself any urges he had to look back.

"Noah, I beg you to reconsider," Jacob argued quietly after the last Council member had left them alone in the Great Hall of Noah's castle.

As he pressed his monarch, Jacob observed his unusually subdued wife out of the corner of his eye, trying to get a bead on her thoughts and feelings. She was shutting him out with exceptional strength, however, shunting him away from their telepathic connection. It was a level of ability he had not realized she had. Even so, it was completely lost on him why she would decide to use it against him in that sensitive and crucial moment. He could have used her input, support, or feedback. Whichever she was willing to offer up.

He continued watching as his wife moved in one direction while Noah moved in the other to stand closer to the fire.

"Jacob, it is your duty to not only uphold the law, but to hold those who break it accountable. I am not an exception to that rule and, as I have already stated, I will not hear argument otherwise."

"You *will* hear it," Jacob said sharply, advancing on his sovereign. "I have been your Enforcer for four centuries, and no one knows better than I how and when to enforce the law. The reprimand you are seeking for yourself is intended to sway future weakness from occurring. It is designed to halt the temptation toward innocents who would fall victim to the potential danger of a Demon out of control. This edict was never meant to reprove those who are striving only to seize their one true mate in life. Especially when taking into consideration that once you do become mated to that person, there is no longer any threat of this insanity overtaking you. By our very own laws and traditions, you have the right to claim what you have claimed. Laws that I helped you draw up, I might add."

"*No one* has the right to do so in a way that endangers the innocents around them," Noah bit back.

"Then consider Kestra if you will not consider yourself," Jacob said grimly, his voice echoing in the stone room. "If you undergo standard procedures, you will be left physically and emotionally devastated. To penalize yourself would mean punishing this innocent. She is becoming a Druid now. You know what that means. She will need to feed off your energy. She needs your full strength if she is to survive such a taxing alteration of her genetic code and physical being. None of us knows what this might do to her, to you both, if you persist on this path."

"No," Noah murmured. "No. I cannot walk away from this without being answerable for my actions. If not standard punishment, then you must devise something in its stead. I demand your compliance in this, Jacob."

"Very well."

Both men looked up when Bella finally spoke, her soft voice—usually so full of her vibrancy and humor—wintry and dead as it fell on them. She had her arms folded tightly around her midriff as she advanced on the Demon King, the bite of her step a warning come too late to her husband.

"*I* will punish you," she hissed at the Demon King, her hand suddenly flying at Noah's face and striking him so hard that the slap reverberated through Jacob's very bones. He could only imagine how it had felt, knowing how powerful Bella was in spite of her compact appearance. But as Noah recoiled from the surprise of the blow, the male Enforcer knew the psychology behind the strike was what would cut to the quick.

"You are never to go near my child again! Do you understand?" Isabella gritted the dictate through clenched teeth, her full fury and outrage finally, after all these hours, taking aim at their first solid target. It was a brutal, tangible thing. "Never! You will not even look at her! Do you hear me? I trusted you! Trusted you with her life and her safety like I would never have trusted anyone else, *and you betrayed me!* You betrayed *her* and used *her* for a wild experiment that could have—" Bella choked on her emotion, her tears finally spilling as she fought for her voice. "How could you do that? How could you put my baby in such horrific danger? *She loves you! I* loved you!"

She raised her hand to strike the stunned King again, but her husband caught her by the wrist and halted the forward-flying motion of her body. Noah turned away from them both, reaching out to steady himself against the stone of the fire-place as the Enforcer enfolded his violent wife into the un-yielding frame of his body.

"Enough," Jacob whispered into her black satin hair as he pressed his mouth to the ear hidden beneath. "Enough, my love."

"It will never be enough," Bella rasped hoarsely. "I will

never forgive you for this, Noah! When I think of all the things that could have gone wrong, it makes me want to scream! I had to stand there and sweet-talk and coddle you while my baby and my sister sat huddled in a corner, beside themselves with terror! You make me sick!"

His mate was screaming so violently by then that it did not surprise Jacob when Gideon's hand appeared out of nowhere and touched Isabella's shoulder. The Ancient medic did not give her any opportunity to fight him, even if she could manage her power enough to attempt to drain his abilities. As hysterical as she was with the emotion that only a mother in defense of her child was capable of, she would never have been able to concentrate.

So Gideon sent the chemistry of her body careening out of balance, tricking it into thinking it was desperate for slumber. The sleep command hit her like a ton of bricks and Isabella collapsed against Jacob mid-accusation. Jacob felt Magdelegna brush past him, hurrying to her brother's side with the ready compassion that was so much a part of her nature.

Noah felt her touch and shrugged her off so hard that she stumbled back several precarious steps.

"Do not comfort me, Legna! Just stay away from me!" he growled savagely. "Leave! All of you. Your duties are finished here."

Noah finalized the order by snapping into a vicious flurry of flame that burned hard and brilliantly, making them all flinch and protect their eyes.

When their vision cleared, the King was gone.

Chapter 7

Kestra woke the next evening with a sigh.

Her clear blue eyes flickered open halfway, and beneath her she felt soft sheets and the plush down of a feather bed. She made an irresistible sound of pleasure. The pillows and the comforter that spread over her were all made of the same incredible softness that could only be down. It was, she began to realize, the very first night in months that she had slept through. There had been no dreams of a shadowy, arrogant lover tormenting her relentlessly with his teasing and touching, wakening her in a sweat.

She rolled over, looking up at the sheer white fabric that crisscrossed the canopy of the enormous bed, the center of the X anchored into the ceiling that was far above the actual posters of the bed itself. Dim light was streaming in from nearly all sides, but it was all muted, silvery colors, speckling patterns over the ceiling, the bed curtains, and the long canopy. Her eyes flicked through the dark to the source, finding two banks of windows on the connecting corner walls, all of which were stained glass. Most of them were a random collection of shapes and colors seemingly dashed together haphazardly on the window glass. A couple of the others had intricate, more defined designs, beautiful motifs in colored glass of a forest and another of a village of cottages.

Kestra put her hands on the mattress and began to slide herself upright so she could better view her surroundings, trying to shed the haze of sleep enough that she could remember what country she was in and what hotel would have such a fabulous old room.

She froze midmovement, however, when she caught sight of a wing chair drawn up close to the edge of her bed, facing her as if someone had been observing her for long hours. She quickly scanned the room, taking note of every dancing shadow created by the fire roaring in the fireplace nestled in a corner of the room. She was struck by the inescapable feeling that someone was there, watching her, even though she saw nothing at all in the shadows.

The mystery ended abruptly. The person made a distinct movement, making her suddenly aware of his location and imposing, half-lit silhouette. Kestra's knee-jerk reaction was one of hostility and defensiveness and she quickly worked up a threat, the words readily bubbling up to her lips.

And there they froze.

As he turned his head slightly and she felt him assessing her even through the dark and shadows, she was flooded with memory, instinct, and emotion all at once. She opened her mouth but couldn't speak. Information and questions overloaded all the nerve conduits in her brain.

Noah said nothing; the only sound in the enormous room was the snap of the fire and her rapidly pitched breathing. He turned his eyes away from her after a painful moment. He had moved away from her only moments before she had awakened, his abilities warning him about the changes in her wakening energy. Before that cautious removal, however, he had steadily occupied the chair she had noticed.

He'd sat in it, watching her every breath and trying for all he was worth to reconcile all the emotions churning in his heart, as well as the thoughts and memories plaguing his mind. Noah had said nothing to anyone about how he'd experienced his first live meeting with Kestra. Besides himself and his intended mate, only Corrine had witnessed it.

How had Kestra come to be in such a situation? Who was she? Why would a human female, seemingly without power, ever put herself in such danger? She knew how to fight, clearly knew how to use a weapon, and showed a remarkable lack of fear for a mortal being, but . . .

What was it she had been doing that had apparently been worth dying for? Did she have any idea how close she'd come to death? That if not for him, death would have claimed her a second or two later? He'd seen it, the picture of it flashing violently in his memory, still terrifying him even though it was over and no longer a threat to her safety and her life. She was safe. Within his reach. Here.

At last.

He should say something to her, he knew, but found he couldn't think of a single word that would be appropriate for such an extraordinary situation. If what he'd intruded upon at his arrival was a commonplace occurrence in her life, it was no wonder she'd fought him so frantically in their dreams. How could a woman who lived so dangerous a lifestyle ever trust anyone? He laughed in his own head over the irony. He'd been high-handed and arrogant, always pushing to get his way, and it seemed he was going to be rewarded for that on many bitter levels. He'd wasted time playing games and struggling with her for the power of the dreams they shared. Now she was here, lying in his bed, looking at him with suspicious eyes, and he realized for the first time that he'd squandered a hundred chances to make this so much easier. If only he'd acknowledged the importance of the dreams months ago, perhaps she would not be looking at him in such a hostile manner.

Now that she was there, what did she think of him in reality?

He could easily imagine the answer to that.

The devastating pain of Isabella's wounded hatred had been more than enough karmic justice to glut him with guilt, and the King didn't think he could face any more recriminations from this woman who was supposed to be the most precious gift he'd ever receive.

However, he was also unaccustomed to behavior that reflected a certain level of fear or even cowardice, so he was compelled to move forward if only to prove to himself that he wasn't afraid to meet his fate, whatever it turned out to be. He moved through light and shadow until he reached the back of the chair he'd occupied for the past twelve hours or so, keeping as close to her as he could, feeding her body with his energy as she fed his emaciated soul with her mere presence and closeness.

As he neared her, rounding the chair, he fell within the range of the lone candle sitting on the bedside table. As the light fell over his height and his features for the first time, Kestra made a startled sound. Noah's eyes darted quickly to hers, the wide pools of startling blue ice reflecting her shock and trepidation. Her breathing doubled in speed and he could sense all the energy of her body focusing and coiling into the reflexes of her muscles, readying her to spring away from him should the need arise. Otherwise, she sat perfectly still, her eyes never even blinking as she kept them on him.

Slowly, Noah continued to take his seat. He leaned back, remaining relaxed in appearance somehow, in spite of the surges of emotion twisting within his stomach and psyche.

He'd never expected her to be as breathtakingly beautiful as she was. It had barely crossed his mind, he realized, except when it came to the sight and feel of her hair. Long, sugar-white, pin-straight, and sheeting thickly to the middle of her back, her wispy bangs the only curve it could lay claim to. Braided as it was, it was pulled back high and tight, still as neat as it had been from the start, in spite of her having slept on it for so long.

If possible, her eye color was even more remarkable than her hair. Her pupils were an astonishing light blue, almost like very lightly tinted glass, faceted like diamonds with outstanding luster. White lashes and blond brows lent eerily beautiful accent to her penetrating gaze. She had a truly gorgeous face, with flawless skin, softly defined cheekbones, and a mouth that looked twice as luscious as it had felt when they had kissed in their dreams. Perhaps it was the inviting pink innocence of their color that made him think so.

The longer he sat in silence, making no moves or declarations to satisfy whatever curiosities she must be full of, the more she allowed her muscles to relax. She slid up against the headboard very slowly, until her shoulder was situated securely against it and she was fully facing him. Noah recognized what she was doing. She was guarding her back. Leaning up against the headboard, she could feel a little more comfortable about keeping her focus on him.

He supposed that, to her, he was no more or less dangerous than the men who had succeeded in killing her a week ago.

"I think you better tell me who you are and why you were in Sands's penthouse. Are you some kind of cop?"

"Why would you think that?" he asked curiously.

"I don't know. I didn't hear you come in, so I figure you were already there. Since you didn't seem to like the bad guys, I figured you were working undercover and had to . . . well, if you're a cop, you couldn't just sit there and let them kill me."

"Excellent logic," he said.

"Ah!"

"But I am not a cop."

"Oh." She squinted at him with apparent confusion. "Do I have to ask twenty questions or are you going to explain this?"

"I see you do not recognize me," he remarked carefully. "I told you I needed to find you."

That gave her pause and she tensed tightly against the headboard. Kestra's eyes moved over him with amazing scrutiny as she tried to figure out why she should know him. She *never* forgot a face. Considering the multitude of people she encountered in her travels, that was truly saying something. But she was positive she'd never laid eyes on him in all her life. She would remember a face like that: dark and tanned, serious, yet clearly prone to amusement and laughter when the crinkles near the corners of his eyes were taken into account.

All that aside, people of power and confidence always made an impressive mark on her. Even sitting in the soft light of the candle and stray beams of color that broke through the windows, she could see and sense that he was a formidable man. Power. A position of some importance somehow in the world. A leader. Something about all she'd seen so far told her he was capable of conquest. He had certainly shown no hesitation or fear when he'd come to her aid.

Damn if that didn't bite her butt. She wasn't exactly the type of woman who enjoyed playing the helpless blonde while Mr. Savior came to rescue her. It was a bad impression to make at the outset. There *was* something about him, though. Beyond all the rest, she felt as though he was right on the mark. She *did* know him from somewhere.

His voice.

More importantly, his accent. Deep, resonant, a careful enunciation of certain consonants, and the tendency of foreigners to avoid contractions. Kestra felt her chest constrict suddenly as all her blood threatened to rush out of her brain.

"Eurotrash."

The breathy identification made him laugh, a rough bark of humor that made her sudden recognition take a leap forward.

"That . . . this is . . ." she stammered. "No. No, no, no, no, no! This is bullshit!"

He was a dream. *Only* a dream! What was worse, he was

acting as if he knew all about those dreams! As if he had truly been there all those times when she had . . . when they had . . .

Kestra put both hands to her temples, squeezing her head hard as if it would pop her rampant imagination out of her brain. Then she jumped out of the enormous bed, taking to the floor on the opposite side from where he sat, pacing frantically across the slightly chilled floorboards. She saw him rise to his feet out of the corner of her eye and she instinctively stepped two feet farther from him, continuing her short, agitated circuit of steps.

"You're not going to make me believe you're some sort of dream that poofed to life. I'm not a child and I don't believe in fairy stories anymore!"

"You once believed in fairy stories?" he asked, sounding genuinely interested.

"Never mind that!" Kestra snapped. "Tell me what's going on here, or I swear I'll . . . I'll . . ."

"Make me 'centuries of sorry'?"

"Yes!" She gasped in horror. "No! How did you—?"

"Because I was there," he said, his tone so low and so soft it was frightening in its truth.

Kestra downshifted suddenly, her spinning wheels finally making purchase as she reached that level of panic that always clicked into a cold calm. It was an emotional and physical reflex she'd had since . . . well, for too long. All emotion was cut off, only logic and instinct remaining as she faced what the overcharged parts of herself had suddenly found so threatening.

"I see," she murmured softly.

And so did Noah. Her energy aura went through a massive shift right before his eyes, something he'd seen before, but on a much, much smaller scale. It was as if she'd cut one switch and fired up a new one. The soft nimbus that he could see around her fluttered from pink and white with rushes of red, to an almost uniform blue with a sense of order and uniformly applied focus. The Demon King felt an eerie sting of sensation flying across his back from one shoulder to the other, causing the hair at the back of his neck to prickle to attention.

"Listen, Kestra, I am not here to hurt you," he said as sincerely as he could, holding out a staying hand. "There is plenty of time for explanations in the—"

"Actually, now is a perfect time for explanations," she said softly, slowly making her way around the foot of the bed, finally coming toward him. "I've known men capable of all kinds of trickery in my time, but I confess that I'm baffled as to how you were able to pull this off. I should've known. The human mind does not function in that way without some kind of psychopharmaceutical assistance." Kestra rounded the second corner of the bed, now only a few steps away from him. "Every day for six months. Dozens of countries, hotels, water supplies . . . how did you do it?"

"It was not anything like that. I admit that, in a way, I am responsible for the dreams, but—"

"You admit that? How magnanimous of you."

"But you are just as guilty as I am," he finished sharply. "You have been haunting my every sleeping moment with your fickle nature and this need you have to always be in control."

"Me?" She laughed hard and short. "I never asked for this! Why would I want some arrogant S.O.B. taunting me and constantly groping at me like some kind of horny adolescent boy?"

"Hey, you give a fair enough grope yourself," he snapped back at her. "And it is not as though I have a choice in the matter. Like it or not, you were made for me."

"I was . . ." She gasped with outrage at his audacity. "I must have missed the part where I stepped back in time. Could you be any more full of barbaric testosterone? Made for you? Well, thank God you found me so I can finally have a purpose in the world!"

"That is not what I meant," he growled, his frustration very clear as he stepped close enough to go nose to nose with her, had they been the same height. Despite his sparking temper, he was aware of the wash of her cotton candy scent slipping around his ravenous senses. "You cannot measure me by the standards you use to measure other men. Trust me when I say all the rules you are used to have changed, and they will continue to do so for quite some time."

"Trust you? A supercilious stranger? I don't even trust people I'm tempted to call my friends! You come on strong with this whole mysterious stranger gig and you think I should flutter my lashes, be weak in the knees, and so very flattered that you took the time to notice me?"

"If I have been mysterious," he retorted tightly, "it has been purely accidental. I do not think you should be anything other than the woman you already are. Although, given a choice, I would delete the sarcastic snobbery and the bullet bull's-eye on your head, but I do *not* have a choice. *You* do not have a choice. The Fates decide, and they do not take suggestions."

"Oh, there's always a choice. It's called free will, sweetheart. I was born with it, and I'm going to exercise it. Starting right now."

Kestra sidestepped him, marched around him, and headed for the nearest door. She yanked hard on it, but it barely opened an inch before the weight of his hand on it slammed it shut again. She found herself trapped between him and the door as he loomed darkly over her, and she turned around quickly in the confined space.

"You are free to leave if you wish, but I will have to insist on a few things first," he said, his voice low and gravelly with what she suspected was deeply repressed emotion.

"Such as?" It was really all she could say or do. She'd already tried to attack him once before. He was too strong and skilled, even for her impressive skill in martial arts. It wasn't worth expending energy on a hopeless cause. She would simply have to outsmart him.

He took a moment while she thought, using it to slide his eyes over her long, well-built body. Even with her feet braced hard apart and her hands curled into fists, he found her extraordinary. Probably even because of it. She was flushed with temper, a condition he could admire even though it aggravated him as well. The element he'd been born to was the epitome of volatility. If she had been easy, compliant, and too biddable, she wouldn't have been able to play flint to his steel. It was just one of many facets she had that made his entire body tighten with anticipation and his heart thrum with uncontrollable stimulation. Her body was hot with her raised temper, and that scent of warm sweetness was intoxicating.

"First, I would have you know my name is Noah, even though it has not occurred to you to ask."

She crossed her arms beneath her breasts and gave him a derisive snort to remind him how little she cared.

"Second," he continued smoothly, "you cannot leave on your own. You are without identification or papers. You would need the help of me or one of my people."

The statement gave her serious pause, her anger shedding sufficiently to make her catch key parts of his phraseology. Why would she need identification or papers to travel? Was she beyond American borders? Chicago was close to Canada. Still, crossing the Canadian border wasn't one of the world's most difficult accomplishments. The way he said it, and taking into consideration the general structure of his accent, she got the dreadful feeling that she'd somehow ended up in Europe. To pull off something like that with an unconscious woman, he would have to be a powerful man. A man authoritative enough to refer to others as "my people." That easy term on his lips gave away the biggest clue of all. He was what she expected him to be, and apparently a whole lot more.

Kestra suddenly realized it would be a very good idea to maintain her composure a little better and pay even closer attention. The last thing she needed was another influential enemy. What was more, she traveled in very highly placed European circles, both lawful and unlawful, and she'd never heard a single reference to a man of his obvious caliber with the name of Noah.

"Is there anything else?" she asked, her tone very subdued.

"Yes," he said softly, leaning closer to her ear as he did so. "I would very much prefer it if you did not leave. I would . . . I wish to invite you to stay, as my guest."

Just by altering the pitch of his voice, he had managed to change everything about the atmosphere between them. Kestra was suddenly aware of so many small details at once that she became a little breathless. He was incredibly warm, even though he didn't touch her. That earthy scent of toasted wood surrounded her as his heated breath skimmed over her ear and neck.

This was what reminded her of how truly potent the chemistry they had shared in dreams really was. Her heart seemed to pound in response merely to his nearness. He hadn't even touched her and was just as able as ever to manipulate her responses to him. But this was a waking moment; he was not some nameless, faceless entity in a dream. Was it some sort of Pavlovian response, born out of months and months of conditioning?

"I won't spend a moment more than I have to near you," she declared in hot defiance of all she was thinking and feeling. She dared to look up at him directly, and his smiling response infuriated her.

"I see. You are afraid of me."

"No, I'm sick of you. After half a year of your games and manipulations, I've had more than enough!"

"A game you played just as adroitly, *Kikilia*. With a skill to outshine mine."

"Don't call me that!" she snapped, the nickname solidifying his claims on her dreams and her memory of her part in them.

Noah understood her pique probably better than she realized. Why it served to fascinate him further was momentarily beyond him. She was used to being in control, used to being the one to dictate terms. It was written in everything she said and all of her actions. A personality trait he could identify with entirely. A trait he found unbelievably intriguing.

"I could easily remind you of the rewards to the games we have played in our sleep, Kestra," he said with that incredible arrogance that grated on her. Only, somehow, while standing so close to him in reality, it didn't feel as grating as she would hope. She reached out the short distance between their bodies to lay her palm on his chest, intending to push him out of her personal space. She needed to breathe, needed to think without his warmth and magnetic presence playing havoc with her electrified senses.

Her fingertips and palm slid up against his solar plexus, nestling firmly into the space beneath the arch of his ribs. Through the heavy fabric of his shirt, a loose, navy satin that was thick and so smooth she couldn't feel a single seam in the stitching, she felt the resistance of abdominal muscles. Tight, impressive ridges of sinew coasted down the length of her hand, heat backing the penetrating thought that he was in incredibly good shape. But hadn't she known that already?

Yes and no. Dreaming was one thing, reality clearly another.

Kestra felt a moment of instant panic as she realized what her touch was doing to her senses and her resolve. He didn't even have to do anything, and she was already contemplating things she absolutely should not and could not think about.

"You've had more than your share of fun, messing around inside my head," she said softly. "Why can't you just leave it at that and let me go in peace? You're stronger than I, a better fighter than I, and clearly prevailing in a dozen other ways. Can't you take a gracious victory and just let me go?"

"Is that what you think this is about? Some sort of contest?" he asked. "That has never been my intention."

"What exactly are your intentions?" she demanded, meeting the unusual gray and jade coloring of his bright eyes. "Why is it so important to you to humiliate me like this?"

"If you feel humiliated, Kestra, it is purely by your own device. There is nothing for you to be ashamed of. Why should what you feel be a source of shame?"

"Stop it. Just stop talking like that, like we are . . . like we know each other! I don't know you. You're a complete stranger to me."

"But is that not how people like you and me relate best when it comes to intimacies with the opposite sex? The less known the better? Passionate bodies without reserve and inhibitions, while our minds and our hearts remain safely put away?"

It was too close to the truth for Kestra's comfort. How he knew that was beyond her. It made her flush uncharacteristically.

"Is that what you want? Is all of this about fulfilling the dream? Will a quick tumble in your bed make you let me go about my business?"

"Quick?" He chuckled, the deep sound resonating across her neck, near where his lowered head hovered. "I am beginning to wonder if you paid any attention at all these past six months."

The innuendo struck its intended mark, causing a burst of excited chills to shimmy over every surface of her skin. Perhaps it was a memory response, because she absolutely remembered the nature of his inference. In her dreams, he had never . . .

Dreams!

It was just a dream! There was no reality to it! In dreams,

a body could do anything it wanted to. No one could have the stamina he had portrayed through the long nights they'd spent entwined in her mind. No man could be that patient and skilled. No male would ever be so sensitive to the needs of a woman's body.

Kestra struck out at him hard, her other hand joining her first, and she pushed him away with all of her might and all the leverage she could muster from the door behind her back.

"Get away from me!" In spite of all her effort, he merely stepped back. He was just as close as ever. "I swear to God, I will hurt you if I have to!" she threatened him, her entire body trembling with fury and frustration.

Even though he knew she couldn't really cause him harm, Noah decided it was best to back off for the moment. He stepped back again, giving her room to breathe. She exhaled hard, relaxing against the door as if she'd just expended more than her limit of strength and energy. She probably had. Her emotions ran just as hot as his did, she just usually hid them beneath a veneer of culture, quick-thinking diplomacy, and logic. Exactly as he did. It was an extraordinary thing, seeing a female version of the most essential parts of himself. It made him wonder what would happen as she began to change. What type of Druid would she become? What power would be at the disposal of the woman meant to be the mate of a Demon King?

Noah knew he should warn her of all the things she would start to experience. He knew he couldn't truly promise to let her go off on her own, at least not for any real length of time. She would be in danger of illness so early in the transformation from human to Druid if she was away from the resources his energy provided for her.

But she was a woman used to her freedoms, and he didn't have the heart to take everything away from her all at once. He would find a way to let her go and keep her just the same—if he had to. He was hoping he could think of a way to coax her to stay. He wished that in all this time he'd learned something more useful about her than the ways around her incredible body. Still, it was impossible to regret a single moment of that time or think of it as wasted.

"I'm going to leave," she said, her breath rapid and deep as she called him on his offer. "I thank you for your gracious invitation, but I'm afraid it's impossible for me to stay."

Noah lifted a single brow at her, and she realized a moment too late what she'd done. Out of habit, she'd fallen back on her finishing-school manners, and by doing so, had given away an important piece of information about herself. Should he decide to look for her, hunt her down in the future, it would make it easier to find her. No one could ever truly cut themselves off from their past. It was her one real weakness, and she'd just given him ammunition to exploit it.

"I will have someone take you to a hotel near a local airport. That will get you as far as Heathrow, but from there you will be on your own, as far as your passport and other things are concerned. You will not need to worry about money. I will arrange for a room in your name and you can freely charge anything you need to that bill. I will take care of it."

"I don't need your charity. I'm—"

"Quite capable of caring for yourself, I know. But I can tell by your expression that you were not expecting to be so far from home and resources. Since that is my fault, it is only right that I correct it. Wait here. I will send someone up to you shortly."

He took her elbow into his hand, gently moving her out of his way so he could pass through the door. She quickly closed it in his wake, leaning back on it and exhaling as if she hadn't drawn a breath in days.

Noah sat before his hearth in the Great Hall.

For all of sixty seconds.

Then he stood up and began to pace across the width of the large fireplace. The fire within gave him little comfort. He felt as though his skin were screaming, as if it would abandon his body and run away if it could.

He'd actually managed to let her go.

True, it had only been a few hours, but already he was strung tighter than he could have ever expected. At the moment, it wasn't because he couldn't control the cravings of his body, although the battle was more intense than ever now that they'd stood in each other's presence. It was the understanding that he'd touched her more than enough to start the emergence of her Druid self, and that she was completely ignorant as to how deadly her distance from him could potentially be these next couple of weeks.

Noah didn't plan to stay away long, even if he could. Unfortunately, time was against him. Just as it had been against him when she had died at the very moment she'd finally been within millimeters of his grasp. Besides her needs during her physical transformation, Samhain was imminent. Come Samhain full moon, Imprinted couples couldn't bear to be apart, even in the slightest, for any length of time. That holy day, as well as the spring full moon of Beltane, called to their basest instincts. It drove them to each other's arms as if it were the last day on earth they would ever spend together. It was violent and hot and loving to the point of making the soul wrench out tears of bliss and agonizing need.

He needed to win her over before that happened.

But Samhain was four days hence, and with a woman like Kestra, trust and acquiescence didn't come that easily.

Noah sat down again, rubbing his right temple as he scowled, the firelight deepening the dark look even as it illuminated it. He would have to be more resourceful now than he ever had been in his lifetime.

Chapter 8

Kestra sat down with a sigh of relief she simply couldn't help.

She ran both hands back over her slick, wet hair, smoothing it back until large droplets of water pattered down onto her back, shoulders, and the plush white towel she had wrapped around herself.

She felt better now, although it had taken a sauna and a shower to achieve it.

Or at least she was determined to feel better.

She was glad to be free again, there was no denying that. At the same time, it had been so easy to leave in the first place that she was completely baffled. She couldn't even begin to get the logistics of how she'd ended up in rural England, in a legitimate *castle*, with a fairly impressive man doing the whole lord-of-the-universe attitude to suit it.

By her tally, she'd used up about half of her nine lives in that day alone. It was a miracle she'd escaped without a scratch, the worst damage being that she was stuck in Europe without clothing, money, or her passport. All of which could be fixed before her hair dried.

She reached for the phone and dialed quickly.

"Yeah?"

"Ah, James. I can always count on you for a cultured greeting."

"Kes! Where the hell have you been? I've been half out of my mind!"

Kestra heard something crash on the other end of the phone and she smiled with the familiarity of it. It made her feel more grounded to hear him do something as habitual as jumping out of his chair so enthusiastically that it fell over.

"James, if you lost the last half of your mind, that would leave you with an empty skull and you would start to collect dust bunnies in there."

"Kes," he growled impatiently. "It's been all over the news for days. Gunfire at the hotel, at the very suite I sent you to a week ago. They found men there crushed into little pieces and I've been freaking out! I thought you were in jail or dead or something like that."

A week?

"I'm in England, actually," she said absently, trying to figure out how she'd lost an entire week. It had felt like a day, two at the very most. Could a person sleep for the better part of a week without waking? Maybe others could, but she never had.

There was silence on James's end of the line, so complete that she thought she could hear his heartbeat through the receiver.

"England?"

"Yes. Long story short? Yes, I had a very bad day yesterday—umm, last week—and I'm still alive and well. I'll try and explain England when I get home, but I can't make you any promises. At the moment, I need money and my passport, and I'd appreciate it if you opened the charge accounts at the usual places."

"Okay, wait a minute . . ." James made a half-laughing grunt. "How the hell did you get into England without your passport? And for that matter, why have you traveled without money for an entire week? Why would you? All you had to do was pick up the damn phone." He interrupted himself. "Wait. I know. It's a long story, right?" Jim sighed into the silence on the other end of the line. "Fine. Consider it FedEx'd by nine a.m. my time. I'll have the money and accounts opened by the time you hang up. Are you at least going to be home in time to do a few more run-throughs of our next gig?"

"I always am. Thanks for your help, partner. I could never survive without you."

"Yeah. Uh . . . Kes . . . one more thing?"

"Mmm?"

"Did we get paid before the deal went sour?"

Kestra's breath hitched tellingly in her throat. She slapped herself in the forehead and made a little sound of frustration. "I knew I was forgetting something."

Noah entered his bedroom from the bath. He ran a towel absently over his hair as he crossed to the large wardrobe situated on the left side of the bed where Kestra had slept off his siphoning of her energy. The Demon King withdrew soft kid breeches from the wardrobe, as well as hunting boots and a simple, loose-sleeved silk shirt.

He thought about her as incessantly as ever as he dressed. More than that, even, because he was unable to help his distinct worry over her dangerous position as she ran around in the world without him. What was more, it had finally occurred to him to *really* wonder what in hell had been going on in her life that had put her on the other end of a hot pistol in the first place. Never mind the potential danger to her health because of their separation; what dangers were out there that had nothing to do with him?

He was worried. It weighted his heart in his chest, this dreadful fear that he hadn't done the right thing. It was bad enough he hadn't taken her from that time and place before she'd been killed the first time around. Had he thrown her back in search of a freedom that would only get her killed once again? And this time, there would be no way of fixing it. This time, after having begun the process of tying her to him and himself to her, he wouldn't be able to bear going on without her. He would already be emotionally incapable. Perhaps he had been for months.

Noah had to turn his thoughts away from that for the moment. In spite of having fetched her and brought her to him, as the Samhain moon approached, he was still in a fragile state of mind. He couldn't help it. In spite of having regained a modicum of control otherwise, he couldn't see straight when he thought about her vulnerability. The more he thought about it, the more he wanted to retrieve her and demand she stay by his side for all time. Which, in all honesty, was what he was supposed to be doing. She wasn't even aware that he was being generous with his gift of freedom.

Noah knew he was merely perpetuating an illusion to try to ease the shock of what was going to happen.

Noah sighed heavily as he finally sat down in the chair that he'd held watch in as she'd slept. He rested his boots beside his feet and leaned back, rubbing at his weary eyes. He could replenish his energy again and again if he wanted to, a blessing of his power that had allowed him to avoid sleep for long periods of time in the past, even when faced with the lethargy the sun induced in his kind. However, there was no true substitute for the repairing comfort of sleep. The body healed and recovered from the long night's exertions when it slept, cycling away toxins and other by-products of an active lifestyle while rest and dreams soothed the psyche.

In all honesty, though, he was afraid of dreaming.

She was so close now.

Would his dreams be stronger, more powerful than ever before? Even more irresistible and tormenting? He'd barely survived those endless nights of imagined pleasure and completion, waking every single evening with it all suddenly out of his reach, falsely played, but remembered by his aching body and desperately pounding heart. In a way, he'd made love to her over and over again already, and yet he was now farther away from her than if they were total strangers.

Were they strangers, or were they lovers? What did she think and feel when she looked at him? Was it anything like the struggle he was currently suffering? If so, how could he even begin to go about easing her way, without allowing his own selfish needs to get in the way?

It was impossible. Especially as the moon waxed and the sacred holiday approached. The Demon King would be unable to resist the need to be with her, in her bed, and inside her body, which had been so perfectly designed for his. The hunger and the draw of her was an instinct of the ages, and no one dared try to circumvent it; those who had were never successful. With the full moon four nights away, Noah knew he had to find a way. He had only one chance to make her understand her future in a way that would make it a blessing instead of an entrapment. He would sacrifice anything to make that happen.

The Demon King lurched impatiently out of the chair, pacing the floor with his hands locked tightly onto his hips. It took a third wide circuit of frustration before he heard the knock at his door.

"I do not wish to be disturbed!" he barked to whoever was on the opposite side.

"My lord, your guest has returned," was the tentative response.

Noah stopped dead in his tracks.

"Seclude her, John, in one of the private parlors. I will be there in a moment."

Why was she back?

Apparently that detail didn't matter to the rest of him. His entire body was quickening with elation and the need to lay eyes on her again. It had only been half a day since she'd left, and already it seemed like half a year.

Noah went to retrieve his boots.

Kestra paced the room with great impatience. She'd decided to take the direct approach and ask her former host if he'd taken her money before whisking her off to England. It wasn't likely he even knew what was in her purse, unless he'd gone looking for identification. It was also possible that he hadn't even bothered to pick the purse up. He'd pointed out that she lacked ID earlier. Since she didn't carry identification under those iffy kinds of circumstances, it could go either way. Her first choice was to swallow her pride and ask. It didn't seem like he needed to steal money from her, when the sheer size and opulence of his holdings were taken into account, but to some, money was money no matter how much they had.

This way she could take his measure eye to eye. If she suspected he was lying, she would come back later and try a more stealthy approach. It wasn't the favorable choice, considering the volume of people that moved about the castle and the fact that she knew nothing of the floor plan outside of what she'd already seen. No backup, none of James's little toy technologies to help guide her. But it wouldn't be the first time she'd slunk around foreign rooms and been successful. Frankly, given her level of edginess recently, it might be fun to try and pull something over on the arrogant bastard.

Kestra turned sharply when the door opened behind her.

She'd seen a great many people and places in her lifetime, so she couldn't understand why he looked so remarkable and vital to her as he shut the door and crossed the room toward her. His clothing was so simple, clean and crisp but cut incredibly close to his body. It looked like he was about to go riding. The only thing missing from his ensemble was a riding crop and coat. Again he wore the black and tan boots of a master of the hunt, which told her he was an excellent horseman and probably hunted for sport. It was a common English pastime, even though he himself was clearly not native to England.

It was rare for her to find herself in the company of men greatly taller than herself. He had to be well over six feet in height because he made her feel smaller than usual. It probably didn't help that she'd already tried to take him down once and had had about as much luck as she would fighting a cinder block wall.

If it came right down to it, she had to admit none of that was what made her heart quicken with trepidation and the sudden urge to run for the hills. In spite of everything else, Noah was one hundred percent magnetic. Electromagnetic, and fully charged at that. Kestra was afraid that if she didn't acknowledge his potency as a male, it would give him some kind of power over her. But how could she do that and still deny the way she felt herself respond to that potency? She couldn't even hope that he was ignorant of it. Not if they truly had met in all of those heated, volatile dreams.

What was more, it seemed this time was even more powerful than any other, her entire being humming with attraction. She turned her focus inward as he neared, making a very conscious effort to keep her breathing even and her attitude strictly businesslike.

"I'm sorry to bother you," she said, hoping that her cold address would bring him to a stop right where he was.

It didn't.

"It is no bother to welcome your company, Kestra. Though I admit I am surprised to see you here again so quickly. I had the impression you wished to be as far away from here as you could possibly manage."

"Actually, I have a matter of business I wanted to attend to with you."

He lifted a single dark brow in surprise and clear curiosity.

"I have more than enough business partners, Kestra. I am not interested in acquiring any others."

"The last thing I want is a partnership with you," she retorted. "My purse was on the floor of the suite. Did you happen to retrieve it?"

Is that all?

Noah couldn't answer right away. He was too busy fighting off a very volatile wash of temper. He clenched his teeth together as he tried to control a rash of temperamental impulses. He usually had a far better rein over the infamous passions of a Fire Demon, but his disappointment over her motivations for returning triggered it like very few things could. Of course he hadn't expected it to be that easy. He was a monarch, and as such expected things to take time and finesse to come about. However, it seemed as though rational thought didn't tarry long when it came to Kestra.

Just walking in the door and seeing her standing in his home had made a whole new impact, as if it hadn't happened once already. Her hair was loose now, long and full of that sheen of white that fairly sparkled. She'd changed from the designer dress and pearls he'd found her in, trading them in for a teal minidress without a single touch of decoration. It was a short-sleeved tube of Lycra that began slightly off her shoulders and ended just above mid-thigh, clinging to every lush curve like a second skin. As a result, she appeared to be little more than a very long pair of legs fitted into ridiculously high stiletto heels. Yet she was perfectly balanced and clearly in control of every fit muscle of her body. All of which were apparent to even the quickest brush of a gaze, right down to smooth, tanned legs she didn't bother to cover with hosiery.

Kestra felt her throat go tight and her mouth dry up as she registered the ominous gray clouding in his jade pupils. He wasn't showing it in his expression, or even in the relaxed pose of his body as he stood before her, but she was convinced that he was seething with emotion. Anger? Hostility? She couldn't be sure, but it was there. Every instinct in her body demanded that she acknowledge it, and demanded that she understand how truly dangerous this man was.

"No," he responded at last, his tone more dead than neutral. "I was more concerned with your safety at the time."

"Damn."

She believed him. Then again, she had figured as much to begin with. That meant the cops had her money, which meant they had Jim's money. Not to mention her weapon and her fingerprints. She would be splashed over Interpol and FBI bulletin boards already. That would make her exit out of England a little more difficult.

"Thank you. I'm sorry to have bothered you."

"It was no bother," he murmured, narrowing his eyes on her thoughtfully as she moved to brush past him. "I do not suppose you would like to tell me why you were caught in the middle of the situation I found you in, would you?"

Kestra turned and faced him, barely a foot away from him.

"I don't suppose you would want to tell me how you found me in the middle of that situation, would you?" she countered.

"It is as I said. I came looking for you."

"Now you do sound like a cop. Or a private detective." She made the accusation with a narrowing of her crystalline blue eyes.

"Why? Do you often have problems with cops and detectives?"

"Right. Like I would tell you if I did?"

"I can hope," he said very simply. "I am curious about this woman I find myself involved with."

"Involved?" She barked a short, disbelieving laugh. "We are not, nor will we ever be, *involved*. What goes on in my life is my business, not yours or anyone else's. After I walk out that door, I will be doing my level best never to set eyes on you again."

"I am afraid that will be impossible."

His tone was more matter-of-fact than it was ominous, but for some reason, it was far more threatening to her because of it. He seemed so sure. Confident, yes, but not with the arrogance she'd attributed to him earlier. Kestra realized then that she'd been mistaken in that assessment. Arrogance implied a certain level of callousness and selfishness. What she suddenly was feeling from him had nothing to do with those traits.

She should have met the comment with outrage at its audacity, but she was unexpectedly overwhelmed with a sensation of fear unlike anything she was accustomed to feeling. Her heart pounded relentlessly, the speed of it ten times what it had been as she'd casually lain sprawled over plumbing while a security guard walked beneath her. Being shot at was far less unnerving than this man suddenly seemed. At least she knew what a person firing a gun at her was after.

"You have . . ." She uncharacteristically struggled for words as his eyes never left hers, becoming more jade every instant as she watched. "You're nothing to me," she whispered, grinding her teeth together when the lack of conviction came through in the softness of her voice.

"I am everything to you," he said in return, his voice just as soft but in no way deficient in conviction.

He took just one more step closer to her, the slight squeak of the leather of his boot sounding terribly loud, somehow drowning the noise of her own body as her heart pounded and her breath came quick and chaotic. Noah reached up, and the sight of his fingers unfurling, displaying his fingertips and broad palm as they reached for her, made her react. Her entire body pivoted into the slap she used to strike him away from whatever part of her was his goal.

With uncanny instincts, her opposite hand darted up to

catch his other wrist as it moved, quick as flickering flame, to replace the one she'd already discouraged. Kestra felt just as surprised as he looked, if she could call the intrigued lift of his brow an expression of his surprise. She was fast, she knew, but it usually took the register of a telltale movement or something like it to justify any action. The point was, she normally wasn't fast enough to do what she'd just done. She was realistic about her own limitations, and with all of her body committed to the original strike . . .

"Full of surprises, hmm?"

Kestra gasped. It was as if he were reading her mind.

She released him roughly. She backed away, wanting to turn and run, only her pride keeping her from doing so.

"I don't know who you are, what you want, or how it is you've done the things you've done," she hissed angrily, "but you will never come near me again. Do you understand me?"

"Every word," he agreed.

Lies. It was lies. She could see it in the predatory look in his eyes, felt it with every fiber of her being as he stepped toward her again and again. She was being hunted. Stalked. Kestra didn't know why he threatened her so easily, but she met the perceived threat the only way she knew how.

Noah stopped midstep when, preceded by movement that was almost too fast for even his preternatural senses to comprehend, he heard the distinct click of a gun being cocked and found himself targeted right between his eyes.

"I swear to God I will," she ground out hoarsely. "Don't make me kill the man who saved my ass. I hate feeling guilty about things like that."

The remark was almost glib, and it amused the Demon King. She had no idea that the little gun was more of a threat to her than it was to him, even under the best of circumstances. It didn't change the captivating question of exactly how she had concealed the weapon while wearing so brief and tight an outfit.

Noah knew he wasn't reacting to her pulling a gun on him

the way she would expect a human male to react. The increasing tremble of her outstretched arm and tightly clenched hand were clear giveaways to that fact. Still, she had to find out sometime that he was no ordinary human male, and there was no patience left within him to wait for her to get to know him a little better.

This time it was the Demon King who moved faster than perception, his left hand grabbing her wrist and removing the danger of the weapon from them both. His right arm snaked around her waist quick as lightning, jerking her up off her heels and forward into the bend of his body. She was so long and lean, so humanly hot to the touch even through her clothes as he clasped her to himself. It was like fitting a lock with its only key. She slid into him hip to hip, thigh to thigh, and breast to breast, as if they'd been born that way and sliced apart at birth. Now, finally, they were completed once more. Noah made a low, rough sound of satisfaction that rang out like the sigh released when agony was comforted at last.

Kestra was shaking head to toe with rage and apprehension and who knew what else, but none of it mattered to him. All that mattered was that he was touching her, that he was close enough to truly take in that unusual scent of sweet sugar that radiated off her in warm, delicious waves. He barely knew what he was doing as his nose drifted over her cheek, her hair, her neck. He'd waited all his life to be this close to her, and would spend all of the rest of it bringing her closer still.

When his lips touched her throat ever so slightly, the end to the strangest act of aggression she'd ever been victim of, Kestra's entire network of muscles constricted in sharp spasm. Still, she barely heard the report of the small .22 she held as it went off, forgotten on the end of her clenching trigger finger. The gun clattered to the floor, though she was sure she didn't release it. It was as if it passed right through her hand and fingers, as if they were no more than air.

She didn't give it another thought. She was far too shocked by the response flooding through her entire body as his lips traced up the artery along the side of her neck. Flooding was the only word for it, because it was as if all of her blood had burst the confines of its vessels, like a heated waterfall beneath her skin, crashing to a halt in . . . in places she couldn't bring herself to acknowledge.

She should have been screaming in protest, fighting tooth and nail for her freedom . . . at the very least kicking the crap out of him.

But she couldn't.

She was paralyzed. Paralyzed with feeling and a rush of thoughts she should never have had. All this because he'd touched his lips to the side of her neck. But in spite of this paralysis she tried to blame for her inaction, her head tilted slightly, as if to give him better access, her hand fitting against the muscles stretched across his lower ribs.

She realized what she was doing, understanding that though everything was new, it had an experienced habitualness to it. *It's those damned dreams.* As if they'd been real, as if they were lovers a hundred times over, she responded when he abused his knowledge of her body's sensitivities and preferences.

Kestra jerked back violently, trying to escape his well-sprung trap. She was successful for all of a single breath, and then he was following her and close to her again. Again flush against her, he stepped with her as she backed across the room, his body strong and heated against hers every single millimeter she moved, like a skilled partner in a perfect tango. She had no space to breathe, everything about his movement so much more deadly and erotic than resting still against him had been.

"Stop," she begged him just before she backed into a solid barrier. She sounded breathless and aroused even to her own ears, and her face burned with a combination of fury and mortification. "Let go of me."

Of course Noah couldn't oblige her. He had waited far too long to hold her like this in the waking world, and he was too heavily swayed by emotions and needs far out of her scope of understanding. He could feel the near fullness of the moon burning just outside the windows behind his back, alternately chilling him and firing him with a hunger that was almost as frightening to him as it was to her. It was to the point where he could no longer tell which one of them was shaking hardest.

"Not yet," he objected on rapid, heated breaths. "Not yet."

Kestra jerked her head back purely out of self-preservation when he feinted for her mouth. All she earned for her effort was a hand at the back of her neck that held her perfectly still. She felt the bite of potential tears in her eyes as alarm and bewilderment warred within her. She cried out, a frustrated growl that grew into an outcry. She struggled even harder, but it was like being a fly stuck in glue, and she made no headway and no impression on him at all. Worse yet, she affected the reactions of her own rousing body even less.

Finally, Noah was able to touch his mouth to hers.

Her resistance and reluctance were nothing new to him. In all those months of interaction, it had become like a form of foreplay for them. He knew she could accept what she was feeling only after she convinced herself that she had done her best to fight him off. The moment his lips touched hers, the soft sound she made gave away her true desires, at least those of the body she had tried so hard to keep away from him. It was enough. Hopefully her mind would follow later.

There was no time for tenderness between them. There never had been. They had always switched gears hard, and this moment was no different. He had barely had a sip of her lips when her mouth parted beneath his, demanding a speed and aggression that was painfully easy for him to fall into. As soft and beautiful as she was, there was always hardness and forcefulness beneath her more delicate exteriors. On some level he understood that it was because she couldn't bear to give him the vulnerability she associated with those things she hid within herself.

All of those finite details meant nothing just then. He let her draw him into her game just as he let her draw him into her mouth. He kissed her, tasting deeply of her antagonistic tongue, the warmth and wetness of her mouth as much like refined sugar as the rest of her radiated in sweet, fragrant waves. She was breathing as hard as he was, the rasping rhythms all either of them could hear over their crashing heartbeats.

Jasmine landed lightly on her feet, her boots scuffing slightly on the asphalt.

The female Vampire took a long, lazy look around herself, then raised her head to the cold autumn breeze. She could smell Demons on the wind, just as she could sense every creature, Nightwalker or otherwise. Either by scent or her heat-sensitive vision, anything existing within a certain proximity was known to her. Life and power, all these things tickled over her senses in one way or another, five centuries of experience giving her the skill to sort through the information adeptly. All she need do was flick down the nictitating membranes in her eyes, and in a glance she could sort out a gathering of Nightwalkers just by the disparate level of heat they gave off. Every one of them was unique, but to her it was like reciting her alphabet. She knew it all in her sleep.

She turned farther into the breeze as it picked up, allowing it to lift the black tangle of her already windblown hair. The loose black satin of her shirt fluttered against her athletic body, the untucked tails lifting until her flat midriff was exposed, revealing the sparkle of a diamond hoop along the edge of her navel and a slim gold chain wrapping through it and around the circumference of her slender waist. She caught the tails of the shirt in her hands and tied them tightly into a knot just beneath her breasts. The original knot had come undone during her flight, but now she could repair her outfit.

She walked up the drive, her long legs taking her up quickly as it changed from asphalt to gravel, then at last to a large path of rocks. There were no vehicles in the drive, as was to be expected because Demons could no more use technology than Vampires could. It forced them to live anachronistically, but Jasmine saw no true loss in not being able to properly use technology. It looked to her like it was little more than an enormous pain in the ass. Then again, that could just be because her Nightwalker chemistry often made those types of human trinkets blow up in her face. That or the fact that most Nightwalkers were born with everything they would ever possibly need to obtain comfort in life. Technology was superfluous to many Nightwalkers, downright primitive to others when compared to what they could do naturally with their power.

Ten minutes later, the Vampire who had so hastily been assigned the task of being her Prince's messenger found herself cooling her heels in the Great Hall of the Demon King's household. After five hundred years on the planet, and by default because she was a Vampire, it never took Jasmine long to get thoroughly bored. She was not the type who could stand still for more than two minutes at a time. She was also not interested all that much in protocol.

The Vampire slowly began to inspect her surroundings, walking with ease throughout the sprawl of rooms in the lower level of the Demon King's holdings. The staff was used to strangers coming and going, their master liberal with his open invitations, so she wasn't questioned as she wandered around.

Of course, being a senior Vampire and quite skilled at becoming a part of the shadows around her, she found it almost too easy to slip past the sentries that *were* posted here and there. Jasmine would have thought that Noah's guards would have more experience detecting her type at this point, what with the traitor Demon Ruth at large and rogue Vampires tagging after her. It was assumed that Ruth and Nico, her Vampire compatriot and an old enemy of Damien's, had survived their last battle with the Vampire Prince and his new Lycanthrope bride. A battle Jasmine had attended. If those turncoat Nightwalkers had survived that kind of devastation, then they were fearsome enemies indeed.

Jasmine left the shadows as she continued to explore. Everything around her was made of painstakingly laid English stone. It made almost every room a uniform shale or dark gray color. Every laid carpet and heavy hung drape was just as elegantly detailed and anachronistic as the rest of the place.

It was equal to the citadel in which she lived as counselor to her Prince. Since Damien had only opened court and living quarters just at the beginning of the year, there had not yet been time to have its blank walls filled or the touches added that would make a home. Here it was obvious that family had lived in the maze of rooms.

Compared to these personalized and elegantly adorned rooms, Damien's citadel was decorated like a monastery. It probably had not improved much over the past nine months because its new mistress had lived all of her life in a monastery. The least Syreena could do was try and be like other Lycanthropes. They, at least, knew what it meant to enjoy the richer comforts of the world. Of course, Jasmine's quarters were decorated with all these elegant comforts and an assortment of sins in mind. Had she been in charge of the—

Jasmine stopped the fruitless thought.

She would never be the mistress of Damien's household again. Not unless some unfortunate accident befell the Princess. However, even she couldn't take delight in contemplating that. Damien was in love with Syreena, and if anything ever happened to her, it would destroy him. Jasmine would never want to see that, no matter how much that woman got on her nerves. Ignoring her deeper personal feelings in the matter, she focused solely on the fact that if Damien were to die any time soon, she would very likely end up taking his place just to keep their race from being run by some arrogant jackass.

Frankly, she wasn't the right sort of Vampire to play royalty, and since she could think of no one better, she would rather help maintain the status quo. Damien had ruled for centuries, and she would see that he continue to do so in as much happiness as she could manage.

Jasmine stopped short in her thoughts and in her steps as she sensed something out of place nearby. Curious, she turned toward a nearby door and touched the handle lightly.

Human.

There was no mistaking the heat and scent of a human, even through the door. It was not usual for Demons and humans to associate. Not full-bred humans, at least. Jasmine was already beginning to know how to sense the difference between usual humans and the Druids that were suddenly being resurrected into Demon society. She could be mistaken, as the talent was new, but she could swear there was nothing Nightwalker about the human she was sensing beyond the door. What was more, the mortal was not alone.

Now, this is interesting, Jasmine thought with delight.

One minute it mattered who and what they were; the next it didn't. The next instant was about nothing but chemistry, wanting, and gripping, starving needs that had yearned for this connection for far too long. The moment where Destiny demanded obedience.

Kestra's fingers slid into the crisp, curling hair at Noah's collar. She couldn't help herself. She had dreamed of him as often as he had dreamed of her. Whether she would admit to her needs or not, she craved the reality of him. The feel of his thick hair curling between and around her fingers was rich realism. Her opposite hand skimmed fast and hot over his clothing in search of far more carnal sensations. Kestra shaped him with her fingers and palm, down his chest, over his ribs, and around to his back, a thorough exploration of the musculature of his flank.

The Demon King responded, his broad hands just as alive and active over her long, sensual shape and fit contours. Her body was truly athletic, firm beneath the stroke of his searching palms, but it was easy enough to find the soft, feminine curves that were generous and delightful. His huge palms cupped her hips and bottom, stroking and drawing her into his body, making sure she felt their tight fit. He traveled upward, curving into her waist.

Noah's hands slid up her sides beneath her arms, only his thumbs breaching the curve of her rib cage, sliding up toward her breasts. Kestra was braced between his body and an equally solid wall. She lifted one stiletto-heeled foot from the floor, her knee drawing slowly up the outside of those soft breeches he wore. The fabric of his clothing was the only thing besides his hair that was soft. The rest of him was like granite baked in the sun, immovably hard and incredibly hot.

The moment they had entered the same room it was flint and steel, with the touching of their bodies becoming the major spark. Once he'd cornered her and kissed her, that was what had truly set her to burn. A single kiss. Just as he was kissing her now, hot and skillful, his tongue catching hers again and again until she burned from head to toe just from the fire of his mouth.

She'd needed this for so long. This wildness and heat and danger. A career of death-defying escapades, not to mention thrill-seeking hobbies that most men would shy from, and none of it had shaken her, stirred her, or brought her to understand the truth of danger.

Now it was here, all around her, invading every pore and

flushing her with adrenaline as it pumped into all corners of her bloodstream. She knew that this was danger in its rawest form, this man and all the places within her he had the potential to reach. She had known it from the very first time she had fallen asleep and then fallen into the dream of his determined hands.

Hands that were now sliding up her body with ferocious intent.

She felt the stroke of his thumbs on the undersides of her breasts with astonishing sensitivity. He broke away from her mouth, using his hold beneath her arms to jerk her farther up between his body and the wall. Instantly his lips were burning trails of flame down her throat. Whirlwind emotions welled up in her. She didn't know how she had borne life without the heat of his mouth, hands, and body pressing against hers. The thought was surprisingly dependant for the fiercely independent nature of her soul.

Noah had learned her in dreams, studied her like he would any of his treasured tomes. But this was like a brand-new language. Soft beneath his hands, warm against his body, delicious against his tongue. She even tasted like candy, sweetly melting beneath his mouth as he stroked his tongue over the rise of her breast where it was exposed by her neckline.

Clothing suddenly seemed wasteful and clumsily hampering.

Kestra abruptly came alive, catching his dark head in her hands and dragging him up to her so she could devour his mouth. She needed that rich, masculine taste against her lips and tongue. She was starving for the reality of it. Even as she entrapped him with her kiss, she began pulling at his clothes. Noah reached out to catch on to something far steadier than himself, his fingers coming to curl around the corner of the stone wall. She managed to free one of the tails of his shirt from the waistband of his pants and her eagerly searching hand found his naked skin beneath it. He broke from her mouth and gasped, unable to help himself. Nothing could burn him, and yet her touch was like fire exploding over the entire surface of his skin, and this time he felt the singe of it soul deep.

Noah was truly hot to her touch. It was hardly a metaphor to say he scorched her palms as her left hand joined the right in her foray beneath his shirt. Instinct ought to have made Kestra pull away, jerking back just as she would if she had touched a hot stove. Mere instinct, however, didn't stand a chance in the face of the pull as base as evolution that now gripped them both.

"Months . . ." he muttered against her ear, following it with a soulful groan as her strong fingers glided up his back beneath his shirt, over his shoulders, and back down again.

Months. Kestra knew what he meant. There was a world of torture and agonizing frustration in that one word, a world she was all too familiar with. Like long-distance lovers reunited after too long a separation, each pushed past any and all simplistic needs. There would be time for all of that later, perhaps. Niceties were not what either of them needed or wanted.

Noah's hand pushed at the hem of her dress as hers fell on his waistband and fly. They alternately kissed and then drew for breath. Noah found the thin holster to her weapon strapped around her thigh and he yanked it from between her legs, the tearing of the Velcro fasteners sounding just as satisfying as the holster leather did when it hit the floor.

Noah heard her laugh briefly at his actions, the humor bracketed by murmurs of distracted pleasure and encouragement. Still it made an impact on him, skipping down every major artery in his body, flooding him with renewed fervor and need, though the initial emotions had never flagged.

"Don't stop," he heard her demand of him. Using the wall at her back for leverage, Kestra made sure he felt every inch of her burning body, broadcasting its message of hunger. The effect was like a heart attack, tossing the beat out of syncopation and stealing his breath away.

It threw him off stride enough to allow her to flip their positions against the wall. Stone bit into his bare back, making him realize she had freed him of his shirt entirely. He did not give it another thought, though, as she ran her hands down the front of his body, seeking out the details of his body's landscaping with bold, efficient fingers. Noah ground his back teeth together as she tested his patience and his sanity. She wasn't shy or hesitant, exactly as he would have expected, instead sliding down the entire length of his body as she investigated him strictly for the sake of arousing him. Her hands went first, her mouth following in a wicked little trail of expectant fire.

Need clutched at him, ferocious and violent in its anticipation. Her hands bracketed his waist so she could lick and nip her way down his belly. It was quick and thorough, meant to tease and succeeding famously. His hands locked into the white silk of her hair, the strands caught into his fists. He closed his eyes because it was unbearable to watch her. He couldn't keep his sanity if he watched her.

Kestra's hands slid down to his hips and without hesitation sought the feel of his straining erection through the fabric of his breeches. The sensation of her sure, strong hands went surging through him with volcanic force as she took in his form and heat, molded her fingers to the thickened hardness of him. She kept her curious, stroking hands against him but she came back up to her full height. She reached for his mouth, licking at his lower lip with a slow sensual stroke to get him to open his eyes. She made a deep, appreciative sound as she noted the hunger he couldn't keep at bay within his gaze.

"You feel so good," she whispered against his mouth, making him groan in response to her observations and touch. Kestra could feel the fine trembling that shuddered through his body. She liked having the power to do that to him. She had always liked it.

She pushed just a little further. Waiting. Wanting.

Kestra slid her fingers over the closures of his fly, releasing him from the strangling confinement of the fabrics. She closed her fingers and her palm around him. He was scorching hot, incredibly hard, and she could feel his pulse surging thickly through him. She went one step further, stroking a sly thumb over the very sensitive tip of him.

Danger.

She felt it explode out of him like nuclear fire. She gasped when he locked his fingers around her wrists, removing her taunting hands, and then reached for her. Both his hands were suddenly gripping her with bruising strength as she was hauled up off her feet. Her limber gymnast's body seemed to fly with the ease it took to bring them together, sex to sex, a burning massage of two pelvises communicating the intent of the same promise in need of fulfilling.

Kestra's hand flew out, bracing against the wall near his head as she threw back her head in a silent cry of overheated anticipation. He had hold of her hips even as the vise of her legs wrapped around him. He made damn sure she could feel the heat and raging hardness she had created.

The thong she wore gave way with a snap as he whipped it off her body. He immediately sought for her once she was exposed to him, his hand slipping between their writhing bodies. She cried out with a sense of shock as his fingers slid over her, searching through ready wetness and heat. Noah caught that cry against his tongue. Kestra felt the flick of a teasing thumb as a long, seeking finger slowly made its way into her body. Kestra shuddered at the unexpected pleasure of it, at how easily he riled her senses. He slid a second insistent finger into her just as his teeth closed gently around her nipple, right through the fabric of her dress.

"Oh!" she exclaimed breathlessly.

Then his eyes were locking with hers, his mouth hovering close to her aching lips. "In all these months," he said breathlessly, "one of the things I wanted most was to hear my name on your lips." But he didn't request it. He merely stated the desire and decided to let her do with it what she would. "I am so delighted you are ready for me, *Kikilia*," he murmured against her lips as he made tight little circles around her clitoris with his thumb, making her moan and arch into him.

Noah withdrew his touch abruptly, and she cried out something close to a rebuke. He made up for the deprivation when he dragged her against himself, wetting his hard shaft with the slickness of her eager body, and unerringly found the threshold he had wanted to cross for so long now. He had no patience, no care, and no sense of anything except the demanding passion of the fire inside himself. She had lit the fuse, and now she would feel the explosion.

Noah thrust into her in one scorching movement, dragging her hips to his with torrid command, and impaling her on himself with barely suppressed violence of need. She was unbelievably hot as she surrounded him. How was it possible that she burned him so fiercely? Her body welcomed him, grasped tightly at him with a voracious sucking of quivering inner muscles. It was heaven and hell, a relief and a torture. He could barely breathe with the onslaught of sensations and emotions the joining of their bodies evoked.

Kestra inhaled so hard she thought her lungs would burst. He was inside her at long last. After months and months of waking to the empty feeling of her hollow body, at last she was filled to satisfaction. Her entire body arched with the overwhelming sensation of fullness, her thighs and knees clenching around his hips like an aggressive, sinuous constrictor. His powerful hands held her suspended against him as she absorbed her initial pleasure.

Then her head snapped back up, showering him in white strands of snow as her mouth sought the fit of his and she began to move with a sensual rhythm in his hands and over his body.

"Months . . ." she repeated on a gasp into his mouth as she moved slowly and tightly over his superheated and hardened body.

Again, it was all understood. But as hot and erotic as taking her like this was, he felt deprived without his hands free. He reached to hook her thigh higher over his hip, making her breath catch as it opened her deeper to him. It also freed up one of his hands, allowing his hungry fingertips to run up her thigh, her hip, and on to her belly and breast through the tight fabric of her dress. He peeled back the teal Lycra, rather like opening a gift, until her breast was exposed, its very dark nipple pulled into a tight point of excitement. Noah cradled her breast in his palm, toying with the rigid nipple with skilled fingers, coaxing her into growing still hotter around him, bathing himself in her sensitive response to his touch. All the while, her agile body curved and wriggled against him.

The Demon King could bear no more. He had needed her for far too long and his body pounded with primitive male urges. He grabbed hold of her, turning and stepping with her until he was near his goal.

Kestra felt her backside skimming over a solid surface, though it was covered in lace of some kind. She realized that he had set her on a huge antique table she had seen as she had waited for him earlier. It only took her a moment to understand why.

He stripped her of her dress in one quick motion, completely lacking in gentleness as he did so. Kestra didn't even notice to care. He was laying her back along the table, allowing him to stand sturdy between her thighs. His hands went to her hips, gripping her tightly as he sank himself deep inside her in that ancient surging need of all dominant males. He repeated the thrust, shunting himself deeper and deeper, as if he wasn't yet satisfied with his depth within her.

Kestra could do little more than grasp his hands where they clutched at her hips. She looked up into his watchful, smoky dark eyes as he looked for her every response, sought every movement that gave her pleasure. Even though he was half wild, even bordering on abusive as he stroked violently into her accepting body, he was looking for her gratification.

Kestra allowed his taxing of her body because it was pure ecstasy to do so. She arched, cried out, and felt stark waves of raw rapture begin to envelop and overwhelm her. Before she could even acknowledge its approach, she flew into a thrashing orgasm, her entire being locked up so tight, inside and out, it was incomprehensible.

Noah said something low and vicious under his breath in his native tongue. He had to stop as she cried out and seized with her climax. She was clutching at him so tightly, bathing him in hot, melted sugar, and he refused to be taken by her. When she finally released, gasping for breath and trying to open her dazed eyes, he began again to move within her.

Kestra was so highly sensitized that she thought she would fly apart as he took that first long stroke deep into her already pulsing body. She felt instantly tight, ready, and needing.

"Hang on, baby," he warned her with wicked masculine confidence.

She couldn't begrudge him his arrogance in this situation. He was leaning over her, his body like magic as it plunged slow and deep this time. His mouth skimmed up over her ribs and sought the thrust of her nipple. He sucked her deeply into his mouth and it sent rivers of fire rushing down her body. She made a small sound, half anticipation, half fear, and he looked up to see her widening eyes. He felt the tension coming, felt her begin to tremble.

He felt her resist.

He pulled her up against his chest, bringing her ear to his mouth so he could whisper softly to her as he began to pick up the pace with which he pitched into her body.

"Do not be afraid," he said, his smoky voice swirling around her like a sensual fog. "Just let go."

She shook her head. Maybe it was less about fear and more about disbelief. It was almost painful, the tension he was sending like a coil through her body. How could he do this? Only through the dreams could he know how to touch her this deeply. No stranger could do this. No one could. Never.

"*Kikilia*," he whispered, his voice taunting sorcery. "I will help you if I must."

Kestra gasped, her heart pounding as she tried to figure out what more he could possibly do to her. He let her fall back onto the table gently, seizing her hip again, sliding relentlessly into her taut body. Then Noah reached to where their bodies joined, slid a sure thumb through wet, white curls, and touched her.

Kestra squealed. She couldn't help it. It was the only sound that could escape her as her body tension ratcheted up to the tenth power and beyond. Colors swirled around her vision; tears actually burned their way onto her lashes.

Then she detonated.

Noah absorbed her power with bracing agony and unrelenting hunger. She screamed out, and he devoured the sound with greed and pleasure. She was beautiful, hot, responsive as all hell, and she was his. Her body licked at his like a live flame and he was definitely burned.

Wait. Wait.

It was a brutal, demanding whisper in his mind, forcing him to hold back even though she threatened his very sanity with her voracious body and capacity for pleasure. So he held on while she whirled away and back again. He wouldn't allow her breath this time. He had need. He hungered. Like fire and flame, he would be relentless. And nothing would stop him now. It came over him savagely, the appetite of a building fire. He gave her no quarter, driving into her before she had fully returned from her last peak. Two wrenching strokes and she was rippling with orgasm again. She took his need and his hunger with equal appetite. Hard as he took her, as brutal as his ability to give her pleasure was, he couldn't exhaust her. She slid now with every thrust into her body as the cloth on the table alleviated friction, allowing him to manipulate her until she thought she would pass out from the pleasure.

The more he made her come, the more she cried out, the more relentless his pace. His touch was everywhere, toying with her, teasing, and setting her off until she was blinded to anything but ecstasy. Just when she reached that point of her personal threshold, she heard him make a low, predatory noise, saw the intensity of the storm in his eyes, felt the increasing thickness and heat deep within her until she thought she was on fire. Noah suddenly grabbed her shoulders, dragging her against his chest and seeking for her mouth with his. She felt the slickness of his sweat-drenched body all over her as his surges into her body became frantic. She fell completely apart, her body jerking with spasms of pleasure that seemed to grip deeper into her with every invasion. She was almost completely senseless by the time he surged hard into her for the last time, succumbing to an explosion of release that poured liquid fire into her again and again. He vocalized, a raw, masculine growl of intense satisfaction, and his hands clenched around her neck and thigh as he shuddered violently from the aftermath.

It was, by far, the wildest and most satisfying sexual experience of Kestra's life. She understood that even before she could breathe again. Every muscle in her body was abused by the tension of pleasure caught and released. Noah had done the impossible. He had made her feel the intangible. Kestra couldn't understand it, and part of her didn't want to try.

But it was also the moment she became aware that she had just made the biggest mistake of her life. She couldn't even begin to list everything that was wrong about this. She wasn't the type to regret her sexual choices, but she instinctively knew that there was far more at stake here than the well-being of her body.

Oh God.

They hadn't even used a condom.

Kestra's heart was already pounding at top speed, so even that frightening lapse in the protection of her body couldn't increase the beat. She was protected against pregnancy, so *that* she wasn't worried about. It was the million other variables that should concern her . . . but didn't. Come to think of it, she realized it hadn't concerned him, either.

Noah hadn't even stepped away from her, hadn't even released her in any way, and he could already feel the buzzing of her thoughts just outside of his awareness. He could easily imagine what someone of her personality would be thinking in a moment like this. Especially because she didn't yet understand that there was no such thing as casual sex between them, and there never would be. But he could let her be with her thoughts easily in that moment. The fact that he could sense the jumbled bustling of them was the first sign that the Imprinting was begun in earnest. She would change even more rapidly now, now that they were mated.

As he looked up at the wall and the table and the disarray of clothing around them, he could see the scorching and burns that had come with his increasing lack of focus on things other than Kestra. Handprints in stone. Burns on the table. Toasted doilies and scorched clothing. Luckily, he had pulled her close to protect her at those last moments, because a glance up at the ceiling revealed the remnants of his total loss of control, a blackened, billowing pattern, as if flame had been thrown up above them in a roiling cloud. As it was, he was hoping her healing abilities as a Druid had kicked in, or she was really going to feel the damage he had done to her body. She was red everywhere he had touched her, though none of it more serious than a sunburn. Still, it would make her uncomfortable. Over time it would no longer matter; she was designed to dampen power surges like those. Soon, he would never burn anything by accident ever again.

At least, not when he was with her.

"Wow. It's like a sauna in here."

Noah and Kestra nearly cracked noses, both whipping their heads around to see who had addressed them.

The tall brunette finished entering the room and flopped down in the nearest chair, kicking up her booted feet until her crossed ankles rested on the ottoman before her.

"Otherwise, I really like this room. It has a more feminine touch than most of the others. I'm going to guess your sister must have had something to do with that."

Kestra was shocked by the audacity it took for this woman to walk into a room with two clearly indisposed people in it, never mind the ballsy way she casually took a seat. She still had Noah standing between her knees, *in her body*, their bare chests against each other, and their arms still wrapped tightly about each other.

Noah released Kestra first, reaching for the lace tablecloth and using it as a wrap to cover her. He realized the fabric was smoldering at his touch, and he took a deep breath in an attempt to cool his sudden temper. It wasn't so much because Jasmine was being rude, either. Jasmine was a Vampire. Public sex and other such liberties were commonplace to her breed. This type of indiscretion truly would mean nothing to her had she come across it in any venue. However, Noah was certain she'd meant to cause mischief. There was no way someone of her years and skills could have been unaware of her untimely entrance.

Still, there was no way for her to know how deeply she'd just messed up his life. Of course, that didn't mean he couldn't find a way to punish her for her brazen troublemaking.

"Jasmine." He greeted her dryly, moving away from Kestra at last and going about the task of straightening his clothes and handing his mate hers.

Chapter 9

Kestra was barely over the shock of what she'd done, not to mention about a thousand thoughts and emotions to follow. This man was a total stranger to her, she realized with a sensation of panic suddenly crawling beneath her skin. For all she knew, he was married to the sultry brunette who had made herself so clearly at home.

What in the world was I thinking?

That thought had come through to Noah loud and clear, probably fueled by the emotion behind it. He was also aware of the emotional defenses that slammed down over her. He could feel the shift, right down to the little hairs standing up on the back of her neck.

"Jasmine, I trust you have a damned good reason for invading my privacy," he said coldly, his eyes a world of threatening promises.

"I beg your pardon, my lord," she responded, her tone nowhere near as respectful as her words. It was clear she was having a great joke at his expense. "I had not realized you had taken up the human penchant for privacy."

Noah's eyes shifted to glance at Kestra from beneath his

lashes. Someone as sharp as she was would not miss Jasmine's casual terminology even under the best of circumstances. He sighed heavily, running a quick, angry hand through his hair as he glared at Jasmine.

"Not another word, Jas. Wait in the Great Hall for me. I will be there shortly."

He could tell she was thinking about carrying on her joke for a little longer, but luckily she realized exactly how seriously pissed off he was. Unapologetic as ever, though, she dropped her booted feet, paused long enough to adjust the thin chain around her slim waist, and then finally stood up. Her dark eyes roved over them with merriment for a moment, and then she left the room, surprisingly obeying his command to keep silent.

Noah rested his hands on his hips, bowing his head briefly in order to cool his temper and gather his thoughts. He felt Kestra slide off the table and backpedal away from him, toward the remainder of her scattered belongings. When he sensed that she was dressed to a point of decency, he turned to look at her. To his surprise, she was moving toward him with his shirt extended in her hand.

"Thank you," he said, taking it from her.

"I need to go," she said in quick, apologetic excuse.

She reached to reattach her holster, and Noah didn't miss the fact that she turned her back to do so.

"Jasmine is an ambassador from another culture," he said quietly. "I will have to remind her of certain common courtesies."

"It doesn't make a difference to me," she said from behind the fall of her hair. "It's not the first time I've been walked in on during an indiscretion."

Noah flinched inside, but he had bigger fish to fry than her terminology. There wasn't even time to waste on the instantaneous flare of jealousy that her words inspired.

"Kestra—"

"Look," she interrupted him hastily, turning toward him

with perfect posture and a practiced air of indifference, "I'm not the frail and fluttery type and I don't need promises or good manners when it comes to something like this. It was fun while it lasted, let's just leave it at that."

Kestra started to look for her gun, another convenient excuse to turn her back on him. Noah wasn't used to uncommunicative people, people who hid their emotions and refused his input or his every address. For a moment he was at a loss, trying to draw on his experiences with the others he knew who had been raised in human culture. Corrine and Isabella were hardly good examples, however. They were both outspoken and incredibly adaptable for their species. They almost never made a mystery out of their actions and their opinions.

Kestra found her weapon, but as she bent to retrieve it, she realized it was melted, even parts of it that were pure steel, into a ball of jumbled materials. It was as if it had been in an explosion or an extremely intense fire, but she had seen weapons found in the aftermath of such things and she'd never seen anything like this. She couldn't even begin to formulate a suitable question for him, however, so she didn't bother.

Noah, meanwhile, was struck with the overwhelming sensation that he had done everything wrong. It was a stark understanding and it filled him with fear like very few things could. Hadn't he read that fairy tale dozens of times over the years to the children in his family and others? The words in Sarah's mind when she had realized she was Imprinted upon a man she very nearly despised began to echo in his brain.

She could keep her heart from him.

Lovers but strangers. Forever.

All she had to do was put her mind to it, walling off her emotions. It was rare, but not unheard of. In those rare cases, it led to a perverse kind of insanity, a fate worse than death. Especially if one partner fell in love and the other one did not.

Kestra felt his fingers encircling her arm, dragging her up to her feet roughly and spinning her into his body as if they'd never stepped away from each other in the first place. The reflexive sensation of coming home as she settled against him made her angry, frustrated over her body's misbehavior when she'd spent all of her life fine-tuning it as a weapon under her complete control. She reacted by bracing her hands against his chest and pushing hard away from him.

Noah didn't let her go this time, using his significant strength against her. What was more, he was able to do it with a single arm around her waist, allowing his free hand to come up and push back her hair, baring her ear to his close, heated whisper.

"I do not know what you think to accomplish, but I can assure you that you will never be able to escape me just by leaving my home. I have been inside you, *Kikilia*. Not only today, but for months. Our hearts have thrummed to the beat of this chemistry between us for so long now. Do you really think distance will work any better now than it did all the while you were an ocean away?"

Kestra opened her mouth, but his audacity left her speechless. Worse, the potential truths of his suppositions were terrifying. However, he didn't know her quite so well as he thought he did, she thought as a familiar flush of very explicit excitement coursed through her. It was a reaction that she recognized all too well.

He had just given her a challenge. What was more, it was a deadly one. She knew it as sure as she knew how to wire listening devices for sound. He was dangerous, she admitted to herself. She had probably known this from the outset, and it was probably why she had felt such an overwhelming attraction toward him.

Let him build his better mousetrap, she thought to herself with almost wicked confidence and satisfaction. *There isn't a cage made by man that can hold me.*

Kestra lowered her chin, flicking up her snow-white lashes until he could very clearly see the danger in her eyes and the gentle tilt of her suddenly smiling lips.

"Would you like to make book on that?" she murmured, flicking her blue diamond gaze down the length of his entire body, clearly taking his measure and just as obviously finding herself unthreatened.

She wasn't expecting the feral smile he sent her in return, though.

"I have all the money and time in the world to make good on that bet, *Kikilia*," he whispered. "Whether you know it or not, you need me now. You will always need me."

Kestra laughed, hard and harsh, a derisive sound that would have cowed any normal man. She was already beginning to realize that he was no normal man, so she didn't underestimate him in that way.

"Listen," she said quietly, "you can threaten and cajole all you like, you can even seduce me until the cows come home and we are both exhausted from it, but you will never, ever own me. Unless you have something better than idle threats, my mind will always remain my own, and so will my life. There is nothing you can do to change that. Now let go of me or I swear—"

"I already have changed it, although I would never want to change the honest essence of who you are. I am not who you think I am, Kestra."

"I don't *think* anything. I don't care *who* you are. You're as much a stranger to me as you ever were! You're rich? Well, so am I. You're strong and clearly have power? You haven't even scratched the surface of my strength and my power. I don't care how many little tarts come traipsing in here calling you *my lord* or whatever it is that gets you off, because I don't impress that easily. Don't challenge me. You'll regret it. Now let me go!"

Noah finally did so, clearly more suddenly than she expected because she stumbled backward in her abrupt freedom.

"Kestra, you have no idea what you are going to do to yourself if you leave."

She laughed, a snorting sound of disbelief.

"My God, you are on a trip, aren't you? I survived just fine without you all these years, and I will damn well do it again. You were an itch, Noah, and you have just been scratched. So, it's been swell, but I really must be going."

Her haughty sarcasm was a practiced art, and she used it too well. His fingers curled into tight fists as she turned surely on her heel and marched out of the parlor with a hearty slam of the door. It took everything within him to control the surge of his temper, to keep his feet planted firmly on the floor and not tag after her like a schoolboy with a sick crush on the head cheerleader. He could have shown her the meaning of the word *power*, could have sucked her into his world with a heartbeat and a whirlwind of smoke and ashes. Hell, he could have blown up an entire country just to show her what she was enmeshed in whether she liked it or not.

But that was purely his infamous temper talking. He could no more harm an innocent than . . .

Noah shook out his fisted hands and exhaled harshly. He had already harmed innocents in his quest for her. The memory of Bella's outrage bit as sharply as the recollection of her slap against his face did. Would Kestra ever know the price he had been willing to pay just to save her life? Did he have the cold heart it would take to throw that knowledge up in her face?

Patience, he told himself, using the word like a mantra to soothe his sparking temper. *Patience.* Time was on his side. He hadn't been lying about that. However, if he were to take advantage of it, she would pay a heavy price. All he had to do was wait, give it three, maybe four days. Then she would understand what it would mean to be without him. She would only grow weaker, sicker, eventually facing no future but her own death, unless she returned to him.

And he couldn't bear the idea of it.

He had to find a better way.

* * *

The Miserable Princess
A Demon Fairy Tale
Cont'd . . .

Ariel made good his promise.

Sarah sat watching contemptuously as he defeated one opponent after another in the exhausting games. She was convinced he was somehow cheating, especially when he was able to best the Warrior Captain himself, the most skilled of all fighter Demons. Maybe it was because he was an Enforcer. He cast a cloak of dread in front of himself just by entering the area. He probably had every last one of them shaking in their boots and they were letting him win in some hope that if he caught up with them on a Hallowed night transgressing, he might be kinder to them. But there was no kindness in him. Sarah did not care if he was only doing his job, a job appointed and respected by her very own father. Even her father would blanch at the idea of having the Enforcer for a son-in-law.

He was going to win, and she could see it coming. Sarah refused to simply sit there like a lamb to the slaughter. She did not care that she was required to spend supper feast with the winner as the reward for the night's games. She did not care that her absence would embarrass her father and the Enforcer, perhaps even infuriating them both. She stood up and walked away at the first opportunity of her father's distracted attention.

She ran to the stables.

She was mounted and fleeing on her fastest and favorite steed within heartbeats. She did not even change or use a lady's saddle, yanking up her skirts and sitting astride like a man so she could get the speed she wanted and that the beast beneath her deserved. She was like a wraith in the night, her slim, beautiful body and fair hair catching the glow of the moonlight, the silk and chiffon of her gown streaming colors behind her like a standard. Mile after mile peeled away beneath the horse's hooves, and the thunderous cadence pounded joyfully through her body. She no longer belonged to the Demon world and all of its traditions, all of its expectations. She was free. She could breathe. There was no future looming with suffocating imprisonment to a man everyone despised.

And then, as if summoned by the thought, the Enforcer materialized out of the nighttime mists, becoming solid right in the path of the racing horse. The animal lurched to a halt with all of its power, its intention to rear back in terror, but before that happened, Sarah was thrown forward over the animal's head, reins falling helplessly from her hands as she became airborne. She would have plowed into the Enforcer, something she would have at least found momentarily satisfying, but the coward dematerialized. But then she was being caught by a heavy cushion of thickening fog and moisture, the sensation soft and gentle as she slowed to a stop.

In a heartbeat, she found herself cradled in the arms of the Enforcer, her heart pounding as though it would burst her chest. Half of the feeling was from fear of her fall, but half was from fear of how flushed with excitement she became when those cool eyes fell on her. His need of her was naked within them. It was an incredible feeling to know that she was what the man who was most feared, most powerful in their world, now wanted. It did not matter that she was a Princess. She had been born to that, had not earned any merit that might come with it. But he was born to be the Enforcer, and had also proven himself for centuries as the one rightfully deserving of the role, al-

though there were other choices from amongst his line who could have vied for the duty.

She struggled to be free of his hold, and Ariel let her go, placing her feet on the ground and letting her try again to put a great distance between them, though in fact it was only a few steps.

"Come, come," he taunted her softly, "all is fair here. You must maintain your part of this bargain."

"I made no bargain!" she cried out in defiance. "I was put up like a mare to be bred, and no one asked me my permission!"

"I am not here for a mare, although breeding has its place somewhere in the things I would like. I want you, Sarah, and all your possibilities. I knew for decades that you were waiting to be claimed by me, but I forced myself to give you time to live, to grow, and to become whatever it was you wished to become. I watched you flourish with beauty and a personality of such light and kindness that it awes me when I think you will shine upon me."

"No! I never saw you!"

"I never touched you, either," he said, his voice like soft clouds in a summer sky. "Until today. Your father was torturing you with his efforts to push you onto others, and I could not let it continue. Though I must say, it brought out that fire in your temper I find so intriguing."

Sarah's hand went to her throat in an age-old feminine gesture of defense, broadcasting her fear and vulnerability. She saw the truth in all he said. Ariel had stood by and left her to grow, given her space that even her own father had refused to give her. How must it have been for him to let her be free, knowing all along that she was destined to be in his arms? She had lived in blissful ignorance, but Ariel had known for a long time—decades, he had said—and he had waited. Stood by and watched. So many days, so many years in such close service to the King, there in the Council rooms every day, rooms she walked through. Feasts and celebrations.

Samhain and Beltane.

Sarah's eyes widened with horror, as she suddenly realized what torment he must have suffered every single Hallowed moon, forced to do his duty, forced to hang on to his sanity, temptation just a breath away, satisfaction just a touch away.

His sacrifice touched her like nothing else in the world could have.

* * *

By the time Noah had composed himself, both physically and mentally, he knew Kestra had long since exited his household. He could still feel the powerful trail of her energy as he followed it out of the parlor and into the Great Hall, in search of another woman who seemed to have it stamped on her to-do list to give him grief. He was beginning to lose count of how many women he had rubbed the wrong way in just the past twenty-four hours. The Demon King figured taking Jasmine to task would probably add her to that growing list.

He stepped into the Great Hall and stopped short with justifiable surprise. Jasmine was holding court with about a half dozen Demon males, their hands and attention on various parts of her slim body as she flirted shamelessly with them. She was thriving on the attention the Demons were giving her in abundance, a generosity fueled by the conditions of the night and the ripening moon.

Since she was a Nightwalker, Jasmine was considered more than fair game nowadays. He could not possibly voice any form of complaint, even if he could form a logical reason for one. It was better that their attention was falling onto her. It would at least keep one or two of them out of the Enforcers' paths, should she decide to fulfill any of the flirtatious promises she was clearly making with every inch of her highly sensual body.

The trouble was, he was pretty sure that Jasmine was an extremely prejudiced creature and that she would consider playing outside of her species to be beneath her.

"Jasmine!"

Jasmine turned her head, looking unconcerned as she faced the very obvious disapproval of the Demon King. She gave him a disarming smile, standing up from her chair as he walked toward her. If he were a thundercloud, she mused as she watched his approach, he could have belched a bolt of lightning right at her head. He certainly was able to clear the room with merely his approach and expression, the other Demons leaving them alone with all speed.

"Good evening, Noah. It is good to see you. I have a message from Damien," she said, as if nothing at all was due her by way of reprimand. She was cordial and matter-of-fact, returning to sit with casual ease before his hearth and looking completely at home.

"In the future, Jasmine, I expect you to restrict yourself to the common areas of the castle. I would not wish you to make the mistake of crossing the wrong threshold and finding yourself perceived as . . . an open invitation for trouble."

Now, that was a threat, Jasmine mused. *Either that, or it was an enticement.* Either way, it delighted the female Vampire no end. Noah was as clever as a cat, and he had just perched himself outside her mouse hole, just waiting for her to make that one extra misstep while stealing the wrong piece of cheese.

"I will keep that in mind," she promised him, the expression on her face and the obvious shift of her sensual body broadcasting her intent to play the tease. Noah closed his eyes briefly, shaking his head once in an attempt to cool his dangerously seething temper before finally glaring at her.

"Enough, Jasmine." He exhaled, managing to calm down enough so he didn't do something rash. Something along the lines of throttling her with his bare hands. That would start a war with the Vampires, and he had enough trouble in his life already. "Do you turn Damien's household upside down regularly as well, or have you spared the honor for me alone?"

"I promise you," she responded easily, "I make my best effort to cause trouble wherever I go."

She reached out to take the hand he held out to her, and he pulled her to his side as he began to walk back toward the gardens where they would have the best privacy. After all, business was business, and she had come for a reason.

"So tell me what I can do for the Vampire Prince."

"Actually, it is more a matter of what he can do for you. I come with a warning."

Noah stopped, turning to look at her as his expression became grave.

"Explain."

"Just that what Damien has been anticipating has actually happened. A small faction of Vampires has taken the recent wedding of their Prince as an excuse to break away from the laws that govern them. I know you have enough to worry about, with Ruth and the Vampire Nicodemous unaccounted for after our battle with them last winter, but until they turn up, Damien begs you turn your attention to this dangerous group of Vampires. Now that Vampires know that drinking the blood of Nightwalkers can imbue them with the foreign Nightwalkers' powers, no one is safe from a group like this who is publicly flouting the law and Damien's rule.

"Of course, Damien is doing everything in his power to call them to justice," she continued. "However, since your people are most at risk due to the variety you have in your elemental powers, he felt you should be put on alert immediately. He has also asked that I remain close to you until they are caught. Between me and Horatio, we will best be able to sense if a Vampire comes close to the court. If they do, we will be in a position to track and deal with them."

"I appreciate the warning. However, I am capable of protecting my own court. While you are always welcome, I am sure Damien needs you more than I."

"I do not mean to insult you, Noah," she said firmly, "but I think you are wrong. There are only three Fire Demons in existence, two of whom are from *your* family. Since you are the only male and by far the most powerful, you will be the proverbial brass ring. You and I know it is insanity to gun for the Demon King, of course, but greed makes for ridiculous bravery. And who knows how much power these rogues will have acquired before they come after you? Because that is exactly what they will do, you know. They will hunt down as much power as they can, gathering it within themselves like a wicked posy. Then, when you are outpowered and outnumbered, they will come for you."

"Which is exactly why Vampires were forbidden to drink the blood of Nightwalkers all this time," he said bitterly. "I am sorry. I do not mean to begrudge Damien his happiness with Syreena. I also publicly allowed a few changes in our laws to suit the introduction of human hybrids into our race, but when Demon and Druids become matched, it has no opportunity to hurt outsiders."

"Hmm. I see," she mused. "So creating a bucketful of Druids who can rob Nightwalkers their power does not affect us outsiders? Better yet, that one Druid in specific, Isabella, who takes on the power she steals . . . she is no danger to us?"

"Point taken," he agreed grimly. "I suppose, as always, it is the character of each individual that tells the tale, no matter how many laws we make."

"Do not get me wrong," Jasmine added. "Far be it from me to defend Damien's current lack of sanity. Frankly, the more time goes by, the more I am convinced this entire marriage of his was ill thought and worse timed. Things were much better settled and peaceful before that Lycanthrope crossed his path." Jasmine countered the causticity of the statement with a brilliant faux smile. "But we are sure to get along famously given enough time."

"Enough time for what?" he countered knowingly.

"For Damien to get bored of her. Or a mishap in childbirth, perhaps. Who knows?" She waved off his expression of disapproval for what could be construed as a treasonous remark. "For now I prefer to deal with one problem at a time. This week, my problem is keeping you and yours protected. You will not begrudge Damien this favor, I hope. If something were to happen even remotely close to you, he would take it very ill."

The way she constructed the observation gave Noah pause where it might not have otherwise.

"Very well," he said softly. "If you insist, I will welcome your assistance. Just remember, while you are here, I expect you to adhere to our laws just as I do your brother and any other visiting dignitary."

"I'll be sure to brush up," she said dryly.

"Jasmine . . ."

"I promise, I will stay within the letter of the law. I do know how to control myself."

"Despite evidence otherwise?"

"Hey, you have your culture, I have mine. Besides, what fun is life if it doesn't keep you on your toes?"

"My toes are appropriately exercised without your help, Jasmine."

She smiled and turned to leave him to his privacy, now that it was no longer important.

"And, Jasmine?"

"Mmm?" She turned back and arched a curving dark brow at him.

"Do be so kind as to refrain from teasing the bloody hell out of my men. I know you have no intention of making good, even if they do not, and I will be seriously displeased if your actions stir one of them up enough to behave lawlessly." He made certain he was locked to her gaze so she would see the seriousness of his. "You know what Samhain is like for us, and it is cruel of you to tempt without relief.

You are a Vampire, and as such you bear a sensuality that is markedly powerful and impressionable. Destiny help you if it turns on you. Or worse, on an innocent."

The Vampire sobered considerably under the warning, all signs of amusement leaving her dark chocolate eyes. Still, it was not in her to apologize, so he had to be content with the purposeful bow of her head in acknowledgment.

Damien entered the citadel by way of the turret that led into their private rooms. They used the small tower as a private sitting room, the circular exposure of windows making for an excellent view of the Romanian mountains in the night. Although, consequently, it had to be locked up and sealed off in the day to prevent even the slightest touch of the sun from disturbing their rest.

He was flushed from a fresh hunt, windblown from the circuit he had made around the leading edge of his property, scanning for any lurking problems or outright threats. Once a threat breached the property itself, he would instantly know it. Since the holdings were so large, he needed to physically run the borders if he wanted to scan even farther than that. True, there was security everywhere in the form of loyal Vampires, but it was new to him to think about trusting others with his safety, and definitely impossible to accept trusting others with the safety of his mate.

Just as the thought of her entered his head, she entered the door to the sitting room. She had sensed his impending arrival, even though he had no made telepathic contact with her. It always impressed him how she was able to do that. What awed him more was the outfit she was almost wearing. Damien felt an instant fire light inside him, his midnight blue eyes devouring her beautiful little body.

Whatever the garment was, it looked like a robe. It swept the floor and had long sleeves rather like the wings of an angel. It was buttoned across her body with two lone buttons, was made of a very fine white netting of silk that was completely transparent, and she wore absolutely nothing beneath it. As she moved toward him, the robe dragged back behind her, parting all the way up to the insignificant buttons that held it closed between her breasts.

Damien felt as though he had been cemented to the spot. It was the only way to describe the hard, heavy sensation that poured through him as his sexy little wife approached him with such clear intent. If he had forgotten what it was like during her last heat cycle, Damien was thoroughly reminded as Syreena pressed her heated body against his and began to fish past his clothing for contact with his skin. Her dark charcoal eyes, with their multicolored flecks, were hungry and avaricious. She wanted. She needed. She made sure he could see it, and now she would make very sure he could feel it.

"Damien," she whispered, her breath quick and hot against his sensitivite neck.

Oh, how well she knows me. She knew every reactive place on his body and how to use them. Her tongue flicked against his throat, taunting him as she laughed low in her throat, the sound so sexy and stimulating that it sent a shock wave of desire flooding through him. It was intensified by the swift seeking of her hands over his skin.

"Is this your idea of a hello?" he asked, his teasing tone destroyed by the obvious sound of pleasure that interrupted him as her hands swept low and sure against him.

"Would you prefer a handshake?" she asked coyly, her fingers circling him in a silky grip that was nowhere near his hand.

"Syreena!"

She shrugged, all innocence as she worked quickly to free him from his clothes, though she did not release her hold on him.

"All right, then," she relented. "I see you prefer oral greetings."

Damien's hand slammed out to brace against a window frame as his wife slid down his body.

* * *

Kestra didn't utilize the nearby airport as Noah had suggested. She couldn't go through Heathrow, even though her identification had arrived on schedule one morning later. Even after a week, her face would be far too hot for such public places of travel. So she decided the safest thing to do would be to spend another week in Europe, although it really burned her to be anywhere on the same side of the ocean as Noah . . . Noah . . .

Oh God, I don't even know his last name.

As soon as the thought entered her mind, she promptly quashed it. She refused to waste any more energy on thinking about that huge mistake. It was done. Over. In the past. Now she was on her way to the North Country, as far away from the south as possible, where she had rented a nice cottage for the week under the identity James had sent her.

She could spare a week. She had a gig lined up and needed to go through it with Jim once more, but it wouldn't help if she got nabbed at the airport because she moved too soon. She had the option of staying the winter if she had to. The job could be postponed. She could stay low here, or swing into Monte Carlo for a little business mingling and social reconnection with certain people. She would have to feel around and see.

It was well into the night by the time she pulled up to the gorgeous little rental, a smaller building on a huge property right out of Edwardian England. The main house was back beyond miles of gardens and lakes, or so it seemed at first glance, and she had the privacy of her own walled-in park as well. She had been here before, as someone else's guest, and had always been determined to capture the place for herself when she found the time. At least she could thank her precarious fortune for that much.

She unpacked her car of all the supplies she'd deemed necessary, although the minute she entered the location she could see that others had preceded her in order to fully stock and freshen up the place. There was already a fire in the large fireplace. The cabinets were full. Wooden floors were highly polished, as were brass rails and marble fixtures. The part she adored was the full gymnasium at the center of the house, built obviously with a woman in mind. A gymnast. It was matted wall to wall, mirrored on three walls, and had everything from a climbing wall to a dance bar.

Kestra didn't even waste time with any other details. She'd been idle for a week, apparently, and it was unacceptable to her. She changed into a red sports bra and snug biker shorts and warmed up. Still, she couldn't help but feel like something was off with the time. She felt fit and well sprung and not as though she had lain lax and sleeping for all that time. She was active and in phenomenal shape, but no one could maintain tone under those conditions. Not her kind of tone.

Or maybe she was merely losing what was left of her mind. After all, she had to be insane to have had sex with a total stranger. It was the only explanation. She'd never done anything like that in her life. Never. Jokes and taunts aside, she honestly had no time or inclination toward a sex life. Though what she did have was brief and detached, she usually knew the person pretty well. In fact, she had a knack for destroying male friendships that way.

As those faces dared to loom up at her, she turned her back on them and opted for the gloves and punching bag instead. Kickboxing made for excellent cardio, and she was definitely in the mood to work up a sweat. She hated having all this backwash of emotion seeping through her mind all of a sudden. She would beat it down if it was the very last thing she would do.

She thrashed the bag, letting it swing and become a moving target. She imagined life into it. Even gave it a face. A dark, arrogant green-eyed face that was far too handsome for its own damn good. She landed a vicious spin-kick, grunting with satisfaction. That would teach him to touch her. Oh, and she just bet he was all kinds of proud of himself now. It had taken him mere hours to get into her pants. Probably wasn't even a recordable event for him. He just *seemed* like that type.

"'Do you really think distance will work any better now than it did all the while you were an ocean away?'" she mimicked, making him sound even haughtier. "Well, it's working now, pal!"

Kestra beat the hell out of the bag. When she was exhausted and dripping with sweat, she stripped off her gloves and dropped heavily to the mats. She did not usually tire this easily, so she had to admit that maybe she *had* been out of commission for a week. It was the only explanation.

She got up, dragging her bottle of juice with her as she shuffled back to the shower. She stripped off sweat-drenched clothes with the remainder of her strength and turned on the taps so water spewed from three different directions to bathe her in relieving heat. She closed her eyes as she leaned against the wall with stiff, bracing arms. The water was brutally hot, but it felt divine, and this even though she had inexplicably gotten a sunburn on certain body parts when she hadn't been paying attention. Her palms, thighs, breasts . . . all toasted red. Still, it was fading fast and didn't hurt.

If she weren't afraid of falling asleep, she would take advantage of the sauna. But being alone and tired, it was dangerous. So the shower would do. The worst she could get here was pruned toes. Meanwhile, the water struck her no matter where she turned; steam filled her lungs, making every breath heavy. Heat soaked into every pore and she felt as though she craved more. She closed her eyes and shut off the cold water entirely. Kestra gasped at the burn, but then moaned with pleased relief a heartbeat later. If she could fall asleep right there in that scalding waterfall, she would have been delighted to do so.

Chapter 10

"You look tired."

Noah looked away from the steady crackle of the fire and glanced at her.

"I am," he agreed, knowing it would be useless to fib to a Mind Demon, not to mention an astute sister.

"You need to sleep, to replenish your energy properly. What's more, you need to fetch Kestra back here and start telling her—"

Legna broke off when Noah turned back to look into his fire, making an obscure sound of agreement that plainly had no connection to what she was saying.

"But you aren't, are you, Noah?"

"What?" he asked impatiently.

"Sleeping! You are not sleeping."

"Magdelegna," he said in the warning, elder-brother tone she knew all too well.

"Do not 'Magdelegna' me," she huffed. "I can understand if you do not wish to discuss this with me, but do me the courtesy of acknowledging I am right and that something is disturbing you."

"Of course it is, Legna! My mate is running away from me at top speed, quite possibly into some other situation where someone will blow a bullet through her little blond head!" he snapped at her. "You are damn right it disturbs me!"

"I meant your ability to sleep, Noah. Disturbing your ability to sleep," she said quietly in the face of his explosive outburst.

Noah caught himself at once. He held out a hand to her in apology, which she took readily. There was nothing he could do to someone as loving as his sister was that would not be forgiven, and for that he was eternally grateful. He was surrounded by such women, and it would be his saving grace, he knew.

"I apologize. My temper . . ."

"Is short because you are exhausted," she said with soft urgency as she quickly moved to kneel by his chair, enfolding his hand between hers. "You can only process energy from outside sources for so long. What is worse, Kestra needs your energy. Pure, healthy energy. She needs you and I know you need her. Noah, I do not understand this. You let her go freely and then you do not pursue. She will become sick, yet it makes you sick to think of it. You will not sleep—"

"Are you *mad*, Legna? Sleep?" He laughed so bitterly it made tears come to her eyes. This was not her lighthearted, contented brother, and it struck at her soul to see him thus. "She is too close to me. It was hard enough when she was an ocean away, but now that she is in my blood, her scent all over my body, and physically within my reach . . ." He shook his head, his speechlessness making more of an impact on her.

"My heart." She murmured the endearment sympathetically, running gentle, elegant fingers through his hair. "What can I do?"

"Nothing."

"Dearest . . ."

"Legna, I do not wish to discuss this anymore."

Magdelegna knew her brother well enough after two and a half centuries of her life to know when he could no longer be drawn out. She stood up and away from him, her heart beating in a rapid, worried tattoo.

Legna walked away from him, her thoughts in turmoil as she twisted one hand in the other. She had just barely stepped into the garden when a sparkling silver light burst into her path, erupting into the astral form of her husband, Gideon. He reached for her, and she stepped into his comforting embrace.

"*Neliss,*" he whispered softly into the coffee-colored hair near her ear, the nickname soothing all on its own. Her thoughts were his. Even over thousands of miles, they shared every piece of logic and emotion as if theirs were a single mind. And because he loved her, he could never ignore the cry of her heart when it was in such clear distress.

"Where is Seth?" she asked automatically.

"Our son is in the lap of a fairly confounded Lycanthrope Queen at present."

"Of all the choices in sitters, why do you always choose her? She cannot figure out the top side of a child from the bottom."

"Siena only pretends to be terrible with children so she can excuse herself for not producing any. And it is not like you to dodge a subject," he scolded gently.

Legna looked up into her husband's tinsel eyes, their sparkling color the gift she had received when they had fully Imprinted, making her eyes the perfect mirror to his. She remembered how that had so upset Noah in the beginning, when their color had changed to no longer match the gray-green of his.

"He will not see reason. He can be so stubborn," she said with frustration. "What does he think to do? Leave her until she is sick from being without him? You saw what that did to Corrine. Bella and her sister both were able to adjust to a new and unexpected life, and so will Kestra. I think he is punishing himself, Gideon. I think he is doing this thing to himself because of what he did to get Kestra back."

"I am not arguing with that. You are a wise woman and an even wiser sister. You are seeing the truth of the matter." Gideon stroked her hair with a long, soft caress of his hand. "But I think he is also angry with himself for their first mating. Noah is very old-fashioned in his way. He had very specific ideas of how he would treat his mate should he ever be blessed with the Imprinting."

"He does not account for the pressure of the Hallowed moon and the volatility of his elemental nature!" Legna broke away from her husband's attempts to soothe her and began to pace. "We are all pressed beyond our natural behaviors now. For example, you and I are a very tender, gentle pair, yet even we get . . . aggressive . . . during the Hallowed moons."

"Tender and gentle?" Gideon threw back his silver head and laughed up at the stars, making her face flush with consternation.

"Gideon!"

"I must apologize, *Neliss*, because apparently I have been sleeping with a totally different woman these past couple of years than I realized." His eyes sparkled with glittery amusement. "Tender and gentle, yes, we are that, but I think I need to remind you of a few places, times, and acts that had nothing to do with Hallowed moons."

Legna's blush deepened as her mind was flooded with those memories, her husband pushing them on her to make his point. She had not realized how very good his memory of their time together was. He even remembered what she had been wearing—to start with, at least. By the time he released her mind, they were both breathing off-tempo and gazing at each other with hungry eyes of silver.

"You are trying to distract me," she said breathily as he stepped up to enfold her in his arms.

"It is nearly Samhain. Even without the Hallowed moon I want you more with every passing hour," he whispered to her. "But it is impossible to resist you when it is so close upon us."

"Gideon, you have to do something. Promise me. We must help in some way."

"Shh, hush, sweet." He soothed her, pulling her close to the warm sparkle of energy his body emanated in his current form. "I will talk to Jacob. If anyone can help, it will be him."

Jacob had known his wife for exactly three years, come Samhain.

In all of that time, Isabella had shown a remarkable adaptability when it came to his culture. She was as Demon as an outsider could get.

She faced transgressing Demons at every Hallowed moon, which pushed even the strictest moral beings into lawlessness. She was an Enforcer, and this was her duty. Bella had met every single one of them with diplomacy, softness, and compassion. She had understood. She had helped bring them back from madness with her obvious forgiveness and her lack of judgmental behaviors.

Afterward, after the punishments had been meted out, she had done what Jacob had never thought to do. She had visited each and every household, every night, for as long as it took until they all understood that she saw them the same as ever, without shame, without reservation. In her mind, their sentence was served, it was over, and she was positive, in only a way that Isabella could believe with her enormous heart, that it would never happen to those Demons again. She made sure they knew that she had faith in them.

But as tenacious as she was in those situations of kindness, Jacob realized she could be just as intractable with negative feelings. He had seen her dig in her heels before on other issues, so he was quite familiar with the signs, but he had never thought Noah would become such an issue.

She had shut Jacob out of their shared thoughts, again shocking him with her ability to do so. He had never experienced such a thing, and she had never even hinted at her ability to do this. They had been sharing every single thought, action, conversation—everything—since the moment they had first spoken in full telepathic sentences. Now there was nothing but dead air, as though half of his brain had been surgically removed. He was lost and sometimes woozy, feeling unbalanced without his other half within him. The pain was unspeakable. Isabella was deliberately trying to hurt him, and she was succeeding.

For the first time, they weren't communicating in any way. She couldn't bring herself to speak about even the most mundane of topics. She didn't speak to him, to Leah, to anyone. Not a single word, her lips pressed together as if she were afraid they would disobey her command for silence. Jacob suspected it was because she was afraid that if she started, she wouldn't stop until she had forgiven everything, and she was determined not to do so.

Jacob was not extensively worried. Bella was only so strong and only so obstinate. She could shut him out all she liked for now, denying him, denying their needs as a couple. It would last exactly two more days. Then Samhain would be upon them and it would come to a crashing halt. It wasn't the sexual intimacy that would matter to him, either. It would be the emotions she wouldn't be able to contain as she was forced to feel joy and pleasure beneath his touch. They would merely break the dam, and then the rest would come. He knew this because he knew her. She was the other half of his heart, of his spirit.

Meanwhile, he was kept busy, as always, with his duties as the moon phase increased instances of insubordination among the Demons. Isabella remained at home with their child, now unwilling to leave her with anyone they knew. She wanted no Demons near their baby, just in case something else happened. No Demons, Imprinted or otherwise.

It was irrational. Prejudiced. Disturbing.

Jacob sensed Gideon's coming even before the Ancient medic arrived in the middle of their living room with a burst of heavily displaced air from the teleport that was no doubt courtesy of his mate. Gideon never excused his entrances or what Isabella considered intrusions on her privacy, so when she looked out of the kitchen to see what the disturbance was from, the acidic glare she cast at the medic didn't faze him in any visible way. Bella quickly ducked back into her hiding place, leaving the two Demons alone while she dealt with her latest surge of disapproving emotion.

"I need to speak with you."

"At least someone does," Jacob said, rising to his feet and putting aside the book that had lain open in his lap to the same page for over half an hour. "I think it would be best if we go elsewhere."

Clearly it made no difference to Gideon. They left Jacob's home, but Gideon didn't wait long past the door before he cut to the chase, as he always did.

"I need your assistance with Noah."

Jacob exhaled deeply, reaching up to rub his temple in anticipation of the headache this was about to cause him.

"The feelings of my wife be damned, I suppose?"

"She must learn to accept things as we do if she is going to suit this culture. What is done is done, and it cannot be changed. The result is what it is, and Leah is safe. I see no reason to dwell on it."

"Isabella seems to disagree. At least I think she does. She would have to talk to me in order for me to be certain."

"How do you feel about the King keeping from his mate?"

"You mean keep Noah from Kestra?" Jacob dropped his laughing irony when he absorbed the Ancient's grim expression. "He just walked through hell and time to get her, and now he wants to keep away from her? Wait a minute. He cannot keep away from her. She will begin to starve from lack of energy. This first week is critical. He knows that."

"Mmm, one would assume so, since he is the scholar among us," Gideon mused pointedly.

"Where is she?"

"I do not think he knows."

"He does not—" Jacob was horrified. "When did he let her go? Sweet Destiny, Gideon, if anything happens to her, we will lose him! He has touched her! He has been with her. The Imprinting is done."

"I know."

Jacob looked at the Ancient as if he had lost his mind.

"Why is no one doing anything about it? Someone has to force him to go to her. Someone has to bash some sense into his thick skull!"

"I know. That is why I am here."

"You think he will listen to *me*?" Jacob laughed harshly. "What of your wife? She has always had a touch with him."

"She has tried and failed. We both believe Noah is indulging in some sort of self-punishment. He is obviously not thinking clearly." The Ancient flicked startling silver eyes over the Enforcer. "He is quite misguided, his need battling with his damaged sense of honor. He is denying something he has always known in his moments of better judgment. He said it to you and he said it to Elijah. The Imprinting is a law unto itself and it cannot be denied. It supersedes all others. Jacob, you are the Enforcer of our laws. I believe you should do just that. Enforce the law. Although I do not think you alone will sway him. But I do have an idea as to who will."

"Oh?" Jacob said warily. "Why do I get the feeling I am not going to like this?"

Jacob turned to face his King as Noah came down the final curve in the stairway. Noah had appointed him four hundred years ago, and by now he had come to know his every mood just by the way he was standing. The brace of Jacob's feet on the marble floor was that of an ageless sentry, set down by

Destiny to guard the secrets of fate. Even more ominous was the tight fold of his arms over his chest and the implacable expression he used when discarding emotions for the sake of duty.

His first thought was that Jacob had come to redress issues surrounding Leah or Bella. It was the only thing Noah could think of that would affect him to such a degree.

But then he spoke.

"You have need of me, my King?"

Noah was silent for a moment as his mind turned over the seriousness of the very specific protocol Jacob was using. Why did Jacob think he needed him just then? "You anticipate me, Enforcer. I have not sent for you."

"Anticipation suggests that I am merely early, not unnecessary."

Jacob watched his monarch think on that for a moment. "Jacob," he said irritably, "I am too weary for riddles. Can we not reach the point of the matter?"

"You are seeking punishment, my lord, and I am he who deals it out. Therefore, I am at your service."

Noah squared off with his Enforcer, meeting his nearly black eyes. "So you have decided to do your duty after all," he mused softly.

"It is my duty to enforce Demon law, even if that enforcement brings me to the doorstep of the Demon who appointed me." Jacob took a slow, thoughtful breath. "You defile this edict actively, although the wise and temperate King I have known has, in the past, always been the strongest advocate of this stellar law. There is one law, and only one, which you are breaking. That is the law which is unwritten."

"Jacob." The King scowled. "What is this?"

"Enforcement, Noah," he said, his stance softening just slightly. "You defile the law of the Imprinting. The ultimate blessing. The ultimate gift. The Imprinting is everything and must be honored as everything. You harm your Druid mate, deny her health, peace, and Destiny when it is your duty to do everything in your power otherwise. I swear to Destiny, Noah, that I will not allow it. And on my wife and daughter's souls, I would have sworn never to see the day when you would be so selfish. So cruel."

"Jacob—"

"As always," he interrupted, his dark eyes glittering with hard inevitability, "my target seeks to cajole and argue his way out of the truth."

"Damn you, Jacob!" Noah exploded, his temper unleashing like a whip. "What of Leah? Corrine? They are abused by me, yet you do not claim justice for them. If you will not, then I will do so myself!"

"Not at the cost of another's safety and wellness, you won't!"

Noah started when Corrine's outraged cry penetrated the hall. She marched out of the shadows, making Noah realize how tired he must truly be if he had not sensed her there. The redhead came at him in a fury, even going so far as to poke an indignant finger into his chest once she reached him.

"How dare you use my name in an excuse that will cause a Druid to suffer the way I did! You think it's noble and self-sacrificing, what you're doing? To starve her? To neglect her? Selfish bastard," she growled. "You know nothing about me if you think this would make me feel like justice is being served." That said, Corrine took a long breath and reined in her outrage. She was still holding herself stiffly, but otherwise she softened, assuming the demeanor that would most make an impression on his beleaguered mind.

"Noah," she said gently, reaching to touch a gentle hand to his forearm, "you're paralyzed. You're unable to move, think, or sleep. You do nothing because you're afraid that if you act you will cause more pain. I understand your fear, Noah. You've hurt those you love, and that is very hard for a man of your honor to bear. But you need to let it go. Let yourself be imperfect, allow for mistakes. Put the past aside and look toward all the futures you hold in your hands. Not just Kestra's, but all of us. How long will our King survive without his mate? I refuse to believe that you're going to sacrifice your entire race over a single act of understandable desperation.

"Just go to her. Do what you do best. Be wise, patient, and loving, and be her guide into our world." Corrine suddenly gave him a cockeyed grin. "And if that don't work, bean her over the head and drag her back by her hair."

"Corrine!" Noah burst out laughing when she made a wicked face of lechery to go with the outrageous proposal.

Jacob sighed heavily, rolling his eyes. *Some things*, he thought, *just run in the family.* "And she was doing so well for a second there," he said dryly.

"C'mon, Noah. If I can forgive you, then you can do the same," Corrine urged him, patently ignoring Jacob. "At least I understand what happened and why. But Kestra *doesn't*. She needs you to explain why this is happening to her and to make it a safe and healthy transition."

Noah wasn't unused to being humbled. He had two sisters who had made an art form of keeping him grounded. However, Corrine snapped him into awareness like no one else could have. She corrected him without trying to humiliate him, clearing his exhausted mind for what seemed like the first time in days. Whether he forgave himself for past behaviors or not, she was right about Kestra. She was an entirely separate issue and he was being injudicious with her needs.

"You are right. You are both right," he said at last, releasing a wry laugh as he reached to slide a finger of affectionate appreciation down Corrine's smooth cheek. "I have no idea what I was thinking." The King shook his head with puzzlement at his own behavior. "I need to find her." He looked to the Earth Demon he knew was the best tracker in their world. "Jacob, would it cause a family war if I asked for your help?"

"Please," Jacob chuckled wryly. "Bella cannot possibly be any angrier with me than she already is."

"I'll take bets on that one," Bella's sister said with a chuckle.

Noah chucked his Matchmaker beneath the chin gently, a silent thank-you that made her smile with pleasure. Then he promptly morphed into smoke so he could follow the stream of dust that was already heading out of the window ahead of him.

"Cygnus?"

"Eh?"

The eldest of the small group of Vampires turned to face the youngest, who also happened to be his brother. When Cygnus moved, it was with the natural stealth of his kind. His face was young and harshly handsome, a heavy lock of dark chocolate hair sweeping in a charming curl over his brow. He had the sensual beauty and lean figure of his people and the elegance of centuries of living. He also had the lackadaisical aura of boredom that plagued so many of his brethren. He looked everything that was young and fit and attractive.

Except for the icy black cruelty of his eyes and the slash of meanness cutting at his lips. His dark brow furrowed into an irritated scowl as he faced the other Vampire, the brother who looked nothing like him.

Half brother, actually. But that was a distinction rarely made among Vampires because it was unusual to have a true full-blooded sibling. Vampires had a fickle nature, their inconsistencies the only constant thing about them. In the case of the brothers, it was a dam they had in common. Otherwise it was different sires and vastly differing centuries to which they had each been born. The younger brother was clearly held in a measure of contempt by the elder, the feeling obvious in harsh dark eyes as he appraised his sibling.

Cygnus had little tolerance for Quinton, with his bony body, weak chin, and unruly mop of dirt-colored hair. Even his eyes were a rheumy, water-weak tan color, as if they couldn't be bothered to be brown and couldn't aspire to be gold.

"We want to hunt," Quinton stated with cold determination. Since Quinton wasn't known for his backbone, Cygnus could only assume that his nerve had been built up by the demands of the others who nodded in silent agreement at his back. Their *silent* agreement unnerved Cygnus's baby brother. He'd expected his supporters to be more vocal, rather than leaving him to be the sole voice to speak up against him.

This was the reason why Cygnus was the one honored with the role of leader, he thought with pained aggravation. The rest of them were just too damn stupid. Lacking in initiative, too, usually. But the group was wound up and hyped about moving on to their next targets.

"In Demon territory?" Cygnus retorted mockingly. "Until we pick a target, that would not be a clever idea." He noted that the urges of the others to defy logic were growing closer together in occurrence. It didn't even take a telepath of his skill to know they had serious moments where they wanted to plot against him. His brother most of all, with his delusions of grandeur that he'd never have the power or intelligence to live up to. "It would tip off the Demons that we are here. I want to watch and make a distinct plan of action before we start hitting the targets we have chosen. If you wish to hunt, go off to an area less populated by Demons and choose human targets."

"Bah! Humans have no power to be gained. Since we tasted that sweet little Mistral last week, I find I crave the flavor of power," Quinton argued, waving off Cygnus's suggestion impatiently.

"Mistrals are easy targets. Catch them young enough and they can barely manage a defense. That mind-numbing musicality of voice does not work so well on older Vampires. Our telepathy dodges that little parlor trick. However, Demons are something else entirely. They are innately offensive. Especially some of the ones we have chosen as potential victims."

"Then I say we skip those more risky choices and go for the young ones."

"A thought that proves to us all why you are not in charge," Cygnus snapped, suddenly losing his patience. He surged out of his chair, rising to his feet with a low, riveting growl of warning. "I am a good two centuries older than any of the rest of you, and my power dwarfs the most powerful of you. Feel free to challenge me if you think yourself more competent to lead than I am." There was silence as he glared at each member of the group in turn. His brother was the only one who appeared to itch for a contest, but Cygnus was used to that. "Very well, then. Go off and hunt in proper feeding grounds, come back and sleep until dusk, and I promise you, tomorrow night we will begin to select from the gems that surround us."

Cygnus turned to stare down his sibling.

Quinton cursed him under his breath, and then with a burst of dark light, changed form to a blackbird, the power he had gained from the Mistral they had fed on. The elder Vampire watched as the others took off through doors and windows, thinking very carefully about how he needed to proceed, and how to keep the others in the positions they deserved.

Kestra shuddered as she looked down into the pool. She couldn't understand her sudden aversion to one of her favorite sports, but the idea of jumping into the chill water made her skin crawl. The water was heated, she tried to remind herself as she took a swig from the water bottle that had come to be ever present in her hand of late. However, even though the pool was enclosed in glass, the late October cold penetrated all around. She sighed, pushing a hand back through her bangs and hair. Apparently, she'd gotten into her suit for no reason.

She turned to look back at the house, biting her lip thoughtfully. There was a Jacuzzi next to the pool, but for some reason it was the sauna that really beckoned her. Was there a rule about how many saunas one could take in a single day? Or rather, night. She'd hardly seen daylight since she'd come to England. She seemed to be sleeping her days away. And nighttime seemed to be reserved for the sauna. If she went back into the superheated room, it would be the third time that day. It was no wonder she was drinking water like a fiend. She was probably dehydrating herself.

Maybe that was why she felt like she was dragging with every step she took lately. Maybe she'd caught a bug and her instinct was to sweat it out of herself. In which case, a third sauna was probably a very good idea.

That logic was apparently all the convincing she needed. She practically skipped on the way to the master suite and the adjoining bath and sauna. Kestra got out of her suit, wrapped a thick white towel around her hips, and stepped into the cedar-lined room, which already had serious steam in it because she'd subconsciously left it running. She dropped her water bottle on the bench behind her head as she stretched out with a happy sigh.

The heat had weight, pressing against her, filling her lungs and coaxing toxins out of her pores. She ran her hands over her face, making sure her hair was swept back, telling herself to simply relax and let the steam do its job. It took effort to breathe, but she didn't really mind so much. Her skin was coated in moisture, beads of it running down her bare breasts, the track ending over her throat where the little rivers tickled as they rolled off her body.

Her fingertips drifted down her throat, sweeping slickly over her collarbone. She resituated herself restlessly as unbidden images of Noah floated into her mind. She had managed not to dream of him for a small chain of days, and for that she was grateful, but she couldn't get the memories of their frantic, explosive lovemaking out of her uppermost thoughts. She had never felt anything like it, had deemed herself incapable of passion anywhere near what he'd coaxed from her body so easily.

She groaned softly, throwing her arm over her eyes as her skin seemed to come alive over every inch of her body just from the thought. Perhaps that was why she'd allowed herself to be so reckless. She'd been accused of being cold, controlling, and even frigid on the few occasions she'd allowed a man to touch her. Every time she hoped it would be different, but it never was. There were too many scars, too much baggage that weighed her down and leashed her tightly away from the ability to be uninhibited. She hadn't even had the vaguest idea about what an orgasm was truly supposed to feel like until she'd first dreamed it with such realistic intensity six months ago.

But even that had paled to the real thing. Things. *Oh God,* she had never once suspected . . . How was it possible? How could he manipulate her stubborn body with such ease? Was he so better skilled than others? What, she wondered, would it be like if he actually took his time instead of being caught up in the torrid needs of the moment? What would she be like?

Kestra brushed a hand down her body, sloughing off water and perspiration, her fingertips sliding over her breast and onto her stomach. She felt heat and weight, but it was inside her body and had nothing to do with the press of the steam around her.

She had a fierce memory for detail and had been able to memorize even the smallest of nuances with barely a blink of an eye. She remembered every single facet of his strange gem-and-smoke-colored eyes, every sharp angle of his rugged face, and every single touch of his vital body against and within her own.

Kestra sat up quickly, gripping the wooden bench fiercely as her head spun with the images and the heat. It was impossible! All of it. She needed to put this out of her mind before she drove herself crazy. She had a wild life and there was no time or space in it for a lover, no matter how much he set her on fire. Besides, she knew his type, knew what men of power were like and the demands they thought they could make. She would rather shoot a hole through her head than give up all she had worked so hard for her entire life.

She stood up and headed for the door.

Kestra stumbled, realizing too late that she had moved too fast to her feet. She was overwhelmed with a sense of vertigo, the world falling away. She fell to the floor, cursing herself for her stupidity. Still, she didn't truly realize she was in trouble until she tried to push herself upright and found she didn't have the strength.

The heat and steam seemed to suddenly attack her, the weight of it pressing her down and suffocating her as though she were trying to breathe in water.

She gasped once. Twice.

She fell straight into blackness.

Noah moved across the porch even as he sensed Jacob leaving the area. Jacob could track anything, and Kestra had been no exception. Now Noah could sense her and smell her. She was everywhere in this house, and his heart leapt with anticipation of seeing her again. He knew he wouldn't be welcome initially, knew she'd be as hostile as ever, but it didn't matter. He had to be here for her well-being. He had to see her. He desperately needed to touch her. He'd worry about the delicacies of her heart and how to win it after he could see she was well and safe. He still hadn't been able to get the vision of her being shot out of his mind's eye and he didn't think he would be able to do so for a very long time.

Noah scanned for her energy patterns, penetrating every

wall and piece of furniture in the house. At first he thought she wasn't there, or that his exhaustion was fouling up his sensitivity, but suddenly he felt that innate warning ringing into his psyche. It was the very same warning that he'd ignored once before when he'd inexplicably stopped dreaming of her. An overwhelming sense of panic rushed over him. It had only been two days and three nights. At the most she would be just as tired as he was, wouldn't she?

Sweet Destiny, I have been a fool.

He went into the house, a dark cloud of building power as he drew on all of the electrical energy being fed into the cottage, replenishing himself as he moved. Lightbulbs began to explode from the power surge. Visible arcs of electricity darted at him like strikes of lightning as this fire made by man arced to touch him, clung as it whipped blinding white and blue, stretching to keep the contact with him as it was consumed by his body with a snap.

It followed his progress through the house, and then suddenly all the bulbs and electronic equipment burst like little bombs. Once the the transformer blew, everything went dark and quiet. All residual energy faded or was absorbed by his body. He practically glowed with the power crackling through him.

That was when he saw the one and only other power source left in the building. It was low to the ground, sprawled out over it, and Noah understood with perfect clarity that it was Kestra and that she was in trouble. He was in motion in an instant, a storming god limned in a bright blue aura as he rushed through the house, his heart pounding with fear and fury, his eyes blinded to everything except the low energy of her body. He burst into the bathroom, seeking, seeing, and understanding. He wrenched the sauna door right off its hinges and looked down to the floor even as he shoved it aside with a crash. Kestra was sprawled out, her head and face hidden by the damp sheen of her white hair.

How long has she been like this? he wondered in panic,

his heart clawing for speed in his tightening chest. He crouched down over her head, took her shoulders gently into his hands, and turned her over against his arm. She was breathing, though it was with soft, rattling gasps because she was starved for steam-free oxygen. Noah stripped the hot, heavily soaked towel from around her hips, then scooped her up and hauled her out of the room as quickly as he could. Her arms hung splayed and limp, her horrifying gasps for breath shuddering through him.

"Okay, baby, okay," he murmured in a soft, breathless voice of reassurance even though he felt nothing but terror. He strode into the bedroom, back through the house, and out onto the porch.

Noah beelined for the pool, not even hesitating as he stepped hurriedly into the water and down the stairs of the shallow end. He sank her into the cold water quickly, right up to her chin, letting her float so he could reach to press her head back as well, wetting her hair. Her face was bright red, and even though he had plunged her out of pure heat and into pure cold, she didn't react even on a subconscious level.

Not until a full minute or two later.

Kestra came to with a staggering gasp of breath, jolting with shock, her vivid eyes flying open and looking straight up into his. Her hands came up and clutched at his arm, her fingers digging into his flexed muscles.

"It is okay now," he soothed softly, the silence of the water surrounding them eerie as it echoed his voice and her rapid but easier breathing. "You are safe now."

Kestra tried to join thoughts and images in her head, but it was pounding with pain and she could hardly see anything other than his face. She focused, understood his words, and took them at face value. Whatever had happened, she was safe now. She had no choice but to believe him, to allow him to be her protector if he chose to be. It wasn't such a difficult thing to do, she realized. There was a stark honesty in those dark features. She took comfort in knowing that she'd never once thought he was lying to her, whatever else she had thought of him.

"How did you find me?" She shivered as she asked the only question she could come up with, curling her rapidly chilling body closer to the heat of his.

"Now, that would be telling," he said with pointed humor, a smile touching his lips. However, she could see that it didn't reach his eyes. His eyes held something else within them. Something dark and primeval.

Fear.

She understood that instantly, though she didn't know how. He'd been afraid for her.

No.

He had been terrified. Terror was the only term to fit the raw pain and panic flickering in the smoke of his eyes. The comprehension stole her breath away, tightening her chest with inexplicable emotion. Why did it matter to him what became of her? She knew it wasn't just a matter of human kindness and the impulse to save the life of another that came to those of good conscience. Kestra saw more. She felt it in the pounding of the heart behind his ribs, the grip of his fingers as they grasped her and released her feverishly, and the deeply etched lines of concern in the otherwise smoothly drawn angles of his beautiful face.

No one ever really worried about her. Despite what Jim said, so long as there wasn't a body he needed to pick up at the morgue, he never really was worried about her. He certainly never feared for her.

Kestra couldn't understand why seeing the emotion in this virtual stranger on her behalf made her feel . . .

She didn't know what it made her feel, and she was far too weak and confused to figure it out. Kestra relaxed in his hold, allowing her body to float in the cool water. She closed her eyes, reaching out with her other senses. She heard the lapping of the water against her skin and the edges of the pool. If she let her ears lower beneath the water, she heard the fast rush of her own breathing, and the equally rapid cadence of his. She turned her head and looked at him. Really looked at him. He was fully concentrating on her, keeping her head abovewater and her relaxed body below it. He was fully clothed, she realized, feeling the fabric of his shirt wet beneath her fingers and against her bare skin. Clearly he wasn't concerned with it. His concentration was completely on her. He watched her steadily, as if watching a ticking bomb.

She was completely naked in his arms, the buoyancy of her breasts bringing them above the water, the shivering cold making her nipples contract almost painfully. As she floated, she felt there was a strange sensuality to her perceptions of contrast. Cold water, warm male body. Nude female, clothed male. He was so powerful and strong as he suspended her in her watery bed, and she was as weak and limp as noodles.

She swept her gaze up to his and saw a darkly troubled expression for a brief moment before he hid it beneath a calming upward sweep of his lips. She closed her eyes, or actually hooded them with her lashes, letting him think he was unobserved as emotions ticked across his features. She understood his suddenly dark expression as his eyes drifted over her exposed body, her breasts, her legs, and the curls at their apex. He closed his eyes and clenched his jaw until she thought he would break a tooth. No doubt he was giving himself a very intense lecture on inappropriate thoughts during lifesaving moments.

Kestra only smiled. Her slightly disembodied state as she floated in the water allowed her to release and confess. She thrived on his hunger, she acknowledged. It thrilled her, left her breathless, and she couldn't even force herself to be offended over trivial things like timing and circumstances. She was glad she had not been a mere itch to him. She wanted him to continue wanting her. It seemed to calm her even as it excited her. More feelings she didn't understand, probably due to her inexperience with the feelings born in interpersonal relationships.

She suddenly shivered, and hard as she tried, couldn't make herself stop. She felt the shivering bone deep, felt it rocking into him like a focused quake. She was flooded with nausea, the sensation making her gasp, and she instantly tried to gain her feet. Instead, he held her tight.

"Okay, baby, time to get you dry."

He swung her up high against himself as he turned and walked them both up the pool steps without so much as a stagger from the regaining of their weight.

"I'm going to be sick," she warned him.

He didn't respond. He walked straight into the house, into the kitchen, and dropped her feet just in time for her to clutch at the sink and throw up. While he supported her with one arm, he drew back her hair with his free hand, holding it away from her face as her entire being shuddered with her nausea. His mouth brushed the back of her head and he murmured softly to her. It sounded like an apology.

After a minute she was able to catch her breath and rinse her mouth. Once she began, she realized she was incredibly thirsty, and she tried to scoop up handfuls of the fresh water in order to quench her thirst.

"No," Noah denied her gently. Taking her hand away from the water, he drew her closer to his warm, wet body and shut off the taps. He leaned toward the refrigerator, looking at it for a moment as if he thought it might potentially bite him. Then he pulled open the door and searched the shelves. It only took him an instant to find the bottled sports drinks that athletes tended to keep in stock. She barely noticed that the power seemed to be out and there was no light. She was too busy trying to burrow into his heated skin.

He was right, though. The electrolyte-balancing beverage would be the better choice over water for now. He handed her the bottle and she cradled it against her body as he scooped her back up to his chest and walked the hallway toward the master suite. She heard a very loud squishing sound as they went, the noise grating on her headachy brain, and she looked down his side. She laughed when she saw water spurting up out of his boots as he walked.

"I did not have time to remove them," he explained, his grin genuine in the face of her laughter at his expense. She was instantly puzzled. She hadn't thought he would be the type to laugh at himself.

"You're getting water all over the house."

"It is only water," he said with a shrug.

He was right. She had much bigger things to worry about. Her head was pounding and she was still nauseated. Her skin itched and her hands and feet were cramping like crazy. He carried her to the bed and carefully laid her in the center of it. He tucked a single pillow behind her head before releasing her and reaching to strip off his dripping shirt. Once he was sure he had minimized getting the bed any wetter, he reached to pull up the heavy quilt over her legs, covering her hips.

"Stay," he commanded her sternly, as if she were a puppy. Since she felt no stronger than a puppy, she couldn't argue with him. She just held her drink and tried to figure out how to get the little plastic top off it as she watched him cross to the bathroom.

He seemed so big compared to everything, especially as he stormed around with such knowing efficiency. She had a direct line of sight into the bathroom and she watched as he pulled a stack of fresh towels down from a shelf. Then he sat on the dressing bench of the vanity and disposed of his boots. Kes had to snicker when water poured onto the tiled floor. He glanced her way, jade flashing from beneath long dark lashes, the chiding look meant to be a scolding of some kind. But Kestra saw the humor etched around his lips and those fine creases at the corners of his eyes. She had been right. It was natural for him to smile a lot.

Her answering smile faded when he stood up and stripped

off his belt. Noah turned his back toward her, but she realized it wasn't because he put any thought into it. He stripped off his pants and stood naked and powerful and hellishly male. There were those powerful legs and thighs that he had used to bear their combined weight against the parlor wall. When God had handed out sinew and muscle, he had taken special care in sculpting Noah. To top it off, Noah had the finest-looking backside she'd ever seen. The angle of his stance changed and she caught the shiver in her own breathing that had nothing to do with feeling sick. There was a difference between feeling something and seeing something, she realized as she stared at his hefty penis. Cold water notwithstanding, he was mighty impressive. She absently licked her lips as Noah reached for a towel and wrapped it tight around his hips.

It wasn't until she exhaled that Kestra realized she had sucked in an excited breath and had held it. She couldn't reprimand herself for it, either. He was sinfully gorgeous, built like a god, and even tanned perfectly from head to toe. Tall, dark, and ultradangerous. Delightfully dangerous.

Jumping-out-of-a-plane dangerous.

Damn him.

She closed her eyes as he turned to approach her, his arms laden with towels. He dropped them on the bed with a plop and reached to tap her on the nose.

"Mmm?"

"Open your mouth."

While you are standing thigh level to the bed in nothing but a towel?

Her eyes flew open. She laughed a little shakily when she saw he held a thermometer in his hand. She obeyed his command and let him take her temperature. He was lucky she felt like crap physically, because otherwise she would never have stood for all this bossing around and whole lying-around-like-a-wilting-flower routine.

Her mind was still sharp as a damned tack, though, wasn't

it? Her imagination was definitely in working order. Oh, and no need to worry about her newfound libido. It was doing quite fine.

Noah found himself smiling. He couldn't read her thoughts yet, but her eyes were more than expressive enough. Her wryness and consternation, accented by an impressive bottom-lipped pout around the little glass stick of a thermometer, made her feelings very clear. She didn't like being helpless in front of him. She would be more determined than ever to prove her ability to control her world after finding herself weak before him. But that would be then, and this was now.

He drew back the quilt and grabbed up a towel. Starting with her legs, he began to dry her briskly. He saw the painful arching in her feet and immediately understood what she wasn't telling him. He let it go for the moment and continued to dry her skin. It wasn't until he reached the area of her hips that she gasped around the thermometer and her hands reached haltingly for his wrists. They were just as cramped as her feet, so it was hardly a detriment.

"Kes, I am not here to hurt you," he said in a soft, reassuring tone that washed over her. He put all of the passion of his intention to keep her safe in his voice, and she could not help but feel it. "I would never hurt you. I would never treat you with disrespect. I want you to believe that."

She relaxed visibly once more, but she closed her eyes as he dried the moisture from her hips and bottom, from between her thighs, her snow-white curls and the dip of her navel, and up her belly and back. He was so incredibly gentle and meticulous, as if he was determined to snare every drop of water.

In spite of her headache and the rest, Kestra was rather breathless by the time he finished with her body, the most intense moment being when he had encircled her upper thigh with his strong fingers, drawing her leg up against his side and tilting her knee outward so he could expose her for his attentions. The brush of the towel had been a dizzying sensation, but nothing compared to the accidental brush of his knuckles against a wetness that was not entirely from the pool.

Having finished drying her, ignorant of how easily he was affecting her, he caught up a fresh towel and raised her head so he could wrap it around her hair. Once the wet mass was contained, he dragged a fresh, dry pillow beneath her head and found a light sheet to cover the middle of her body with. The cotton was crisp and cool, allowing for any excess heat to leave her body, but keeping the chill off.

Noah checked the temperature of her body by sight alone. The thermometer was strictly for her benefit. She frowned when she looked at it.

"It could be much worse. You are very lucky that I am a persistent man," he told her quietly. There was an edge to the remark and she felt it keenly. There was regret and irony for him in the statement. It surprised Kestra that she felt she was getting very good at reading him. She usually missed those little nuances about people that allowed ease of understanding and building blocks that led to forming friendships. Usually when she looked at individuals she saw threats. She saw only their potential to harm or be dangerous, and once that evaluation was made, the other subtleties never seemed to matter. Noah was different somehow. In him she was seeing more. She was taking the time to stop and do a further observation for some reason, even though she knew he was hazardous to her general welfare. Did that make him different, or did it just make her very, very stupid?

He was extremely straightforward, but it was very clear that it was a selective honesty. She would get certain information from him if and only if she asked the right question. He had a code of honor, one she had seen in brief but powerful glimpses. Certainly enough to impress her. He was tough as well as gentle. Wildly confident enough to ravish a stubborn woman to within an inch of her life; determined enough to chase after her when said woman ran away like a chicken. Or rather an ostrich. However, her head was coming out of the sand. Making herself hate him wouldn't change her attraction to him. Neither would denial of it. No matter how much she wanted to quash it, it was what it was and it most certainly wasn't going away any time soon.

She wondered what he did for a living. How had he earned his money? He didn't strike her as a spoiled heir, and it was clear that his household in general held him in enormous esteem. Now that she thought about it, there were a few things that had happened that were a little—

"Hey," he said suddenly, drawing her attention. He bent over her, looking straight down into her eyes. "Stop the merry-go-round," he advised, tapping a soft fingertip to her temple. "I know you must have a hell of a headache. All you should be doing is sipping your drink, closing your eyes, and not thinking about a thousand things you cannot possibly do anything about at the moment."

Again, he was right. It was an annoying habit, but his wisdom had its charms as well. She did what he said, relaxing and not thinking, even when he picked up her foot and began to massage the fiercely cramping muscles.

"Rest," he encouraged her, the low timbre of his voice rich and soothing. "Let your body heal. Tomorrow is another day. You have plenty of time to yell at me, be cranky, and hate me. Tonight just rest."

"I don't hate you," she argued softly, toying halfheartedly with her drink bottle.

"Well, that is nice to know," he said. He tried to sound neutral about it, but she could tell he was pleased and amused.

She was pleased, too. His hands on her feet worked like magic. Within minutes the muscles released, a pleasant tingle left in the wake of his fingertips and palms. He slid his broad hands up her calves and she could tell he was checking for cramps there. Then he took up the hand nearest to him and gently rubbed his thumb into the palm of it. It was a soft, circular motion, and that tingle started again, like the littlest sparks of electrical current. Warmth spread over her hand as he slid his fingers over hers, weaving their hands together and using the free one to continue the massage. Kes watched him very carefully, watched as he studied her hand with an almost singular amount of attention. It could be that he was looking for the best way to ease her cramps, but she didn't think so. If she had to venture a guess, she'd say he was memorizing her.

Noah traced every finger, every fingerprint, the whorls and swirls on her skin fascinating to him. She had calluses on every possible point of contact, even some unusual ones in between her knuckles themselves, though they were not as thick as the others. Her hands were those of someone who worked hard, but they had the elegance of someone trained to hold her hands in a specific way. Posed. Poised. He turned her hand over and looked at her wrist. He could see her pulse beating, but he also saw an incongruity. He almost missed it, but when he looked a moment longer, he saw the small tattoo of a dancer in silhouette. It was done in a soft tannish pink, and it almost blended in with her skin. But it was clear she wore it with a great deal of pride.

"Cyd Charisse." She said it before she realized it, her sleepy eyes opening to meet his curious gaze. "She was a dancer during the time of MGM musicals. She was told she was too tall . . . but she wasn't. She was the most beautiful dancer I had ever seen. The silhouette is of her."

"A role model for a tall girl who wanted to dance," he said, looking at her beautiful face with suddenly understanding eyes.

"I wanted to do it all. Dance, gymnastics, anything I could try. Except basketball. Everyone wants to stick you in basketball when you're tall." She rolled her eyes with her honest exasperation. "I wanted ballet. Floor exercises. Rock climbing. Kickboxing. Yoga."

"And I am willing to bet you got every last one of them."

"Yeah," she said, clearly victorious. "Still learning new stuff all the time. Last year it was bungee jumping. This year . . ." She shrugged. "Who knows? I haven't decided."

"I am sure something will come up," he said.

And she knew immediately that there was something veiled behind the seemingly innocent remark. She was too tired to really inspect it, though, so she let it go for the moment.

"Is this your only tattoo?" he asked.

"Yes. You can hardly see this one. Other than that I have no identifying marks."

Noah didn't react, but he found that to be an intriguing way for her to have put it. He filed it away. This was the most he'd learned about her outside of sexual knowledge. Even so, he felt as though he needed to know her better. He wanted more. Craved more. Both body and soul.

"You have a scar. You have a lot of scars." She reached up to point to two of them, touching the spots on his left upper arm and shoulder where iron nails had been shot through his body in battle. Her fingertips skimmed down his chest to the third scar on his ribs, then the fourth on his side just above his hip. He tried not to be stirred by her touch, but the brush of her hand was so soft and so clearly sensual, he was fighting a losing battle. The rush of blood heading between his hips had no conscience at all when it came to her. "The worst one is on your back." She slid her hand around his side and touched the ridges of the evil scar left by an iron dagger that had been dragged through his flesh. As she did this, she leaned low and close, her breasts brushing over his belly, the rigid tips drawing a teasing pair of lines over his taut skin. He took a deep breath as he felt the demands of his completely flushed body surging up beneath his towel.

"You are very observant," he murmured, reaching around to take her hand from his burning skin, settling it gently between his palms for a moment as she finally settled back onto her pillow.

He noticed that she didn't ask how he had gotten his badges of battle.

"You have two scars." He returned to her, reaching to slide the cotton sheet all the way up her leg. She had a long white line, about five inches long, down the back of her thigh. "One . . ." he counted, running brief fingers over the ridge of it. Then he hesitated before resting his hand low on her belly where the second scar lay beneath the sheet. He actually expected the hand that clasped his defensively. "Two," he finished, respecting her feelings and not tracing the white scar slashed horizontally just above her pubic bone.

She looked at him with wide, vulnerable eyes for a long minute.

"No one ever notices that one." She sounded like she didn't know whether to be impressed or upset. Perhaps she was a little bit of both. Noah knew she expected him to ask questions, but that wasn't in the rules of the game. She'd set that boundary clearly enough, and he would respect it.

He slid his hand out from beneath hers, bringing it back to the first spot he had pointed out, his fingers absently tracing the jagged texture of it.

"I know someone who has a blade scar that runs from the back of his skull to almost the small of his back."

"Really?" She was practically envious and Noah suppressed the urge to chuckle. "How did that happen?"

"Someone jumped him from behind with a sword."

"A sword? Who runs around with a sword?"

"A madman. My friend was lucky to survive."

"I can imagine." She took notification of the act of violence in stride, though. It was clear neither one of them was a stranger to it. "I know someone who got their throat cut ear to ear. Walking around with the scar to this day."

"Ouch." Noah had to wince.

"Luckily, the guy who did it had watched too many movies."

"What does that mean?"

She smiled, her ice blue eyes sparkling with her knowledge.

"It means that you aren't supposed to jerk someone's head back when you slit their throat. If you pull their chin up, all the crucial structures, the veins and arteries, get pulled deeper into the neck. So you miss them. Plus, ear to ear . . ." She traced the path under her chin. "Worst you'll hit is the larynx."

"That is very educational," Noah remarked, his lips lifting in humor. "Perhaps tomorrow we can go over techniques for suffocation. I find those to be excellent topics to discuss with a strange man when I am all alone in the house with him."

"I'm not afraid of you," she retorted smartly, her chin lifting. "If anything, you should watch your back around me."

"If you are not afraid of me, then why did you run away?"

Noah wouldn't retain or withdraw the question. It needed asking, and he needed the answer. He watched her very carefully as she absorbed it and formulated a response.

"Okay," she breathed, absently pulling the sheet up over her breasts in a clearly armoring gesture. "I suppose that's a fair question."

"If . . . if my intensity frightened you, I have no excuse for it," he offered, his eyes never leaving hers as he spoke. "I know what you think of me, Kestra, but you are wrong. I was not using you, and I was not looking for another conquest. If I could do it over again . . ."

"It would happen the same way," she told him softly. Kestra moved to sit up slowly, drawing up to him so they were intimately close, her breath warming his face. "I know what drove you, Noah. I know it so very well because it drove me, too. After all those months of empty promises, I'm amazed it didn't happen in your bedroom the minute I woke up. We're only human, and what human being doesn't want to fulfill his or her fantasies at least once? I'm sorry I was so bitchy. I'm frankly impressed that you ignored the queen bitch and came after me. I acted like it was nothing, like I'd used you and that it was easy for me to walk away. I can be very nasty like that, and I'm not going to promise it isn't going to happen again, because I assure you it will."

"No doubt," he chuckled. "But I can also understand why you were so upset. I have a way of coming on very strong in certain situations. I could not . . . I was not very considerate."

"Oh, I wouldn't say that," she said, a blond brow lifting teasingly as she smiled.

Noah was bemused and baffled, and it came through in his laugh.

"You know, after the other day, I had visions of your wanting to beat the hell out of me. I was not expecting candor, or any latitude for that matter."

"Well." Kes smiled to herself as she recalled her session with her punching bag. "I had some time to think and work out my emotions." She hedged. "And I'm feeling mellow because you saved my life *again.* Plus you made my cramps and headache go away. Well, mostly."

"That's the liquids and being out of the heat," he told her, amusement shining in his smoky eyes. He reached for the nape of her neck, his fingers sliding over it until he found tension. He gently began to massage as he had done for her hands, and again she felt warmth and magic flooding her like a powerful balm. She sighed contentedly, not caring about vulnerability as she let her head drop forward. He continued the massage until she swayed and caught herself, looking up at him with sleepy eyes.

"Is it safe to sleep?" she asked.

"Yes. I will watch over you and wake you in an hour to get more fluids into you." Noah glanced around to see the enormous windows and their potential sun exposure. She would be safe, but as exhausted as he was, the direct touch of the sun could render him comatose. "I am going to cover these windows so you do not get any sun or heat on you. That would be contraindicated for heat exhaustion. You know, you are very lucky you did not have a stroke."

"I think I did have a stroke." She yawned and lay back, snuggling into the bedding. "Otherwise, I probably would have beaten you up by now, instead of being nice. I'm never nice."

"Well, then you will pardon me if I do not run to get the doctor to fix you."

"Mmm, just wait till I'm feeling better."

"I will await it with bated breath, *Kikilia*."

"I told you not to call me that."

"Yes. I am ignoring you. Now go to sleep."

Chapter 11

Jacob had done some pretty daunting things in his lifetime, even surviving a battle with a fairly moon-altered and infinitely powerful Gideon at one time, but nothing would ever compare to this if even the slightest thing went wrong.

And nothing would compare to it even if everything went right.

The Enforcer glided down to the ground, altering the effect of gravity on his weight with such skill that he set down softer than a feather. He paused before his doorstep, still unused to the silence of thought and greeting he would be getting. Leah would be long to bed by then, and though he loved her, even her jubilance as he walked through the door couldn't replace the tender, loving warmth of her mother as she greeted him with a kiss.

He swore softly, changing his mind and remaining in the growing sunlight as the early morning hours moved forward. He sat down on his stoop, his long legs braced about halfway down the short set of stairs leading to the pathway. The lawns and gardens around him were perfect, flourishing in the sunlight as the dew from the chill night slowly burned off. It was one of the benefits of being an Earth Demon—greenery and flowers anytime he wished. But Bella was partial to autumn, yearly sojourns to take in the seasonal color a part of growing up in New York. It was because of this that sturdy old oaks and dozens of other leafy trees surrounded a house that had once had a clear view to the cliff side.

The ground was littered with leaf debris, the colors bright and fascinating, and weak little piles were dotted around here and there. He could have cleaned it all away with a thought, but Bella insisted on raking them up into piles, which she and Leah immediately destroyed by jumping into them.

They played the game in the dark, of course.

Jacob knew she wished her child could safely see the things that sunlight illuminated, but it was what she called a "soft regret." One that would fade over time, perhaps when Leah grew strong enough to do just that.

And it was this adaptability that made it so hard for him to understand why Isabella was so impenetrably angry with Noah. And with him.

"Because just once I wish *I* wasn't the one who had to adapt."

Jacob hadn't heard her speak in so many days that, when he turned to look at her, his heart felt as though it had twisted full around in his chest.

"Bella . . ." he murmured.

She stepped off the threshold and down the steps until she was taking a seat beside him. She was in a cable-knit sweater, but even so she had to hunch deeper into it to keep warm.

"But then I look at these trees and I play in the leaves with our daughter and I realize that you've done your share of adapting as well."

Jacob watched as she swiped at her eyes with her fingertips quickly, one of those strange human habits meant to hide emotion when it actually drew attention to it.

"Growing trees is nothing to me. It is natural. Part of who I am, little flower," he told her softly. "Just as it is natural for you to be angry with someone who endangers your child."

"She is your child, too. Which means your customs apply to her. By your customs and culture, the earlier a child shows and uses its power, the more she is to be respected and encouraged to use it. By that perspective, I can understand why no one agrees with my anger. But what about *my* culture? What about the human customs I have that say you should be livid with Noah for what he did? That a father should beat the crap out of someone who exploits his child for their own ends?" She laughed shortly, shaking her head. "The only person who understands that and agrees with me is Noah, for God's sake!"

"I know," Jacob said quietly. "And you are right. What Noah did was wrong and dangerous . . ."

"But?"

"But you love him, and you have to forgive him."

Bella nodded once, and burst into tears.

Kestra stirred and cautiously opened her eyes in the face of the lancing pain that shot across them and through her head. It faded as she focused, though, and she sighed softly in relief, waiting it out completely before she dared to move an inch. As she rested, she became aware of weight lying across her back.

She was lying on her stomach and the room was completely dark, although she had pretty good night vision so it didn't really matter to her so much. But usually there was a hint of light from somewhere, even if it was a street or porch light from outside. There wasn't even a single ray of moonlight.

The weight against her back twitched, bringing her attention back to it. It really got her attention when fingers slid softly up her spine for a few inches as their owner stirred restlessly beside her. She waited him out, waited for him to settle, and then gingerly turned her head to look in the opposite direction. She held her breath, and it was a good thing, too, because she was suddenly just about nose to nose with him. He was out like all the rest of the lights, so she carefully exhaled and allowed herself to breathe. She'd never slept beside anyone before, her inability to trust making it an impossibility. She found it wasn't really at all upsetting to realize that she had done so, or that it had been with this particular man.

She could see him with surprising clarity in spite of the darkness. More impressive were his features as he slept. Even in repose he reeked of authority and strength, the planes of his face and the unruly curls of his dark hair making him look stormy and wild. There was nothing innocent or boyish about him, even when totally relaxed. The smile lines on his face were gone while he slept, so even they weren't there to soften him. That was okay, though, she considered. He was positively arresting, and his dark lashes and widely cut mouth were incredibly sensual. She closed her eyes briefly, remembering the feel of his mouth, its taste. That memory quickly led to others and she flicked her eyes open before she got carried away.

Only to find tempestuous green and gray eyes looking at her.

She was suddenly breathless, totally speechless, and she couldn't so much as blink. What did you say to a man in your bed? It wasn't as though they'd covered these things in etiquette class. She'd already thanked him for saving her life, hadn't she? She frowned in consternation and told herself she wasn't allowed to do it again. Getting almost dead was a very bad habit. Needing a rescuer was a worse one.

"You have been conscious for all of five minutes and already you have something to frown about?"

It wasn't a criticism. She could tell he was honestly puzzled by that. It was funny to her, though. She hadn't thought him to have a regularly sunny disposition himself. Perhaps it was his looks. Or maybe it was because they always fought. She hadn't exactly given him a fair chance at showing his true colors. Besides, she just assumed the worst of everyone and moved on. It was easier that way. That meant no surprises, and no one ever disappointed her.

Although, she had to admit, he was full of surprises so far. He had certainly caused her to surprise herself.

The thought made her entire body blush and she found she couldn't maintain eye contact. She was afraid he would be able to read her suddenly carnal thoughts.

He chuckled softly. "That is definitely an improvement," he teased her, his voice low and full of speculation. She instantly looked up at him, fire snapping in her crystal eyes.

"You better not piss me off first thing in the morning. Wouldn't want me to frown or anything," she warned him.

It was clear by his sexy, overtly masculine smile that he was completely unconcerned. "First of all, it is evening," he corrected her. "Secondly, it is my fondest wish never to piss you off again."

He said it with such sincerity, such seriousness in his smoke-dusted eyes, that she couldn't help but grin and laugh softly. She bit her lip against the humor, tried to look daunting, and even reached out to give him a shove.

"Don't you dare use that Eurotrashy charm on me, mister. It won't work." She was miffed that her shove seemed to have no effect on the wall of his body at all. He didn't budge a millimeter. Even his hand remained on her back. She felt his fingers move, the tips drifting up over her skin briefly before his palm settled back down again. She suddenly realized that the slight caresses were a need, one he couldn't control despite his best efforts to do so. He was struggling to keep from really touching her, trying to satisfy himself with those little strokes. There was something very exciting about knowing that. The idea that even though he was clearly as used to controlled behaviors as she was, he could not maintain that perfect control around her.

"I would never try to charm you. I would never insult you like that."

Noah was completely fascinated. She had the fastest-changing thoughts, expressions, and moods that he had ever seen. So fast that he could hardly keep track of them. He wished their mind contact would kick into gear. He was dying to know what she was thinking. He slid unobtrusive fingers over her back again, cursing himself for the slight petting but unable to help it. Her skin was so unbelievably soft, like refined silk beneath his fingertips. She was so warm, her humanity making her naturally warmer than he was, and he found that heat addicting. He wanted to check her over, to see how she was functioning after yesterday's close call, but he couldn't make himself do anything that would rob him of the opportunity to keep touching her.

That was all he needed. Just this. Lying there talking and gently touching. He could be very happy like this.

"Where are you from, anyway?" she asked suddenly. "I know you aren't originally from England. You don't have that haughty Brit thing going on at all, though I think you have been here long enough that you learned your English here."

"You have a good ear," he said, honestly impressed. "Clearly you are no stranger to Europe yourself. You do not speak like an American."

"And you know a lot of Americans?"

"I know a few. I find New York accents to be particularly charming."

She laughed at that. Only a European would find that accent "charming."

"Hey . . . you dodged me!" She said it suddenly, lifting her head from the pillow so she could glare at him accusingly.

Noah was suddenly in threat of losing contact with her. He pressed his fingers to her moving back and hastily rectified the situation.

"I apologize. It is an old habit. My people have been

through a lot these past years, and I have gotten in the habit of being impersonal and diverting attention in order to gain information. My family is from a region in the Czech Republic. Many of my people have roots there, though we are scattered now or are concentrated here in England in small groups. It is more peaceful here, less skirmishing over land and borders."

"You keep saying 'my people.' What people?"

"My culture. I am a leader of my culture, and people look to me for guidance and the traditions that define our culture." He smiled at her. "Now what about you? The American without an American accent. Your speech is refined, almost as though you are purposely eliminating any hints of accent."

She felt a chill walk down the back of her neck. He was frighteningly accurate in his assessment. She had never met anyone with such an understanding of detail, and she moved in shrewd circles. Her first instinct was to give him the same cover story she gave everyone. She never told anyone any truths about herself. She made up a story and made it a truth right before their eyes. She wasn't honest like he was.

"I went to a Canadian boarding school as a very young girl. A school for young ladies of culture. We were trained to speak perfect French and to speak with perfect elocution. We learned to walk and act with precision and grace and to excel in manners and etiquette. I suppose I have retained some of my skills from those years." And that was a truth. She felt her heart pounding with the instant kickback of fear brought on by the exposure.

Noah felt the sudden rush of the fearful emotion. It rang through him with heart-stopping clarity, instantly making his heart race to catch the rhythm of hers. He held his breath a moment, almost too excited to focus. At last, a sign of their minds beginning to open to one another. He let the feeling wash over him, savoring the connection. After a moment, he slid his hand up her spine to the nape of her neck and soothingly began to rub the sensitive spot.

"And you travel a lot," he managed to say with a level voice, totally belying the pitch of his delight.

"How did you know that?"

"You maneuvered through England like a professional traveler. Only people who live in a variety of places have that confidence."

"You know," she murmured, "you have to be the most astute man I've ever met."

"Well, when you get to be my age, you tend to acquire a bit of wisdom."

"Oh yeah, you're a regular sage. Shouldn't you be sitting on a mountain somewhere cultivating a long white beard waiting for knowledge seekers to come to you?"

"Have I mentioned that sarcasm has the potential to be detrimental to the natural beauty of your face?" he countered.

She laughed, but breathily, because the compliment had come to her in so casual and backhanded a manner that she hadn't recognized it at first. She had learned to thank people graciously for such things, but this time she was speechless. His hand was moving gently against her neck, relaxing away all tension and every bit of anxiety their conversation might bring up. It was also leaving the heat of his fingers and palm forever imprinted on her skin, that magical sparkle of energy spreading out over the entire expanse of her back, shoulders, and even her scalp and face. She wished she knew how he was able to do that. For the moment, she hoped he wouldn't stop.

"I will try to refrain in the future," she said quietly.

"Is that a promise? If so, I will hold you to it."

"I said *try*," she pointed out. "I promise to *try*."

"I think I shall have to be satisfied with that," he mused with humor flashing in his beautiful eyes.

"Yes, you shall," she mocked him with an aggrieved expression. She chuckled when he did. He had a wonderfully easy laugh, rich and male from top to bottom. It was rather infectious, bringing out those little wrinkles at the corners of his eyes that so fascinated her, making his pupils flash with jade lights and misting smoke.

Noah nearly jumped out of his skin when she inexplicably reached out and touched his face. Her fingertips went to the corner of his right eye, smoothing over the skin there as she blossomed into a breathtaking smile that went deep into her fair blue eyes. He closed his eyes, unable to help himself as his starved senses raced to memorize the softness of her touch, the sweet scent of her skin as it brushed near his nose and lips. It took all of his willpower not to catch up that beautiful hand and place a kiss or two in the palm. He didn't want to do anything to possibly upset her when she was being so surprisingly receptive for a change.

"Noah?" His name on her lips instantly opened his eyes. She drew her full bottom lip between her teeth for a moment as she scanned his face. "Why do you do that?"

"Do what?" he asked, unable to weed out the hoarse undertone to his voice.

"You stop. Everything. One minute you're laughing or upset or talking, then suddenly your eyes close and you go very still."

He just looked at her for several beats, at first trying to formulate a plausible explanation, but he was a lousy liar and he hated the idea of being dishonest with her in any way.

"I suppose I do it as a defensive or protective gesture because I am experiencing something out of context or inappropriate to a specific situation."

"My, my, them sure is some fancy words, mister," she said, affecting a hillbilly accent. She switched instantly to her usual sweet tones. "Would you put that in layman's terms for those of us who know you're trying to snow them?"

"I am not trying to snow you." He sighed when she cocked a brow at him in contradiction. "Damn, you are the most . . ."

"Infuriatingly observant woman in the world?" she supplied when he was at a loss.

"Yes, something a lot like that," he conceded with a sigh.

Noah rolled away from her, suddenly getting up out of bed. He ran both hands through the long, wild waves of his hair as he tried to gather his thoughts. Kestra was frowning, feeling the loss of his remarkably soothing touch. She was also sorry that she had obviously said something upsetting to him. He walked away from her and out of the bedroom. She turned over immediately, grasping the bedsheet and twisting it around her body. She sat up and went to stand up, but the entire room took a massive nosedive and she gasped with the shock of it. She fell back across the bed, closed her eyes, covered her face with her hands, and began to lecture her lurching stomach on the joys of antinausea.

"Hey, are you crazy?" came a masculine scolding several minutes later when he found her lying in that very position. It was obvious she had tried to get up. He sat down beside her on the bed, leaned over her, and she could feel his warm breath against her hands. She sighed, feeling the heat of his body and finding it somehow comforting. "Feeling a little dizzy, are we?"

Well, he doesn't have to sound so smug about it. She frowned and dropped her hands. She daringly opened an eye and found it was much better with her eyes opened after all.

"I understand you have this whole Wonder Woman thing going on," he mused, reaching to stroke his thumb under each of her eyes, somehow making her feel more focused as he did so, "but I doubt you will be walking around much tonight."

"I don't do invalid," she grouched, making the face to match. "Just give me a minute and a very big anchor and I'll be fine."

He laughed, the energy and sound of it making her smile in spite of her pique at her situation, and she beat on his chest in punishment as he made her laugh with him. "This is not funny!" she insisted irritably.

"No. Your illness is not funny, but you are. It never occurred to me that your acerbic remarks could be used for good."

"Evil of the world, beware," she announced halfheartedly with a fisted salute that ended with her arm flung across her eyes. She made a long, growling sound of frustration. "I hate this. I hate it so much."

"I know, baby," he said softly, reaching to stroke through her hair in sympathy. "But I promise you, in a few days you will bounce back far better than you were before."

"You bet your ass I will. Don't get used to this whole macho man in shining armor thing."

"I know. I know. You do not do maiden in distress."

"Exactly!" She lifted her arm to look up into his face. "You catch on pretty quick for a . . ." She trailed off, biting her lip on the completion of the prejudiced remark.

"For a man? Another promise for you, Kestra. I am not like any man you know. So that insult does not bother me in the least."

He pushed off from the bed and walked out of her sight again.

Noah leaned on the kitchen counter, having come in under the guise of getting Kestra one of those sports drinks in order to continue her rehydration.

The fact of the matter was, he was running out of time. In so many ways. She was already asking questions that required carefully worded answers so he would not lie to her. When she asked for a light, he was going to have to explain how everything in the house had gotten fried electrically, why phones wouldn't work, anything like that. He could possibly come up with something clever about that, but he was already growing weary of avoidance. He had to tell her the truth, had to come up with a way to help her accept it and him, and he only had twenty-four hours to do it in. Samhain was gnashing at his heels, he could feel it with every fiber of his being; every muscle and blood cell beat with the rhythm of the full moon hidden behind the thick towels he had hung over the windows and the storm that was gathering outside. But none of this would help him tomorrow. He wasn't even sure if it would help her. Was she far enough into the change to be affected like he would be?

He didn't even know if her illness was all heat exhaustion or if some of it had to do with his thoughtless absence those couple of days he'd struggled with indecision. He needed a plan and he didn't have one. It wasn't in his nature to work off the cuff. Leaders planned. They got counsel and advice and thought things out meticulously. His last action of impulse had probably destroyed his friendship with Isabella forever.

Nor was he used to so much indecision. Corrine was right, he was paralyzed. Nothing in his life had ever given him such a sense of fear as when he thought of losing Kestra through the mistakes of his own actions or inactions.

He just had to bite the bullet, as the saying went. He couldn't keep it a secret, and she was definitely smart enough to start figuring things out on her own. He wouldn't feel right touching her again without explaining what she was getting herself into, and Destiny knew he was dying to touch her again. His entire psyche was screaming for it. It almost had nothing to do with his body at all. It would be a whole lot easier on him if he didn't remember how she felt, how she tasted . . . how she *sounded*. Her impassioned cries echoed loudest within him, making him howl out for more from deep within his soul. He was no stranger to his animalistic side, but this possessive craving was entirely out of his realm of experience.

He pushed off from the counter, taking a deep breath or two before moving back toward the bedroom, having affected his own hungry body with his thoughts and memories of the woman who was far too real and close for his sane mind to handle at the moment. He needed to draw from a completely different well of need. The need to know her, to learn her, and most of all, the need to earn her respect and trust.

At least he had used enough sense to put his pants on. Somehow it felt a lot safer than his temporary alternative of the night before. The fabric was damp and chilly, but he figured he didn't deserve much better and it could help in the long run. Then again . . .

He entered the bedroom, his keen eyesight picking out her hands-and-knees position on the center of the bed all too easily. The sheet around her body was not so much around it as it was half on and half off it. She was rummaging in the bedside drawer for something. Unfortunately, it was the bedside drawer on the near side of the room, the side facing him. He supposed she'd expected to hear his approach, but out of habit he made no sound when he moved. Demons were night creatures, natural-born hunters, and moving with stealth was as innate to them as breathing.

Kestra's face was hidden by a curtain of white hair, made almost iridescent in the darkness, at least to his eyesight. He could see every single curve of her body, from breasts to taut belly to the silhouetted space between her thighs. The sheet was draped over her back and buttocks, so it left all the rest exposed as she searched, clearly having little success because she was swaying dizzily and trying to fight it. She looked incredibly tempting, far too delicious, and adorably stubborn. Noah almost turned around and walked back to the kitchen so he could breathe all over again. But, he thought with a sigh, even a King was only so strong.

"Looking for something?"

She didn't start or react with any kind of shock. She tossed back her hair, and after a dizzy moment of regretting the habitual action, she blew at a stray strand and cocked a brow at him. Noah was ridiculously pleased that she didn't rush to cover herself up.

Pleased being the least volatile of adjectives at the moment.

"Yes. I am looking for my flashlight. None of the lights seem to be working."

"Yes. I believe the transformer overloaded last night. Most

of the lights blew out, and as for the rest"—he shrugged—"I guess they have not restored the service."

"Oh." She sighed. "Well, considering how rural this is, I won't be surprised if I spend the rest of the week in the dark. Aha!" She pulled out the small metal cylinder she had been looking for, dragged the sheet across herself, and sat down. The strong little light flared to life and she flashed it at him, making his maladjusted eyes smart. He hid a grin and walked over to the bed.

With a violent pop, the bulb in the flashlight blew out.

"Grr! Isn't that just the luck?"

"Yes. I was so looking forward to running around in the dark with a tiny beam of light to show me the way. Here, drink this."

She took the bottle absently, shaking the light as if it would make it work again. She sighed.

"You're right. It's not as if it can heat bathwater. God, I hate cold showers."

"Yeah, me, too," he said softly. She looked at him and he could easily see her eyes narrowing. "Although, if you are feeling better after you drink that, we could always return to my holdings. Plenty of light, plenty of hot water. I believe I even have a tub my sister claims all women will consider divinity on earth."

"Sold! To the man in the shining armor!" She laughed. "So much for Wonder Woman. She who hates to be without amenities. And a gym."

"Mmm . . . the best I can do there is the training yards. A lot of violence and sweaty people. Oddly enough, I can picture you right in the thick of it."

"Hoo-yah!" She laughed. She clutched her head and slid into a reclining position. "Well, maybe just hoo . . . the yah can wait a few days."

"I am inclined to agree."

"So I guess this means you're driving."

Noah went very still.

"You're stopping again," she noted immediately.

"No. My eyes are still open."

"Well, it's dark."

"Okay."

"But something is bothering you. I can feel it. Your energy gets all prickly."

Now he was definitely stopping, and he couldn't help it if she noticed it. He closed his eyes as an anxious yet exhilarating wash of emotion flooded over him. It was not very likely that the average human being could detect changes in energy, never mind "prickly" changes in energy. Did she even realize what she was saying? Perhaps she was chalking it up to her extremely impressive instincts and intuition, but it was too uncannily coincidental for it to just be that. Energy. Heat. Power. Those were a part of him. Were they now becoming a part of her? What kind of Druid was she going to be, exactly? They had no way of knowing. He was overwhelmed with the urge to find out, even as he wanted to delay it all just a little while longer.

"Damn it."

"What?" she asked quickly.

"Nothing." Then he sighed and rubbed his forehead just over his nose. "No, wait. I apologize. What I mean to say is, it is nothing for you to be concerned with. Just a lot of thoughts running amok and trying their best to give me a headache."

"I see. Well, don't expect pity from me. I won't be impressed until you at least have some nausea or . . . blood coming out of your eyes or something."

Noah looked at her with utter disbelief. "Have you seen much of that in your lifetime?"

"You know, some questions are better left unanswered."

The really frightening part about her response was that he didn't think she was making a joke. Noah was instantly taken back to the first moment he had seen her in reality, and how it had ended so abruptly seconds later.

"I have a plan," he said absently, pushing that aside for more pressing concerns. "Let us get you dressed and then you can rest while I prepare for our trip. Considering how you are feeling, I would not be surprised if you sleep the entire trip." He purposely looked away, turning to find some clothes for her.

"I'd be surprised if I did. I don't like to sleep while driving."

"Actually, I was thinking of flying."

"Flying? Quicker, but on such short notice?"

"I have means of private transportation," he said, again purposely vague. He withdrew a brief cotton dress out of a series of dresses that didn't seem to go past midthigh. She was clearly a modern girl who loved to flaunt her femininity and her hard-earned body. Every dress was stylish and light, not conservative but not garish, either. She had a small selection of very sophisticated evening dresses from some pretty exclusive designers as well, confirming his suspicions that she had more than her fair share of resources. He wasn't certain that the brief dresses were at all appropriate for an English October, but she had worn one that he had seen already and it hadn't seemed to faze her.

"Actually, I have a red velvet dress in there. I would prefer that one," she said before he could turn and show her his choice. It seemed such a domestic thing for him to be doing for her, choosing something for her to wear. "If you can see it in the dark."

He already had it in hand as she was saying that. He draped it over the bed and then turned to the only dresser in the room. He selected a bra and underwear with just enough care to make her blush uncharacteristically. Kestra told herself it was because she didn't like being ill and waited on. Then she told herself she was a coward and the blush was because she liked his choices, that they were sexy and she had bought them after they had made love, probably with temptation in her subconscious.

Sex. Had sex. Not made love, she corrected herself hastily.

"You were not wearing hosiery the other day . . . ?"

He let the unspoken question hang, the memories of that

torrid meeting crowding between them both. Kestra shifted beneath the sheet, the fabric suddenly overly stimulating against her skin. She casually crossed an arm over her breasts in an attempt to hide the sudden thrust of her nipples.

"I . . . wear garters and stockings, but I haven't found any I like yet," she managed to say in a passably even tone.

"Oh. I forgot you had to buy—"

He stopped again.

She watched his eyes slide closed and was sorely tempted to call him on it, to know what he was thinking that very second. After a moment he looked at her and smiled in a way that didn't reach his eyes. "We will not be leaving your clothes behind this time."

"Barneys and Saks will be very sorry to hear it," she joked. It was clear there was no enthusiasm behind it, but he smiled again anyway.

Noah moved to the bed, coming to her side and sitting down so his hip contacted hers and he was facing her. He reached out to push back a strand of her hair as he found and held her gaze. Kestra could see the seriousness in his eyes and she felt her throat constrict with an anxiety that she couldn't make herself understand.

"When we are settled at my home, I would be very grateful if you would allow me to talk to you about some . . . unusual matters between us."

"Unusual matters?" She looked perplexed. "I don't believe I have ever heard it put quite like that before."

"Believe me, you have never had a discussion like this before."

"I wish you hadn't done that," she said with a frustrated sigh.

He looked at her with bald confusion.

"Now I'll spend the entire time from here to there worrying and wondering what it is you want to say to me that's unusual," she clarified.

"Worrying? I do not think worrying is required. As for

wondering, you will have no success, so you should not attempt it."

"Just like that, hmm? You think telling me not to worry and not to wonder is going to make it happen?"

"I am appealing to your logic," he said, a grin already playing over his lips. "But you are beginning to sound suspiciously like a woman."

"Ooo." She squinted her eyes and wrinkled her nose at him as she shook a scolding finger. "You just said that because I almost made that man comment."

"I told you, the man comment did not faze me."

"Uh-huh." She clearly didn't agree.

"Come. Dress," he ordered her. "Unless you need my assistance?"

"No!" She snatched her clothes from him, fighting back a wave of nausea as she moved too fast. "You go take those lethal hands elsewhere," she commanded, not thinking about her phrasing.

"Lethal hands?" he echoed, his tone suddenly careful.

Kestra froze, bit her lip, and cringed slightly when she realized she'd spoken the words aloud.

"Yes. Lethal," she said, facing the music. "Deadly. Dangerous. Otherwise unwise to be in the vicinity of."

"I see."

"Are you leaving so I can get dressed?"

"Yes."

"Well, might I say it is a very slow departure?"

Noah got up and walked out of the bedroom. He ended up back at the kitchen counter. He was smiling, unable to help himself.

Chapter 12

Banda ran for his life.

He had been caught in the city. He'd had no choice but to go, but for every shadow there was light. He felt them coming, slipping shadow to shadow as he was, just as adept, more than powerful enough to seek him out. He didn't understand what they wanted with him. Their people were not enemies. Banda hadn't been making any mischief on any of their kind.

As he ran flat-out among the streetlights he felt the glow touch his skin with irritating prickles, touching just his arm but running the entire course of his nervous system, whenever he had to run out of the shadows to cross the path of the frightening light, the blessed light that created shadow sanctuary as well as representing imminent death.

The young Shadowdweller could hardly breathe, he was running so fast. Besides the pounding of his feet on the pavement, all he could hear was the coarse and violent rasp of his own breath as it labored in and out of his body. The Vampires were faster than he, and the light didn't hurt them at all, unless it was sunlight, which Banda was very unlikely to find at this hour. All the better. He'd rather get caught by the threatening Vampires than get caught by the deadly sun.

There were too many of them to fight, and his powers were too untried to go up against those that were clearly very potent. His only hope would be to contact a more mature Shadowdweller, one more powerful than himself, more powerful than the Vampires. The odds of finding one in the city were very low, but better to try than not. The fact of the matter was he couldn't even attempt it while blindly on the run and shuddering head to toe with fear.

Banda had to stop, if for no other reason than that his body ached from the running and the harsh slaps of light that burned him. He tried to control his breathing as he stepped back into the deepest shadows and tried to hide. He blended, phased, and because of his desperation, found the power to become a perfect shadow, indistinguishable from the shadows that belonged against the building made of gray and pink brick.

Cygnus stopped a block away from his quarry when the slippery little 'Dweller up and disappeared. Cursory scans did nothing to find him, the little chameleon having exceeded himself this time. But Cygnus and his counterparts knew the 'Dweller had been just ahead of them a minute ago and that there were very few places he could hide. Especially if they got close enough to him. 'Dwellers could not trick Vampires for very long when they were as young as this one. And Cygnus had watched and purposely hunted this young one. While Vampires already had the ability to blend into the shadows unseen, to fog the minds of passersby from noticing them, Cygnus knew 'Dwellers had other abilities, powers that they did not advertise. He knew this because he had seen them.

It had been about a century ago. Ironically enough, he had been out hunting with Damien at the time. Hunting Shadowdwellers. A little pack of them who had taken to causing trouble for Vampires along the borders of some of their territories. This little pack had been unwise enough to nibble at Damien's hunting grounds. The 'Dwellers would taunt whatever Vampire they found in the area, chasing off prey by scaring them or playing poltergeist tricks.

'Dwellers taunted humans as well. Though it was not blood they took, Damien did not appreciate the sloppy remains of a pack's roving that was left behind for authorities to question, making it harder for Damien to hunt and for Nightwalkers in general to remain incognito. Luckily, humans had a way of making up reasons for things they could not explain, and Damien had quickly caught up with the pack and given them a sound thrashing that had sent them back to New Zealand . . . or Alaska. Whichever it was at whatever time of year that remained darkest most of the day and night.

But before that had happened, Cygnus had been tracking a stray, a 'Dweller who had somehow gotten separated from her pack. He had chased that one, exactly the same way he was chasing this one. Only that time, when he had found the little bitch, she had looked at him, right into his soul, and twisted something around inside himself. It had taken him three days to come back to his senses. Three days to remember what had happened. He had never explained to Damien what happened to him, figuring the information might come in handy one day. He had never expected to be so right. He was very interested to see what exactly he would acquire when he stole this new aspect from the young 'Dweller.

Cygnus stilled suddenly, his senses flaring as he neared a brick building. Now that he knew the 'Dweller was there, the trick was separating him from the rest of the shadows.

Banda held his breath. He could hold it for up to six minutes if he needed to. But he would release it and redraw every time the Vampire passed far enough out of hearing. Which was not often, because the Vampire could hear very well. Then the leader's cohorts caught up to him, making it much worse. Banda's odds plummeted as they crowded around. They were very focused on the building he hid against, so they knew he was near. All he had to do was maintain perfect concentration and he would stay safe, perhaps long enough for them to tire of the chase. He doubted it, though. Vampires were tenacious, and as hunters they could be extremely unhurried.

The lead Vampire passed Banda's path a fourth time, and the 'Dweller had to push down the fear that rose in his throat. He tried to hold his shadow. Tried like hell to focus. The Vampire suddenly whirled on him, reaching into the nothingness with unsheathed claws and grabbing Banda by the face. As Banda stumbled out of the shadows, he felt those talons puncturing five separate holes in his cheeks and forehead. The Vampire resituated his grip, creating five altogether different holes. He dragged the struggling Shadowdweller up against his chest, laughing and making his partners laugh as well.

The Vampire jerked Banda's head back with undue violence, nearly decapitating the boy with the force exerted against his light bone structure. Banda made a strangled sound of protest or fear, feeling the burning rip of claws again as the Vampire tore the collar of his shirt off his shoulder. The leader's palm prevented him from crying out, actually suffocating him in the process, forcing him to hold his breath again. He felt a cold, slimy tongue and hot, unnecessary breath licking over his neck, and he shuddered with revulsion. The tongue suddenly stopped, and Banda could feel his own pulse beating against that wet thing that sought it as fear pumped through him.

Cygnus reared back and struck with the speed of a snake, only he did not puncture and remove to feed as all of his kind did. He used his fangs to rip the 'Dweller's throat open on the side, blood spurting and welling all over his mouth and clothes as he took several long, drugging gulps of the powerful, fear-laced Nightwalker blood.

The others pressed forward for their turns.

* * *

"Sweet . . ."

"Mmm?"

"I really need to patrol the border. With those rogues out there, I cannot feel safe unless I do."

Syreena looked up at her husband from her position sprawled over his naked body. She had been lazily kissing his chest and neck, adding those sinful little licks against his throat that she knew drove him just shy of madness.

"Damien, you know they won't come here. It's certain death. With you, Stephan, and Jasmine in the same household? The household staff in itself is a small army. Did I mention the full guard and their meticulous security measures which you and Stephan both planned out?"

"Jasmine is not here," he pointed out, reaching to rub her irresistible shoulder, the pale line so graceful and elegant. Damien knew she tended to see herself more as a scrapper, a stalwart and steadfast support rather than a thing of great feminine beauty. She always insisted that her siren of a sister Siena, the sexy Queen of Lycanthropes, had inherited all the womanly genes along with her mountain cat aspects. He had very different opinions on the matter.

"Oh yes." Syreena sighed with happiness and snuggled back down to kissing his neck with a contented chuckle. "That's right. I was enjoying the peace so very much I had almost forgotten. Have I ever mentioned . . . ?"

Damien groaned and suddenly moved, dumping her off his body and gaining his feet. He ignored her laughter.

"Whatever it is, I would prefer you continue *not* mentioning it," he warned her, a storm of seriousness sweeping his dark features.

Syreena's continuing giggles told him she wasn't fazed by his warnings as she sprawled in their bed with her head hung over the edge, facing him, her charcoal hair snaking off the mattress all around her like a thousand little serpents. Since her hair was alive, with blood flow and feeling from root to tip, the imagery was completed as the soft waves sprang up to keep from touching the cold floor.

"Damien," she crooned as she looked at him upside down from her position. "You must have noticed that she has an incredibly bad habit of concocting urgent situations that always seem to coincide with our lovemaking."

Damien had known she was going to bring that up. Why wouldn't she? Jasmine had been subtle at first, but it was clear she was growing bolder and less caring about getting caught in her mischief. Jasmine's singular intention was to give Syreena grief and to play a power game with her.

The Vampire Prince looked at his wife, his response delayed for a moment by the sight of her irresistible body being spread out like a virgin sacrifice across the rumpled bedding. He also wondered if she was aware that she was absently running her hands over her body as they spoke. He could see no purposeful seduction in the movements, only that unending craving for stimulation that came with her current state of heightened sexuality. He made a soft, predatory sound in the back of his throat as his body instantly responded with hard flashes of heat and molten need that he knew would never be satiated, even after they'd been together for centuries. He loved her. Everything about her. From flaws to perfections, she was unbearably exquisite to him. And he wasn't even describing her physically, although he would confess to a partiality for the next few weeks.

He saw her smile, knowing her eyes were fully on his body, that she was taking a great deal of satisfaction in the way it was reacting as he watched her. She lifted an arm and crooked that naughty little finger at him again, beckoning him to her, knowing he would come and the knowledge of it flashing with smug confidence over her entire being. She purposely licked her lips, and Damien suddenly was made aware of their current positions and all their intriguing possibilities, if only he took a few steps forward.

"When she gets back, I will have a talk with her," he said before taking those few steps and once again forgetting all about patrolling his borders.

Kestra woke with a start, sitting up and blinking against the muted light as she tried to adjust.

Light.

The importance of light was instantly superseded by the smell of soap and steam. Then she saw Noah moving into the room from the far door, a towel swathing his hips and another in his hands as he dried his dripping curls. She found she was holding her breath as she watched him move. He was far too graceful for someone of his build, but too beautiful to be denied, either. His muscles flexed and moved beneath his skin with that repressed power that reminded her of a panther as it stalked slowly and with purpose through its natural habitat.

Likening him to a predator was only natural. He was just as polite and polished as she was, but as a woman she had advantages when trying to hide her dangerous and deadly sides. Simply, no one expected a sugar-haired blonde to pose a danger. But a male of his physical caliber fought the opposite prejudice—that all he could be was male and aggressive and quite possibly capable of violence, just as he was clearly built to be. But she was learning that there was far more to this man than his obvious virility, a depth that instantly sent a sensation of warning creeping across the back of her mind. She was getting too comfortable. She was beginning to like him. She couldn't afford attachments or, even worse, entanglements. Watching him stalk with such ease of power around the room, she realized she could be in over her head, and that if this man decided he wanted her, there would be nowhere she could hide.

The problem was, she had known that from the very first time she'd laid eyes on him. The crisis part of the equation was that she was aware it was already far too late to jump off the road that was careening so wildly in his direction.

Okay, fine, she reasoned. *This could be fun. It has great potential. He's damn sexy, an incredible lover even with a far too brief sample to go by, and he isn't an idiot who will bore me to tears.* She was attracted to him. Okay. Correction. She was hot for him. And he had that nice sense of honor and morality going on so that if she did want to bring it all to a crashing halt, she could just tell him what she did for a "living." Yeah, that would chase him off pretty damn quick.

All she had to do was keep from doing anything stupid. Like falling for him. Actually, in his case, it was probably best to reserve *all* emotions. Because for all his physical size and aura of power, the danger in Noah came from the threat he posed to a heart starved for even a small sense of closeness, anything beyond the camaraderie she shared with the only person she considered herself close to: James. And that was almost a stretch of the imagination in many instances.

"Hey, you are conscious."

The teasing remark drew her attention to Noah as he moved toward the wardrobe near the bed. How was it that she always ended up in his bed or in a room with one or both of them being half to fully naked? Just her luck, she supposed. Question was, was it good luck or bad luck?

Good. She watched him move and held back a sigh. *Definitely good*. The man was a walking sin waiting to happen. After all, she had already sinned *and* burned for it all at the same time. She was still burning for it. She could feel the physical ache of her body increase as he neared. Her libido remembered him on sight. Her mind did, too. If she could keep her heart and soul out of the equation, one plus one could equal two happily orgasmic people.

She knew he wanted her. She also knew that was an understatement. There was outright hunger in his eyes, though he tried to hide it behind clouds of smoke gray and his polished manners. Kestra reached up to toy with the neckline of her dress as she fixed her eyes on her target and didn't look away. Water beaded on his dusky skin, rolling down his chest, arms, and back with a tempting slowness. His muscular form made gravity work for its claim on the clear droplets of liquid. Kestra absently licked her lips as she thought about catching the drop currently running down his abdomen toward his navel.

That naturally focused her attention on the path of dark hair leading down to the edge of his towel, the cloth spoiling her fun and forcing her to skip lower. The dark hair on his thighs was wet, slicked down onto his skin. She had to confess to a weakness for the sheer power and maleness that seemed to be reflected in the rock-steady brace of his thighs. Kes shifted, warmth infusing her entire body as she thought about having the opportunity to touch, to taste . . . to smell up close the sensual scent of masculinity and smoldering sweet wood.

No, it wouldn't be so bad to enjoy him for a time if he shared her lighthearted intentions. She craved what he had made her feel. She was starving for it, in all honesty. Partly, she feared it was a fluke that had only come in the heat of that long-awaited moment in the parlor. She was afraid of never feeling that intensity again, that release. God, how she needed that release. It stirred within her so hungrily that a fine sheen of perspiration broke out across her skin. She had to draw in a shaking, cooling breath before she jumped him like a demented sex maniac.

This was so unlike her. Why was she thinking this way? Feeling this way? She was aroused and her body was seeking him even though he was ignorant of it as he moved easily around his bedchamber. If he took a moment to look at her, to see the glistening of her skin and the thrust of her straining nipples beneath red velvet, what would she do? Pull him down to her? Invite him to fill the hollow place he had left between her legs when he'd withdrawn from her the last time? Would that be such a crime?

Noah opened the wardrobe door and stepped out of her line of sight, carefully hiding his expression and forcefully tamping down the surges of emotion and need twisting through him like a storm. He bent his head and tried to breathe, tried to cool the raging torrent of heated blood flooding him into iron hardness until he throbbed painfully with it. Even if he hadn't seen the obvious sensuality wending sinuously through her body, even if he'd missed the rampant flush of her rising body temperature, he would have known her thoughts. They were so powerful that they had burst the confines of her mind and crashed into his. Not words or sentences, but bold impressions of her desire for him, of her cravings and the demands her body wanted to make upon his.

He had been used to receiving thoughts and impressions from his sister Legna. As a Mind Demon, she had always shared emotional impressions and experiences with him as practice and just because it was a knee-jerk response to their close sibling relationship.

But all of that was a mere shadow compared to the power of reading the wild thoughts of his Imprinted mate. To feel and to know of her appetite for him, to understand with undeniable clarity what she wanted on so base a level, it was intoxicating. However, she didn't know he was becoming able to read her thoughts, or that she could possibly read his as well. He had to be careful. With her inexperience, it could be *his* needs she was mistaking for her own. She could inadvertently be mirroring his own savage desires if she tapped into what he was trying so hard to repress. He had some mighty powerful passions locked up inside himself; Kestra endangered his control like nothing else could. While many of those passions could be intensely pleasurable, there were potentially dangerous ones as well.

Noah didn't think that even Demons fully understood the emotions that came with the element of Fire. They thought emotions were attributable to females and therefore, less dangerous. They thought he was all about the physical, the fire, and the energy. The emotions were for Hannah, his sister and a female Fire Demon.

But there were never absolutes when it came to Demon power past a certain age, or perhaps even in a certain genetic combination. As time ticked nearer to making an Ancient of him, his power grew, but additionally, his emotions grew more and more volatile. Only his study, responsibilities, and iron will had kept them under control thus far. Jealousy. Anger. Rage. Hatred. Passion. Love. Devotion. Hurt. Loyalty. Joy. Ecstasy. The potential was staggering. The times when others had thought he'd lost control? They hadn't suspected that he was actually still half in control in those moments of volatile overflow, that he wasn't truly flinging himself wildly into the emotional discharge. There was no true release for him, and he did not think there ever could be. Even so, losing half his control had made for some pretty impressive and damaging displays. He couldn't think about what he would be capable of if he ever lost completely his grip on his inner serenity. He had come so close before Kestra had arrived, before he'd finally touched her and smelled her sweet and soothing availability.

What would happen if someone as green and as unsuspecting as Kestra was were to accidentally tap into that volatility? With no training and no grounding? Noah had to prepare her. He was running out of time, and dawn would be approaching in only a few hours. What could potentially happen between them on the night of the Hallowed moon? No one knew. His kind was a rarity, his power phenomenal and unheard of at this age and level.

What if she wasn't yet strong enough to dampen the power surges he might give off in the heat of any given moment? He already knew he couldn't maintain control around her. His ability to protect someone close to his body from fire would protect her, but what of a castle full of aides and visitors? Servants and friends? True, on Samhain they were likely to be elsewhere, the holiday releasing them of duties and obligations by tradition, but those who had nothing to do or were afraid of their own needs were always welcome to stay.

Noah reached to rub at the tension in his temple. He was giving himself a headache with all of these thoughts and worries. There was too much to do and no time in which to do it right. That included taking his beautiful mate to bed the way she deserved, with nothing but honesty, truth, and full disclosure between them. The tension in his head exploded into tightening pain that coiled down the back of his neck and shoulders.

"I can't believe I slept the whole way here," Kestra offered at last when she got tired of trying to stare at him through the wardrobe door. "How is that possible? Car to plane to car and all the way up the stairs? I never sleep like that. I must have been boring company."

"You were exhausted and recovering," he countered, slowly looking through his clothes before settling on the more modern convention of slacks and a matching black polo shirt.

She supposed she had to accept that. She had to confess that she'd never remembered being so tired, so drained of energy.

Kestra's brow furrowed and she rubbed at her temple as an unexpected flare of painful tension shot across it and down the back of her neck. It was an instant tension headache, but she couldn't understand its sudden source. She was the calmest she'd been since she'd been rescued from Sands's apartment. Noah was pulling on his clothes behind the cover of the wardrobe door, so she was able to push the pain away and formulate a halfway decent smile by the time he emerged fully dressed. He walked around to her side of the bed and took a seat, once again by her hip, facing her. Since she was sitting up, it brought them very close and she could see the lines tucked at the corners of his eyes were not all there because of his smile. There was tension bracketing his lips. She reached to smooth the lines away with a gentle touch.

"Hey," she said softly, her heart suddenly hitching with confused excitement as it tried to settle on anxiety or exhilaration.

"Hello," he returned, his charming smile reaching the jade behind the smoke of his eyes.

"Are we going to have 'the talk' now?"

Apparently her reminder disturbed him. He reached up to his temple, rubbing at the spot with a strong thumb. At least she wasn't the only one rattled by all this, she thought with amusement.

"Kes . . . are you happy in your life?"

Kestra's breath stopped midexhale as the question impacted her. Her knee-jerk response was to tell him that she was really damn happy with her life, thank you very much, so go piss up a rope. She knew why he was asking. Her heart pounded her ribs into a pulp because he was asking.

"Sometimes." It was all she could force out of her clogged respiratory system. It was a lame response! She was supposed to be taking a stand here! What the hell was wrong with her?

"You strike me as the sort who leads a very full and busy life."

"I do," she agreed with more ease. His acknowledgment compensated for everything she hadn't gotten across to him. "And an unusual one. Both business and pleasure take me all over the world. I see and do things that make my life very . . . not run-of-the-mill."

"I can understand that. My life is not run-of-the-mill, either."

That she didn't believe. He had roots here in his big, anachronistic castle. She sensed he had a large network of supportive friends. He was just the type who would engender that type of loyalty. All she had to do was remind herself how easily he had slipped past her rather prickly defenses without her even realizing it. That took a skill with people that, frankly, she envied. It was a skill that produced attachments and ties, however, so she had long ago decided she was better off without it. She could see that he didn't make enemies easily, and while she tried not to, it almost invariably happened.

He'd said he was a cultural leader, which, while it could mean anything, implied responsibilities of a political nature. He was clearly some kind of rallying point for his people. He had to be. Only people with that kind of power and devotion used the term "my people" with such soft ease.

"I don't think your life is anywhere near as wild as mine is. I have some fairly hair-raising hobbies."

"Like?" he encouraged.

"Whitewater rafting, spelunking, cliff diving, base jump—" She broke off because she was watching his expression turn to very still stone. Not anger, not rage or irritation. Just still. "Noah," she said carefully, fending off disappointment, "don't ask me questions if you can't handle the answers. I'm trying to be truthful and I'm not by nature a truthful person."

Noah blinked at the rebuke, as gentle as it was. She was right. She was also using her enhanced intuition to see past the mask he tried to use to cover up his reactions to her death-defying list of relaxations. How could he explain to her how terrifying the thought of her being hurt or killed was for him? He couldn't bear life without her. Imprinting or no, he couldn't live in a world without touching her sugar-soft hair, tasting her sweet mouth, laughing at her barbed humor.

She was proving to be wise, stretching her limits to communicate with him, which proved her ability to adapt and be receptive if she wanted to be. He knew there was pain, that all of those hobbies and the rest of the danger she subjected herself to were an attempt to kill off a fear that she couldn't touch no matter how hard she tried. The closer her mind got to his, the more positive he was of that.

Still, he had no right to judge or to place limitations on

her. He hadn't even given her the courtesy of telling her that her life would change.

But he would.

"Kes, if you are looking for dangerous things, they are far closer than you might think," he said softly to her, reaching again to touch her hair. "You were born to be great. You were born to be in a position that will always be dangerous."

"I already know that," she said, looking at him with surprise and confusion warring in her features. "I just don't know how you know that."

You were born to be mine.

Noah looked dead into her blue-ice eyes and pushed the thought into her mind with all of his mental strength, with every trick Legna had ever taught him to help her read his mind.

Kestra felt a ferocious chill burst over her skin, her headache flared, and then . . .

The words entered her mind with a growl of permanence, impossible to be her own because they were in *his* voice, loud and clear, rich and sexy. There was no mistaking it, and there was no mistaking the look in his eyes that repeated the phrase over and over.

You were born to be mine.

"No," she whispered, instantly shaking her head and trying to dislodge the hand in her hair at the same time.

He only tightened his grip and brought them closer, very nearly placing his mouth against hers, their breath hot as it mingled against their faces in rapid rushes.

"Listen to me very carefully, Kestra. Look into my eyes and remember only one thing. Trust yourself. Trust yourself if you do not trust me. You laugh in the face of fear, remember? It is in everything I have seen and heard you do. I need you to be fearless for me, for just a little while, long enough to hear me out. Do not run away from me without letting me explain."

Kestra's eyes were wide, her breath was quick, but she couldn't form honest fear when she looked into his eyes. Not fear of him. Oh, she was terrified of what that thought floating in her head made her feel. She was screaming with that fear from top to bottom. But that had nothing to do with his belief that she was born to be his, and everything to do with the fact that she believed him.

All the way to her soul.

He shifted his hold on her head, his hand sliding to catch her around the nape of her neck, that soothing, protective grasp that so disarmed her, so relaxed her. God, his touch was like magic. It *was* magic. She was convinced of it now. He was some sort of magician and he was about to pull a bunch of bunnies out of his hat.

She laughed, not caring that it sounded a little hysterical.

"Okay," she said a bit breathlessly, "explain. Tell me all your secrets and I promise not to run screaming until afterward, if running and screaming are merited."

"Baby," he breathed against her lips, communicating with that single word how he ached to kiss her but wouldn't do so until he felt it was an honorable act. "I swear to you I can never do anything to hurt you. I need you to understand that. It is impossible. Hyperactive lovemaking aside, I will never willingly harm you. Do you believe that?"

"Hyperactive lovemaking?" She found herself grinning in spite of all the emotions holding a civil war inside her. How did he do that? Make her laugh when she was at the worst disadvantage with him? "That's a very good term for it. Elegant, tasteful, yet honest."

"Thank you," he said, eyes sparkling.

"You're welcome."

"But I need to know you believe me."

She did, but she couldn't speak for a minute. She was trying to piece something together in her head. Why had he mentioned their lovemaking, as if he had hurt her? They'd been pretty wild, very intense, but he hadn't truly hurt her. She was tougher than that. Perhaps he thought he had. The male ego could be an enormous thing.

Then she remembered her sunburn. Rug burn? No, no rugs involved. How had she been burned? She hadn't been in the sun, certainly not nude in October, which is what she would have to have been to get burned on her . . .

Noah could not help himself. Watching her thoughts and her struggle to hide her expressions was painfully poignant, and she looked so damned beautiful it hurt. Before he could curb the impulse, his mouth touched to hers.

Lightning.

It was instant reconnection, hunger, recognition, and a whipping burn of need that didn't like being held in check on either side. He'd meant to reassure her, to express some form of solidarity and faith in her ability to cope. Noah hadn't planned on the instant conflagration that came with kissing Kestra. *Why not?* When had he kissed her without these levels of passion arising like a wildfire?

Kestra made a sound of pure want, her hands coming into his hair to pull him closer, to push her tongue into his mouth because she needed to taste him. He was as hot as fire, tasted like smoky passions deeply repressed, waiting to be unearthed. She felt the tremor through his entire body everywhere her body contacted his.

She tasted like every sweet confection, her wonderful aggression pure aphrodisiac. Noah dragged her across his lap, needing contact with her, needing to feel the intensity of the heat of her body. He had no idea how he had kept control these past few days. How had he managed to deny himself after the way it had felt when they had come together?

Kestra was asking herself the exact same question. Why had she left him? She couldn't remember. What insanity, to walk away from so much feeling. As she settled into his lap eagerly, she felt how even just her kiss aroused him, the evidence of it snuggled against her bottom. God, she loved knowing that.

"No!"

Noah suddenly surged to his feet, pushing her back down to sit on the bed and forcing himself to back step away from her. He closed his eyes so he could regroup without having to look at the flush of passion on her mouth and the curve of need in her sensual body. Mostly, it was the confusion bordering on hurt in her eyes that was going to kill him.

"I mean . . ." He cleared his throat, cursing violently in his head at the waxing moon and all its influences. He could control himself. He knew he could. He had to. "Kestra, as badly as I want . . . Talking must come first."

The statement had his desired effect. The hurt was replaced by understanding, and he even saw respectful gratitude as well. Saw or felt. Their connection was getting stronger with every touch. Every moment.

"Thank you," she said softly, her hands smoothing down her skirt. "Not many men would . . ." She trailed off, already knowing he understood.

"Kes," he said, her name ardent on his lips as he added the passionate gesture of catching up her hands and kneeling before her feet. "I am not the man you think I am. Not in physical terms." Unbelievably, she arched that smug, knowing little brow at him and made him laugh. "That is *not* what I am talking about," he scolded her, squeezing her hands as if it were a punishment.

"Then please explain."

"I am not human, Kestra."

Okay, I was not expecting that.

The thought came through loud and clear.

What were you expecting?

Kestra's eyes went fabulously wide, her white lashes flickering with shock.

"Oh my God, you can read my mind!"

Kestra exploded out of his grasp and reach, stumbling across the room as a dizzy spell threatened to take her to the floor. She fought it off long enough to glare at him.

"Stop it right now! No mind reading! How long have you been—?" She broke off, remembering all the things she had been thinking since he'd come to her rescue.

"Relax, Kes, I have only just become attuned to your thoughts within this past half hour or so. I only catch the powerful ones. Our connection is not that strong yet."

"Oh. Okay. I feel *much* better now." She could not have gotten snider if she had paid others to help her. It cut him as fiercely as her passion did.

"The connection of our minds is a natural evolution to two extremely complementary souls, Kes. You can read my mind, too."

That seemed to give her pause. Instantly she began to concentrate, clearly attempting to read his thoughts of the moment. Her lashes blinked hard a single time.

"You think I am sarcastic and stubborn," she accused.

Noah gave her a charming half smile.

"See? I told you that you could read my mind." He rose to his full height and walked up to her, reaching out to catch her arm when the action of tilting her head back to maintain eye contact with him wreaked havoc on her equilibrium. "Did you get to the part where I think you are so beautiful that it almost hurts to look at you? That it takes every ounce of my willpower to keep from touching you? Kissing you? And nothing stops me from needing you. Soul-deep need, Kes."

Kestra instantly fell into the soft green and gray need reflected in his eyes. She couldn't understand why she wanted that so much, to be needed like he said he needed her. She had never wanted it before, was convinced it wasn't a part of her makeup. The words "I need you" had repulsed her from the beginning of time.

She blinked.

From the time she'd last heard them.

Noah felt the black rush of memories and fear explode over her like a violent malevolence. He had felt her answering need a moment before, but then she had taken a turn into a dark place, a place where evil lurked in her mind, scarring her in a way she thought could never heal. *Should* never heal. This, he realized, was the heart of her need to fight fear with dangerous hobbies and probably dangerous work.

"I don't do need," she said hoarsely, trying to pull her arm free. "I don't need anyone, and I resent you needing me for anything. You have no idea who I am. You have no idea what you're touching! I don't know you! I don't even know what you are!"

"I am a great many things, Kes," he countered calmly. "I am a King. I am an immortal Nightwalker called Demon. I am Fire. I am a brother, an uncle, and a friend. Most of all, I am your soul mate. We were born into this universe meant for each other. You are for me and I am for you. Your fear will not change that. Do you know what you are? Are you sure?" he pressed before she could speak. "You are Druid, Kestra. You are no longer just a human being. The day we met, the day we came into contact, you became much more than human. You will grow in power, though I do not know how, and you will become immortal."

"The day we met?" she asked weakly.

"When you were born, it was with a specific genetic code. That code is attuned to mine. As mine is to yours. That is why we searched for each other, how we found each other in our dreams. Once I understood you were somewhere out there for me, I must have opened my mind to you. Then, when our bodies came into contact, when I first touched you, it triggered a cascading change in your genetics, birthing your power, making you ready to be my other half, connecting us in life and death for all time."

"You are a madman," Kestra gasped, this time succeeding in yanking free of his hold and backing away from him. "You're crazy!" she screamed, hysteria edging her voice.

"No, I am not. Do you see me?" he demanded in cold, blasting severity. "Do I seem crazed or manic to you? Have I acted rashly and with intent to harm you?"

"No, but you will! I know!" She was gasping for breath, clutching the furniture. "Oh God, how stupid I've been! You think I was born for you? You think we are destined to be together forever? You think these promises are *poetry*?"

"Kestra, you do not understand, baby. Please calm—"

"No! I do understand!" Kes dragged in a breath, wheezing and hunching over into herself like a wounded animal, grasping at the agony clawing through her chest. "You're insane. It doesn't stop. And I can't . . ." She shuddered and shook so hard that she couldn't finish speaking. Her face turned a florid red and she collapsed to her knees and hands, trying to breathe and hold herself up at the same time. Noah was there instantly, dragging her into his body, finally realizing that this wasn't just about hysterics or normal disbelief in the face of the unbelievable. He realized she was having a violent panic attack.

His Kes. His fearless Kes.

And suddenly he understood.

He held her as she flailed for breath, gasping, clutching at the incredible pain in her chest, tears of agony streaming down her face.

"Easy, baby, easy," he soothed her in a fast whisper, trying to penetrate the screaming of her brain. "It is not what you think. Shh . . . I swear it is not. I did not know, *Kikilia*. I did not know. I would have found another way to say it if I had known. I am so sorry. Shh. Breathe, baby, breathe."

She couldn't. Not when she thought he was like the one from her past. The one who had caused the evil scars within her. The one who had given birth to the fear she tried so hard to fly in the face of.

The one who had hurt her in the name of his love for her.

How could he make her believe that this was not the same? That this was truth and she would know it if she just listened to her own spirit? How to make her believe this was not about obsession, but about Destiny?

How could he make her breathe?

For all his power—the energy, the Fire, and the force he could compel—he could not compel her to breathe!

Noah closed his eyes and tapped that power, his entire soul screaming out in fear and fury as Kestra passed out in his arms and went deathly still.

Every Elder Demon in a hundred-mile radius felt the raging torment of their King. Even some of the adults were sensitive enough to hear the cry. But it was not a summons for them to answer. It was meant for one and only one Demon to hear, and those who were up to date on the workings of the court feared she was too far away to receive the message.

Chapter 13

Legna leaned over her son, her incredibly long hair falling like a protective curtain around him as she reached to kiss his tummy, making him squeal with laughter. The beautiful Demon mother glowed with love and patience even when her sixteen-month-old son grabbed her hair and held on to his prize for dear life.

"He has his father's penchants," Gideon mused, looking on from a chair very close to where they were settled on the floor at his feet. He leaned forward and stroked loving fingers through her cascade of coffee-colored hair. He wore a necklace made of her tresses, the only jewelry he had ever worn in his Ancient lifetime. It had been a gift from her just after they had wed. The day they had learned their son was coming.

Legna extracted herself from Seth's death grip on her hair, sitting back on her heels and smiling at her husband as his hand lingered on her back.

"That is all well and good, but I think I will have you braid my hair for the next few years. He is a little hard on my poor scalp."

Instantly Gideon reacted. He reached for her abused hairline, his powerful healing abilities more than compensating for her soreness. It was gone in an instant, and she reached to kiss him in gratitude.

She never quite made it. To Gideon's shock, his wife was suddenly plucked from his grasp. She flew backward across the room—a full ten feet—before she crashed into the wall, as if she were a rag doll thrown by a spoiled child having a temper tantrum, and slid to the floor limply. Gideon instantly went to move, but she was still in the air and only halfway across the room before the backlash in her mind reached her Imprinted mate.

Gideon roared with the pain exploding in his head. He heard the answering cry, the torment, felt the path arcing from the brother to the sister and overflowing into the husband. The medic's brain, as powerful and sophisticated as it was, was not made for the abuse. Blood vessels burst and his nose began to bleed in a torrent. It was a tribute to his powers of healing that he didn't lose consciousness, that he managed to avoid the hundreds of little strokes popping in his brain with devastating potential.

He couldn't succumb. If he was suffering only backlash, his wife was being bludgeoned to death. Gideon gasped as he gained his feet, fighting himself to step over his son without falling on him. He staggered to his wife, healing himself internally the entire time with a calm that belied his horror at the sight of his beloved mate lying unconscious on the floor, blood leaking from her nose, ears, and eyes.

Never in all of his life had he suspected Noah was capable of such power. Since Gideon knew Noah would never knowingly harm his sister, he doubted Noah even knew it himself. Gideon laid hands on his wife, rapidly healing her, focusing everything he had on her, now ignoring his own pain and injuries. He said a fast prayer of thanks that he had been there, that he had been with Legna when this had happened. What if he had been abroad on some errand? There were no Demon healers in the Lycanthrope court besides himself. In his unleashed fear and fury, Noah would have unknowingly killed his adored sister.

Gideon gently wiped away her blood with his fingertips as she stirred. He bent to kiss her forehead, finally able to breathe again now that she was moving appropriately.

"You are all right, *Neliss*," he soothed her. "I have to go to Noah."

"No, wait." She cleared her throat, trying to rid it of weakness. "Do not tell him."

Gideon understood. "If I do not tell him and he does it again, he could kill you if I am not with you. He nearly did in spite of my presence."

"It will destroy him if you tell him." Her beloved eyes were begging, though she knew he would always do anything to secure her happiness. "Warn him. Tell him less. Only enough to moderate him. Only do not tell him of this."

"As you wish, my love," he whispered. "Can you teleport me?"

She sat up with his help, but she nodded.

"I will ask Elijah to care for Seth. You will rest."

She didn't give him a single argument.

Gideon entered Noah's bedroom with a pop of harshly displaced air. Gideon saw the King clutching his mate, his face ravaged with panic. She had passed out and now lay pale and limp in Noah's arms, gasping for breath in little hitches. Her lips were blue.

"She had a panic attack. I thought when she passed out it would get better but . . ." Noah became speechless, explanation unnecessary to the great medic.

Gideon wordlessly reached for Kestra, his fingers touching her throat as he closed his eyes and sank into her struggling body, searching for all the signals and warnings that would lead him to his answers. She had a very healthy body overall, which made it much easier to sort out minor glimmers of illness from that which was serious. When the body entered a crisis, it pooled all resources and sent them screaming to the area of alarm. Gideon was swept along for the ride.

"Asthma. She has asthma, set off by her panic. Her lungs are completely closed off."

As he assessed Kestra, the medic also reached to touch Noah on his shoulder. He made it appear to be a gesture of masculine support, a comforting grip of reassurance, but he was far too aware of the volatility of Noah's emotions in the moment. He covertly, gently, manipulated the chemicals pumping too much adrenaline into the Demon King's body.

Noah instantly began to calm, to regain composure. He had no reason to doubt Gideon's medical skills, he remembered. Gideon could heal with miraculous power and speed. The medic had managed to heal himself from death once, only one of a dozen miracles Noah had seen him accomplish over the years.

When Kestra took her first full breath, a long ragged gasp that echoed into the room, Noah actually sobbed with relief, unable to help himself. Another harsh breath, much-needed oxygen coming with it, and her color began to return. Noah dragged Kestra to his chest as Gideon was forced to find a new touch point of access into his patient's body. The nearest point was her hip, so he allowed the King to purge his emotions and simply touched two fingers to the supple red velvet covering Kestra's pelvis.

Technically, Noah shouldn't be hugging her, as it would restrict her breathing, but given another minute, even that wouldn't matter, so the medic said nothing. He would have her healed completely of her crisis. As her eyes opened and she gasped a deep breath, Gideon also removed the remnants of heat exhaustion from her body. There was some small damage and weakness from her temporary removal from Noah's energy too early on in her growth into a Druid, but it would heal quickly enough in spite of Gideon's inability to aid her in that respect.

Gideon couldn't explain why, but suddenly he was sure he was the center of Noah's mate's attention. He looked up and met her eyes, a pale and glittering gaze, like blue glacial ice cut into gems. She didn't speak, nor were there any traces of her initial panic. Gideon had soothed her body chemistry into perfect balance, but that didn't mean she wouldn't ruin his work with chaotic thoughts.

However, it wasn't that knowledge that allowed a strange sensation to walk down the back of his neck. It caught hold, capturing all nerve impulses and cutting off his brain from his spine until he was relaxed into a paralysis that he found fascinating and even a little frightening. He probably could have broken away from her, but he didn't, his curiosity as a scientist of the Body getting the better of him.

In her eyes he saw clarity and understanding. There wasn't even a blink of an assessing expression. Her comprehension was instantaneous. He realized then that she *knew* what he was. She knew he was Demon and all that this meant. She now held in her mind a blueprint of his capabilities, his peaks of power and, most of all, his places of weakness.

Noah finally realized both Kestra and Gideon were staring at each other and sitting still as statues as they did so. His hold on Kes loosened, and it allowed her to sit forward. She reached toward Gideon's face, toward the edge of his silver eyes. She laid her hand against the side of his cheek and they continued to stare at each other as if entranced. Noah was beginning to understand that this had nothing to do with common curiosity, that there was an undercurrent of something else.

That there was power.

He felt it suddenly, though it had been growing the entire time as Gideon and Kestra had threaded together through their joined gazes. His heart skipped a beat, only to pound all the harder to make up for it. He didn't know what to do and didn't understand what exactly was going to happen. He wasn't precisely afraid for Gideon, because even Bella couldn't affect him with her awesome power to steal ability from others. So he let the exchange continue, standing ready and waiting.

Gideon felt her following her blueprint, her mind technical and calculating as if she was very familiar with reading and interpreting complex schematics. He felt her tracing within him with a cool sapphire light, a small concentrated orb of color and energy mapping over every path of power, through all the access points to his gifts, examining them one by one, voracious with curiosity.

"Astral projection," they said softly in unison, startling the Demon King, though he didn't show it or allow it to disturb them.

They spoke in tandem because Kestra's mind now controlled all of Gideon's autonomic and voluntary impulses. His vocal nerves picked up the signal of her brain when she sent the desire to speak to her own systems.

Kestra continued on, the sapphire orb of inquisition examining his ability to astral project, measuring it, admiring its scope and all the things he could do with it that no one knew he could do. Then she went a little further and traced the energy slightly into the future, traced the paths of potential he hadn't yet reached or discovered, and saw what he couldn't do, but one day would master.

"Astral healing," they said as they understood that potential for what it was. Gideon's low voice blended with her strong feminine one, and it was almost like music, a symphony she was directing. Gideon had always suspected that one day he would be able to heal in his astral form, and he had even experimented with the possibilities. He had felt on the verge of it, had known it was possible, and yet hadn't attained even a glimmer of success. Now he knew he would. He suddenly knew how he could find the path.

Because she had shown it to him.

Instinctively, he broke into her control over his motor skills; his free hand came up to circle the wrist of the hand against his face. It was not a restriction, but a show of gratitude. Gideon was also aware of the burn of power it was taking for her to chase her curiosities within him, that she was fascinated enough to continue on until she had examined every last power and its potential. She would flame out long before then, her untried power not yet ready or trained to go any further without ultimately damaging her.

"Kestra," he said quietly, firmly. "Release yourself from your task. Pull back toward your own energy; find your home in your own body. I know you are curious, but you have all the time in this ageless existence to discover more."

"Kes," Noah said softly into her ear, adding the familiarity of his voice to the call, "I know this is exhilarating and new, but I also know you are a thrill seeker, not one who has a death wish. You know the difference between using safety measures and being reckless. Be safe now. Harness this. Let us talk awhile about this and plan your next adventure."

She blinked. Gideon sighed and sat back with the release, freeing her hand but instinctively maintaining his healing touch against her hip, although his focus had disallowed any healing while Kes had studied him so closely.

Kestra looked at Noah, met his eyes, but he brushed his hand gently over her gaze.

"No, *Kikilia*. I know your thoughts. I know you. Knowledge removes fear, and you think if you know me, know my power, then you will learn not to fear me. While this is plausible, it is not safe for you to do right now. But I promise you," he added with a great intensity of emotion that drove his sincerity home to her, "I promise you that we will do this together, and you will know me like no other knows me. This is the way of Imprinted mates, and I am not afraid of it. Not with you."

All at once, Kestra understood the enormousness of responsibility and the trust that would be required for something like that. Even the silver-eyed healer had allowed her unprecedented access, never once thinking of shutting her out, of not meeting her with trust. She now knew him to be an enormously powerful being, one who didn't reveal his weaknesses to anyone. But she knew them all now. Some she herself could exploit just with her human skills, others she could never manage, but she was grasping quickly that there were those out there who could. There was an entire network of beings who wielded gargantuan power just as these two men did. Not just their breed, but several differing breeds.

"Nightwalkers," Noah whispered to her, making her aware once more that he was in her thoughts.

"So." She paused to clear her throat. "You weren't speaking metaphorically about all of this, then?"

The way she cast her eyes up at him, her lips pressing back her wry smile, made him chuckle low and soft, relieving him so very much that he dared to press his lips to her temple.

"I am not the metaphorical type, baby," he informed her.

Kes flicked her eyes back to the medic. "Thank you. For what you did. I haven't had an asthma attack in a very long time."

"It was brought on by your panic and the addition of this heat exposure you seem to have had." Gideon didn't even look at Noah, but the King felt his reprimand anyway. *She should have been to a medic immediately*, Gideon was thinking. "But I am happy to inform you it will very likely be the last one you will ever experience. Between my skills and the changes in your body, you will no longer be susceptible. Your body will rewrite a lot of your weaknesses and old injuries as you become Druid. Your ability to heal is stronger already, though a fraction of what it soon will be."

Gideon completed his sentence, but an expression chased over his face and she could see the abrupt end to one thought as another was formulated. His head and eyes moved almost imperceptibly, but it was the slide of his fingers from her hip to low on her belly that made her understand. His fingers sought her scar, and her heart lurched with a thousand feelings. Fear again. Dread. Pain and loss. But the worst was the sudden flare of hope, a wild surging that she didn't even know she was capable of. She struggled to smash it down, turning her face away and into Noah's chest, her hands gripping the fabric of his shirt.

"No."

She whimpered the word, her pain causing Noah instant agony. He saw the track of Gideon's fingertips and struggled with blinding impulses. The touch was too intimate. Jealousy. It was hurting Kestra. Protectiveness. It released the memory of trauma and that connection to evil that blanketed their joined minds in blackness so thick it was suffocating. Resentment. Fury. The blinding necessity to lash back, to fight, to destroy the source for all time.

"No."

This time it was Gideon who said the word.

It fell hard and harsh, a warning to the King and his whirlwind of uncontrolled emotions, and a rejection of the hand that reached out and clamped around Gideon's wrist. In his rush of emotion, Noah would crush Gideon's bones to dust if that was what it would take to make him cease hurting his mate.

"What manner of accident caused this?" Gideon directed the question to Kestra, who was already shaking her head in refusal. "This trauma is very old. You must have been quite young. They repaired your uterus, but you lost an ovary. Just the same, this level of scarring makes it impossible for you to carry a child."

Kestra sobbed as Gideon aired out her dirtiest laundry. Noah's death grip on Gideon's wrist fell away like dust in the wind. Kestra was keening, a terrible sound of grief and hurt unlike anything he had ever heard. It tore into him like thousands of blades, scorching him with agony, as if he were standing on the surface of the sun. He clasped her even tighter, sealing her to his pounding heart as he cradled her head in his hand. He felt her hot tears touch his skin at his collar. She then laughed a slightly wild laugh against Noah's neck.

"Are you ready for forever now?" she asked in a hot whisper. "Are you ready to be a King without an heir? A man with no hope of a child? Will you see me with all that beautiful, mindless passion now? Or will you look at me like all the rest—broken and defective?"

"Kestra," he said with soft, scolding pain. "I am ready for only one thing, and that is you. You are perfect for me. You are perfect *to* me." Noah raised hard eyes to the medic, but Gideon was moving to make his retreat. Legna was already in his mind and she snatched him out of the room with a teleporting pop.

"Look into my mind, baby, and understand me," Noah urged Kestra gently. "I have always thought to have a child one day, but I have lived over six centuries without one and felt no great loss, because my house literally runs over with fosterlings and *very* short kin who leave too many toys around. There is only one thing I have ever craved with all of my heart and soul. From the first time I saw my parents kiss and look at each other with the boundless love that only comes with the perfection of mated souls, I have hungered for my soul mate. She who would be Imprinted on me for all time. I have aspired to nothing as much as I have yearned for this one thing. Not my throne, not my power, not my scholarship. None of these has mattered to me with the intensity with which I have wanted the one who would look into my eyes with that level of love and devotion I saw in my parents' locked gazes, who would long for the same from me. The one. The only one.

"I have finally found you, baby, and nothing but Destiny herself can take you from me. Nothing you say will drive me from you. Nothing. Do you understand? You will be my love. I pray that I will be yours. I pray that I am worthy enough to earn it."

"Why me?" she asked, huge tears refracting the crystal blue of her eyes as she bored her gaze into his. "Why waste this on a woman who has never known love? Who can't even be sure she can feel it? A barren woman. A woman who is afraid of nothing except this one thing you're asking of me. You offer devotion, obsession, centuries where you believe you won't tire of me? I'm not that naïve, Noah."

"Why do you use that word? Obsession? You keep using it, like a talisman to ward me off. I feel and know that scarred place within you, and it has nothing to do with your womb, Kestra. Tell me of this one who haunts you," he demanded fiercely. "This one who makes you so afraid to be loved and adored by me. The one who blackened those words for you forever, making them a curse instead of the blessing they truly are."

"The one who loved me so much that he would kill me rather than let anyone else have me?" She shuddered. "The one who couldn't accept that I never loved him and never would. He did everything so sweetly at first. His words were like poetry, and he was just as charming as you are, but jealousy and possessiveness reared up and he became ugly. Then the ugliness would fade back to charm as he begged for forgiveness. I forgave once, but never again after that. I turned away from the pretty words and the cajoling and he screamed for me. Day and night, walking in my every step, my every move interpreted as an invitation, my every rejection everyone else's fault except mine and his. Two years he haunted me. Stalked me. He hunted me like an animal and I lived in fear. I was fifteen when I met him, and I was seventeen when all that love and obsession finally turned to hatred and rage. I was seventeen when I came home from school and found my mother stabbed to death in the bathroom, my father slaughtered in the garage . . ."

Here she sobbed once, hard, the memories flooding her, flooding Noah, and he struggled to keep the violence of his reaction down. He knew what was coming. Like a tidal wave, it was an inevitability.

"Tell me," he managed to choke out, his arms tightening around her, his kiss in her hair.

"It never occurred to me he would still be there. I . . . I couldn't leave even if it had. Leave my mother? My father? What if they were still alive?" Her memory of being covered in her parents' blood washed into him, her vain attempts to stem the flow from fatal stab wounds in her mother's neck and throat. Blood on her hands. Blood on her cheerleading uniform.

And then hands in her hair.

Noah saw it without her recitation, and she knew he could see it. Hands in her hair, dragging her to a fresh point of slaughter. Fists against her face and body, endless pain as a rage she didn't deserve was loosed upon her. Now her blood, broken teeth, broken ribs, broken arms and hands as she tried to fend off the blows. An offensive hit that threw him off her body. Rolling over, crawling.

Screaming, fiery pain as the knife slammed through the back of her thigh, tearing through her flesh, the tip breaking off against her thighbone.

And then he was on her, beating her again, but refusing her the bliss of darkness so she would be awake for the rape that went on endlessly. The police arrived while he was still inside her, trying to spend himself again on the pleasure of her pain. In his final fury, he plunged the blunted knife low in her belly, a purposeful attempt to make himself the last to ever use her as a complete woman.

Even as she lay in shock, begging God for mercy, death, or at least unconsciousness, she watched them shoot her assailant in her own living room. It was the end of evil, but it didn't matter. He would never die now. He would always be there. Buried deep within her like the knife.

Yet she never shed a tear. She couldn't. *He* would win every time she did. And she swore from that day she never would. She would never be a victim again, and she would never love anyone for fear . . .

For fear.

And she never had. Until Noah. He had touched her. He

brought with him urges that she found she couldn't resist. He resurrected wants and needs that had died with the plunge of a knife when she was only seventeen. She used sex as a control, a tool. Men who got too close were used and discarded coldly, assuring an end to friendship and caring. The very thing she had tried with him.

Except none had touched her like he had. None had made her burn, lit forbidden fires and desires. None but Noah had given her pleasure. She had thought pleasurable sex a lie or fairy tale; she had thought lovemaking an impossibility. Noah had come along and had changed everything, crawled under her defenses, and terror gripped her until she felt as though she were once more lying in helpless shock, waiting to see what horror would happen next.

She could fight anything; she could detonate the entire globe, sabotage the most powerful men in the world and bring them to their knees with both bombs and femininity. She was lethal, every step she took a danger to others.

Yet Noah had stripped her of her power, just as surely as he was setting off the changes to give her new ones. The Demon who claimed to be her Imprinted mate, claimed dependence on her for all time, promised the poetic possibilities of a depth of love unlike any she had known.

But one *he* had known.

Kestra suddenly raced into his memories, desperately needing to see what he knew. There was no stopping her as she rushed through them like a microfilm scanner, zipping to the one thing she wanted.

Sarah and Ariel.

His parents. Imprinted. The love, the touches, the need. Endless, beautiful need. Not obsession, but uniformity of living. Ariel had been so different from Sarah. He had passed on his position of Enforcer to his brother in order to marry her. He had become a warrior instead, just to please her. Still a fighter for his people, only different now. He was athletic in build, as dark as Sarah was light. Eyes of ice and blue like

Kestra's, only far darker. Hair as black as night. Sarah was blond and light, delicate in frame and petite against the height of her mate. He was aggressive and spoke his opinion like law; she was more temperate, willing to see all sides, and lovingly willing to coax her husband into seeing them as well. She mediated when he stormed. She railed and he teased her to frustration. She enjoyed riding through the night, so he bought and bred her beautiful animals on which to do so. He worried she missed her life of royalty, knowing he was too intemperate to ever become King. She worried she couldn't give him the son he wanted so badly. But through it all they had loved. Rhythm, movement, and thought, all the harmonious symphony of two separate souls joined to make one. One in love. One in understanding. One in allowing those things that needed to be separate about them to maintain individual identity.

Ariel and Sarah. Hannah, Noah, and Magdelegna, the treasures of a wonderful union that had lasted for centuries. Sarah had given Ariel a son. Ariel had given Sarah a future King. Kestra saw them both within Noah. Aggression and excessiveness of desires and emotions, restricted by temperance and diplomacy. A scholar like his mother; a warrior like his father. The dark good looks of Ariel; the gentle, loving heart of Sarah.

Then she saw the tragedy of their deaths, as little dealt with as her own pain, as horrific as what she had suffered.

"Oh God . . ." she gasped, reaching to wrap her arms around his head, holding him tight and close. "Oh, Noah . . ."

The King fought back pain as she slid into his memories of that day, the day he and Gideon had found Sarah flayed apart, raped and eviscerated by one of their own. The very same horror as Kestra had suffered. Only, it had been a random act out of the blue instead of a purposeful torture, instead of a bomb ticking away waiting to explode. The child Magdelegna, only a few years old, looking for her mother and finding her before they could protect the scene. How to live with that child's expression? What choices to make? To suddenly be the head of the household as Sarah's mate fell into despair? How could Ariel exist without Sarah? He had felt every thought, every moment of torment and pain before she had died. Too far . . . too far from her to stop it. Failing her. Failing his children. Failing his heart and soul as halves of both were ripped away. Too far to stop his son from finding her. Too far to stop Legna from seeing what no toddler should ever see.

They had lost both parents that night. Ariel's devastation couldn't be assuaged. No Imprinted mate could survive the grief of such loss. They knew he would be gone within a year, one way or another, and there was nothing they could do about it. They didn't want to do anything about it. They wanted him to have mercy, to go and be with their mother beyond this lifetime. But even the dignity of his own death was denied Ariel. He was Summoned shortly after, taken by black magic and Transformed into a horrific monster. And Noah, having been made King by then and the pride of his parents, had to send his Enforcer out, ringing the death knell that would save the world from his ruined father. Jacob. Jacob, who had never known how much gratitude and love Noah had felt toward him for doing that service, for freeing his father from torture and torment.

And so ended a fairy tale. A love incorruptible.

"No . . ." Noah whispered against her ear as he heard the bitter ring of that thought. "You have to understand that the end of the story is unimportant, Kestra. All stories end. All life ends. Nature makes it so. And you know that it can be peaceful or it can be violent and cruel, but it is not the end that matters. It is everything that happens right up until that very last minute that matters most." He stroked fingers through her hair, knowing she listened as she held him tightly and breathed against his neck. "I know you understand this concept more than anyone I am likely to know. You had two paths before you when that terrible thing happened to you." They closed their arms tighter around each other in impulsive support. "Be forever a victim, or be anything and everything that savage thought he could take away from you. Oh, you make so much more sense to me now," he breathed, making her laugh, the tone low with spent tears.

"Don't get cocky. You don't know half the things about me you think you do," she taunted weakly.

"I am living in your mind," he reminded her in an intimate whisper. "I see the fire. I know Fire, Kestra. Come see mine, see the things I have done, justly and unjustly, all a part of learning my way through life. I see the fury you try to express with explosives. I feel the craving for deeply burning passion that you try to fill with danger. You are notorious? A mercenary? This is supposed to shock me or impress me? I wish to please you, so do let me know."

"You're mad as a hatter, you do know that, don't you?" She sighed the phrase, but there was no rancor to it, no power, and she was relaxed completely in his embrace. Her fingers slid into his loose hair, the curls still damp from his shower. She stroked through them slowly, the sensation singing through Noah as if a tuning fork had been struck to him. The vibration traveled from her fingertips and straight to his toes with some interesting pauses in between. "Nightwalkers, hmm?"

"Yes," he said carefully, not sure where her mind was going in spite of his newfound access to it. "Demons . . . my people. Vampires. Lycanthropes, Mistrals, Shadowdwellers, and more recently Druids like yourself. Although, your combined human DNA makes it possible for you to live in the sun, whereas we cannot."

"Thus the term Nightwalkers," she said dryly. "This sounds like a plot for a computer game or something." She paused a beat. "Why can't you go in the sun? I mean, what happens? Do you poof into dust—or is that just a Vampire thing?"

"Each species has a weakness to the sun, each reacts differently. For Demons it is like walking into a sleep chamber.

Everything about it is designed to make us fall deeply asleep. In muted light, or light colored through stained glass, the effect is wonderful and comforting. We sleep beautifully during the day when the sun filters in." He slid a hand beneath her hair to palm the nape of her neck. He just felt better when he was touching her, soothing her somehow as he talked of wild and strange things. "Direct sunlight, for the young, is deadly. They can die if exposed too long. Adults will feel debilitating lethargy, making it impossible to move or defend themselves. Elders feel it, too, but those of us who are more powerful can defeat the effect for a period of time with tricks of power manipulation and the like."

"You're very powerful."

It wasn't a question. Especially not for one who could clearly look into a being and gauge exactly that. Plus, she had access to all of his thoughts and memories now. Some, when touched, would show a conflagration of power and furious firestorms.

"You will be, too," he told her. It wasn't meant to patronize. It was a stark truth. She had to be powerful in order to dampen his passionate fury. Very powerful. "They will develop faster now that you are remaining close to me. A Druid's power comes from the touch of his or her soul mate. Druids need to feed on that Demon's energy in order to recharge themselves."

"Feed?" She sounded momentarily horrified as she tensed against him.

"Mmm. Like a battery. A toy feeds off the battery to function. In our case, that means being in each other's presence. Being close. Over time, it will not be so restrictive a symbiosis. But we will always need to remain in contact."

Kestra slid out of his lap, kneeling to face him and sitting back on her heels. Noah trailed his fingers off her neck, clearly reluctant to let her go. She shook out her sugary hair, the straight fall settling a little wildly around her shoulders. Her bold eyes regarded him for a moment.

"I don't care for the idea of being dependant on anyone."

"It is not a dependence, Kestra. It is a symbiosis. I provide for you, and you provide for me. It is the Imprinting. I could not survive without you any more than you could without me. Look into my thoughts. See what it has been like for me. See the nights of the Hallowed moons and their waxing and waning the weeks around."

He showed her. Kes was struck instantly with memories of those nights. Dark and gripping urges. Primal impulses to give in to the elemental nature of his power. It was like an endless whisper, growing louder as the moon waxed, begging him to respond, to obey. It cried for fire and mischief. Flame and passion. The body burned with need, a violent ache that even a menagerie of women couldn't sate, so he'd stopped trying. He hadn't taken a woman to his bed during Samhain or Beltane for centuries now. He'd suffered alone, burned alone. For ages he had been saved by the loving presence of his sister as she grew into her wondrous powers of the Mind. Her humor and knowing ways, her ability to ease his emotions just with the power of her voice. It wasn't a cure, but enough to keep his sanity.

But he had been so afraid when she'd left his home to be with her mate, Gideon. And he'd been right to be fearful. Not for himself. No. He never truly thought of himself. He thought of the others. The innocents. He was certain that if he lost control, he would destroy everyone he loved. He had hung on, every year worse than the previous, but never showing it. Never showing his torture, in order to be a figure of support for those who looked to him for their own sanity.

The recent years had been hell. Without Legna's calming influence, he'd suffered and screamed and blistered. He'd waited until he knew he would be alone, then gone to a cavern he had found a few miles away. The entire cavern was burnt and blackened from the release he had found. He'd scorched everything. Blasts, explosions, and streams of flame—his body covered in sweat, soot, and smoke, his power igniting until he exhausted himself beyond consciousness. He'd wake shortly after because he *was* energy, and his body easily regenerated. Then he would return to the Hall to try to study, or he would lose himself in sleep.

And then, last Beltane, he'd dreamed of her. He had lain in the cavern, exhausted and gasping for consciousness, and he'd dreamed of her. Her fire and her fight, her passion marking him for all time, the blaze between them more than anything he could create, blissful beyond anything he could imagine. He had awakened that time and every time after screaming with need, his body aching, heavy, and hard until he was in unfathomable pain. As empty as she had felt, so had he felt unfulfilled.

And then . . .

Lost.

He found her one second, and the next she was lost. Kestra saw what he had seen; saw the death she had met. The aftermath was a conflagration of rage and blind devastation. But he had rescued her. He had found a way. The path through hell. A walk through the defection from all he believed in, all he held most precious in morals and love and his very soul.

Again, lost. Control lost, friends lost, respect lost. Love and trust lost perhaps beyond repair. And as Samhain loomed so close, time was lost as he desperately tried to bring her into his world as smoothly as he could. As he tried to know her and let her know him. Their encounter in the parlor hadn't even begun to satisfy him, to satisfy her. The physical was an impulse; the emotional was an essential. It was her soul and her heart that he needed to soothe the beast of Fire inside him. It was her feminine power, her back-burn that would stop him in his path and forever keep him from causing harm or uncontrollable destruction. The passion of their bodies was just a symbolic explosion of their symbiosis, perhaps one day of their love, and definitely an outlet for the Fire within them both. One that would cause no harm to them or to others when their symbiotic relationship clicked into perfect position.

Kestra struggled to her feet, aware he was following her every movement, but he didn't touch her, knowing she was overwhelmed again and needed to just breathe and think. She sat on the bed and took deep breaths, not looking at him but feeling him hovering at the foot of the bed watching her, probably reading her mind. It was such a vast responsibility! She would be responsible for the sanity of a King, the sanity of a being of such enormous power, a power meant to be contained by her parasitic presence.

But as frightening as that was, she wasn't afraid of facing it. She felt inside herself that place of equal measure that was growing. She suddenly understood that she had scanned the power of an Ancient and powerful being, had taken him by surprise even. She'd shown him a path he'd been seeking for for centuries. In one heartbeat she'd started him in the direction of power that even his vast wisdom had been unable to find.

Her body was growing stronger. She'd be able to heal rapidly, she'd been told. Yes, this she was more than capable of handling. She worshipped strength, embraced the undiscovered thrill of the future she'd have as a being of power and the responsibilities that came with it.

She looked at Noah, understanding that helping him abate his Fire was going to be her top priority. It would mean passion beyond her wildest imaginings. This made her heart race, but there was no fear. There was hunger. No. *Starvation*. She was thirty-two years old. In all that time, there had been nothing but a frigid, gray existence where her body only felt alive flying in the face of danger.

But here lay a potential feast of feeling, spread before her in the form of a beautiful man, a magnificent lover, and a good soul. He would set her body to burn in a thousand ways, and she could see it in his quickly clouding eyes. Noah was in her mind, so he knew her thoughts. His hand was wrapped around a post at the foot of the bed, his knuckles white and lips pressed with restraint. Honor. Nobility at its most extreme.

Find the fear, Kestra, she thought to herself. *What should you be afraid of? Where is the danger? Don't walk in without knowing the danger.*

She was afraid she couldn't love him as he deserved. She was terrified of the danger that would cause to herself and others. He'd proved her body wasn't frigid. Could he do the same for her unpracticed, unwilling heart?

Noah came around the bed, walked to her, and took her chin between his fingers. He tilted her face up until their eyes met. "In this one thing, I ask you to trust me. I can show you the way. You think you are incapable of loving, but you also treat yourself as if you had no life before you were eighteen. You have pushed away the love of your parents, your friends, and your remaining family. But it was once there, Kes. You did love."

"And they suffered for it. I suffered for it," she said icily. "I will not love only to lose. What if—"

"No." He cut her off instantly. "Do not go to that place. You do not belong there. You never second-guess, never doubt. You only prepare, be safe, practice, learn, and grow in skills. These have been your precepts for all of your adult life. You chose not to live in fear in all things save love. It is time you apply those principles to that which frightens you the most. You look into your heart, see its needs, see its penchants toward me, and all you see is danger." He leaned closer to her, his sensual mouth smiling slightly as it hovered close to hers. "Jump, Kes. Just jump off and trust all your safety systems to work. Jump, throw your arms out, and feel the rush. It is incredible, and it is worth every second of it."

Chapter 14

"Now, the trick with Demons," Cygnus lectured, as if he were a professor at Cambridge, "is to know their element. The ideal is to catch them in the daytime, when they are sleeping, but that way is very painful."

The others chuckled, except Cygnus's brother. Quinton was not amused. He had to grudgingly admit that Cygnus was really good at stalking Nightwalkers. They each now had aspects of Mistral and Shadowdweller in addition to their Vampire skills. They were confident they could take down a few of the lesser Demons. An adult. The women were not powerful and not worth it, so it had to be males.

"However, there is an advantage we mustn't overlook. Samhain." Cygnus grinned. "It's tomorrow. I have something good planned for tomorrow, but tonight is pretty powerful in itself and, well . . . let's just say there are going to be a lot of horny Demons out there. Catch one while it is rutting, and he will never have a chance. Capturing the power of a Demon for ourselves, no Summoning necessary." He chuckled with the others. "The trick is, what element to choose?"

"We need no telepathy or healing."

"Do not rule out Mind and Body. Mind Demons teleport and Body Demons have astral projection powers as well. For both reasons, however, it would risk exposing us if they got the opportunity to warn others. I would say a Water Demon. Or Wind. Both have weather abilities. Shape-changing to mist or wind, that would be very advantageous. Earth Demons are dangerous even at an early age."

"No Fire?"

"Fire," Cygnus mused. He made a show of tapping his chin in thought, and then he gave an evil grin. "That is what Samhain will be saved for. There is only one male Fire Demon. The Demon King. It would be the best time. He will be alone. The castle will be abandoned to the holiday after festivities. I figure if we get Water and Wind tonight, he will not be able to fight both with his Fire."

"It would be wise to wait. To practice untried abilities," Quinton argued. "There is time for Beltane."

"Perhaps. We shall see what happens tonight. I have other ideas as well. We will have a glorious time either way. Follow me, I think I see our first candidate."

They fell into the shadows behind an unsuspecting young Demon male.

Noah kissed her then, feeling their hearts beating the same wild rhythm. His mouth stroked against her softer one, gently tasting her lips, little sips of that natural sweetness that he simply couldn't figure out the source of. He had to believe it was just Kes, only Kes. His Kes.

"My Kes," they said together, against each other's mouths. Noah smiled just as she reached to kiss him a little deeper, and she laughed into his mouth just before their tongues touched.

"Do I really taste like sugar?" she asked between breaths and kisses.

"Find out for yourself," he encouraged her, the invitation somehow sounding sexy and forbidden. She pulled back, looking at him curiously, taking a moment to think. He reached to stroke a lone finger through her bangs, completely under the spell of watching her think about so many things, feeling her struggle with small surges of caution and apprehension.

He met her eyes with purpose, lowering to touch her mouth, sweeping his tongue playfully across her lower lip. He made an appreciative sound, licking her taste off his lips, his eyes gleaming with a smoky dare.

Kestra reached for the back of his head, securing him by lacing his hair between her nestling fingers. She held his eyes, searched them for a moment, and then he felt her flickering through his senses, felt her adjust for a moment to being behind his eyes, focusing on herself and how he saw her to be.

"You are beautiful," they said, her merge into his thoughts so perfect every time that she kept mistaking his impulses to speak for her own.

Noah left his eyes open, wanting her to see and feel everything he could provide, wanting her to know what a blessing it was for him to have her. He took her mouth gently, ignoring the inviting parting of her lips for a moment so she could pay attention to the full effect. He inhaled slowly and deeply, catching her scent, bringing it deep into his lungs where it stirred up sensory memory of over a hundred cotton candy dreams. They made an aching sound of pleasure as just these small traces of data sent stabs of heat streaking like hundreds of little fireballs down through his body.

When he finally nudged his way into her mouth, sweeping her taste onto his tongue, she could feel his heartbeat quickening, could feel his arousal as if it were her own, so unbelievably heavy, a straining need for her, for even the slightest detail of her. She did taste like sugar. At least she did to him. And she was shocked to find it was the truth, although she hadn't truly doubted him. His senses were so different than hers, so much sharper, so focused and powerful. She could hear her own heartbeat through his ears; she could smell the teasing flirtation of her own excitement.

Kestra gasped, jerking back away and into her own mind, her eyes wide with wonder and her cheeks stained with a ridiculous blush.

"I d-didn't realize . . ." she stuttered softly, pressing her hands to her face. "Your senses are so . . . so strong." She laughed. "I have the strangest and most desperate urge to take a shower."

"You do not require one," he said. "But I am ever the gracious host."

He reached for her hand and jerked her up from the bed and against his body. He secured her to himself with a tight arm around her waist, fitting her to every detail of his incredibly healthy form. His gray and green eyes were dark and knowing with his blatant desire for her. She was mesmerized and couldn't look away. He kept her feet barely touching the floor, moved, leading her backward across the room, again that debilitating tango that destroyed her equilibrium and every other thought that had nothing to do with him. He drew her entire focus, body and soul, making her feel his body, his eyes showing her his soul.

Forever.

She saw it. Maybe she heard it. But most of all she felt it. She felt his certainty of it, and knew it was the truth. He would never tire of her, he'd never be able to hurt her, he couldn't betray her and could protect them both from all the dangers she could imagine and even those she hadn't yet come to know. It wasn't an absolute. Life and death were absolutes in and of themselves, and no one could change what would be.

Except he had defied that. He'd cheated death for her. Who else would ever give her such a gift? Who else would ever need her so much? Need but release when she required a separate peace. Argue but reason. Communicate though speechless.

They entered the bathroom, gaslights flaring brightly to life though he touched no switches. Candles flamed on their wicks, then lowered to muted softness. He moved her, his masculine body rippling with power and grace against her with each step. He smelled so good that she leaned in to him to breathe the smoky scent of his essence. He stopped their progress, simply feeling the sensations running over him as she did this, knowing she took pleasure in it just as he took delight in the fragrance of her.

"You showered, but you still smell like me," she noted on a whisper under his ear.

"I could not possibly wash you away even with a thousand showers, baby," he said, his intensity giving her a delightful shiver. "You are a part of me now."

"Why is it when you call me 'baby' I don't want to punch you out like I usually do when men think they can call me that?"

"Mmm, I have an answer for that, but I will keep my counsel on it for a little while longer." She lifted her head and narrowed her ice blue eyes on him. He covered the glare with a hand, making her laugh. "No fair reading my thoughts. Not about something I have just deemed semiprivate. You have no scruples."

"I confess I do not. Well, I do have the important ones." She watched as he reached into the shower stall behind her and turned on the taps. Steaming water streamed into the huge cubicle from all sides. "I just believe that if you have a resource, it should be utilized."

"You may revise your opinion when you are in a roomful of telepaths and empaths." He tested the temperature of the water with his fingertips. When it met his satisfaction, he looked into her eyes.

Kestra felt her breath clogging in her throat when she read the blatant craving in his look. Her hands came to his biceps reflexively, clinging to him as she waited with a pounding heart for his next move. He made it, stepping back from her, though his eyes never left her face and body as he watched steam tumble from the shower, casting opaque clouds around her.

"Undress for me, Kestra," he instructed her in a low, male command, his voice rumbling with sheer sensuality of purpose.

Kestra leaned back against the glass of the shower for a breathless minute, her heart throbbing painfully in her breast. Slowly, she reached for the hem of the red velvet dress.

"No. The other way, Kes," he huskily scolded her, his eyes flickering like jade gems with their intensity.

She understood. The neckline of the dress was such that she could easily step out of it. She reached for her shoulders, slipping the dress down. She had a natural sensuality that made every movement sexy and riveting. She felt it within herself, but now, under the fixed hunger of his gaze, it became amplified. Her gymnast's body always stood posed in a perfect curve of the spine and thrown-back shoulders, but her desire to be tempting to him added a slink to her backbone and a tilting curve to the pitch of her shoulders. She wriggled her arms out of the sleeves of the brief dress, then slowly peeled the top down.

Noah watched with total possession, welcoming the instant need gripping and clawing its way through him this time. He remembered the bra he had chosen earlier, a demicup of black and scarlet jacquard satin, the straps thin and black and doing so little to contain so much soft, enticing flesh. She hooked her thumbs in the dress and slowly worked it down her body, revealing the bra and all the lush beauty of her skin and curves. Noah's breath left him in a violent decompression of air. She was more beautiful than he could bear. Her skin was so perfect, her face, hair, and body all so flawless and so unbelievably tempting. Perhaps he was blinded by prejudice, but if it were so, then he welcomed his ignorance with open arms and a body she had turned to steel with longing. He wanted to learn every inch of her, he thought as she slid the dress past the curve of her waist and on to the swells of her hips.

Kestra watched Noah's hands curl into rock-solid fists, his stance becoming visibly more rigid, his jaw tightening perceptibly. A smile of feminine satisfaction blossomed in her mind as she watched him. She purposely shifted her legs, sliding one thigh against the other, causing a soft undulation of her hips just as she pushed the dress farther down. She tilted her head down so she was looking at him with blue flames in her eyes, staring hard at him through her lashes. She looked predatory, aroused, as if she knew exactly what she wanted, and it was no illusion. She released the dress and it fell to her ankles. She took a single step out to the side, widening her stance. She listened. She watched.

Noah was rooted in a web of his own making. He watched as she flared into erotic life, as she turned his own game against him with painfully artful ease. She slid her hands up her hips, palms spreading out over her belly as if she were touching herself as she would want him to touch her. She turned wickedly meaningful eyes on him as her hands slid up over her ribs, then her breasts. Noah's entire psyche screamed out with voracious need. He had to forcefully drag in his next breath, though it did nothing to oxygenate blood that was pooling in one specific place on his body. He felt as though he were hard from head to toe. His clothes were strangling him. She purposely looked below his belt, smiling a sexy little smile of satisfaction as she flicked open the front catch of her bra and peeled it back from her skin. Her gorgeous breasts and their darkly colored nipples were thrust forward as she shrugged her shoulders back and allowed the bra to glide easily from her arms.

Kestra hooked her thumbs into the tiny fabric edges of her panties, but this time she didn't play him as she removed them with a sexy little slide down her legs. Her eyes were still on him, the hunger making him pulse with painful need, which pumped up in intensity with every step she took toward him. She crossed to him in no time at all, because he hadn't gone far, and she pressed her naked body to his clothed one.

"Kiss me," she demanded on a hot, hoarse breath.

He did. With all the fire and desire and want raging through his entire being. She slid tighter and tighter against him, making him groan as he felt the heat of her skin through his clothes, the curves of her body rubbing sensually against him. Her hands reached for his, and she guided his palm to her breast, moaning into his mouth with relief and pleasure as he cupped her tightly in his hand. He was a little rough, bruising in his fever, but she didn't mind. In fact, it wasn't enough for her. She released him once he had his touch on her and slid her hand down his chest, over his belly and buckle, finding the straining swelling behind his zipper with a firm, sure stroke.

Noah swayed, unable to keep from surging against the powerful temptation of her palm, unwilling to pass up the pleasure of her strong, assured fingers. His free hand grasped hers, holding her tight against himself as he ground forward into that torturous touch.

She laughed at him, the sound throaty and excited with the power she had over what he was feeling. Acting torridly, Noah suddenly shoved her away. She stumbled back, her breasts swaying. She was laughing at him still as she openly licked the flavor of his kisses from her lips. He yanked off his shirt in a single movement, throwing it at her face as she continued to chuckle with her eyes so obviously full of naughty thoughts, and the thoughts to match drifting blatantly in her mind for him to read and know.

She seemed to abruptly remember that the shower was running just as he grabbed for his belt. She stepped back twice, all that was needed for her to meet the torrent of sprays. The water hit her like a thousand stars, beads and rivers of prismatic crystal light that glistened off her face, lashes, breasts, and her long, heartbreaking legs. She sighed with delight, reaching to brace herself against the glass and tile with a hand on either side of herself. She only opened her eyes when she felt his body finally come close to hers. She held her breath as she looked at him, a long, appreciative appraisal.

"Noah," she murmured, her tone sultry and soft, the antithesis to the raging hunger in her eyes and the eager trembling of her hands as she reached for him. She said his name twice more, under her breath, like a private mantra as palms and fingertips slid over the map of muscles on his chest, shoulders, and arms. Her eyes traveled over him just as relentlessly, at last settling on the jutting evidence of his voracious need for her.

You are so hot. Her voice was a seductive whisper in his mind as her tongue reached to lick water off his throat at his pulse point. *I mean in terms of sexuality, not temperature.*

Oh?

Yes. I thought you might need the clarification, as you are elementally challenged. Although, touching you, hot also applies here as well.

He laughed, amused by the compliments in her statements, even as he surged with pleasure at the knowledge that she found him attractive. At the same time he was inundated by his own very elemental heat as her hands and now her mouth traveled over him. She avoided his attempts to touch her, chuckling against his skin as he was forced to be satisfied with his hands in her soaked hair. She inched down his body, her hands paving bold swipes over his wet skin, her mouth flitting fairy lightly in their wake. Occasionally he would feel the nip of her teeth, making him jolt with the shock of liquid lightning pouring heavily into his already agonizingly expectant body.

You are killing me.

He groaned aloud to punctuate the accusation, the tormented sound echoing off the dripping walls. Kestra smiled against the toned skin across his belly and swept both hands into the lee of his hips, finding him eager for the touch of her very interested hands. She slid her fingers over him, wrapped them around the ever-thickening shaft, relishing the surges in heat and amazing hardness that her touch coaxed from him. Then she lowered to a single knee, dragging her mouth down into the play. Noah's response was vocal as her tongue slipped over the very tip of his erection, a teasing flicker that destroyed his control, then a soft sucking draw of her lips as she closed around him and brought him into the heat of her mouth. His grip on her hair was fierce; the sounds of pleasure escaping him were unhinged and primitive. Kestra drank it all in: his response, his flavor, and the helpless way he thrust into her eager mouth.

She knew she could give him pleasure like this, that she could take away his entire sense of control and of chivalry. She could make him forget all about the pleasures he felt she required, if only for a violently pulsating moment. It didn't matter. Pleasing him was like ecstasy to her. Every sound he made, every twitch and shudder he couldn't contain, the steel need that was now nestled in her mouth; this was all mind-numbingly exciting for her.

Kes!

It was a forceful mental command, coupled with the upward tug of her hair in his hands. She had no choice but to follow, releasing him as she came up to meet his eyes. She stepped closer then, allowing the rigid tips of her breasts to stroke provocatively against his chest, his now-neglected erection coming to nestle against the lowest part of her belly. He could feel the tickle of damp, tight curls against himself, the touch painfully erotic because she had left him raw with sensitivity.

Kestra ignored the accusing heat from Noah's eyes as she reached for a bar of soap. His soap. She kept his gaze as she smelled the clean, masculine scent of it, a perfect complement to the scent of fragrant toasted wood that always seemed to cling to him. Kestra began to soap her hands, but then stopped as she arched that brow in humor and mischief, the white-blond arc maddeningly impish.

"Oh, wait, you already showered." She tossed up the soap so he had to catch it and did a swift about-face. "Do me, baby," she said, provocatively snuggling her bottom against the hard length of his shaft, fitting herself tightly into his hips.

Noah almost dropped the soap, his instinct being to grab the little vixen by her hips and end her game with a savage thrust. Instead, he gritted his teeth and allowed her the victory of the unstoppable groan she wrenched out of him, as well as the surge of heat pulsing against her bottom. He drew a fast lather from the soap, then reached out to whip her hair into his fist, jerking her by the wet mass so her back curved, her shoulders contacting his chest, and his mouth was planted firmly along the side of her neck.

With his free hand, Noah reached around to the front of her body and caught up her breast. Soap smeared over her, a lavish wash of sensation under the ardent sweep of his hand. Her chest foamed with suds as he kneaded her flesh, tortured her with the rub of his fingers as they slipped quickly over her hard nipples. He brought his other hand to the task, making her moan, her body pressing back against his sensually. He slid both breasts into his palms, soap fitting him to her with perfection, her nipples so hard he could not resist rolling them between his fingers even when her cries warned him of how sensitive she was becoming.

When he wanted more, he slid his hands down to her belly and hips. He grasped her hips, keeping her against himself with a taunting grind of his pelvis as he leaned her forward so he could wash her back. Soap slid down between them, the connection they were using to tease each other becoming slick and slippery.

Kestra moaned long and deep, unable to help wriggling into the alleviation of friction. He slid right between her legs, right through heat hotter than the steaming shower, slick lubrication far more efficient than soap.

She heard him curse violently, felt him seize her hips, and then heard the sound of soap hitting the tile. She wanted to tell him, but she was gasping at the feel of him, at how near he was. Until she remembered her new voice.

Take me, Noah. Like this. Now.

His response in voice and mind was a growl of primal demand. He found her, breached her, and thrust as hard and as deep as he could. They would have fallen over had she not braced against the walls as she had felt his gathering surge of possession.

But at last he was there.

"Noah," she rasped as his hands dragged her hips even tighter against himself. She felt him inch deeper inside her, stretching her to accommodate his thickness, scorching her with a blinding and intense heat. Noah shook back his wet head after he had a moment to absorb the bliss of having her so tightly around him again. It was a fantastic strangulation, how she embraced him with honey and heat.

What to do now . . . ?

He teased her with the contemplation, although Kes could hear the strain of pleasure that was on him. She responded by flexing inner muscles around him in blatant suggestion, laughing when he swore again.

That's how I know I'm getting to you. You swear like a sailor on leave.

Impudent wench.

Noah withdrew and stroked deep in return, lifting her onto her toes with the collision of their hips. Her cry made her entire body shudder and he felt it in ripples of response within her body and her mind. He decided to leave teasing to another time. Her need was too great, as was his own. He could sense how she felt, raw and craving, hunger for satisfaction pressing on her. He felt the call of Samhain within her for the first time, the power of it blinding to one so inexperienced with its compulsions. It would be torture for him to withhold what she needed so badly. He grabbed her around the waist and turned her to face a single wall, both of her hands bracing against the tile. Even those simple movements seemed to drive her to distraction. He fitted her into his hands tightly and slowly found a deep stroke into her. She moved with him, using her leverage against the wall to push back until he was hitting her with a rhythmic, magic contact. He knew he had achieved it instantly, even without her sudden chain of encouraging gasps and pleas that accompanied each thrust into her body. She called to him with her mind, a cadence of his name that drove him crazy.

"Come for me, baby," he said roughly. "Come, *Kikilia*, I can feel you." And he did. He felt the tension, the tightening vise, her frantic pushes against him to increase his depth, and her louder and louder cries for him.

Her orgasm was phenomenal, a ripping explosion and loss of control unlike anything he'd ever experienced. He had to grab hold of her as she seized with her pleasure, her body ferociously demanding his, clutching him with velvet violence until he could no longer bear it. She snatched away all his intentions, all control, forcing his compliance. She did not stop until he was roaring with release, pumping hotly into her until she had drained him completely.

They collapsed against the wall gasping, her body crushed beneath his, her cheek pressed to the tile. She was trying not to cry, but it was too easy for gasps to turn to sobs. Noah knew why she cried, and he felt she was entitled to a joy that moved her to tears. He knew she still couldn't grasp the existence of so much pleasure, or that her body, which she'd thought she'd known so well, was capable of producing it and surrendering to it.

He moved from her, only to turn her toward him. He swung her replete body under the water, holding her with a single arm as he washed her gently, without trying to stimulate her in any way, letting her recover quietly as he took care of her. She gasped when he washed her in tingling places, but the feel of his tender hands filled her with warmth. After he had made certain her body was clean, he washed her hair, lathering it richly and lingering over the long ribbons of wet silk. When he felt it was satisfactorily washed, he suddenly dipped her down along a single arm, bending her back under the fall of the water, rinsing her hair of soap as she laughed. When he was done, he kissed her behind her ear and shut off the taps. He engulfed her in towels, wrapped her hair, and they moved back into the bedroom.

Kestra suddenly gasped when she looked up at the windows.

"Daylight is coming."

"Yes," he agreed.

"Don't you have to sleep now?"

"While that is the generally accepted practice for Demons," he drawled as he led her to the bed, "I had considered making love with you for a couple of hours first. Although not for too long." He herded his body against hers until she fell to the bed and he followed. "I have a feeling you are going to be exhausting come Samhain."

"Hmm." She contemplated that as he slid between her thighs and pushed aside her towel so he could start licking water off her skin. "It is plausible," she agreed graciously. "I'm in peak physical condition. I'm wholly sexually deprived, as you know. And I find that I'm really quite horny. So I'd say conditions are favorable."

"Horny?" He laughed until she pinched him on the shoulder.

"Yeah. I'm hot for your body, you big jerk. But if you want to laugh at my expense, I could find a subzero freezer to sit in instead. After all, Samhain is only twenty-four very long, long, interminably lengthy hours." She sighed for dramatic effect.

"I think your days of deep freeze are very much over," he told her as he licked a long line from curls to navel to cleavage.

"Mmm. That would be nice." She lifted a shoulder, nudging her nipple against his sexy mouth, practically purring when he obliged her skillfully until she was wet with want all over again. "And the daylight?" she gasped.

"In twenty to thirty minutes, the sun will hit the eastern windows," he said, pausing over her body to point them out. "The stained glass will catch the light and it will bathe your body in a kaleidoscope of colors. Since I love colored light, I can do no less than to worship it in entirety with the reverent kiss of my mouth."

She swallowed convulsively at the thought, her pulse pounding tellingly in her throat.

"Twenty to thirty minutes?" she asked. "What will we do until then?"

"Practice, of course."

He slid down Kestra's body, his mouth dragging hotly over her skin in a direct descent to his training grounds.

Noah woke, feeling that strange disorientation and lethargy that the daylight brought, even before he opened his eyes and saw the spray of colors still gilding the room. Not understanding why he had wakened, he rolled to feel for Kestra, who had fallen asleep snuggled up to his back while toying lazily with his hair, her fingers combing through the waves and curls so rhythmically that he had barely felt her fingers stilling before he himself had given in to rest.

She wasn't beside him and his heartbeat jumped. He sat up, sharp eyes sweeping the room. He exhaled hard with relief when he saw her standing before one of the floor-to-ceiling windows, tracing the patterns of color with a slow, thoughtful interest. His heart literally ached for her as he saw her color-splashed body, wrapped in a sage-colored sheet, her lower lip firmly between her teeth. He realized it was still before noon, the slant of the light in the eastern windows still too strong to be anywhere beyond.

He silently moved to his feet, crossing to her and resting his hands on her shoulders. She settled back against him with a small sigh that sounded too sad and too troubled for his peace of mind. His fingers slid over her collarbone and up along her throat, a soothing gesture as he struggled to keep his questions to himself. He couldn't rush her, could never expect her to settle for him and all he had revealed without a qualm and without a great deal of thought.

"You're so wise," she remarked softly, suddenly breaking the silence and letting him know she was aware of his thoughts, as well as his struggles. "I think more than anything your wisdom and confidence of conviction have had an effect on me." She reached up to draw a finger down the back of the hand resting against her throat. "I was wondering how I was going to explain to you that this isn't settled between us, and suddenly you wake and it's in your thoughts that you already understand that."

Kestra finally turned around, looking up into his eyes, her expression soft yet serious. He instantly cupped her throat between his hands, his thumbs stroking back along the line of her jaw.

"I am not so noble that I do not fear every ounce of your independence when it comes to this topic, Kes, but I am enough of an honorable man to know that I could never hold you without it. I hope you understand that I do not expect everything at once? That I only need you to stay close while I try to . . ." He hesitated, checking his immediate phraseology.

"Try to convince me that you're right?" She gave a wry little laugh. "There's a possessive streak within you."

"It . . ." He made a sound of frustration, unused to second-guessing his every spoken word. "I almost said that this is because it is true of all Imprinted mates, but that would be a half-truth. You are right. I have always been possessive and protective over that which I deem my own. I am used to those being necessary qualities in my life and my rule. How can a King not be those things for the good of his people? If I care too deeply, and if it is a failing, I cannot make myself regret it. Apathy is the curse of those who live long lives, and I will not neglect my responsibilities. I believe this is how a nation falls into disrepair, when a monarch or leader no longer cares to protect his people as though they were his family."

"I can actually understand that. I don't condemn you for it, Noah. I'm simply not used to it."

"I feel I must warn you, Kes," he whispered softly, leaning to touch foreheads with her, closing his eyes briefly. "The night of Samhain is tonight, and it is a night of extremes unlike anything you have experienced—or will ever be likely to experience. It has a way of magnifying all that is wonderful, and all that is volatile, in our emotions."

"I know this, Noah. I saw your memories. I felt your pain and your need."

"Need." He laughed, but without mirth. "Tonight you will learn a new definition to that word. So will I, I suspect. No," he said quickly when he felt the sudden surge in her heartbeat. "Try not to be afraid. If you embrace it, make the power of it your own, then you will not feel fear."

"Sort of like going down a hill in the snow and slipping on the ice? What does it matter how you get to the bottom? You were going that way anyway."

He chuckled at that, kissing her lips gently in tribute to her wonderful humor.

"Something exactly like that. The difference being a few bumps and bruises along the way. But I will try not to see you hurt, Kes. I promised you I would not hurt you, but if there will ever be a time when that would become an issue in the physical sense, it will be tonight. I am of Fire, and there are such dangerous things within me."

"I'm not afraid of danger," she whispered in reminder as she moved to kiss him soothingly. "And I'm not afraid of you. Not physically, at least."

"Well, you should be," he said, straightening up a little sharply and giving her a small shake. "You act so confident about things that even I am not sure of. Do not underestimate me. Not this night. It is the first night, do you understand? It is the first Hallowed moon I will have with you, my one true mate, and I am entering it with a keen and painful awareness that your heart is not mine and that you are afraid to give it to me." He felt her hands circling his wrists tightly and he looked away from her, drawing a deep breath in an attempt to control his rising anxiety. "I am sorry. That sounded like I was blaming you, but I am not. I understand your needs, truly I do. I only wish to make you aware of what mine will be."

"Noah, I know what your needs will be. But you can be as volatile as you like and it will not change the essence of who you are. Your sense of honor is remarkable, unlike anything I have ever known. It won't simply disappear."

"You have more faith in that than I do," he said with a candid bitterness. "I would have agreed with you not five . . . six days ago. But after what I have done recently, I cannot be so sure."

Kestra felt the phrase like a stinging slap. It wasn't his intention to blame her, but she felt responsible just the same. Circumstances had placed him at odds with all the values he held dear. He didn't feel guilt, because he couldn't make himself regret his choices, but he did feel remorse for the fallout of his actions. She regretted it, too, because her careless actions had put him in the untenable position.

"Noah, you just told me I needed to embrace the unfamiliarity of what I'll experience tonight. Doesn't the same hold true for you? Your own fears will be what makes this so difficult for you." She ran her hands soothingly along his forearms. "I haven't closed my mind to you. In fact, you should be encouraged by the fact that . . ." She exhaled shakily, laughing through it because she wasn't used to thinking with her heart. "The fact that I'm willing to stay with you and learn if I can . . . if I can have the courage I'll need to . . ."

"To love me, Kestra," he said with impatience. "You cannot even speak of the idea!" He cursed under his breath as soon as the words passed his lips, releasing his hold on her so he could run agitated hands through his hair and quell the unwanted emotion surging through him. "There is an example of logic and honor for you," he said with bitter sarcasm, "and dark has hours yet to fall." He sighed when he saw she was regarding him with a level gaze. "Whatever else you believe of me in the coming hours, Kes, believe that I truly understand your limitations in this matter and intend to be as sensitive as I need to be to help you cope with it."

"That doesn't mean you have to be happy about the situation, Noah. Don't be so unreasonable with yourself. There's nothing wrong with you wanting someone to love you. I'm only sorry that I—that you've chosen to want someone who feels so much panic when she's faced with an individual who wants her to love him."

Her regret was agonizingly sharp in her eyes and he felt pain choking off in his throat. He reached for her, enfolding her in his arms and hugging her as tightly as he dared to his sheltering body. Kestra instantly felt protected, the sensation so amusing to her that she laughed.

She was the one protecting him at the moment. She probably would be for the remainder of the day and night. Guarding him from these surges of power she knew nothing about, but was supposed to be innately able to conquer. She wasn't afraid of the challenge. It's what would come later that would be more difficult.

Kestra had learned a very long time ago that when it came to dangerous things, a dangerous life, it was best to stay focused on the moment and not let herself be distracted by uncontrollable details. She hadn't liked the idea of not having a real choice in the matter, but she also realized that a tantrum wasn't going to change the facts. Besides, she had to confess she was getting increasingly curious about this night that so powerful a being as Noah seemed to dread, worship, and crave all at once. It was a fascinating combination of expectations. And she'd always wondered what it'd be like spending a day in bed with a great lover and making love like bunnies.

Noah broke out in a coughing laugh, suddenly reminding

her that he was skulking around in her brain. She reached out to pinch him, but he caught her fingers in his hands and diverted them to the kiss of his warm lips.

"You think the most incredible combination of thoughts," he said. "One minute impressively brave and philosophical, the next irreverent and bordering on adolescent."

"Mmm, well, I don't think *you* want to criticize *me* on adolescent thoughts," she remarked with a well-bred tone of haughtiness. It completely belied the warmth seeping up her arm as his mouth rubbed over her fingers and palm. She did snuggle a little bit more cozily against him.

"I am under the influence of great cosmic forces," he excused himself, a brilliant sparkle of mischief in his eyes.

She contemplated him from under her lashes for a moment, letting him distract himself with her taste and scent, allowing herself to feel how it sent heat dripping through him when he noted the scent of their lovemaking was etched over them both so deeply it was almost permanent. She did the same, inhaling their combined fragrance off his skin, slow and deep, filling her lungs with the intoxicating and stimulating scent. She understood her senses were sharpening, and it excited her, but not half so much as smelling him on her own skin. She didn't understand why, she only felt her every sense coming to attention. She felt sensory memory playing tricks on her body, heating and tingling in deep places as the scent called to mind a certain touch, the fine stroke of his body inside her, his kiss and tongue playing over wickedly sensitive places.

She began to wonder if this was normal or if *she* was under the influence of cosmic forces. Then she wondered why the hell she was worrying about it. What did it matter?

She smiled up at him, reaching to stroke a hand along his ribs and waist. She was fascinated by the feel and strength of his flesh. Its warmth and power left her envious and breathless. Kes inched her body back from his so she could slide her hand over the firmness of his belly. She felt the muscles clench beneath her touch and there was a sudden nip of teeth against the hand he'd been kissing. She raised a single brow as she looked up at him with mischievous intent. She knew the expression drove him nuts.

"Kestra, I really do need to sleep at some point," he reminded her pointedly. "I am burning energy just to be talking with you at this hour."

"Then by all means, let's put you to bed," she murmured softly against the strong column of his neck as she reached to kiss him there with all seeming innocence. He nodded, the shadow on his jaw abrading her cheek and catching on stray wisps of her hair.

Noah let her grasp his hand and lead him to the bed. She had him lie down; then she made a show of yanking the tuck of the sheet she wore from between her breasts, the light green fabric suddenly billowing free of her breathtaking body. She placed a knee on the bed near his hip and swung one of her extraordinary legs over him. For a brief but ecstatic moment, she straddled him, settled the center of her weight against him so that he was suddenly flush against scorching feminine heat and moist secrets. He could swear the little minx even rubbed against him before she continued to climb over him to her side of the bed. She slid beneath the coverlet and snuggled down as if perfectly ready to obey his request for sleep.

Meanwhile, her slight erotic dance across his body had pretty much set an all-time speed record for inspiring a completely rigid state of arousal. Never one to be outdone, or easily manipulated for that matter, Noah was faced with a conundrum. It didn't take him long to decide that, in this case, he could accept manipulation and go right for not being outdone. Though he almost changed his mind when he heard her try to muffle a feminine snicker of victory.

He gave in, reaching for her with lightning speed, flipping her onto her back and rolling himself atop her cozy body and right into the nestling cradle of her thighs. He did it fast enough to earn a somewhat satisfactory gasp of surprise from his temptress. In a heartbeat he was breathing softly against her lips and returning her sliding caress of intimacy with a deadly accurate undulation of his hips. Her gasp was far more powerful and extremely satisfying this time, as was the slick heat and nectar of her expectant body.

"The sun," he lectured her softly, the low timbre of his voice against her lips, the smoothness of which was marred by the slightest grunt of pleasure, "though a great distance away from Earth, emits enough radiation to reach the planet, bathing it in what we call sunlight." He moved his lecture down to her throat, although he slid his rapidly thickening arousal against her at the end of the sentence. "Radiation is one of the purest forms of energy available on this planet."

"Oh?" she managed to say, following it up with a groan as his hips shifted again and his mouth lowered so his hot breath was cascading over her breast and its already painfully erect nipple.

"While this energy is best absorbed as a Demon sleeps," he continued, using a significant pause to draw her nipple into his mouth, sucking on it hard and with obvious hunger before releasing it. He felt her response in her sound of pleasure and the flood of fresh wet heat seeping from her body. "For the male Fire Demon *especially*," he stressed, shooting her a look that made her throw her head back and release a throaty laugh. "It is not entirely impossible for the male"—he stressed the word *male* with another taunting slide of very male parts and a leisurely lick of his tongue—"Fire Demon to utilize the sun's radiation in order to maintain a wakeful state"—a slide for punctuation, a swift, ferocious sucking before he shifted weight on his arms so he was above the opposite breast—"during the daytime hours."

"That," she gasped, "is fascinating." Kestra's hands had long since grasped his broad shoulders, and for the moment she was just helplessly taking her lecture and punishment as if she were a very good girl.

"He can also maintain a state of power by using this same source," he said, his voice turning a little rougher before he attended her waiting breast. Kestra barely had a moment to feel him smile against her skin. "However." He thrust into her with a single, savage stroke, forcing her to inhale on a long, hitching gasp of surprise. He reached for her hip, tilting her pelvis so he went fully inside her. His lecture barely missed a beat. "Although this energy can be a satisfactory source of necessary supply . . ." Noah caught up her nipple as he stroked into her again, pleasing himself with her outcry. She was as hot as a forge as she surrounded him, and he could easily have lost himself in the ecstasy of it if he had not been so determined to make a specific point. He lifted his head and grinned down at her. "It is far better for the Demon's state of mind and state of health for him to recharge using the natural resource of sleep." He once more hovered against her lips, looking deeply into her eyes, which so blatantly radiated her bodily bliss. "Especially the day before Samhain night. Now, I just wanted to make sure I have made my point, Kes."

Kestra nodded speechlessly as he chose an exceptionally deep rhythm into her slick heat.

"Are you sure?" His words tumbled over a groan as his pitch inside her was met with a flexing of limber internal muscles. "Because I have learning aids." He chuckled, momentarily destroying her concentration as she broke into hysterics. Her body shook with every outrageous laugh, clenching around him in a way that made him want to be a much funnier man. "My Kes," he whispered softly before he caught her last giggles with his kisses.

Her hands slid from his shoulders and into his hair.

"I think, then," she said with a smile, "that this should be a quickie."

"Which is what you wanted all along," he noted, his scolding look making her laugh again. He closed his eyes and savored the sensation rippling over him, pausing in his stroke again to do so.

"I heard only a lecture, not a complaint," she pointed out.

"The complaint comes next," he teased, showing her his hand back and front purposely before placing it on her breast and sliding it down her ribs and belly. He slid through wet curls in search of sensitive flesh to play with, in the process feeling himself sliding into her body, giving himself an erotic shiver up his spine. "There we are," he said silkily as he found the very spot he was looking for and began to stroke her with sure fingers, "the root of the problem."

Kestra bucked beneath him as a soundless exclamation shuddered up through her along with the blinding ripple of sensation he created. In the end, all it sounded like was a sharp exhalation bursting out of her throat. She searched a little helplessly for his gaze, knowing it would be there because he loved to watch her face as he gave her pleasure.

"Do you like that?" he asked knowingly, tossing back his sweat-dampened hair. She nodded furiously, then gasped as he hit her with a double sweep of magic, both inside and out. He groaned, almost as if he were in pain, but never broke his cadence into her building body. She was tightening around him with whips of tension and it was an incredible feeling. "Is this going to be quick enough for you, baby?" An important question considering how she was driving him crazy. She was using her astonishing legs to meet his every push into her body, reaching just as he was for the ever-deeper surge and connection. They were a whole, a completion, when they were joined like this on a journey to mutual bliss.

"Yes," she said breathlessly, the word punctuating a half dozen sounds of lost joy. "Hurry . . . please . . ."

This was definitely not a problem for him. He felt how ready she was, and he was burning with his impending release. He thickened inside her until the feel of it overwhelmed him with mindless instinct. He came first, a crashing wave spewing forth, only it was so hot he thought he would burn her. She felt him go off like dynamite inside her, heard his heedless cries and felt the helpless thrusts of his hips as he lost himself. The culmination of her little manipulation of him hit her like a ton of bricks. She couldn't breathe, couldn't move, and could barely see. She arched up, meeting his final strokes, and then truly screamed as tidal swells of release washed over her with the violence of a riptide, tearing her first one way, then another.

Noah held himself above her as long as he could while the squeeze of her body took him for everything he had. Finally he fell against her, into her waiting arms, matching her gasp for gasp as their hearts crashed together at the juncture of their chests. He wasn't capable of the casualness it would have taken to roll off her and say good night as if they'd just been talking about the weather, finishing the joke between them. He was incapable of leaving her at all, not even to give reprieve from his weight. But she didn't complain. She held him, her hands alternately in his hair or sweeping his back. Her legs were curled around his. Buried inside her still, it was as full-bodied a hug as was mutually possible.

The Demon King came to understand then the true power of a mate for his soul, and why the everlasting nature of an Imprinting was so necessary. He lifted himself up onto his elbows, an easing of his weight on her and a way to look down into her eyes as his hands stroked through her hair. There was no such thing as complete fulfillment and contentment without someone to share it with. All the most valuable things in life were so wonderful that he wanted to share them, and felt empty when he could not. Weddings. Births. Deaths. Accomplishments. Knowledge. Family. Frustrations. Even the most painful tribulations were in essence things of wonder, deserving of respect and the most honorable of things to be shared.

I want to share my life with you.

The thought was between them before he could censor it. He caught his breath, blanking his thoughts of expectations or regrets or any baggage that would have come with such a deeply felt confession. He feared putting pressure on her that would shut her down or send her away from him in panic.

"Noah, I've been reading your thoughts for the past five minutes," she chided him softly. "It's the most beautiful thought anyone has ever shared with me." She blinked, a single tear dropping out of her shining eyes. "You have such an incredible soul. You can't frighten me with such honesty and purity of feeling."

Noah felt his heart clenching tightly with emotion, and he bent to catch her tear on his lips, treasuring with all of his soul the acceptance that had created it. Finally, he rolled with her, taking her weight and warmth onto his body so he could hug her now. He wanted her to sleep like this, blanketing his body, her beautiful hair a soft sheet like white linen across his chest and arm. She lifted her head to look at him, quietly searching his eyes for a minute.

"So I guess this means you are . . . tired." She sighed on the word regretfully, her eyes sliding over him a little too suggestively.

"If you dare do what I know you are thinking, I am going to have to—"

"Lecture me again?" she asked hopefully.

"Kes!" He laughed at her impudence, feeling her lips on his chest as she tried to unobtrusively slide lower against him. "Kestra, you have to think of the long run," he complained, though clearly halfheartedly. She arched that damnably naughty brow at him and he realized he was lecturing her again. "Kes, I am going to be dead by dusk if you keep this up!"

"Keep *this* up?" She asked the question while stroking fingertips against him that had somehow wriggled between their bodies.

He groaned softly, closing his eyes and covering them with both hands for a moment.

"Human females reach their sexual prime around the ages of thirty to thirty-five," he began, making her laugh victoriously.

Chapter 15

Kestra woke several hours later, realizing that darkness had fallen and she was alone in Noah's bed. The presence of a couple of new towels, most likely damp ones, draped over the foot of the bed on his side attested that he had already showered and had begun to make his way through his evening.

Well, he *was* a King, after all. He probably had a great deal to do. Kes didn't understand why he wouldn't wake her, though. Or for that matter, why he wasn't still sleeping beside her after giving her so much guff about how important his sleep was. Still, it was well after dusk by the look and feel of it. He was probably being considerate, letting her rest up from their heavy-duty lovemaking of the morning.

And early afternoon.

His pained remark floating into her awareness was incredibly welcome and she laughed as expected. Her entire mood lightened and she bounced out of bed.

Thought I had abandoned you, Kikilia*?*

Momentarily, I confess. She quickly crossed the room to the bathroom and gasped when the lights flared to flaming life though she had done nothing to initiate it. She realized that Noah had anticipated her and set them to flame for her. Feeling inexplicably pleased, she began to run the shower.

My apologies. I had an urgent matter to attend to. Samhain festivities start soon and I wanted to get all business out of the way. Otherwise, there is nothing I would have wanted more than to wake next to you as I did the evening before this.

Kestra recalled that gentle wakening, lying together talking, his hand softly touching her back, nothing on his mind but comfort and caring. She suddenly felt his laughter ringing richly in her head.

Believe that if you like, but I was not entirely innocent.

Now, that I do believe.

She made sure the thought was in her haughtiest tone. She felt the surge of his amusement even though he didn't laugh. This connection was so remarkable, she thought with hasty appreciation. She unexpectedly felt fortunate. How many women had this advantage? The opportunity to see directly into a man's mind? To actually know what he was thinking, feeling . . . telling the truth or lying about? Any other situation, she might have been left to feel uncomfortable and a little neglected for waking alone. This way, he instantly put her mind to ease. What was more, Noah had sought her out. He'd kept a part of his thoughts dedicated to her, seeking her needs as she'd wakened. She hadn't even thought to search for the answers within his mind when she'd felt her doubts, but the potential was there.

Baby, Imprinted mates cannot lie to one another. They do not even feel compelled to do so. The joining of our minds is one of those precious blessings that help us to communicate more smoothly, with love and less misunderstanding. For instance, I must tell you to shower and join me in the Great Hall when you feel up to it. That I must focus on my task here for the moment.

Of course. Thank you for thinking of me.

I am always thinking of you.

The thought was so incredibly pleasing that it warmed her entire time in the shower. She was surprised to find her toiletries settled comfortably next to his in the shower and along the vanity. Perhaps *surprised* was an inadequate word. It was just like everything else he did. Thoughtful, subtle things to make her comfort a priority to him. It was strange to have someone who was always considering her and her needs, even before she might consider them for herself. She wasn't used to being taken care of. She wasn't used to being cared for.

It was becoming very clear that Noah cared for her a great deal.

The idea left her a little breathless with a combination of exhilarating emotions. It was rather a lot like base-jumping off a "no access" building, hitting the ground running before the authorities caught up with her. Then again, she had done that twice and had never felt quite so alive as she was feeling at the moment. She was sitting at the vanity drying her hair with a towel when she realized there was no hair dryer. There were no electrical outlets, for that matter. Then again, it was a castle. It even had gas lighting systems. But the water was always hot. It had to get that way somehow. And didn't water work on electric pumps?

Without realizing it, she had sifted into Noah's brain and extracted the answers to her questions. She leapt to her feet, knocking over the vanity seat.

No electricity . . . ever?

There was silence for several beats and she began to tap her foot in expectation, her hands going impatiently to her hips, still clutching a towel in one of them as she glared at her own reflection as if she were glaring at him.

Kes, I need you to put something on and come down here. Now, please.

The request was a command and nothing less, no matter that it was couched in softened words. Normally, that would have pissed her off in a snap, but there was something in his tone that sought out that spot in the back of her brain telling her to pay very close attention to the details of a situation, versus her emotional reaction to it. She forgot her gripes about the missing modern technology and hurried to throw on one of her simpler dresses, a china blue and white gingham cotton minidress that made her look about fifteen years old, but it was the most casual, low-maintenance outfit she owned. She dashed from the room barefoot, flinging back her long, wet hair in an effort to order it, feeling it soak through her dress instantly. Her feet flew over the beautiful Persian runner that graced the third-story hall and continued on down the stairs. She took curving stone steps two and three at a time, a rushing descent that turned several times before the stairs emptied into the main room on the first floor. Without a railing to stay her, she would have shot clear off the last step and run to a stop. But just as she touched the marble floor, a powerful arm reached out and caught her, halting her flight instantly with a speed-absorbing swing into a hard body.

"Uh, Noah . . . I think you're missing something."

Kes looked up, impressively up, at a blond giant of a man whose hair was as purely gold as hers was sugar white. His merry green gaze regarded her for a minute as he set her back onto her feet safely. Kes would have thanked him, but her hands had inadvertently lain against his biceps as he'd caught her and she had to take a minute to marvel at the monstrous size of the muscles in comparison. No wonder he'd plucked her out of the air as if she were no more than a dust mote. He was enormous.

"My thanks, Elijah," a familiar voice said near her ear as Noah drew her back against his body. Kestra shook her head bemusedly. She'd never been picked up and tossed around so much in her entire life. It was such a strangely feminine thing, to be lifted by men who never gave a second thought as to whether they had a right to do so. They just assumed it was a natural-born privilege.

Kes felt Noah's arm around her waist, holding her back against his amazingly warm body, the sensation of coming home as she settled back against him so overwhelming that she raised a hand to fluff her bangs, hiding the flustered blush that burned cheeks that *never* blushed. That was when she realized there were more people in the room.

More men, rather.

The healer she recognized instantly. How could she not? His silver eyes and silver hair were a bit on the outstanding side. More importantly, she seemed to be able to see an aura around him now. A lavender mist all around him, dotted with splashes of color rather like random spray-painted graffiti. A quick glance at the others around her told her that everyone else looked normal to her.

Another man who was slimmer, and yet almost as tall and broad in the shoulders as Noah was, stood off slightly to the right of the healer. He was leaning one shoulder casually against a nearby stone wall, his arms folded over his chest. He had dark hair, either brown or black, and eyes that matched. She could hardly distinguish his irises from his pupils. He held himself with an air of confidence that hinted at the power just beneath his calm exterior.

In a nutshell, she was in a room being dwarfed by the four most powerful men she had ever laid eyes on. This in spite of the fact that she was of significant height for a woman. She suddenly felt at an extreme disadvantage, being held by Noah like some kind of blond-bombshell trophy and looking the part in her silly little dress. Kestra unexpectedly felt Noah's arm drop from around her waist and he stepped around her. She felt a prickling over her skin she was beginning to recognize for what it was. An energy overflow. One that Noah gave off when something disturbed him.

She had somehow upset him. She knew it without a doubt, though she did not understand how. She folded her arms beneath her breasts defensively as he walked to the center of the loose circle they made.

"Kestra, this is Jacob, my Enforcer. Behind you is Elijah, my Warrior Captain. You have met Gideon, our medic. Gentlemen, this is Kestra, my . . . our latest Druid to join our lives."

"Greetings to you, Kestra," Jacob said, pushing away from his wall and reaching to shake her hand in a gesture that made her feel abruptly equalized. "An Enforcer is what you might call . . . police. I am in charge of policing our own."

Elijah tapped her shoulder and engulfed her hand between his enthusiastically. "Hey there. I have to say, I'm tickled to death to meet you. I'll enlighten you, too," he added quickly when he saw Noah's scowl of warning over her shoulder. "Warrior Captain means I am the head of our armed forces, as pertains to our defense against foreigners."

"Foreigners?" She said it carefully, her gaze quickly sliding to Noah. He stood stiffly, not helping in the least. "You mean other Nightwalkers?"

"Sometimes. It is complicated. We have a relatively sound peace with all the other races at the moment, but like with any society, that has not always been the case. And, of course, there're always other threats."

Light dawned instantly and she spat it out on a bitter tone. "Humans."

"I am afraid so," he said with honest regret.

"It doesn't surprise me," she said. "I have dealt often with the seamier side of humanity. I don't blame you for taking precautions or actions to protect yourselves."

"Hey, Noah, I really like her!" Elijah exclaimed with a laugh, chucking her in the shoulder hard enough to make her step back in spite of having her feet braced.

Kestra merely nodded to Gideon as she contemplated this new information. It had never occurred to her that Demons would look on humans as enemies. She had the knee-jerk reaction to go filing through Noah's mind for information, but she also found herself feeling as though it would be an invasion since he seemed unreceptive to her at the moment. What she was left with instead were the only memories she had of Noah's interactions with other humans. The encounter in Sands's penthouse. He had killed both of those men without batting an eyelash. Of course, they had also been massively armed with an intent to kill her and she would be dead if not—

That thought ended abruptly and she looked up to meet Noah's eyes. His gaze was infinitely softer this time and she saw his subtle hand gesture near his thigh. A calming press of his hand downward. A signal to ease her thoughts and to focus on the moment. Explanations and information could come later. He needed her . . . wanted her to stay in the moment and not tangle herself in trying to understand Demon motivations.

The group moved toward the desk set back by some colossal bookshelves, equally enormous leather-bound volumes stacked into them. Two chairs sat in front of it, one behind. She only had to look at the wide comfort and mellowed wood of the chair behind the desk in order to picture Noah sitting in it for hours on end. The armrests shone yellow-gold where the years and his hands had worn at the wood of the sturdy oak. The cushions, royal purple velvet fabric, had that soft paling of wear in the pile that bespoke frequent use.

Noah didn't round the desk to take his familiar place, opting to lean back against the front of the desk. Jacob took a casual seat in front of him. The rest came closer and stood like sentinels, waiting for Noah to begin. Instinct galvanized her, and she moved to the desk and hoisted herself up onto it, her hip near Noah's hand. They exchanged a look but no thoughts. The prickling had stopped and she could feel that he'd calmed down.

"Very well, gentlemen, let us get this finished. We all have . . . places to be and personal engagements." Noah had not meant to hesitate midsentence, as if it were some kind of leering, manly innuendo.

Damn it. He was editing his language of the word *mate*, purposely, so as not to make Kes feel pressured in front of others. Even so, she had come up with that blond-bombshell crack in that thick skull of hers. He had been truly peeved about that. Unusually short-tempered, actually. Eventually, after a few seething minutes, he had appreciated that unreserved affection with one's mate was a cultural difference she would not be used to. Demons were very open about their mates and their importance. Affections, and even the outright acknowledgment about where they would all be ending up after the Samhain celebration, were commonplace. Had Bella or his sister been present, each would be held with far more blatant love and intimacy by her male counterpart than a simple arm around the waist. It was simply their way. A way, he tried to realize, that was practically an alien concept to Kestra. She was not used to affection of any sort. She had come a great distance in a short amount of time in their private moments, and he had to acknowledge that.

"We have a report of the Vampire rogues," Elijah began as soon as he had total attention, his no-nonsense tone abruptly intimidating in the wake of the easy, almost jovial personality of moments ago. Kes was instantly aware that title of Warrior Captain was a far more physically invested position than, say, an American four-star general would be. "Tristan sent word to Siena of a death of one of the younger generation of Shadowdwellers. He was found with his throat ripped out in a human city. Tristan said the subsequent investigation and autopsy were a disaster. The rogues have exposed the 'Dwellers to humans in a way no one has ever done before."

"Does Tristan need help with damage control?"

"His emissary said they had it under control, but you know how these things go. When innocents are involved, you can't just kill off everyone who got a whiff of forbidden information."

"A few Mind Demons might help," Noah insisted. "Erase some short-term memories."

"Tristan said he had it covered." The giant shrugged a huge shoulder. "You can offer, though."

"Shala has gone home for the holiday," Noah mused, speaking of the Shadowdweller Ambassador. "I will make the offer through her when she returns tomorrow. Hopefully it will not be too late to be effective by then." Noah turned to Jacob. "How goes the hunting?"

Kestra could tell there was a wry sort of pain behind that statement. This time she didn't resist her impulse. She sank into Noah's thoughts and found out about this other, more sinister side to the Hallowed moons. The side where burnt caverns were no longer enough, control was lost, laws forsaken and morals discarded, and the Enforcer sent to lay down the law against his own people. Sometimes, battling them, the Enforcer would put his very life on the line in the name of protecting innocents, the laws of his King, and the transgressing Demons themselves. And then the retributive punishment that Demons deemed unspeakable. She had only gleaned glimpses of these awesome responsibilities in her earlier forays into Noah's troubled memories of the Hallowed moons of the past few years, and the very tangible troubles that made the actions of the Enforcer so very necessary.

There was more information still, a link to further understanding his father's death, but she knew he was reliving every thought and memory she touched in him. Since she didn't move as silently through his mind as he did through hers, she didn't want to disturb his composure. Noah's hand left the desk and reached out to link fingers with hers. Kestra felt his silent gratitude, so she couldn't even feel embarrassed about the small affection.

"I have no active beacons at this time, but I have a few warnings. As you know, I cannot tell until it is almost too late who it is. I have noticed a few twitches, and I will keep watch."

Elijah snorted with laughter. "Who's sitting the little hellion so you and Bella can pursue . . . ahem . . . *twitches* tonight?"

Kestra's eyes grew wide and she bit her lips in a repression of shocked laughter as her gaze swung to the austere Enforcer.

"And I suppose your little pussy cat is not going to get the lion's share tonight?" Jacob flashed back, the barb partly some kind of play on words that went right over Kestra's head, but she got the meaning well enough.

She looked expectantly at Elijah.

"Gentlemen." Noah's halting demand ended the sparring. "We all have multiple responsibilities tonight. I would like us to try to manage them with a modicum of maturity. Gideon, anything to add?"

"Only this. The rogues are killing, not merely feeding. There is no telling how this will affect their powers. I think there should be a serious warning placed out over the network."

"I will send Jasmine to start the chain," Noah said. "Anything else?"

All three men shook their heads.

"Great. See you at the festivities. Let us try to enjoy this holiday."

Kestra felt him squeeze her hand. No sooner had she smiled at him, though, than a massive arm swept her from the desk and urged her across the room toward the fireplace. She barely touched the floor as she followed Elijah. She didn't have much of a choice.

"So, tell me all about you. You're spunky, right? Tongue like a blade? You're in good shape for a human . . . err . . . Druid, I mean. That's a compliment, so I hope you are taking it that way." Before Kestra knew it, she was seated in front of a cozy fire and Elijah had pulled a chair up across from her so they were only a foot apart. She glanced up in search of Noah, but he was speaking with Gideon.

"Do you always ask so many questions?" she finally managed to interject.

"Only under special circumstances." Elijah's eyes sparkled with humor and it was too infectious. She grinned back at him as he leaned conspiratorially forward. "My mate gave me specific instructions to find out all about you, and I have to say I am damn curious myself. You don't mind, do you? We've all waited a very long time for you to come along."

"Actually, I'm an extraordinarily private person," she hedged. Again her gaze shifted to Noah. His darkening expression made her wonder what he was talking to the medic about.

"Noah, the next occasion you require my services, I ask you tone down your call. Legna found the power . . . extreme. Painful." Gideon tried to broach the subject he hadn't had an opportunity to discuss before then with as much gentleness as he could muster. A gentleness that had not existed in him and *would* not exist in him had it not been for his mate.

Noah's full attention came around to the medic, his eyes finally leaving the figure of his mate, who was being herded across the room by Elijah.

"Painful?" It took a moment for the information to register on the Demon King. "Was she harmed?" he demanded. He knew how sensitive his sister's powers had become since she'd mated with Gideon. He was a powerful Ancient, and the infusion of his power had advanced her ability beyond her years. It had never occurred to him that his pain would harm his sister when she was so far away in a Russian province.

"It was nothing I could not heal." Gideon paused a beat and Noah had the feeling the Ancient was editing his next thoughts. It wasn't like him to do so. Gideon was as blunt and straightforward as they came. If he was holding back, Legna was behind it. "It was quite a feat for a nontelepath to reach that far and with that much . . . clarity, Noah."

"Legna is a Mind Demon. We are brother and sister. We have always had a strong connection. Though I admit I am impressed as well. I do not even know what my intentions were at the time, Gideon. I was acting purely on instinct."

"And your instincts are like nothing any of us can imagine," the medic said. "Even you do not understand the full scope of your abilities. You have been King since a fairly young age. You have lived a life of restraint, as your position requires. Perhaps . . ." Again a significant pause. "I am grateful you have found your mate, but I believe it would be wise for you to truly examine the scope of your power, Noah. The tie to your emotions is too great, the potential for harm to others equally great if you do not examine and adjust to the ways your power has grown. You have worried too long about things other than yourself. Take this time of adjustment to your mate to find your own depths. Only then can you truly control them."

"Gideon, you sound strangely like my *Siddah*," Noah said quietly, no humor in the statement at all.

"I am your *Siddah*. I will be *Siddah* to you until the day I leave this plane of existence. No matter how many centuries pass, that bond is never broken. When I see my fosterlings floundering, it does not matter to me their age and their position in this society. I taught you to embrace your power, to always plumb its depths for your best abilities, and you have always done so . . . up until I believe the moment your own power began to intimidate you."

Noah's eyes clouded with an ominous darkness, his expression and stance turning to stone.

"Kes is here now. If I were *intimidated*, as you say, then you know it will end with the balance she will bring me. You waste your conjecture and worry on me, Ancient One."

"Do I?" Gideon raised a silvered brow. "Tell me this, Noah. When your uncontrolled power strikes your Druid mate, what consequence do you suppose it will have?" Gideon moved so that he was side by side with the Demon King against the edge of his desk. He leaned in to speak softly to him. "I have complete control over every nuance of my own power, Noah. This alone makes me the most powerful Demon in history. That management includes the ways in which my abilities link to my emotions.

"You have seen how your sister has been affected by the connection we have. It has been over two years since we fully Imprinted. She is still growing in leaps, still struggling to compensate for this growth. Isabella," he cited further, taking no apparent note of the King's flinch, "became an incredible Druid under Jacob's immense power, but even now she cannot fully control it. In the beginning she was bludgeoned by her abilities. It will take her decades to understand how to tone down her premonitions alone.

"When your mate looked into my eyes the other day, she whipped through my entire essence in a heartbeat, without even knowing what she was doing. It was pure instinct. What followed after her initial summary was an ability I have never seen before, and I will be much surprised should I ever see it again. You and your Fire can draw on power and energy, you can even take its quantitative measure by reading a power aura, but no one can map out a precise schematic of another being's powers *and weaknesses* like Kestra can now do. Untrained, I might add, yet with full comprehension of what she is studying all the same. What was more, your newly fledged mate reached inside me and unearthed the path necessary for me to heal others while in astral form. She showed it to me, and I have already begun to examine it. She was not only accurate, but chillingly so for one who had only learned of our existence shortly before. Information, I am assuming, that was responsible for her panic attack."

"No," Noah said numbly. "It was something else. Though perhaps this was partly an exacerbating factor," he admitted. Then he focused on the Ancient fully. "I knew something was happening between you. I even understood she was caught up in a reflexive use of her new power, and that taking the measure of a power was a part of that ability. But I never suspected anything like this talent to lead even *you* to an undiscovered resource within yourself." The King looked across to Kestra. "I could not touch her mind while she was seeking so deeply within you."

"The communication between you is young yet. Already stronger than it was then, I am assuming. And here we come back to my point," Gideon pointed out quietly. "Great power requires more than just great control, Noah. It requires understanding and management. You would put a cork into the mouth of a volcano and expect the pressure to never seek relief? Stop merely controlling what you fear in yourself. Do this before you lose the opportunity to manage yourself with knowledge and the same wisdom which you use in all other things. Be aware that there is an inevitability here. You have your mate to help you now, and you will help her as well, but do not allow it to come to the point that she taps into a part of you that you cannot help her understand because—"

"Because I do not understand it myself," Noah finished softly for him. The monarch reached to rub the back of his neck as tension pooled there in a dull, twisting ache of clenching muscles. He looked over at Kestra and Elijah, and found her breathtaking blue eyes fixed squarely on him, her concern clear on her face, a small frown pulling on her pretty lips as she flicked a wary, assessing gaze at Gideon. For the second time that day he found himself relaxing under the balm of her concern and giving her a calming smile. Noah looked into Gideon's expectant gaze. "Thank you, *Siddah*," he said, nodding his head in a rather formal bow of respect for his old mentor. The King had a sudden thought that sent shadows over his features. "Gideon, is there something you are not telling me? Something I should know?"

Gideon knew he could not hesitate and sound truthful. He wasn't one to lie, and he would never betray Legna's heartfelt request to spare Noah the truth about how he had hurt her. So he gave the question his own interpretation in order to satisfy all conditions.

"I believe I have told you everything I needed to impart to

you," he said easily. "Now, if you will forgive me, your sister is rather adamantly requesting my attendance, as well as the Captain's, at Siena's festivities for the night."

"I will miss you here this year," Noah found himself saying suddenly. He instantly chided himself for it. Holidays had paled for him since his closest friends and family had scattered across the lands to do their duties as mates and ambassadors, duties *he* had often asked them to take on as their King. He had been determined never to show his personal feelings on such subjects, so he would not make others feel conflict with their other lives. "But next year," he added with quick ease, "Seth will be older and perhaps I will host a multicultural Samhain or Beltane, bringing all my distant emissaries home and their foreign friends and courts with them."

"A fine idea," Gideon agreed. "Though I doubt the xenophobic Mistrals will attend, I do not see why all the other Nightwalkers would not. I suspect it is time to engage in this manner of gathering. Peace and Destiny be with you tonight, Noah," he said in farewell, reaching to clasp arms with the King. "Legna and I are pleased to see your future happiness secured in this woman," he said, nodding toward Kestra. "She is strong and intelligent. A fit mate for you. However, she is greatly scarred on an emotional level. This will be a difficult passage for you both and we wish you luck, as well as offering any assistance you might need."

"Thank you, my friend. Give Legna and Seth my deepest love and fondest wishes to see them very soon."

"After the moon has waned some." Gideon smiled with unusually suggestive humor. "I do not think we should dare to pop in until you and Kestra are done becoming acquainted."

Noah laughed and, with a clasp of his shoulder, sent the medic across the room to fetch Elijah.

Kestra had been split between the two conversations, neither of which required much of her input. Elijah chattered a stream of amusing statements that she realized were directed at teasing Noah about her presence and the effect it promised to have on the King's bachelor lifestyle. Apparently, Noah had taken great joy in busting the chops of his newly attached attachés for the changes in their behaviors since they'd taken their women into their lives. Or so Elijah felt. She rather liked the warrior's easygoing manner, but she couldn't fully enjoy it while she was worried about what was disturbing Noah as he conversed with the healer. She felt it pulling at her skin and blood, her very heart and spirit, the urge to somehow be a part of anything troubling he faced.

She had been considering why he had so urgently called her down to him earlier. She'd thought there was something wrong, but now she understood that he'd done this so she would be at his side as he faced potentially disturbing news from his commanders. He had wanted her to be involved, if only to begin learning how his monarchy worked. If only to meet these men who meant such a great deal to him.

She leaned forward, drawing on all her grace and manners to lay a warm, elegant hand on Elijah's arm. "I'm sorry to interrupt you, but could you explain these rogues to me, the ones who killed the Shadowdweller?"

"Yes, of course," the warrior said, not even batting an eyelash before he launched into an explanation about the lawless Vampires who were killing other Nightwalkers to accumulate power through the drinking of their blood.

"I have met Jasmine briefly, but what is her role in this?"

"She's Damien's right-hand adviser. A Vampire," he said, in case she didn't know. "Recently we created a network of Nightwalkers, Vampires mostly, and spread it out across the world to catch any Vampire who thought that this would be a fun way of gathering power. It's a young network, not even complete yet. We had hoped to have it complete before anyone had enough time to think about doing this thing that was once forbidden."

"Forbidden?"

"Until recently, it was forbidden for a Vampire to drink Nightwalker blood. It was mostly a mystique factor, folklore of horrors that would happen to a Vampire if they did such a thing. Wisely, it was a method of stopping this very thing from happening."

"What changed?"

"Damien took a Lycanthrope bride and took her blood. That and we found a hidden Library of great and ancient works that showed Vampires had once married interracially, blood exchanges included. It seems they sabotaged themselves in the matter of love and soul mates in the process of reining in a threat, just like we Demons did when we slaughtered the Druids a thousand years ago."

Kes paused only a single beat before her eyes lit with comprehension.

"Druids are meant to be Imprinted with Demons. You destroyed your own soul mates?"

"Yeah. I'm thinking our ancestors weren't too clever."

"Barbaric is a better word. But"—she held up a hand—"I understand it must have been a barbaric time. So you're saying Vampires cut off access to their own soul mates when they made the taboo about taking Nightwalker blood. Damien made a choice, take his soul mate or leave the taboo intact, right?"

"And he chose Syreena, his mate." Elijah nodded and looked pleased. "We've all ditched a lot of foolish prejudices these past few years."

"But at a huge price," Kes noted.

"Anything worth having is worth paying a huge price for."

"I would have to agree."

She tapped her foot in a rare giveaway about her own high emotions on the topic. Her long glance at Noah made her equally readable. She was unaware of the genuine pleasure that shone in Elijah's eyes. It was the same for all of them, this almost heartbreaking joy they felt to know Noah had at last found the one who would save him from himself, the only one who could truly protect their King from an agonizing lifetime of loneliness and potentially endless shame and pain.

"Are you a soldier?" he asked her suddenly, startling her.

"Why would you ask that?" she asked.

Elijah tapped the side of his nose once, lightly. "Gun oil, for one. The cut of your body is extraordinary for a human woman, I know that much. And I know a fellow warrior when I see one. The way your eyes drift over the exits regularly, the way you are sitting so you can see everyone in the room, and you aren't sitting back relaxed, you're perched on the edge of your seat as if you want to fly out of it the instant you have to."

"Actually, I was a Marine once," she confessed, again surprised at her honesty. "Seemed the natural course for me after . . . after a childhood and college career full of athletics. I went to Annapolis."

"Really? An officer, eh?"

"Yes. I went right out of high school. My parents had died, so I was able to commit myself completely. You can go pretty far if you dedicate yourself."

"When did you opt out?"

"Now, who says I opted out?" she asked with a laugh.

"Because of how Noah found you, Kes. We all know about it. You weren't in uniform at the time."

"True," she agreed. She was becoming increasingly uncomfortable with his logic and line of questioning. Luckily, she saw Noah and Gideon break apart and head in their direction. She was on her feet instantly, wiping her hands against her short skirt before taking the one Noah offered out to her.

"Our apologies, Kes, but we must be going and will not see you at the festival," Gideon said graciously, bowing his lavender-hazed head toward her.

See through my eyes, quickly.

She felt Noah look at her, but she didn't look away from

Gideon. She only strove to keep him there a moment or two longer in order to give Noah time to work his way into the front of her mind.

"I'm very glad to have met you both," she said, reaching to shake each of their hands again, making sure to look at each man distinctly before releasing them.

Kestra gasped when they both popped out of existence right before her eyes. Noah laughed softly at her surprise.

"It is teleporting. My sister is able to teleport herself and others at a thought. She was clearly waiting for her cue."

"Did you see Gideon? What was all that spray paint around him?"

"It is called a power aura. I can see them, too. All Fire Demons can. Apparently you can, too."

"So why him and no one else?" she asked, slapping her thigh in her frustration.

"I would say it is because you mapped his power last night, Kes. Relax. This is how it is going to be for a while. Luckily, I could explain this one."

"This one?" She rolled her eyes. "But you don't see everyone like that, do you? Because personally, I would get eyestrain."

"I can control it. So can you. We will test this ability another time. You need your energy for tonight, and playing capacity parlor tricks will wear you out."

"Oh, is that right?" Her attention was immediately on him as he curled her tightly to his side.

"And did I mention how damn adorable and sexy you are in this dress?"

"You mentioned nothing of the kind," she said, allowing herself to sinuously cuddle up against his hard frame until she was content and comfortable. "In fact, you have been rather silent since I came down here."

"I had business to take care of first," he reminded her.

"Yes, but I couldn't escape the feeling that I had done something displeasing to you," she said pointedly.

He didn't bother to deny it in the least. "It was that moment you thought you were standing amongst us as if you were my blond trophy. It upsets me that you have been in my mind and yet do not realize how such a behavior is in no way part of my makeup."

"Oh," she said, the dawning understanding causing her to look away. "I'm sorry. It was unfair, I know." She sighed softly, reaching to draw a pattern with her fingers against the fabric over his chest. "I'm still getting to know you, but that isn't a fair excuse. You've never given me cause to believe you capable of that level of chauvinism." She paused, absorbing the heat of him through her fingertips, the appendages sipping at him like hungry little straws. He was so warm. He always felt so damned good. It was almost addicting. "I'm also now realizing I have to learn about myself as a person connected to you, and I was feeling a little off my mark with such powerful strangers around me.

"To be fair to myself," she added, "I'm also not used to someone monitoring my every callous thought. I can have a very cynical, bitter mind sometimes. A defense mechanism, I suppose. I warned you I was normally not a nice person."

"And yet you exhibited flawless manners and etiquette with Elijah just now," he countered, leaning forward to brush his lips through her bangs. "Something of a contradiction, are you not?"

"I wouldn't agree. Everything I do is designed to get me something I want or need. I'm a mercenary, remember? I needed Elijah's information, and I wanted to make a pleasing enough impression so that I wouldn't be perceived as a threat to you by him. I'm a tough gal, but I'm *not* tough enough to go up against your own personal Goliath."

Noah choked out a laugh. "He *can* be intimidating at first sight."

"Intimidating? That's what you call it?" She snorted indelicately. "He's a pit bull. He figured out I was military-trained in-like-five seconds and then he dogged me for my entire résumé."

"That is why he is in charge of my fighters." Kestra didn't mistake the swell of pride beneath Noah's humor. "Let me know if he tries to recruit you."

"You'll be the first to know," she assured him. She smiled up at him as she slid her fingers around the soft waistband and leather belt of his breeches, these dyed a piratical black in harmony with a black silk shirt. His black and tan boots had been replaced with entirely black Hessians as well. "You look very Prince Goth tonight," she remarked. "Hair slicked all in order into a tail." She teasingly reached for his hairline and he dodged her mischievous fingers. She then kissed his cheek and rubbed her pouting lips along the line of his jaw, murmuring, "Hmm, freshly shaved and aftershaved. Feeling so soft and smelling so pretty." She laughed when he placed a hand over her face and tried to push her away, but she had already slid her hands into his front pockets, securing herself to his body very tightly. Defeated, he had to slide his hand down from her face, stopping when she nipped at his passing thumb with possessive lips. He began to rub her lower lip with speculation shimmering in his eyes. "One would think you had a hot date tonight."

"I do have a hot date tonight," he agreed. "I am expected to make an appearance at the festival."

"I see. Deep in a dark English forest," she mused. "Where couples frolic behind every bush and tree."

"No," he chided. Then he smiled. "I told you, frolicking comes *after* the festival."

Kestra made a small adjustment of her hands, seeking him through the soft fabric of his pants as she licked her lips, and subsequently his nearby thumb, her eyes shimmering with mischief.

"All frolicking?"

Noah was watching the sexy slide of her tongue when the

touch of her hands seemed to come out of nowhere. He sucked in a soft, startled breath as her fingers rubbed him from their covert hiding places. She chuckled low in her throat as she watched the gray in his eyes cloud over darkly.

"I want you to know," he said roughly, pausing to close his eyes as she caught his thumb in her mouth and slowly, with a sweep of her tongue, sucked it with sexy suggestiveness. His entire body went into instant meltdown as she toyed with him. He barely managed to complete his point. "I am required to make this appearance."

Kes slid a hand free of his pocket so she could fully cup him through his zipper. She made a soft sound of admiration as he blossomed into rigidity beneath her insistent fondling. His hands had come around her shoulders and were squeezing her tight enough to bruise her. She reached for his mouth and he obliged her instantly.

Here *he* was the one in charge of the aggression. His lips crushed down on hers in a full-out assault. He delved into her mouth wildly, a reward and reflection of the fire she had lit with so simple a match. She caught his tongue, sucking it suggestively now as her palm pressed up the hot length of erect male flesh beneath her touch.

Noah groaned loudly, unable to help himself as she ripped the sound out of him with her skillful playing. He felt her take a step and he automatically stepped back under the press of her body. Before he knew it, she had him backed into his desk and she wrapped herself around him like a snake, taking his wild kisses with delighted little laughs of encouragement, her hand taking his and placing it on her backside. He could feel the ridiculously short hem of the minidress she wore right at the tips of his fingers. He slid his hand beneath the thin gingham and felt the shock of completely naked feminine flesh filling his hand warmly.

"Sweet Destiny, Kes," he gasped, "you have nothing on under this dress!"

She shrugged and actually batted her lashes at him, the little minx. "I was in a rush."

She heard him curse roundly, and she burst into laughter even as he flipped their positions against the desk, seating her on the edge and grabbing both of her thighs and hooking them onto his hips. He kissed her savagely until she was too breathless to laugh, his hands sliding up under her dress with heat and eagerness. He behaved as though he hadn't touched her in weeks, rather than hours, and she reveled in the power of his craving for her. His hands ran burning paths up over her hips, one breaking to settle in the sensitive small of her back, the other continuing on until he was cupping her breast, kneading the full flesh with enough passion to bend her back over his bracing hand.

Noah wanted nothing more than to shuck the slip of nothingness she called a dress off her body and devour every inch of her skin. He could not believe she had stood there conversing with a roomful of men in what had amounted to nothing but a—well, he couldn't think of a metaphor at the moment. Her hands were driving him to distraction.

The Demon King was no fool, however. He was also very cognizant of the benefits to the immodesty of her apparel. He slid his hand down from her breast, sweeping over her belly until his fingers crept between her thighs, playing a fair game of turnabout as he sought sensitive, damp flesh.

"My, my, my," he murmured against her ear as he stroked through rich, honeyed folds. "Someone has been thinking some *very* exciting thoughts."

"You would know," she gasped, her voice so low and sexy it caused heat to claw at his groin in response. Everything she did seemed designed to make him swell beyond reasonable capacity, and he ached with the pleasurable pain of it. Without any further preamble, Noah slid a finger inside her. She shuddered, and he felt it from the inside of her body outward.

"You know what?" he said suddenly, removing his touch and making her exclaim in consternation at the unexpected deprivation. "You will forgive me for my impatience, baby," he whispered hotly as he reached to rapidly free himself from his pants, "but you pick the damnedest times and the worst places."

Her response was to nod vigorously in understanding. He reached for her, cupping her buttocks in his hands and dragging her to the very edge of the desk. He settled his throbbing length against her and she gasped with that sensation of first touch, so exciting and anticipatory at the same time. Her hands instinctively dove into his hair at the back of his neck, her fingers cupping his head as he fastened his mouth to the line of her throat as if he would devour her even as he claimed her. He slid like pure heated steel against her, and her entire body trembled as tongues of fire licked up inside her from that contact point. She felt him poise himself against her entrance, tickling her with inevitability.

Kestra felt him hesitate. Hold back. She made a whimpering sound of complaint, her body trembling in his iron grip as he denied her needs. Then she felt his hair brushing her cheek as his head picked up and his entire body went still as death. She could feel the hackles along the back of his neck rising beneath her sensitive fingers. She pulled back to look at his face, her heart rate suddenly picking up for all new reasons as she saw the darkening expression on his face.

"What is it?" she asked warily.

"Trouble." He looked at her and, cupping her head between his hands, kissed her regretfully. "Sorry, baby, but we have to finish this later."

"Of course." She immediately let go of him, letting him step away in order to resituate his clothing. She hopped down from the desk, smoothing her dress back down into place. She self-consciously rubbed a hand over her bruised lips, but it was the restless shifting of her needy body that she couldn't seem to hide.

"*Kikilia*, do me a favor and stand in front of me for a minute or two?"

She laughed, grateful for the release of her keyed-up tension as he leaned against the desk and pulled her back against him.

"Play trophy blonde?" she asked.

"Human shield is more like it," he said dryly. "And do not wriggle that backside of yours or so help me . . ."

"I will do my level best," she promised. "And it's *Druid* shield," she corrected on a quick whisper.

"How could I forget?" he said softly, unable to contend with his feelings about the remark that indicated her acceptance of who she was becoming, versus the wall of dread and torrential rage approaching them from an outside source. Noah was no empath, but the energy of these emotions was something he knew all too well.

They both looked up when a shower of dust blasted into the hall through an open plate in one of the high windows. Jacob materialized with a vicious twist of dust molecules, his dark eyes blazing with outrage and his fists clenched even before he began to speak.

"Noah, Benjamin the artisan has been murdered."

"What?" Noah's voice pitched so low and so dark so suddenly that Kestra felt ice walk down her spine even though his breath was hot on the back of her neck. Leaning against him as she was, she felt every muscle in his body coiling into a position of flexed fury.

"His throat torn open, among other sadistic wounds. I saw the body myself." The usually steady Enforcer actually shuddered slightly. "It was an accident, really, that I should come across him. It being Samhain, I keep watch for hints from nature of things out of place, as most Demons leave signs of their struggles even when they manage to cloak themselves from me in other ways. I saw carrion birds and . . . the kill was fresh. Last night, right before dawn, I would wager."

"The Vampire rogues," Kestra said. "Clever to just beat the dawn in such a way, when the Demon himself was probably more focused on getting home to bed. He would get a little sloppy, not be paying any real attention as he paced himself against the coming sun."

"That is exactly what I thought," Jacob agreed. Kestra took note that the Enforcer accepted her input in equal stride, no hint of ego or the usual macho nonsense she had dealt with in human society.

"Jacob, do you have a trail?"

"To be honest, Noah, I did not even bother to check. I came right here. Benjamin was a Water Demon. Adult level, about the midrange."

"They knew he was just powerful enough to be of value, but as an artisan was likely to be unskilled in battle tactics," Kestra mused. When both men looked at her with surprise, she shrugged and tilted a wry grin at them. "What? It's what I would do."

Jacob opened his mouth to speak, but closed it with a silent snap.

"It is a long story, my friend," Noah offered him gently. He moved his mate aside, letting her lean back beside him so he could see her as she contributed to the conversation.

"This means they are on our territory, Noah, during Samhain, our weakest, most vulnerable time save Beltane. And I hate to say it, but I can only think of one reason why they would choose Water."

"To countermand Fire, of course." The trio looked up to see Jasmine standing in what Kestra had to classify as a classic superheroine pose. Feet braced in heeled boots of burgundy that climbed to her lower thigh, tight wine-colored shorts that were very much just that—short. And a midriff-baring sweater in the lightest of pinks that was, in a shocking bid for modesty, long sleeved. Her hands were on her hips, one of which was thrust to the side, causing the gemstones and silver linked around her waist and through her navel ring to catch the sparkle of the light. "Or so they would like you to think. Your power is not truly all about Fire, though, is it?" she mused aloud, even though it was clearly rhetorical. "You manipulate energy. Scads of energy. You could put the lot of them to sleep like that!" She snapped hard, the sound echoing in the room. "They would have to be insane to pull a stunt like coming after you."

"I do not know, Jas. If there's a time to try, Samhain is it. Plus, the extra burden of a new mate," Jacob pointed out. "This makes him very vulnerable." He suddenly raised a staying hand to Kestra. "No offense."

"No . . . *offense* is exactly what this is about," Kestra countered. "They want a target that is powerful, yet vulnerable. One who they can hit offensively who puts up the least amount of defense or resistance. The proof is in the victims chosen so far. Youthful. Nonwarriors. That doesn't describe Noah, with or without me. Do you want to know what my suspicion is?"

Noah arched a brow at his mate and, in spite of the grimness of the situation, allowed delight and pride to swell over him, hoping she was reading his mind just then. She paused to smile ever so slightly before continuing, letting him know the answer to that.

"I want to know why the body was left out in the open. Knowing carrion birds are in the region? Knowing a missing Demon would be searched for? Forgive me a minute if this sounds callous in regard to your fallen friend, but . . . why not burn? Why not bury? Why would anyone leave fresh meat lying in your path?"

"A trap. A hunter's trap. Fresh kill lures the prey," Jacob said.

"I think it's more of a decoy." Jasmine spoke up suddenly, meeting Kestra's eyes so Kes could see the understanding dawning. "Oh, lookie over here at what we found. Buzz . . .

buzz . . . busy bees trying to figure out what it means. Meanwhile, it has been left like some drugged-up hunk of meat for us to get fat and lazy on while all hell breaks loose elsewhere."

"And our backs end up turned away from the real game." Kes looked fully at Noah. "I have used this ploy hundreds of times. It's a classic diversionary tactic. Even the best trained people will fall for it for at least too long to realize they've been had. Look at what Jacob did, for example. He came straight to you, to raise the hue and cry. No offense," she tossed back to him with a soft wink.

"None taken," he said, looking at Noah with an expression of pure amusement.

"It didn't occur to him for a moment to play it close to the vest, whatever his reasons—protocol, experience, outrage—and if your enemy knows enough about you, they can predict this."

"If there is one thing we Vampires know, it is how vengeful Demons are over the death of one of their flock," Jasmine pointed out. "We learned that during the wars."

"Yes, I remember teaching it to you the hard way," Jacob remarked with a flash of cockiness and a side shot of humor sharp enough to defuse any insult the Vampire might have perceived.

He underestimated her humor, though. She chuckled quite readily.

"Okay, so we won't run around like chickens with our heads cut off. But how do we figure out the real target?" Noah asked.

"Wrong," Jasmine said suddenly, her head picking up and her heels snapping hard against the marble flooring as she came closer. "Actually, you need to send out a whole flock of chickens." She shook her dark head at their blank expressions. "Vampires are telepaths. If it's a lure, they left someone behind to report when it gets taken. If no one shows at the sight of the body, they will call off their assault."

"Well, maybe that is the best idea."

"Yes, until next time when we have no warning at all," Noah countered. "At least tonight we have a slight advantage."

"I did not sense a Vampire. I would know," Jacob said.

"Would you? With all these stolen powers in them, Jacob, would you know?" Jasmine paused to drum her fingers on her thigh as she gathered her thoughts, clearly already knowing that Jacob would concede her point. "Something stinks about this. I know Vampires. They will think in circles trying to outlogic an enemy. They aren't just after another kill this time."

"It's a game," Kes realized. "Catch me if you can. Serial killer modus operandi."

"That means it is about enjoying our pain and our fear," Noah realized, his jaw clenching briefly with anger as he absorbed this sadistic intent. "Jas, what do we do? They are your brethren, you will understand them best."

"Distraction technique," the brunette began to tick off on her fingers, "enemy knowledge, taunting with pain and fear, making themselves out to be smarter than all the rest of us . . ."

"Least likely target," Kes said suddenly. "Jas, if you were a . . . okay . . . uh . . . I mean, as a Vampire," she corrected herself, making them all chuckle with a release of growing tension, "who would be the last person you'd ever dare to go up against?"

"You mean besides me and Damien?" she asked with a sparkle of danger in her eyes. "I'd have to say Noah."

"That is what I thought in the first place," Jacob said with exasperation.

"Wait! Wait." Kestra's hands flew out to stop the others from speaking, her voice a sharp command that cut into their attention. "Besides who, did you say?"

"Me and Damien. The Prince."

"Why wouldn't they go after you?" Kes demanded.

"Imminent death and destruction?" Jasmine snorted.

"That and Vamps don't gain power when they feed on each other. There would be no point. Except to gain the monarchy."

"That would be a reason, Jas," Jacob pointed out dryly.

"Then explain to me this: Why Samhain? There's no sense to doing it on Samhain. Vampires aren't weakened by it. Why not wait and gather more power if they are going after Damien's crown? We have a celebration tonight, too. The first festival for Samhain since Damien returned to the homeland. The place will be packed with Vampires. It would be suicide."

"Or the perfect cover for an assassination attempt," Kes mused. "Invite the enemy onto your territory."

"No. Damien knows these rogues. He's being very careful. He promised me. He could sense Cygnus and his bunch in a heartbeat if they entered the castle."

"Are you sure? Even with all this power gathering?" Noah countered her in return.

"It's *Damien*, Noah. Damien can sense any and every Nightwalker on the planet." She made a disgruntled sound at her perceived disparagement of the capabilities of her Prince. Kes was forced to wonder if she was too biased to see the truth.

No. She is right. Damien is not the kind you can sneak up on when he is on the alert.

"Provided he's on the alert," she argued with Noah aloud, her thought so irritable that she forgot all about telepathy.

Out of the corner of her eye, Kestra saw Jasmine stiffen suddenly. She jerked her head up when she caught the telltale reaction. The men noticed it, too, and Jasmine suddenly had all eyes on her as her face paled even more than it naturally was.

"Oh no. Oh, *damn*!"

"Jas!" Noah snapped when she made a move as if she wanted to take off.

She turned back, fury exploding in her dark eyes, fangs exposed as she snarled at the Demon King.

"They know I am here, and Damien is unprotected without me!"

"You just said—" Jacob protested.

"Add it up. Samhain leaves access to the castle; Damien thinks the rogues are headed here. And I myself put him on his guard and made him promise me to be careful!" Jasmine growled, ferocious black flames leaping in her eyes.

"Jasmine," Noah said helplessly, "I do not understand your point."

"I knew the Lycanthrope bitch would be the death of him!" The Vampire hissed furiously. "*She's* the one they're after, Noah. Low offensive, low defensive, you said, right?" Jasmine confronted Kestra. "Make noise in Demon territory and keep Jasmine far away from Damien. Kill the Lycanthrope, get her very extraordinary powers, extraordinary even among her own kind, and you get a two for one. Damien will never survive the anguish if something happens to . . . to . . ."

"His soul mate," Kestra whispered.

Chapter 16

Damien didn't even want to breathe the sigh of relief he felt when Syreena finally fell into a fully exhausted sleep. He levitated gingerly out of their bed, floating over her to retrieve some clothing from across the room with all the stealth he, in all his power, could possibly muster. He had been through one of Syreena's heat cycles before, but it seemed like this time she was driven beyond even her own capacity. Frankly, he couldn't remember the last time his body ached so much. She was enough to wear out even an Ancient like himself, he thought, a fond smile and a repressed laugh lighting his eyes.

He slid on his trousers. Syreena was driven by multiple incentives: fear, need, and desire. The desire was for him, no more or less than it always was between them, just magnified in frequency perhaps. Her need was for a child. A child of their love, an heir for them both, each of them being in line with a throne of their peoples. A child she had longed for and, until they had met, thought she would never be privileged to know the joy of. Just as she had never realized her dreams of so loving a mate and marriage would come to fruition.

And the fear was the most obvious of all. She was terrified she would not have that compatibility of chemistry they needed. Not that he would be incompatible with her, he was beginning to realize, but that she would be incompatible with him. She was afraid that her singular genetics, the mutation she had suffered during her childhood, would prevent her from conceiving. She feared barrenness.

Damien tucked in a heavy linen shirt at his waistline as he cast a long look at his sleeping wife. She could very well be right, he realized, and he had to come to terms with that if it were true. But unlike her, he did not feel such a pressure to discover the truth of the matter. He loved her. He wanted children; right away was fine with him, but later was just as fine. He was not worried and did not see why she should put herself under so much pressure because of one failed heat cycle. It wasn't entirely unheard of, in spite of what she would have him believe. He had been affiliated with the world of Lycanthropes long enough to know that much.

For the moment, however, he had exhausted her for what he hoped was a good couple of hours. It was more than enough time for him to run a circuit of his territorial borders and then make a fairly decent showing at the Samhain festival downstairs, which his keen hearing told him was already well under way. She would be extremely peeved with him when she woke to find him gone. But as soon as she came searching for him, he would pull himself away and tend to any needs she might have, with more than enough love and attention to mollify even her spiky little temper.

He also needed to hunt. That meant leaving Vampire territory and seeking human holdings. Damien sought within himself to judge the time, even as he slid on his shoes and cinched his belt. It was early yet and he would easily be able to find prey. Then, as he combed his fingers through his hair, he scanned the interior of the citadel for specific energy sources. As expected, there were no hostile entities. He would have felt those immediately, no matter the holiday and the influx of Vampires. Then again, it was always the threat you *didn't* expect that was most dangerous. For that he had Stephan. The Vanguard leader was stalking the halls and the celebrations belowstairs with his usual brooding thoroughness. Though home defense was usually Jasmine's venue, she being far more willing than he was to make a merry fight with one of her own, Stephan was more than capable of facing any threat no matter what face it wore. Damien sent a brief telepathic warning to Stephan that he was leaving the premises and that Syreena would require a guard at her door until he returned. Once he had Stephan's acknowledgment, he slipped into the tower room and took flight out of the window.

To Stephan, nothing was more important in that moment than seeing to the protection of the Prince's woman. He knew very well how crucial she was to the Prince's well-being, and Damien's well-being was always his top priority, just as it was Jasmine's. The 6'5" Vampire made his way through the crowd slowly as he sent a telepathic order to one of his most trusted lieutenants in the Vanguard.

He attracted attention as he always did. Between his size and his sheen of blond hair, he was something of an anomaly amongst his own breed. They rarely produced blonds for some unknown reason and it made him a curiosity with some, attractive to others. Most remarkable was his size. He, like Damien, did not have that slimness and almost gaunt athleticism that was to be expected of his breed. He was bulky across the shoulders and chest; his muscular waist was thick and his legs were as long and dense as tree trunks. This was what he preferred to be noticed for. His overwhelming size was sometimes all the deterrent he needed when dealing with those who would contest him.

So it did not come as a surprise to him that a path opened up for him no matter what direction he headed in, no matter how thick the crowd in the common levels of the citadel. He considered sending a second guard to Syreena and Damien's quarters. There were a great many Vampires crowded together, a large cross-section of a very powerful population. Unsurprisingly, there were also Demons and Lycanthropes milling about. Not many, but more than had ever attended a foreign Samhain celebration in the past. He suspected it was a combination of factors: the recent exchanges in ambassadors that had opened up the cultures to one another, and the loosening of Demon cultural restraints that had them seeking the highly promiscuous newness of Vampire partners that hadn't been previously open to them. After a few centuries, Stephan supposed, the same faces over and over would definitely be cause for searching out new ones.

Frankly, if Syreena was anything to judge by, Lycanthropes had a fair sex drive themselves. On par with Vampires, if not—and he would never have thought to say such a thing—exceeding it. He had not seen so much as a hair on Damien's head for the past four days. Their telepathic contact a moment ago was the most he'd heard from him in all that time, except for a hastily prescribed instruction to take over the rounds of the territorial borders until otherwise ordered. He supposed they were taking advantage of Jasmine's absence. That woman made no bones about how she felt about Damien's marriage and the can of worms it had opened, but Jasmine blamed Syreena for the entire boatload, whereas Stephan was more inclined to lay the majority of the blame at Damien's doorstep.

Still, he could hardly complain. He'd been fairly bored up until Damien's marriage, even considering going to ground for only the third time in his life until a more exciting era came along. In all honesty, all of this peace was bad for a soldier's disposition and attention threshold. Sure, he could train and learn various war forms and run drills and all that, but he was 633 years old. Exactly how much could a person dedicate to the same calling, and for how long, with no one or nothing to exercise the skills upon? Sometimes he missed the eras of serious warfare. Human wars were amusing. Damien had always loved a good human war and would take along all comers for the party back in the day. But after a thousand years, Damien had grown tired of losing his companions on the battlefields and had become peace loving.

The best had been the war with the Demons. That had been an awesome century for battle. The Demons were extraordinary fighters and cunning strategists. Their keenest skill had always been the ability to reason out their enemy's movements and plans of actions—an impressive trick when the Vampires were fully telepathic and Mind Demons had barely begun emerging at the time.

Yes, he had loved warring with the Demons. He'd only been two hundred some–odd years old at the time, just a minor soldier in the Vanguard, but that was how he had begun to make his name for himself back in the day.

This domestic protection gig was not his scene. This was Jasmine's territory, watching Damien's back. She was like a cat, able to sit and watch for prey for hours, just waiting for the bat of an eyelash to pounce. He found it boring, making the same circuit again and again. He longed to be out on the network. Sure, it meant hunting his own, but a battle was a battle, an enemy an enemy. No matter what, he would always be loyal to Damien. His area of expertise was in the defense and offense against those with Nightwalker powers, and if lawbreaking Vampires started accumulating these powers for themselves, he and the Vanguard were by far the best solution.

He decided to send an exterior guard up to the tower turrets to guard the exterior access to the royals' bedchamber until they saw or sensed Damien's return. He felt infinitely better knowing there was now extra protection for the Princess, and he turned his attention elsewhere.

* * *

Cygnus received the message the moment Damien crossed the border of his territory, heading out to hunt. The Vampire Prince wouldn't circuit his borders until he had been refreshed by prey, habitually choosing to not face any potential dangers without nutritional fortification first. It was what any Vampire would do. And therein lay their advantage.

Hiding from the Vanguard had been no easy trick, but Damien was the only true wild card. No Vampire could claim equal skill in detection of a threat as Damien. With the exception of perhaps Jasmine. She had an uncanny sense, that one did. But she was all the way in Demon territory, tromping over the Demon murder scene with the rest who had come to investigate it and to try to track him and his gang. His spy in Noah's lands had telepathed as much to him, and he had known it was soon going to be upon him to make his move.

The only significant risk at the citadel now that Damien was gone was Stephan. Even though the Vanguard leader was ensconced in the celebration on the first levels of the citadel, he would be on full alert and would instantly be aware of any and all intrusions. However, Cygnus's comrades were ready to cause a distraction that would lure Stephan elsewhere. Then the attack would take place, completely undetected, before Damien was even flushed with the heat of his prey.

"I don't understand!" Kestra fumed, stalking after him, running to keep up with Noah's hasty, ground-eating strides.

"That is just my point, Kes. You do not understand. If you comprehended the power of the creatures we were going to face, you would not dare make such an insane suggestion!"

"Will you stop and look at me!" she yelled at him, panting softly from their third circuit over the stairs to the second floor and back. Although it was more about being furious with him than it was about being winded.

Noah stopped midflight of stairs and obliged her, looking at her face, if not entirely into her eyes, his clouded gaze hooded by the length of his thick lashes. He finished tugging on a leather wrist sheath with its tiny knife tucked within while he waited impatiently for her to continue.

"Thank you," she managed to say, even though it wasn't quite the full attentiveness she'd wanted. She was suddenly learning that Noah could shadow his thoughts from her when he wanted to. His age, power, and experiences with a Mind Demon for a sister had given him an advantage over her. Now she couldn't even force him to reveal his true feelings.

"Noah, I think I have been in your mind thoroughly enough to know exactly what you will be coming up against. I'm not—"

"Reading a memory and accepting a concept is nothing like feeling the strike, feeling the supernatural power of a being in comparison to a human being, which, I remind you, you will always share fifty percent of a heritage with." He stepped up to her and finally made eye contact, his smoldering temper a breathtaking wall of hot emotion that she could feel against her skin and scalp. "You are not coming, Kestra, and that is my final word on the matter."

To her shock and outrage, he turned his back and continued to descend the stairs.

"Your final word?" She stormed after him, fury flushing her features. "Does this look like the damned Crusades to you?" she demanded. "Do you think I'm going to just sit here doing . . . doing embroidery or something while you wage war, praying you come home in one pigheaded, chauvinistic piece?"

She screeched to a halt when he whirled to meet her abruptly.

"Do not even dare to label me in such a manner!" he

roared into her face, the blast of his emotions manifesting in a hot explosion of air that blew back her hair and clothes violently. "There is not a woman among my people who would dare, or have cause, to utter such a thing! How am I to believe you have even the smallest idea of the enemies we go to face when you cannot even master the simplest understanding of your mate's personality?"

"Oh, I don't know," she huffed sarcastically, hands on hips, head tilted, "maybe . . . mmm . . . gee, maybe because I've only been in your magnificent presence for a max total of three days? Only *one* of which I have had access into that thick skull of yours! You aren't even listening to me!"

"I listened to you, Kestra. Your input and logic were invaluable to me tonight, and I thank you for it with all of my heart." This at least he said with sincerity, but it didn't change the stubborn set of his mouth. "But you will not come with us to battle power-drunk Vampires. You have no defenses, no offenses, and would basically be little more than . . . than a walking blood supply! I will not watch you get your throat ripped out, and I will not be bathed in my Imprinted mate's blood!"

These last statements were the ones she had truly been after, and Kestra sighed as he finally confessed them. She reached out to slide a hand around his upper arm muscles, drawing close and ignoring how hot he was with his overflow of temper.

"Noah," she said softly, causing his eyes to turn instantly troubled as she looked straight into them from her position a step above him on the stairwell. "If it's fear of my death or of my injury motivating your actions or reasoning, then I would appreciate you saying so, rather than disparaging my capabilities to face and understand my enemy."

He looked into those stunning blue eyes of hers while his body shook in a fine shudder against hers. Agitation and terror fueled the tremor. He'd been doing too much soul searching since he'd come close to her, since she'd begun to share his mind. He was too recently inundated with memories of beloved women who had been victims of violence. Each time she begged him to take her with him, he felt the terror of losing her, of finding her with her pristine white hair lying in a sea of blood. Then there was that awful moment, the memory he couldn't banish, of her very own death. A gun muzzle shoved against her fair head, forcing her spirit explosively from her body as she went limp and fell into a lifeless sprawl on the penthouse floor. Worse still, the vision of a rapist thrusting a butcher knife into her womb.

So much pain and abuse, so much horror, and he couldn't bring himself to purposely expose her to more. Expose her to beings of corrupted power and their perverse propensity for toying with their food before killing it? No.

Never.

Noah knew it wasn't fair of him to hold her responsible for his inability to cope with his fear of her being harmed. After all, she'd survived a very long time, most of it unscathed, as a Marine, a mercenary, and extreme sports fanatic. She had gleaned so much information in so short a time, had managed to so easily slip into a military intelligence mind-set, able to grasp strengths and weaknesses of Nightwalkers enough to reach high levels of conceptualization and reasoning.

She was right. He knew very well she was well versed enough in the ways and means of Nightwalkers, able to plot out intelligences for and against them, to decipher and profile their logic. She was completely aware of what she would face should she end up face-to-face with any Nightwalker with enemy intent. But even he didn't fully understand what he was going to be facing this night, the unpredictability of the rogues making this an exceptionally hazardous venture.

Her comprehension of their enemies wasn't the issue, and she was right to call him wrong for trying to make it one. But it was more than just his fear of her coming to harm, although that in and of itself was enough to compel him to lock her up like the chauvinist she'd just accused him of being.

Noah was a being who sought peace above all else. This mission was about protection and redemption. It was about removing a threat. An unwelcome and distasteful task, but a necessary one.

Kestra was just hungry for a conflict. Yes, she understood the morals of the situation and was on the proper side of the issue. However, while her morals might be sound, her motivations were skewed. She was thinking only of a woman in jeopardy at the hands of males and the opportunity for retribution. She wished to play the role of an avenging angel. She didn't realize her own motivations, or how dangerous it would be to indulge in them.

"Kes." He swallowed hard, searching for words that usually came so easily for him. Where was his effortless diplomacy when he needed it so badly to ease his way with her? Truth. It was so hard to speak the truth. "Yes, I fear for you." He reached up and palmed the nape of her neck until he had drawn her forehead to touch his. He sighed deeply with the contact, feeling relief for some reason. "I fear your being hurt. I disapprove of your vengeful motivations for wanting to be a part of this. And in spite of your exquisite intelligence and unquestionable skills, you are not up to this. Even I am uncertain of everyone escaping this conflict with their lives."

She was silent for a long minute and he lifted his head so he could see her eyes. Her mouth was set in a grim line, her eyes averted from him, a tense muscle stretched taut in her jaw. Then her sharp, cool eyes flicked up to meet his gaze and he saw acceptance seated firmly within their breathtaking facets.

"These are arguments that I can accept and understand, Noah. I'm not happy that you feel the need to insulate me from danger, but I can understand it and I can also work with you on it. As to the rest, your reasons are sound and logical.

I only wish you had been this honest to begin with and saved us argument and misunderstanding."

"I must apologize, *Kikilia*," he said softly, "for my behavior. My emotions have the better of me lately."

"I know," she said gently, wrapping her arms around his neck and settling against him. He automatically reached to hold her snug against himself, drinking in her scent and vitality. "I'm trying to remember that. Everything is so volatile lately. My head is buzzing with it all."

Her mouth drifted down onto his and his entire body lurched with excitement even before he felt her lips. Heat crawled up his neck and face, warming both their mouths as he met her kiss with a tangle of tastes and tongues. *This*, he sighed, *is what I should be doing today*. It was Samhain, and he should be doing nothing more than slowly drinking in the flavors and the heat of his mate.

"I am Fire, Kes," he said in a fierce whisper against her lips, "and it is Samhain. It is the worst time even for *me* to consider battle. I would rather be here, focusing these passions inside me toward making love to you all night until you begged me to stop. But I cannot do that."

"Well, of course not. I would never beg you to stop," she countered, licking his lips teasingly when he laughed at her. She sobered softly, though, meeting his turbulent eyes. "And I could never enjoy such a thing knowing another man could lose his wife because I selfishly kept you by my side. I'm not that type of woman. I'm not one who would beg you not to risk yourself."

"I never thought you were," he assured her. "I only meant to point out that with the volatility of Samhain upon me and my element, I will be capable of emotions and brutality none of my kith and kin have ever seen. I have but one anchor in this world to keep me to my senses and hold me to the code of honor that means everything to me, and that is *you*. I need you here, connected to me and within my mind." He touched his forehead briefly and then drifted a finger through the bangs on hers. "Your clarity, your logic, and your intellect will guide me back to my peace of mind if I overstep my emotions." His hand engulfed the back of her head and he pulled her close until her ear was beneath his lips. "You," he breathed into her soft hair, "are my tether to this world now. I have waited for you for a hundred lifetimes, praying to Destiny for a woman of strength and courage who would one day temper my soul, ease my way in this world, and She has finally answered my prayers."

Kestra tensed briefly in his grasp, but then sighed with acceptance and absorbed his fevered feelings. He had such faith in her, and she couldn't bring herself to shatter that faith, no matter what her fears might be.

"I know you fear dependence on me." Noah laughed low in his throat and she heard the harsh sting of irony. "The truth is that *I* am dependant on *you*, Kestra. I hope this is not an added source of fear for you. I know it is a hard responsibility."

"I'm not afraid of you," she murmured softly into his ear. "You may keep trying, but it won't work."

"But I am afraid of me," he said heatedly. "Of me without you. I would not have borne many more holy moons without destroying myself, baby. I know it as surely as I know how sweetly you smell, taste, and feel. My life was half lived before you came into it." He took a deep, shuddering breath. "And now that you are Imprinted upon me, my life will end a heartbeat after yours. It has to, Kestra, because nothing and no one could ever bear the violence of my grief if it did not. Do you understand, *Kikilia*?"

Kestra's heart was lodged so tightly in her throat that she could only nod against his cheek. Her chest felt as though it was going to burst apart. She was greedily soaking up the ambient heat of his fervent emotions. He tightened her to his body in a snug hug that sealed them together.

"You're just saying that because I'm so good in the sack," she choked out on an emotional laugh.

Noah laughed softly at her tension-defusing humor, but hugged her tighter, eliciting a pleased grunt from her as the air rushed out of her body.

"I hardly have enough data to make that a truthful supposition," he taunted her quietly. "Something we will work on when I return."

She pulled away from him, glancing down at the small group on the first floor awaiting their King's pleasure. She looked back at him, reaching to draw his face between her soft hands.

"I can't believe I'm going to kiss you and send you off to battle like some antebellum romance heroine." She sighed when he smiled, and leaned forward to kiss him softly. Noah immediately drew her closer, needing to take her flavor deeply into his mouth, sweeping her into his senses so he would carry her with him and remember what he would be fighting for, and what he needed to return to more than anything else.

When she finally drew back, flushed and breathless, she reached to tap his forehead.

"Knock, knock," she whispered.

Instantly, Noah opened his mind to her, connecting them as firmly as he could, sharing everything so she would be with him fully in spirit. Then he turned and descended the rest of the stairs, moving to meet his companions in this endeavor.

Stephan was focusing too hard. He could tell because he was starting to feel overwhelmed by all the presence and power milling about the citadel. Everything was becoming a steady, indistinguishable buzz, with no definition or clarity. He telepathed instructions to the guards on the lower levels and quickly moved toward the nearest exit. The moment he stepped out into the cold Romanian night, into the darkness and atmosphere of his homeland, he shook off all sense of the indoors and drew in a deep breath of cleansing refreshment.

He took long strides away from the din of celebration. All was well inside, all protected, and he was due to scan the out of doors anyway. He had to confess that he had a partiality to this side of his duties. Air. Darkness. The life of stars and mountains breathing into him. Mostly, if he sectioned away the court and castle and all that social nonsense, there was the peace of solitude.

And the tremor of trespass.

Stephan's attention snapped to with a crack of neck bones as he whirled about and into a low crouch. There was an intruder on the Prince's territory. One deemed an enemy. The eddy of evil and tainted power fluttered into him like the wings of a swarm of dragonflies. The Vampire launched into the air, flying with ferocious speed away from the citadel, casting soft but firm warnings to the guards left behind him.

It was a single being, one Stephan was more than capable of defeating all on his own, but it did not hurt to keep the others alerted to the trouble. The blond Vampire raced toward the enemy with an enormous surge of excitement flushing through him at the prospect of battle. Life rushed into him, as did power.

He saw his target instantly, a skulk in the shadows. A child's trick. Stephan landed boldly in the open.

"Rubio," he commanded, his voice booming and full of the compelling fear that all in the Vanguard could project, but none so well as Stephan. "Come forth, coward, and meet your fate." Stephan had barely finished the statement when a vile odor wafted through the crisply cold air. It was the stench of corruption.

He saw shadows flutter and he narrowed his glittering eyes, watching for tricks but not concerned enough to go in after Rubio. The weaker Vampire who thought to defy the throne and laws of their people would come crawling out to him.

"There will be order in our world," Stephan said, his voice pitching low, compelling, and seeking the weaknesses in the enemy's spine. "Your taint must be washed away." He beckoned softly, like a priest to a penitent child. "Come and be cleansed."

There was a hiss and a rustle of bushes and Rubio stumbled out of the shadows. The compulsion in Stephan's commands had proven too strong for him. As Rubio stepped closer, a small flock of birds startled, flying up between the two Vampires and then settling somewhere beyond their battleground.

"You think you are so special, so powerful," Rubio growled, struggling for composure amidst fear and the compulsion to kowtow to his sentenced fate. "Even the Vanguard can fall!" he declared.

"The Vanguard will never fall," Stephan intoned. "Strike me dead and another will blossom and grow, using my blood to feed his soul for the hunt." It was the motto of the Vanguard, known by heart for all his centuries, and probably the only truth he felt passionately about.

"I'm so glad you feel that way."

Stephan whirled with shock at the sudden voice at his back. A Vampire, whom he had no sense of, stood there. Suddenly another appeared and another, until half a dozen surrounded him.

The birds, Stephan realized.

Rubio had been but the bait, and the birds the camouflage used to squeeze him between the teeth of the trap.

"So be it," he whispered before the six leapt for him.

Chapter 17

Syreena was quagmired in the depths of her sleep. She had spent the first century of her life growing up in a monastery, where everyone went to bed late after a hard night of work, and woke early to greet the dusk. She had learned to sleep hard and sleep fast. Damien had often teased her for her ability to remain nearly comatose once she had committed herself to sleep. He had threatened to see if he could actually make love to her while she slept through it. So far, he had been unsuccessful.

So when she suddenly felt herself being pulled toward consciousness, she only partially resisted it. Syreena was confused, of course. Damien had clearly needed a good hunt and was inclined to disengage himself from her insatiable appetite whenever the opening arose. She was completely understanding of that. He wasn't of her species and wasn't drawn so overwhelmingly at these times as she was. Although he had no problems keeping pace, he also enjoyed his respites when the opportunities presented themselves.

Syreena was lying facedown in her bed, the heavy cashmere blanket barely pulled up over the swell of her backside.

She was cold, the tower off their suite making drafts as others entered and exited. It destroyed the valiant efforts of the fire Damien liked to keep burning. She wasn't cold enough to bear the icy touch that fell across her back and backside with a bold sweep, however, and it shocked her into wakefulness with a gasp. It was one of the meanest tricks in Damien's arsenal that he used to wake her, the chill of his hands prehunt on her naturally hot Lycanthrope skin.

But even as she jerked awake and rolled over to throw off the offending hand, a small clang of warning went off in the back of her head. She knew Damien's touch. She knew it like she knew how to breathe, and this wasn't right somehow. She cranked open her heavy eyelids only half a second before a weighty hand sank into her hair, wrapping it into a fist so tight the sensitive strands cringed and she cried out in pain. A second hand slid over her mouth and she had the violent sensation of being lashed to the bed, hands and feet, until she couldn't move, could barely breathe, and the hold on her hair was forcing her visual range in a single direction only.

Her heart raced in panic. She was helpless. With her hair bound, her Lycanthropic forms were lost to her. In four-point restraints, her fighting abilities were few, if not nonexistent. The only thing she had at her disposal was her young ability to cast illusions . . . and Damien, wherever he was. She was able to see down to her hand on the right side, shocked to see that it was lashed with some kind of thick mist. In fact, the entire floor was covered with a pea soup fog. It was a phenomenon she had seen her sister's husband perform. As a Wind Demon, Elijah had control over all forms of weather.

It was unlikely he would pull such a heartless stunt. He knew how she felt about being bound and helpless, ever since the Demon Ruth had used Syreena as a means to revenge herself on Siena and Elijah. As she was trying to formulate a logical supposition, she felt the heat of a fetid-smelling breath rushing up over the web of her neck and her throat. Her heart gave a jerk at the scrape of canines over her skin. She had been bitten by Damien more than once, and it had always been an ecstatic experience, but this was such a foul sensation that it made her skin crawl with terror. In the blink of an eye she understood. She knew why this attacker had come.

They wanted what Damien had had. They wanted the power of her blood.

"Such a smart girl," a voice whispered beneath her ear, spilling more of that vile-smelling breath across her senses. "One of the best parts about how easy this was is that you have no telepathy. You cannot even call out to him, can you?" He laughed halfheartedly. "So unfit a mate for our Prince. But to each his own. It matters not any longer. And as much as I would love to play, Princess, we must be going."

Where were the guards? What of Stephan? How was it possible that this enemy was able to get into the citadel, never mind able to put his hands on her?

"Dead, Princess. All dead. And even alive they would not sense us anymore unless we wished them to. Come. Time to go for a little ride."

A frightening sensation flowed over Syreena's flesh, as if she were coming physically unraveled, becoming a part of the mist that entrapped her. There was an explosion, then another, a force of air being blown out briefly, then sucking back with a pop that sent the fog in the room swirling madly. Suddenly she saw powerful legs standing in front of her eyes, and she looked up the length of the body until she could see the face of the Demon King.

He said nothing, only reassuring her with a brief glance before a ball of fire exploded into his hand, a tidy round projectile that held meteoric chaos in its center.

"You will back away from her instantly," he commanded, his voice as cold as the fire in his hand was hot.

* * *

Noah was horrified to see the Vampire who was phased half in and half out of a mist form. Either way, he was a breath away from the Princess's exposed throat. Mist was lashing her into paralysis, the Vampire's hand tightly seizing her hair. The Vampire chose a form, returning to a solid state, knowing that Noah could harm him either way if he chose to, but that he could best harm the Princess in his more easily powered form.

I will rip out her throat if you even blink, Demon King.

The telepathic voice rang through Noah's brain gratingly, and it infuriated him that the Vampire would invade him so easily. This was an Old One. One who held pure Vampire power of great maturity. Now more power than ever flushed his paled body as he had farmed abilities from unfortunate others.

To punctuate his point, the Vampire leaned a millimeter closer to Syreena, his canines puncturing her skin just enough to cause two dark trickles of blood to roll slowly down her neck. Syreena's eyes slid closed, an attempt to hide her agonizing fear, useless as two large tears escaped her lids. Noah could practically taste her impotent fury. It swelled with volcanic proportions as she felt the Vampire's tongue sampling her blood, a gift meant only for her mate, tainted with violation now.

For Noah it was like suddenly dancing on the oldest, deepest question within his pained heart. What would he have done if he had been there, in that room, when his mother had first been seized by her murderer? How would he have delivered retribution if her fragile life had hung in the grip of an unbalanced mind? Here fate had dealt him that wished-for hand, and now all he wanted was to wish it away; anything to erase the anguish written across the Princess's features.

"I will deliver you to justice, or I will deliver you to hell," Noah warned one last time, the hoarseness of his voice telling enough to make the Princess open her eyes and look at him with wide, charcoal-gray pupils. To his unending agony, he saw forgiveness flashing in those eyes. Syreena was forgiving him, in case he should fail.

"You cannot touch me," the Vampire swore.

And like that, he vanished, the Princess with him, the fog suddenly dissipating around the King's ankles. He clenched his fist, breaking up and reabsorbing the fireball as he quickly sought for the trick. His mind and thoughts whirled through information and experience. It was like dealing with a half dozen Nightwalkers at once, a powerful and frustrating puzzle. At least with a single breed there came a single expectation, a specific set of rules by which these games must be played. This Vampire and those like him who had chosen to corrupt themselves were maddening wild cards.

Noah sought for energy, somehow certain that what he did *not* see was a glamour, that both were still in the room in spite of his inability to see them. He saw the imprint of the Princess's body heat on the abandoned bed. He even saw the shadow of the Vampire's energy as he had leaned over her. But these were ghosts of the past, and there were no shades in the present. He searched for heat, for energy, and nothing in the dark room, not even a light, showed power.

Materializing out of the dust, Jacob finally took form across the room from Noah. They had teleported in from opposite sides, Jacob maintaining a dissipated form so he could have the advantage of surprise should the occasion call for it, and also to minimize discomfiture for popping up in the Vampire Prince's boudoir should the situation be a more embarrassing one, albeit one they had hoped for.

Seeing Noah floundering, he knew he needed to relinquish himself to solidity. Noah nodded to the Enforcer, a silent signal, and the Earth Demon closed his eyes, his spirit settling softly into the center of his body, his focus leaving the confines of all things man-made and reaching for the beauty of the natural. He spread this awareness into the room and into the nature around the citadel tower, slowly expanding in radius and intensity.

He suddenly jerked to look at Noah.

"Quick. Light the room. Bright."

Noah reacted without thought, his entire body bursting into flames so blindingly bright that no corner of the room was left dark, forcing Jacob to throw up a shielding hand and to flinch regardless. There was a scream of pain and Jacob and Noah watched as the protection of the shadows was torn away from the Vampire who had now dragged the captive woman to the very edge of a windowsill, only the deeply colored glass preventing his escape. He had been using his stolen Shadowdweller power to become shadow with the Princess in the darkened room. Unfortunately for the devil, it also made light extraordinarily painful to him. He had absorbed the weakness along with the ability. It was a useful piece of information that was taken note of by both Demons.

Noah lit all the torches in the room, dispersing the flames around his body, robbing the Vampire of any further useful shadow. Rows of needle-sharp teeth were lying fully against the skin of Syreena's throat now, as if the Vampire would feed even at the risk of getting caught or losing leverage. His wide eyes shifted warily from one Demon to the other. Noah heard glass cracking as the Vampire leaned his weight against it.

Threats aside, Noah couldn't burn the vile creature while he held Syreena so near. She would be just as badly burned. Unless he was somehow closer to her, he couldn't protect one from flames and destroy the other with them at the same time. His first instinct was to keep the Vampire from gaining the air, from leaving the room, but if they found their way out over the earth, Jacob's abilities would come into play and could make a great deal of difference. The Earth Demon could manipulate gravity, making Syreena far too heavy to lift, but that would only enrage her captor.

Noah felt himself reaching out for the comforting touch of Kestra's thoughts. She was thinking as hard and fast as he and Jacob were, working on even less information than they had, and she had nothing to offer. She settled for sending him supportive thoughts and her confidence that he would prevail.

Jacob, stuck in the same quandary, was examining the enemy more closely, with totally different senses. The Vampire reeked, a stench that Nightwalkers associated with corrupted souls, vile in odor to those with clean spirits. It was a mark of having gone against the natural order of their species, murdering their prey . . . murdering *Nightwalkers* for power. Jacob's kind had always been sensitive to this taint. Jacob knew Noah could smell it, and as a hunter, he knew it would make the Vampire easy to track should he escape the room.

A small pane of colored glass popped out of its leaded frame as the Vampire leaned harder and harder against it. The dark colors were meant to block out all light, but now the pane was missing, and the silver wash of the light of the full moon could be seen. Jacob contemplated demolecularization, of either the enemy or the hostage, and knew that without the benefit of touch, the transformation would take too long to prevent any damage the Vampire could do in that brief interim.

Suddenly the Vampire snarled and clamped vicious teeth into the Princess's throat. She screamed behind the hand that bound her mouth. Then, as if she had been planning it, waiting for the necessary moment, she dragged her weight forward just enough to touch the flats of her feet to the floor . . . and then launched back with all the strength in her willowy frame.

Syreena pushed just hard enough to send their combined weight back into the window, shattering glass and leaded threading and sending herself and the greedy Vampire over the sill and plummeting down toward the rock outcroppings at the base of the citadel. Noah and Jacob burst out of the room after them, rushing to see the Vampire struggle for a minute to keep his prize before realizing it was folly. In a blink he went from Vampire to bird, shocking the Demons with the transformation.

"Mistral," Jacob shouted to his King, and they both understood there had been a murder they hadn't yet heard about. Only a Mistral could change to a bird in such ways, with such speed, excepting the Vampire Prince himself, who had earned the nimble aspect from the blood of his beloved Lycanthrope wife.

Noah broke from Jacob and gave chase to the dark crow that zipped into the cover of the Romanian mountain forests. Jacob speared toward the tumbling Lycanthrope. She streaked too far and too fast ahead of him to be caught, but even as he reached to alter her relationship with gravity, her now-liberated hair streamed out over her skin, finally free to do its natural calling, and she burst into the form of the falcon almost too fast for the Enforcer to perceive. She swooped, defying a craggy death by mere inches, but Jacob knew instantly that her danger was not over. The bird lofted, tumbled, and hit the ground rolling. By the time the tumbling stopped, the Princess was in human form and lay across the shale ground gasping for breath, blood pumping from the gap in her throat.

Jacob landed next to her with a skid of his boots, kneeling quickly to press his hands to her throat in an attempt to stem the flow of blood.

Kestra had been seated before the fire in the Great Hall, feet drawn up under the seat of her bottom. All of her focus was turned inward, helplessly watching Noah struggle to find advantage in an untenable situation. She felt every moment of his agony, the pulse of pain from his memories of his mother throbbing in her throat and belly. It was the first time she'd ever heard those two words enter his thoughts or his actions.

What if . . .

And she realized how right he was. It was a road best not taken, because all that would lie down that path were endless twists and bends that led nowhere but back upon themselves.

He would rather live with the regret of a hasty choice than live with wondering how to change the unchangeable. He knew this because of experience, she now understood, because he had allowed a single what-if to plague him for over two centuries.

Kestra's heart clenched with a terrible fear. Oh, he was too good a man. Too noble. Too wise. Too intelligent. Too easily able to love anyone he deemed worthy. So much personal pain and loss over so many centuries. Making choices that ended lives. The years of futility in search of peace. And yet he loved. How could he bear it? How did he willingly give away pieces of his heart, knowing they could be wrenched away so violently? This, over six centuries of life?

When she hadn't survived two *decades* with the ability to love intact.

Kes turned her eyes onto the burning flames in the fireplace, letting the glare burn at her retinas and blind her. Destroying this exterior sense drew her back to the dilemma facing Noah. She gasped aloud when glass shattered and bodies fell; she felt the swell of rage in the King of the Demons as he gave chase.

"It did occur to me that there is more Nightwalker blood than remembered by most. So glad am I to see it so readily available."

The voice came from close by, not from her place in Noah's thoughts. She leapt to her feet, instinctively cutting herself off from Noah when he needed to focus on his quarry. It was no different to her than shutting off a microphone to conceal her location.

She was blinded by huge spots of changing color in the center of her vision, an effect of staring too hard into the fire. But she heard the soft slide of a sole on marble, the whuff of an eager breath of triumph, and even the rustle of clothing.

Kestra suddenly realized that they hadn't followed the logic far enough. They hadn't considered a two-pronged assault. They had not realized that there were multiple targets, and she was one of them. But how had rogue Vampires learned of her existence?

"Actually, my dear, it was just happenstance. I was looking for a random target. But a Druid . . . now, this truly is a prize."

Kes felt the clutch and throttle of her heart hammering beneath her breast as a familiar sensation of helplessness washed through her. Vampires had telepathy. He had a direct line into her soul.

No! She was no victim any longer! That girl had died over a decade ago! She had paid her dues with lack of love and affection, with no one to touch her and no one who would care if she lived or died. She had perfumed herself in gun oil and lived in backwater barracks filled with the most terrifying men on the planet just to prove she didn't fear them and wouldn't fear any again. She'd sacrificed pompoms and proms, girlfriends and love.

And lovemaking.

Lovemaking. A lesson only begun, under large hands that wielded fire in so many ways, yet expressed more tenderness than she could ever truly bear.

No. Nightwalker or no, she would be no one's victim. It was time to put her money where her mouth was. She'd told Noah she knew her enemy, and she would prove it.

"So you have come to lay siege in the castle of the Demon King?" she asked softly, blinking so that her vision would clear more rapidly. "You're ballsy, I'll give you that."

Her adversary laughed, and like radar she used it to home in on him, place and position. Ten feet across the room, northeast, facing slightly away as he perused his surroundings, his voice echoing tellingly into the higher corners of the ceiling.

"Your mind is unusual. It fades in and out of my perception," he mused, as if it were an amusement to him. "You are young, barely fledged," he accused, and by then Kestra could see his handsome pout.

Boyish, slim, and very beautiful, he was an artful deception of looks. However, she could see the avarice in his eyes and knew great strength was hidden in his lean frame. He had hair like silken chocolate, a forelock falling rakishly over his brow. His eyes arrested her, and she was again struck by the lustful greed within them. She was used to that. She'd felt it many times from men of a different kind of power.

She knew this greed.

She cocked a hip, linking her arms behind her back as if she were bound. It was submissive, and it allowed the fullness of her breasts to push tightly into the girlish gingham dress. She paced with him as he moved to peruse Noah's belongings, keeping the same distance between them as he moved and turned, occasionally looking at her as if she were a fascinating dessert on a tray. Whether it was her blood or her sexuality that tempted him, she didn't care. Still, she allowed her hips to sway softly with every step.

"You are not afraid of me," he noted with surprise. "Why is that?"

"Because of who I am," she said, giving a careless shrug. That time she saw his eyes flick to the rise in the hem of her dress as she made the gesture.

"And who are you? Who leaves you here unprotected on a night as dangerous as Samhain?"

"I can protect myself."

He looked at her again, silent, and she imagined he was trying to rifle through her mind for information. His consternation reflected on his face. "What is your power?"

Good question, she mused. She had no idea what her power was or what it would be.

But she thanked him for reminding her of it.

She blanked her mind from his sporadic insights into her thoughts, moving fluidly around the room until she was at Noah's desk. She casually slid onto it, her bottom gliding into the exact spot where Noah had last begun to make love with her. She leaned back on her hands, letting the memory be the only thing guiding her mind as she leaned back on her hands, her fingertips curling softly against a silver letter opener.

"Ah! You are the King's woman!" Her companion chortled with sudden glee as he popped the plum from her mind.

"Yes. Hence my lack of fear." And the reason she'd replayed the memory of their interlude.

"Mmm, true . . . you must have great power to be the woman of the Demon King."

Kestra crossed her legs, her skirt riding up along with the corners of her lips. He was coming closer to her, and she was thinking of anything other than what she would do next.

Noah chased the twice-cursed crow as a ball of pure flame, a meteor streaking through the sky, scorching tree braches and anything else that got in his way. He was going to burn the bastard's feathers off one by one. He was going to stick a spit right up the middle of his miserable carcass and light the roasting fire himself. The midday sun would seem balmy compared to the fire of his fury.

Within minutes he was toying with the frantically flying Vampire, literally hot on his tail. There was no escaping him now. He would burn all the woodlands in a heartbeat if need be.

The Vampire seemed to grasp that he was defeated in his stolen Mistral form, and with a clumsy change to his natural form, he crashed to the snow and leaf debris in amongst the ever-present bits of shale broken from the Romanian mountain. The fiend of fire that was the Demon King landed with the utmost speed and grace as a wall of flame caged them both in a perimeter so tight that the Vampire cried out and hurried toward the furious King in a last effort to escape its heat.

"Please! Do not kill me! I have . . . I have information!"

Noah's flame-coated hands lowered to his sides, burning the entire while, and like any flames they attracted the Vampire's attention.

"I have all the information I need," Noah said carelessly. He raised his immolating hands.

"No! You do not! If you did, you would not be here! You would be protecting your home!"

The panicked remark sent a chill through the Demon King like nothing else could, powerful enough to quench all the incendiary ability in his body and soul.

"Speak," he said hoarsely. Then a violent roar. "Quickly!"

Even as he made the command he sought for Kestra, suddenly realizing she had left him. How could he not have noticed? Had his thirst for vengeance so blinded him to her? Had she called for his help, his volatile need to satisfy his rages suffocating the breath of her cries for him?

"My brother infiltrates your castle even as I infiltrated Damien's. He sought you, great King. A worthy adversary. He did not expect you to come to Damien's aid yourself."

"Fool!" Noah spat the word, unsure who he aimed it at. "It was what was intended all along! *You fool!*"

The woodland exploded in outraged flame.

Jacob hit the deck, barely in time to cover the Princess as a wave of flame roiled out of the tree line just far enough above their heads to keep his hair mostly unsinged. He had felt that one coming, and after it passed he flung his head up to try to see why such a display had occurred. Sweat flew from his hair as he rose onto his knees, straddling the Princess protectively. His hand still plugged her wounds, though Noah had almost cauterized the bloody thing just a moment ago. The Earth Demon could see nothing, feel nothing except the earth as he absorbed the screams of the natural life all around him. Noah's abuse had caused great damage to flora and fauna alike, and Jacob was impacted enough to feel a fury toward Noah he had never felt before.

He whipped his head around, sending another spray of perspiration arcing out like a liquid halo as he searched amongst the lightly toasted scrub for what he wanted. His black eyes fastened on a promising plant and Jacob called it to himself instantly, forcing it to ride a rippling wave of earth so he did not have to leave his position.

The natural coagulants in the roots of the plant would help save Syreena's life. He shoved several in his mouth, chewing the dirty bulbs until the juice broke free of the roots. He spat the dubious salve into his hand, then spat again to rid his mouth of the foul taste that remained even as he smeared the concoction over the gaping flesh of Syreena's throat. How she would survive such a wound was beyond his comprehension. Even now he was watching her eyes slip closed with increasing frequency.

"Syreena, do not close your eyes. If you succumb, Damien will never survive. Come!" He slapped her face, making her jerk back to consciousness. She tried to speak, but could not, her damaged throat refusing to work. But by the fire in her eyes, he guessed she would have cursed him pretty efficiently had she the voice. Over the centuries of the war between their peoples, some pretty fine epithets had arisen from the lips of Lycanthropes in regard to Demons, and the reverse was also true. "Yes, yes, I know," he sighed, "I am the foul son of a hunchbacked Demon whore."

His self-deprecating humor made her laugh, another step toward consciousness despite being little more than a wheezing breath and a sparkle in her eyes.

"Strange, I was just about to say the same thing," a deep voice mused. "Enforcer, would you mind telling me why you are lying over my naked wife?"

Jacob and Syreena both twisted to see behind Jacob, whose body was blocking Damien from seeing the state Syreena was in. Damien caught the painful relief in the Demon's eyes, and then the flat-out pain in his wife's. Jacob went flying as Vampire strength shoved him out of the way without heed for anything save Syreena. Damien grabbed her up, a hoarse sound of fury gurgling from his throat when he saw his wife's wounds up close.

"Sweetling," he whispered. "Oh, love, what have you done to yourself?"

It was a rhetorical question. He was already in her mind, mining her memories, learning the truth. Her eyes went wider, and she knew it took a monumental effort for him to tamp down the need to vocalize and act on the outrage that would have blinded him to everything else . . . had she not needed him so badly.

She brushed weak fingers against the least damaged side of her throat, her eyes speaking where her voice could not.

"No, Princess, I cannot. You are too damaged." But even as he held her he was watching precious rivers of blood run down her naked skin, pooling and soaking into the soil. Jacob's actions had eased the flow, but there was massive arterial damage. He was afraid the spurting had stopped only because there was no longer any blood to power the force of it.

He needed to stop the bleeding, but he could not bring himself to strike her on the neck where she had been so savaged already. Aware of the Enforcer looking on with wary, ready eyes, Damien chose the nearest access to the largest artery in her body. Laying her back down along the ground with infinite tenderness, he slid back to cup her knee in his hand, raising her leg as he bent to press a brief apologetic kiss on her kneecap. His fingers slowly pressed up along her soft flesh, the stroke having an intimacy to it that made Jacob turn his head and eyes to the side. Damien appreciated the gesture as he was compelled to lift Syreena's calf to his shoulder, bending until her knee hooked onto his collarbone. He glanced briefly into her beautifully trusting eyes, their multicolored flecks glistening with tears for him because she knew he was afraid of hurting her.

Then he struck for the femoral artery in her thigh.

His canines flashed in and out of her flesh after a deeply

bruising hit to the crucial blood pathway. Instantly she was bleeding, and he had no choice but to seal his lips to her skin and let the sweet warmth of her blood fill his mouth. What he sought to do was to trigger the age-old instincts of the workings of his body. Only by striking and feeding sufficiently would his body produce the urge to strike again. When he felt himself reach that point, this was exactly what he did. A second strike, just as sure and deep, only this time a flood of coagulants and the antibodies of numberless diseases he had been exposed to pumped out of his teeth like venom from a snake. They would enter her bloodstream, rushing to all sites of torn tissue, and cause the immediate clotting and sealing of all wounds so that no more blood could be lost.

Jacob only looked back at the couple when his peripheral vision caught the Prince leaning over his wife so he could give her a kiss on her extremely pale lips.

"She needs blood and a healer," Damien said, the command inoffensive because Jacob was used to both the majesty of the Prince's position and his overriding demand to care for his mate. He knew that feeling all too well.

"Where can I find your best healer?" Jacob offered.

"We have none. Vampires heal themselves. Damn me, I should have considered this!" Damien cursed himself again, desperately trying to keep Syreena awake with the sweep of his hand over her hair. "She needs a Monk of The Pride. She needs a healer from her sister's court."

Kestra kept her eyes averted from the Vampire approaching her. She waited, wanting him to come closer before she allowed him to look into her eyes. She heard the soft compulsion in his voice, trying to soothe and lull her. It was layer and underlayer, the obvious and the subversive. This was something she had experience in. She'd always had a sense of the seditious. Sands had been an example, though a poor example, because she'd ignored her instincts that day.

So as the Vampire spoke and attempted to charm her like a cobra in a basket, she allowed herself to relax. She wasn't touched by his hypnotic coercion. This, she realized, was a strength. Druid or human, it didn't matter. It was an advantage and she'd use it to its fullest. The whys and wherefores were thoughts best left to later. Although she had to wonder. It seemed that this was the second power he'd used on her that, as soon as she was made aware of it, had become increasingly difficult for him to use against her. When he'd first arrived, he had read her mind in a snap. As soon as she'd realized he was doing so, it had become difficult for him to utilize the skill. Even now she could see the curl of his brow as he warred to hear all the thoughts he wanted access to so badly.

Yes. Of course. It was like setting charges. *You find the supports first, and then go for the bang. Once you know what holds everything in place, it becomes an easy target for destruction.* It suddenly made sense that some innate part of her would destroy all the advantages he'd have in an attack, one by one, weakening his position of power. If she kept blowing out his supports, eventually his advantage would collapse.

He was coming within reach. She tried to reconcile this handsome face of deception with human Vampire lore, though she didn't want to rely on anything she didn't know to be fact. She suspected he was capable of speed beyond her own, but he was moving leisurely as if he expected the Demon King to never come home. The thought sent an inexplicable wave of panic through her and she had the impulse to reach for Noah, to see if he was alive and safe. She tamped down the urge with all her might, focusing once more, telling herself it was ridiculous to worry about a being of such vast aptitude as Noah.

The Vampire closed in, and she could smell him, something foul, like he had rolled in sour trash. She tried not to wrinkle her nose in distaste. She appeared relaxed, and she knew that if she calmed her mind she would have as fair a chance against him as she could manage.

"What manner of man, I wonder, allows so pretty a lady to be here all alone, unguarded?" He asked this conversationally, as if the question itself weren't a threat.

"I believe there were guards aplenty posted outside."

"Those who are not at the Samhain festival, you mean? Well, one had a fairly eager girl on her knees behind a distant bush. They might be done soon, though. She seemed somewhat relentless." He leered in what she supposed was a further attempt at charm. "The rest are easily misled by shadows and the like. Besides, Vampires are not Demon enemies. We have shared the holidays before."

"I wouldn't know much about that," she said, hefting out a sigh. "Frankly, I find the whole thing boring. And I can tell you I don't appreciate being left behind like some . . . some mistress who sits around waiting for her lord and master's urges to fall on him. Somebody around here is living in the Dark Ages." She gestured pointedly to the castle.

The Vampire chuckled, a deep, pretty sound, also full of that coaxing compulsion to relax.

Wait . . . wait . . .

He came closer and she began to raise her eyes, saying all kinds of intense little prayers to herself.

Contact.

Their eyes clashed, the brilliant glitter of her pupils searing the unsuspecting Vampire to the quick, rendering him into shocked immobility. It was at just that moment that Kestra felt Noah flare to furious life in her mind. She ignored him, afraid of accidentally breaking off the tenuous paralysis she had over her target. It had worked, just as it had worked on the medic. Instantly his aura flared into her vision, and then his powers independently revealed themselves to her. She didn't understand all the hows and small details of this power she was wielding, and she knew it was dangerous to wield weapons without experience, but she had no choice. She didn't even fully understand the Vampire's abilities as they jumped onto her mental chart, but she wasn't actually interested in those details at the moment. It was the paralysis in and of itself that would serve her.

She knew from her lone experience with Gideon that next would come the Vampire's flaws, the weaknesses and back doors to circumvent each of his skills. Then she'd feel the urge to map down each power with the precision of the best cartographers. This was what had quickly exhausted her before, and she didn't want that to happen. She would need all of her strength, every ounce of it. She'd need to act, to quickly reseat herself into her own mind and body, and take action before he came around from his paralysis.

Weaknesses. She'd been armed with human mythology just as anyone who had seen a half dozen Vampire movies would have been, but there was no instant death from a stake in the heart for his kind. Even the sun didn't kill them all in a rush. It burned and smoldered them, like a low-temperature kiln, taking hours before it finally reduced them to ashes.

But Vampires could be forced into a torpor. It required a massive blood loss in a short period of time. If a Vampire lost too much blood too quickly, he would have to crawl beneath the safety of the ground in order to restore health, a forced death-like sleep that allowed him time to heal from mortal wounds.

Also, decapitation and cutting out the heart would suffice to kill a Vampire. But since she didn't see herself finding a butcher knife any time soon, she doubted she was going to find either of those routes to be plausible. She believed she'd have only a single shot, while he was unaware and in this stupor. She knew on some level that once pain became involved, the Vampire would break away from her captivity. She felt Noah, a small but powerful presence, waiting and watching, following her thoughts and holding his breath.

Kestra leapt off the desk and plowed into the Vampire in a single movement, dragging the dazed Nightwalker to the marble floor. His head cracked into the tiles with a sickening thud. He barely had an inkling of what was going to happen when he saw the firelight gleam off the silver-plated letter opener she raised sharply into the air. He thought, somewhat stupidly, that silver was a Lycanthrope weakness. Unless . . .

Unless the sharp object was thrust with unerring accuracy and shocking strength into his soft belly and used to bisect the aorta running down the center of his body. This was a most effective maneuver. He would not bleed to death within a minute or two like a normal human, because there was no heartbeat in him at his age to speed the process along, but he would eventually bleed out.

The trick for Kestra would be to remain safe until then.

The Vampire didn't scream until she'd already scrambled off his body, the deadly damage done. She ran as if the hounds of hell were after her, exploding out of the castle and into the gardens, feeling suddenly disoriented.

Go right, straight, to the left . . . now straight.

The instructions were crisp and commanding, a little breathless in reflection of Noah's fear, she thought. She didn't blame him. She was scared to death, too.

She suddenly felt the Vampire on her heels, running after her, not caring that he was forcing himself to bleed into his belly by exerting himself. His speed was unbeatable, but she had to try. She hurdled perfectly groomed bushes and hit straight lawn.

Suddenly she felt hands like talons catching roughly at her shoulders, and legs wrapping around her waist. She was soaring upward a second later and she had to quell the screams of fear rising within her, purely because she didn't want to give the creature the satisfaction. She felt Noah's heart leaping into his throat. His inability to hide his fear was terrifying to the point of calm. She watched below herself with fascination as the lawns flew away and the dark English woods cropped up with a rather apropos October boniness to the scraggly branches.

Branches!

Kestra threw up her arms barely in time to protect her face from the topmost branches of the old oaks and their hapless partners in the crime against her. At the speed with which the Vampire flew, her skin was flayed from her arms and legs, her thin dress instantly in tatters.

Noah!

Hang on, baby, help is on the way.

She had to believe him. What choice did she have? She needed to get the upper hand, but she could be killed if she dropped from this height. Then again, better this than higher. Or having her blood drunk out of her gaping throat.

I will never let that happen!

Noah's roar of conviction made her a believer. She could feel his heart pounding as hard as hers was, and she understood that he would find a way to help her if it was the last thing he'd ever do. Again that calm hit her, that confidence that his arrogant ways could infuse within her. It was the belief that only an individual of great power had—that he wouldn't be defeated, no matter what the enemy. This was his gift to her, and it was empowering.

Suddenly the Vampire pitched downward, and swallowing a scream as bark tore at her skin, Kestra acted.

She had never relinquished her weapon. With a wrenching movement to free her arm, she twisted her hips away from his bear hug on her and stabbed him right in the face. Kes was aiming for an eye, but she settled for a scream. Unfortunately the letter opener stuck and was left behind as she plummeted to the ground like a stone.

Until a branch not much thicker than an uneven bar zipped up the length of her body and she instinctively caught it. She swung; wood creaked and cracked, and then held. Unfortunately, her arms and shoulders had other ideas. The pain from the beating of the branches went shoulder deep and she couldn't hang on despite a dozen years of gymnastics training. She crashed down to the forest floor, catching more bark and bruises on the way, and finally hit years of leaf litter with a back-breaking crack and a grunt of expelled air.

She was aware of crashing and smashing off to her right.

And then her left.

It was like something out of *Macbeth*. To her starry eyes and pounding senses it was as though the wood had come alive and gone on the march. The noises were deafening, branches and stars duplicating in a macabre little dance of indecision. Then the night sky and trees were blotted out by the sudden appearance of a pixyish face and an enormous cloud of raven black hair. There was a very small woman leaning over her, hands on her knees as a brace, and she was smiling at her.

"Hi there. You look like you could use a hand."

"Noticed that, did you?" Kes wheezed.

"My name is Isabella. Noah sent me. You're safe with me."

This woman is a beautiful and trusted friend.

There was almost too much admiration in that sentence, and Kestra felt a nasty twinge of emotion in response.

Yeah. Thanks. I can see the beautiful part without the description from you.

I was speaking of her heart.

There was far too much smugness in that thought. Well, Kes hoped he was having great fun at her wounded expense, because she was going to smash his perfect white teeth down his throat later on. So maybe she'd been momentarily jealous. What of it? He'd been alive since forever, and she couldn't even bear to think how many women that meant.

Then she did think it, and instantly wished she hadn't. What the hell was she doing worrying about things like that when she was lying wounded in a forest with a Vampire out there somewhere trying to kill her? God, the man was turning her into mush.

"You're hurt pretty bad. Don't move at all."

"Vampire?" she whispered, shocked that she could breathe to speak.

"Oh, I, umm . . ." The brunette looked sheepish. "I wouldn't worry about him." Isabella suddenly staggered and dropped to her knees, her hair sweeping against Kestra's face. "Wow. What a rush," she murmured.

"Huh?" It was all Kestra could say, but she had a fine idea of what Isabella was talking about. She knew that look. The look that base jumpers and cliff divers and spelunkers got when they pitched off their ultimate goal in life. It was intoxication and adrenalization and a speedball high all banged into one. Isabella looked like she was ready to lie down on the forest floor beside Kes and contemplate the spinning stars for herself.

Noah?

I am coming as fast as I can, baby. Hang on until we get you some medical help, okay?

Oh, I'm fine. But I think your girl here is looped.

There was a significant pause, and during it, Isabella had taken, or rather fallen into, a cross-legged position by Kes's head. The brunette snorted a laugh, as if to some private joke, and muttered under her breath.

"Oh, bite me!" she finally said aloud, grasping her knees as her back straightened in irritation. "What was I supposed to do? Invite him on a damn picnic?"

"Are you okay?" Kes asked, breathlessness overwhelming her voice again. She was finding it harder to take each subsequent breath.

"Yes," Bella grumbled. "My husband is bitching me out."

That was the first time it truly occurred to Kestra that there were others who shared the same kind of bond she was developing with Noah.

Her *husband.*

Kestra gasped in a breath, wondering why she wasn't getting any oxygen. Maybe she was panicking again, or having an asthma attack. But hadn't Gideon said that would be unlikely to ever happen again? And she couldn't be panicking. She felt too calm. Relaxed, even. And the stars were damn pretty framed by the tree branches like they were.

Baby, you are going into shock. Try to concentrate.

Chapter 18

Noah and Jacob were streaking toward the closest sanctuary. Their only hopes for all involved were in the Lycanthrope court. It was distant, in the wrong direction—away from their mates, who were both in trouble—but they needed to aid Damien's wife as well. The Lycanthrope court would hold all the answers. A Monk of the Lycanthrope's much-revered Pride would be called on to heal Syreena. Legna could teleport him to the holdings in Romania after taking the image of the location from either Jacob's or Noah's mind. She was powerful enough to do that now.

Then Legna could send Noah, Jacob, and her husband, Gideon, to the English forest where Noah's mate was closing in on death and Jacob's was trying to purge herself of the evil taint of powers she had ripped out of the Vampire who had attacked Kestra, leaving him as weak and helpless as a kitten. A state that would probably kill him in light of his existing injuries at Kestra's hands. No one could help Isabella to do the necessary purge, but her husband needed to be with her just the same. She had never before absorbed such pure evil, having learned to use her ability with great discretion because of the huge psychic consequences.

Noah felt Jacob's fear as keenly as he felt his own. He had asked a great deal of his Enforcers when he had commanded Jacob to send Bella away from the festival and back toward the castle to help Kestra. Both had obeyed without question, loyal no matter what his crimes had been against them.

But even as he and Jacob streaked toward salvation, the only thoughts he could give true focus to were those sliding through the mind of his mate.

I am going into shock, she mused with a mental chuckle. *And here I thought I'd forget what it felt like. It's exactly the same. Right down to feeling so damn cold.*

Noah felt her shivering, felt her teeth clattering together, both so violent that her eyesight was blurred by the vibration.

You are going to be okay, baby. You are strong and a fighter and you are a part of my power now. That is not an easy thing to damage. Noah hoped he sounded more convinced than his fear was allowing him to feel.

You mean I'm too stubborn to die.

Do not even speak the word, Kestra! he commanded her with ferocity, as if his tone alone would stave off the Grim Reaper. *Do not even allow the option to ghost into your thoughts! I will not stand for it!*

You know, we're really going to have to discuss this whole "lord of the manor" thing you have going on. I don't respond well to commands.

She was teasing him.

He was afraid for her life and the little wretch was having him on.

Kestra, he warned, his tone so daunting she swore she saw the stormy smoke of his eyes. She sent back the mental equivalent of a derisive snort. She wasn't impressed by his threats. Noah decided to change tactics. *Tell me how Bella fares.*

Kestra had lost track of the woman beside her as she'd floated in her own world of semiconsciousness. Isabella was sitting with her elbows on her butterflied knees, her face buried in her upturned palms. She was muttering softly to herself, rocking back and forth so that her hair swung like a wild fringe of black silk. She sent the entire image to Noah, knowing it would speak far louder than her words and also knowing he wouldn't care for false reassurances. Kestra suspected Bella's muttering was a rapid-fire dialogue with her husband, one that escaped the privacy of her mind as distress ebbed through her.

What did she do? Why is she like this?

Bella has an extraordinary power. She can steal the abilities from another being and make those skills her own for a while. She has done this to incapacitate your attacker. Bella has never taken in so much corrupted power before. It has endangered her.

Kestra took in one of her small breaths, struggling to hold it in. She was used to risking her body, her life, and even sometimes her soul in the dangers she undertook, but she'd never dragged an innocent into the fray with her. It had always been one of her few true morals.

Hush, Kikilia, *hush,* he soothed in the softest of tones, feeling and knowing her disturbance instantly. *She has come to your aid for her own reasons. One, because I requested it; two, because Jacob requested it; and three, because it is in her nature and in her power to help innocents who are in danger from darkness. This is what she was born to do, who she was born to be. Do not punish yourself because a stranger is merely fulfilling her own Destiny, and that Destiny just happens to cross with yours in this moment. Now hold a thought of me. I strain to maintain this distant contact while moving with such energy burning. We are near. So very near. Hang on.*

Kestra didn't understand how he could be too far and yet as near as he claimed. She looked back to the brunette, who she realized had far more understanding of these things than she did. Isabella lifted her head and smiled wanly. She looked terribly pale, a sickly pallor that was nowhere near whatever normal was for her, Kestra was sure. But she did have remarkable eyes, a bright lavender in the silver of the full moonlight. Kestra gasped for another breath, coughed, and didn't even need to taste the blood in her mouth when she saw the expression that crossed the Druid's fairylike features.

"Oh God," Bella murmured, leaning over Kes with concern radiating out of every pore. She instantly reached to tear at her pretty blouse, untucking the silk from her jeans to do so. Kestra recognized the expensive designer blouse, and she wanted to laugh at the incongruity of it being paired with well-worn denims several years out of style. The fact that Bella tore into a six-hundred-dollar blouse without even flinching gave her more understanding about the woman than she'd gotten in all her conversation with Noah.

The small woman used the ragged patch of silk to dab at the blood leaking from the corner of Kestra's mouth. It wasn't even a patch to stanch blood usefully. Isabella had simply done the deed to keep blood from rolling down the sides of Kes's face and into her hair. A gentle, useless kindness, like catching tears. It was meant to have no purpose other than to give comfort.

"Is everyone so nice?" Kestra hitched out the sentence as she reached to lay weak fingers on the arm reaching over her.

"Shh. Don't talk," Bella scolded. She took a moment to contemplate this woman who was dying so quietly on the forest floor. She bit her lip against a surge of emotions, then slowed it all down and sorted it out. There was a blackness of rage, envy, and covetousness that she knew had nothing to do with her own feelings. These were echoes of the Vampire's emotions. She pushed them aside. Her own reaction was still one of anger first, even though she knew it wasn't fair to blame Kestra for Noah's actions. But love for these grand men in her life had already healed a great deal in a very short while. These negative sensations were merely ghosts of what had once been, fading as forgiveness moved to the forefront.

Noah's mate was a gorgeous creature. What Bella would call a polished beauty. Beneath the battering, the bruises, and the debris of half a forest, Isabella could easily tell there was refinement and grace. It didn't surprise her that Noah's companion would be of this type. His sister Legna was this sort of woman, as was his sister Hannah. Destiny could give him no less than what would hold the most meaning to him.

There was a world of woman beneath that polished coating, though. Bella could sense it on a hundred different levels. Had she been too delicate, she would be whimpering, crying, and very likely dead by now. There were ferocity and claws beneath her perfect manicure. *Here lies a fighter*, Bella thought with surety. There was no luck involved with the precision of the wounds she had briefly seen on Kes's Vampire attacker. She knew that now. Kestra had calculated and executed her attack like the coldhearted killer she'd needed to be in that moment in order to save her own life.

Well, good for her!

Bella smiled and recalled the question she had been asked, using it as a means to keep Kes conscious.

"There are no absolutes. Though we tend to be a little nicer than humans." She watched Kes smile in response to the fair answer. Kestra was trying to reconcile herself to this new world and culture calling to her in Noah's voice. She didn't want pretty promises. She needed truth. "There's danger in this life," Isabella confided softly. "Though I believe it's rather like cost of living from one place to another. Everything's relative. If you earn more in power, expect to pay a higher price when pain comes."

The Druid seemed lost in her own thoughts a moment, and she absently stroked Kestra's snowy bangs. Kes found it surprisingly soothing. She was once again taken aback by how much she'd been touched since coming into Noah's realm, and how easily receptive she was about accepting it. She found it bizarre that so delicate a creature, with her happy features and light touch, could speak so candidly about such deadly matters. Noah's view on bringing her into his world was stilted by his emotions of need. He had not hidden his knowledge of the dangers she could face, but neither had he brought them under any emphasis.

She wished she could express her gratitude to Isabella for her truthfulness.

"Noah has waited a very long time for you," Bella whispered suddenly, leaning closer to Kes as if she didn't want to be overheard. "Believe me, I know the pressure that comes with that. But this path you're on is one of inevitability. Don't think you have a choice in the matter, because you don't. Fate or Destiny or whatever it is has made up its mind about this one single factor in your life, and it can't be denied. It's designed so it can't be denied." Bella took a break, but continued when Kes's eyes continued to pay rapt attention. "A greater power than us has created these wondrous, inexplicably complex men, maturing them in intellect and power until they're at peace with almost everything in life. Their only disquiet is the yearning for the women who will be their complements, and who will begin to lead them on the next stage of their journey.

"So Destiny plucked you and me out of the cosmic soup and told us to be whatever we wanted, but it'd make this single demand on us that we must obey. We must love these beautiful men with all of our hearts." Isabella's voice became breathy and shaky with a rush of emotion, her fingertips coasting all the way through Kestra's hair now. "I don't think that's so much to ask, actually. It's sort of like commanding us to eat chocolate during PMS. You don't exactly want to refuse a dictate like that." She hushed Kes when she laughed painfully. "My point is, you have to resign yourself to the fate of being a Druid, of spending your life always connected to Noah. Not controlled by, not dependant on, not indebted to, or any of that feudal bullshit they can revert to every now and then, but a partnership with someone who's been chosen to be your perfect complement. Course, they think *we* are *their* perfect complements . . . but it's the other way around.

"When you accept that, Kes, then you find something better than chocolate. Better than life. Better than anything." She sighed and Kestra saw joy illuminating her features, an expression unlike anything she'd ever seen on a woman before. "Imprinted love is love on a cellular level. It's a matching of genetics, but it's a weaving of souls as well. It isn't even what humans think soul mates are. It's beyond that. Beyond the ecstasy of the body." She broke off into an aside. "Although if it stopped right there, *I* wouldn't be complaining." She traded a smile with Kestra. "There is peace in this life. As much as you see the warfare, the peace is just as powerful. I want you to understand . . . *to know* . . . how very, very lucky you are to have Noah."

No sooner had she finished this statement than an enormous explosion of displaced air blew back weeds, brush, and debris, forcing Bella to curl her body over Kestra to protect her from the fallout. She looked up to see her King, her husband, Gideon, and Legna with Seth settled on her hip standing in a small clearing just a few steps away. She sat back, allowing Jacob to rush into her arms, hugging him so tightly that his breath compressed out of his lungs.

It wasn't until Bella let out a sob that Kestra comprehended how upsetting the entire situation had been for her. She didn't strike Kestra as the overly weepy type, so she had to admire her for her ability to hide her trauma. It touched her to know that the other Druid had put her own pains aside to take the time to reassure her about what it meant to join the world of Demons.

Trying not to get choked up herself, a condition she told herself was caused by her current state of injury, she turned to look up at Noah when he scooped up her hand and leaned over her, concern etched in every inch of his features. She was lost the moment she saw the expression in his eyes. The pain and regret, the guilt and tragedy . . . and most of all, his unabashed love for her.

Suddenly tears were welling out of her eyes, dropping into her hair, her repressed urge to sob causing agony to rip through her rib cage and lungs. Then she felt long, cool fingers sliding into her hair, the contact incredibly soothing. She blinked to clear her vision and looked up to see Gideon leaning over her from his position on his knees behind her head.

"Tears are not recommended, Kestra," he chided. "You cannot breathe because you are bleeding into your chest and it has been slowly compressing your lungs. It will be healed shortly."

She appreciated the information, but she'd already known that. She turned her attention back to Noah as she felt a tingle skip across her scalp. She squeezed his fingers in reassurance and then glanced over to Isabella and Jacob. A lovely woman with a huge braid of coffee-colored hair had knelt beside them and was handing a baby to Jacob. She then picked up Bella's hands and closed her eyes as if concentrating.

"My wife."

"My sister."

Gideon and Noah spoke at the same time, drawing her attention. She found herself laughing on an easier breath as they exchanged wry smiles over her prostrate body.

"She should not have brought the baby," Noah reprimanded Gideon.

"You saw me try to discourage her. You know your sister bears your trait for stubbornness," was the calm retort.

"You clearly did not try hard enough."

"I did not see her listening to you, either," Gideon pointed out.

"You have allowed her to become far too willful," Noah complained.

"I dare you to say that within her earshot," Gideon said with as much evenness as ever, though this time his silver eyes flicked up to glance pointedly at his King. He looked down into Kestra's eyes with a small smile. "Do not fear. This attitude of chauvinism is not his norm. Legna is the baby of the family and as such has been cursed with Noah's overprotective brotherliness."

"I'm not afraid of him," she said, flashing an impish smile when she realized she could speak and breathe almost normally again. She took a deep breath just for the sake of being able to do so. "And he knows better than to treat me like that."

"Hmm. I believe she has your number, Noah," Gideon mused with far too much pleasure for Noah's liking.

"I will thank you both kindly to shut the hell up," he grumbled. But in spite of the temperamental remark, his grip on Kestra's hand tightened and he brought the back of it to his lips. "Just make her well, Gideon." He brushed pained glances at the wounds that striped her soft skin as if she'd been brutally flogged. She realized then that all of her pain had been his, that he had forced himself to function while absorbing her agony, and had reached out to soothe her and anchor her at the same time.

Emotion overcame her, too much all at once, and she inadvertently jerked her hand free of his to cover her face. She felt panic because she knew she couldn't hide from him. He was everywhere. Everywhere. How could she sort through her own thoughts and feelings privately? Would she ever know total privacy again?

"You only need to ask."

The remark was bitten off with more chill than the October air. She dropped her hands and looked at Noah with surprise. His expression had turned to stone, a mask of hurt and anger she felt welling up from him. Confused, she tried to understand what had effected this change. Noah wasn't the unreasonable type. He would understand her thoughts about wanting privacy. So why this hostility so suddenly?

"Samhain."

The word was whispered from above her, Gideon's head bowed close in supposed concentration as he healed her. When he whispered the single word into her ear she suddenly remembered. Everything was magnified. For her. For him. For all of them. They'd all suffered attacks and stresses tonight that made her wonder how they could all seem so calm and so controlled. All save Noah, at the moment. His struggles went deeper somehow. Something unsettled him.

And she knew she was responsible.

Kestra looked around at the faces of those around her, felt the eyes that were surreptitiously being cast toward their monarch. But beyond that she understood there was a sense of complete serenity between the other two couples. It was the peace of mind that came with total confidence in the love they shared. She couldn't offer Noah that measure of confidence and security, and she was sorry for it. This was the root of his outrage: her inability to commit herself completely into his trust. It conflicted with his desire to care for her, to comfort her. He couldn't bear the gray area because he was afraid he would make unreasonable demands on her or would try to force her to feel for him, and where would be the security in that?

Kestra reached out to touch his arm, the hard muscle twitching beneath his skin. He turned eyes of emerald fire and dark smoke onto her and she heard a menacing rumble of sound escape him. She didn't let it faze her.

"Please," she said softly, making sure she drew his attention, "just be patient with me."

The simple request seemed to take the wind right out of his sails. He expelled a pained breath, emotion shuddering out of him physically, his body hunching forward with exhaustion of both the mind and spirit. He'd spanned the world trying to help others tonight. He didn't have the strength to help himself. Instinct reigned, emotion its partner, and the man of learning and logic was subverted by fatigue and the Hallowed moon.

Kestra was finally able to sit up. She felt strange, like a rag doll having been knitted together. She was also tired. She realized Gideon burned as much of her energy as he did his own in order to heal her.

"The rest of your body will heal by tomorrow evening. It is best to let you regenerate on your own power."

"Thank you," she said, taking another deep breath just to reassure herself. She placed a hand of warmth and comfort on Noah's shoulder. He sat back on his heels, his hands fisted atop his thighs, his dark head down. "Noah, let's go and rest now." Then, more softly, hoping only he would hear as she leaned close. "I need you to hold me."

He looked up sharply, searching her gaze roughly, her thoughts as well, checking to see that she was sincere and not just tossing him bread crumbs. She remembered not to be offended, allowing herself to simply feel peace within her own mind and let him deal with it as he would. They couldn't afford for them both to be hotheaded tonight. She was done with warfare for the evening. Now she wanted peace, and quiet, and tenderness. Kestra met his gaze, her mind full of images of them snuggled warmly together, of comfort and companionship and her terrible need that she honestly felt only he could fill.

The change that came over him was miraculous. His sullenness and hostility vanished, his features lighting up with the gift she had meant to remind him of.

There was hope.

If only he would be patient, help her enjoy her life slowly, day by day, then there was hope he would find in her what he needed as well. She needed faith, and he needed hope. They could give it to each other if only they had patience.

Kestra and Noah both took deep breaths of the crisp night air, exhaling twin clouds. Then Noah looked to his companions. He stood up, helping Kestra, and walked over to his sister and the Enforcers who still sat on the forest floor. Gideon also crossed over, taking his son from Jacob and checking him for sufficient body heat.

"How are you faring, Bella?" Noah asked.

"Better." She gave an involuntary shudder and Noah caught a meaningful glance from Legna. "I still feel like he's crawling around in my body. The corruption . . . But so much power, Noah," she breathed, her eyes brightening. "You can't imagine what it was like. It was a Nightwalker cocktail, poisonous but a force to be reckoned with. I'm the only one . . . the only one who will be able to stop these Vampires if they take the time to learn and master what they steal." Her eyes seemed to glaze over as she muttered softly under her breath for a moment, making Jacob look to Legna with concern.

"She is overloaded," the empath said in dulcet tones. "It's like an overdose, of both power and of evil. She has purged most of the power, but the stain of blackness fights to gain foothold within her. She will win eventually because her psyche is so purely good, but I think it best if I go home with you and help guide her. She will be herself more quickly this way and can find peace."

"Agreed," Jacob said, reaching to scoop up his wife as she drifted out of lucidity.

The group gathered close to Legna, but she hesitated briefly to speak to her brother. "Be at peace tonight, Noah."

They all disappeared with a sinus-popping jolt.

Kestra sighed, feeling suddenly alone in the looming woods, in spite of her powerful companion.

"Actually, I need to leave you for a minute for a little unfinished business." He gave her a smile and kissed the corner of her lips.

She watched him stride off, and as soon as he was gone she shivered madly. She hadn't realized he had been using his body heat to keep her warm. Or his power. Either way, she now stood in a ridiculously tattered dress, making her wonder what she had been thinking when she had gone shopping. She folded her arms to her body and watched until he disappeared out of sight.

After a minute, there was a roiling explosion, like a focused bomb had just gone off. Kestra suddenly realized that the Vampire had been dealt with, whatever was left of him, with Noah's form of finality. She felt no pity, remorse, or even horror. In fact, she admired his efficiency. She would love to have that kind of firepower at her fingertips. Without using black-market C-4, that is.

You have a very interesting mind. I never know what you will think of next. You always keep me guessing, and you always keep me fascinated.

Unless I try to keep my thoughts to myself. You don't like that.

She felt his hesitation even as she heard him approaching through the woods. She gave him time to think.

I do not mean to be intrusive.

Oh, honey, it's not intrusive. It's new to me. I'm used to privacy. I'm used to hiding my feelings and double-checking what I say before saying it. I would like some privacy sometimes just to mull things over, but I don't mean to shut you out by doing so.

He had marched right up to her as she thought this to him, and now he seized her by the arms and pulled her to his very warm body. The temperature change gave her a wicked chill and she shook like a leaf. He stiffened and looked down at her sternly.

"You need to buy some real clothes," he grumbled, enveloping her in extra warmth as he drew her to his side and led her in the direction of his home.

Kestra happily tucked herself beneath his arm, her arm sliding around his waist as they walked. She realized she was terribly sore still. Her skin was no longer broken, but the bruising was still there, including a tightness around her chest and her newly healed ribs. It was nothing she couldn't ignore, however, and she concentrated solely on using the slow walk to shelter as a way of winding down.

"So you saved the Princess?"

"We think so. We had to come to you, so we do not know

how the healer fared. Their skills are not what Gideon's are, these Lycanthrope healers."

"I don't think anyone's could be what Gideon's are."

"True," he relented with a smile. His smile faded as they hit the lawns. Noah stopped suddenly and turned to look at her, his hands grasping the moonlight tendrils of her hair with a sense of desperation. "I thought I was going to lose you tonight," he whispered, his voice so low and hoarse she almost missed the statement. "When I realized I had been tricked, that my guards had failed you, I was paralyzed with fear."

"Noah," she soothed softly, moving to rest her body against his, instinctively knowing he would find great comfort in it. "I'm fine. I took care of myself." Then she relented with a crooked smile. "For the most part."

"You were magnificent," he breathed, drawing her forehead to the fervent press of his lips. "I do not mean for my emotions to indicate you were incapable of . . ." His eyes slid closed and he could not speak for several beats as those emotions threatened to strangle him.

"Noah," she chided with a soft laugh, "it's okay! I was terrified, too! And you were right, I was a poor match for a creature of that power." She slid her hands up his back, drinking in his vitality with her fingertips. It was good to be alive. It was even better to be with a man who made her feel that life right to the core of her soul. "I'm glad you had more sense than I did about that. Actually," she said with a touch of wonder, "I'm glad that we were able to make sense of it together."

She suddenly withdrew from him, stepping back and looking at him with a strange expression of surprise and confusion. Noah felt cold from her abrupt departure, the sensation almost making him laugh in his shock that she was able to do that.

"Kes?"

She shook her head mutely, staying his outreaching hand, and wrapped her arms around herself. He saw a shiver shudder through her.

"Kestra," he said, adding a touch of sternness to his tone, "you are worrying me."

"I . . . I don't mean to," she told him softly, the pain lacing her tone sending an invisible dagger through his heart.

He wanted to leap into her mind, plow through what was disturbing her, and kill it quickly with whatever reassurances she needed, but he was beginning to realize that she would need a great deal more time than he had needed to adjust to the connection between them and what she considered a fully invasive disruption of her privacy. Over the span of centuries, he had grown used to telepaths and empaths and their easy way with traveling through the psyche. He had also been raised in a culture of bluntness and honesty in words, meanings, and emotions. Kestra was human, and humans had a great many idiosyncrasies when it came to expressing themselves. Privacy seemed to be a key one. One he was willing to respect if it would make her happier.

"Come." He beckoned her with a twitch of his hand. "We are both tired now and in need of rest. There will be time enough for worrying."

Kestra easily stepped forward and took his offered hand. She didn't hesitate to thread her fingers through his, and she felt his relief and contentment at the intimacy. She felt bad for disturbing him, but she hadn't known how to handle her sudden revelation. She'd been skirting the issue since she'd first laid eyes on him, but she'd suddenly understood with clarity a fact she couldn't deny: This wasn't just about sex, or a quirky attraction, or even a mere twist of her fate she'd have to adjust to before moving on. This was a full-blown, balls-out relationship. More so, it was becoming a damn good one. Fast. Too fast.

Kestra closed her eyes, letting him lead her as she struggled with her thoughts. The thing that had thrown her into the comprehension so abruptly had been the understanding that they had argued, yet managed to communicate, and then compromise. Each in their own fashion, each to their own satisfaction and better understanding. Wasn't that what couples did? Good couples? Her heart began to thump in a rapid tattoo of anxiety and she struggled to quell it. How was it she could face a crazed Vampire, but she couldn't remain levelheaded about Noah?

Because she knew how to beat down a Vampire, just as she could beat down any physical challenge. Noah was a challenge of the heart, and a dangerous one at that. An ultimate one.

She stopped short suddenly. So suddenly that it yanked her hand out of his. He turned back to look at her with surprise etching his handsome face.

"I . . . need to walk. I'm . . . I need to walk."

The stammered explanation was all she could manage before she ran away from him. Noah was left speechless and torn. With a Vampire threat so soon behind them, it was not safe for her to risk being alone and out of touch with him. Not only that, but in a dress made of a fabric little more effective than gauze, she was going to freeze to death. He swore violently into the cold night. How could he protect her while allowing her the opportunity to protect herself as she wished him to, all at the same time?

"Damn!"

How could he give her respect and privacy, yet provide the care and comfort she needed? As well as take care of his responsibilities in the easing of her heart and mind? How the hell could he serve as a true and loving mate when she refused him access at every turn?

She was exhausted, cold, frail after her attack, and twisted into knots he could help untie if only she would let him. What was he going to do? What should he do? *Sweet Destiny!* He had never been so indecisive in his entire life! How many times had he orchestrated the fates of the lives of others with such glowing success? He had brought Jacob and Bella together, more certain about their success than they had been. He had done the same for Elijah when the warrior had questioned his feelings toward the Lycanthrope Queen. Why couldn't he handle Kestra with the same confidence of thought and emotion? It was making him crazy!

Positive he was going mad, Noah began to pace a wide swath of the lawn, his breath clouding on the air reminding him that Kes was as good as naked in that blink of cloth she had called a dress. He should fetch her back. He should demand she see reason. He should at least bring her a damned coat. He ran both hands through his hair, growling in frustration under his breath. Abruptly, his pacing was disrupted by a sharp implosion of displaced air and the solid body of his sister.

"Legna! What are you doing here?" If he sounded impatient, he did not care.

"Hmm," she mused, swinging back the huge braid of hair that had come over her shoulder during her teleportation. "I am an empath, Noah, and I am your sister. Add a dash of Samhain where it is all magnified, and I believe you will come up with the answer."

"I appreciate your concern, but I have not asked for your interfe—your assistance," he corrected hastily.

"I know you have not. First . . ." Legna reached out for him with both hands, holding tight when he would have shrugged her off. "Gideon is watching over her in astral form. She is being looked after."

"She will sense him or see him if he is not careful." Noah laughed without humor. "Then she will blame me."

"He will be careful. Trust him as you would trust me."

Noah looked at her with surprise, suddenly jolting out of his self-absorption.

"I have trusted Gideon all my life. Longer than you have even been alive. He was my *Siddah*, fostering me since I was a boy. Why would you think I do not trust him?"

"Perhaps because you have not been acting like it since the day you discovered we were Imprinted."

Noah was shocked and dismayed right to his soul that Legna would think such a thing. "That is untrue. I have long since accepted your marriage. It was merely the shock of it in the beginning . . . and because I feared he would be a key reminder for you about . . . the day Mother died." He reached out to tug her hair out of age-old habit. "Come now, surely you do not believe I hold ill will toward Gideon for stealing you from me?"

"You have been all politeness," she said neutrally.

The flatness of the remark cut him to the quick. His tender-hearted sister, speaking without emotion? His heart filled with dread as he raced through his memories of the past two and a half years of her marriage to Gideon. He needed to know what he had done to make her think these things.

"Legna . . ." he said helplessly.

"Do you never wonder why Gideon does not visit socially with me when I come? Oh, he attends all Council matters now, and I know you are glad to have his voice back at the Council table," she amended quickly, "but he does not feel welcome in the home of my brother. The home I grew up in and lived in knowing the greatest of love and memories until the day I wed. When was the last time you called on him? I mean truly, in a social capacity, and not when you needed him for some emergent medical or political problem?"

Noah's mouth hung open as he searched his memory for several examples. Surely he had—the man was father to his nephew, his *Siddah*, his sister's husband—surely he had sought to make time for them socially.

Noah flushed with sudden shame. What was more, he could not believe Legna had said nothing to him before now.

"I do not tell you these things to make you feel bad," she said gently, her love for him coming through powerfully as she reached to smooth soothing hands down his arms. "I only wish to make you aware. I think . . . I think it hurts him. I think he feels used, though he would never say so outright. You sometimes forget that, for all his age and wisdom, Gideon is still a being of great emotion and love. He may not show it like his wife does, but he is."

"I know," Noah said hoarsely. "I have known him all my life, and I know his love. I am sorry."

"I know you are. Yours is an enormously sensitive soul, Noah. And a passionate one."

Noah instantly sensed the redirection of Legna's comments. She was no longer referring to Gideon. "It is overwhelming to be a receptacle for your emotional extremes. It is mind-numbing to be the focus of your love. This is not a bad thing, my love," she assured him with a soft touch to his warm cheek. "Only, you must allow that for Kestra, there will be an adjustment period."

"I am trying. Legna, I feel as though my hands are tied. I need to protect her, but she sees that as an insult to her independence. One moment she agrees that the threats out in the night are too much for her to handle. The next she runs into the dark, making me stand here impotently because I know she craves privacy. To chase after her would betray her trust in my understanding of that."

"She is not thinking about danger at the moment. You would know that if you touched her mind."

"She does not like my intrusions into her mind. I always thought the intimacy of the touching of Imprinted minds would be a beautiful thing, I always craved it, but she balks at it. I fear she even hates it."

"She is not familiar with it. It is a disturbing thing for humans, one they accept easier with time and when they fall in love with their mates. You have altered her life considerably, Noah, and she is struggling to maintain shreds of her former identity."

"Tell me, Legna, do I press my suit on her, or hold back? Tell her my feelings for her, or protect her from them so I do not scare the hell out of her? One moment she is empowered, the next a frightened chick. Legna, I cannot make heads or tails of it!"

"Easy, darling, easy," she said softly, pitching the power of her calming voice in an effort to relieve her brother's turbulence. "I know that to love a wounded woman is like walking a high wire. Balance is crucial, and so easily lost if you are not careful. But you are the kindest, most patient and loving soul I have ever known. Center yourself. Calm yourself. Try not to let the volatility of the holy moon affect you so. You are letting it run away with you. Be at peace in the knowledge that whenever you have loved someone, Noah, they have always come seeking more. Be easy. Be patient."

Noah felt that peace stealing over him with every word she spoke. Legna was right, of course. She always was. He longed to have it back, that clarity of thought that came with perfect calm. He was being unreasonable, almost like a child in a tantrum, to expect Kestra to fall into line like a good Demon or Druid should. He had promised her patience, but had found it impossible to provide. She kept begging him for it, reminding him of her need of it, and he had barely managed to remember that fact from hour to hour.

Noah took a deep breath and looked into his sister's tinsel eyes.

"Thank you," he said gratefully. "I have been behaving poorly . . . in many ways."

"I know it has been torturous for you these past couple of years since my departure. I had buffered your emotions during the Hallowed moons for so long, I was shocked to feel the release the first time after I was away during one and living with Gideon."

"You felt that? All the way in Russia?" Noah was shocked. He hadn't comprehended how sensitive Legna was.

"How could I not? It was so horrible for you." Legna shuddered with the memory. "It took me a while to realize that was why I kept having nightmares about you every holiday. Gideon helped me to figure it out."

"I see. I am sorry."

"No. Do not apologize for our bond with each other or you will upset me," she said sternly.

"Yes, madam," he said politely with a bow of his head

and a laugh. "You are correct. It is not in need of an apology."

"But it is ended now," she added, her exhalation of relief profound. "She is everything that you need and more. Her power builds with great speed, astounding even Gideon. You will not have to fear for her safety for much longer. Though all you have seen is passive power, Gideon feels sure that on the near horizon she will rival you in ability. You must help her prepare for that." Again, that stern tone. "Let the rest flow naturally. All will be as Destiny decrees. You, my love, are just along for the ride. Pick the waves to surf, instead of creating them."

"You know," he said, throwing a brotherly arm across her shoulders and turning her toward the castle, "you are beginning to sound like a certain pompous Ancient I know. Perhaps this marriage was a poor idea after all."

"Noah!" Legna punched him in the ribs.

"Ouch." He pouted. "Is that any way to treat your King?"

"Yes, when he is being a jackass!"

Noah reached behind her head and lovingly pulled her hair.

Hard.

Then he ran.

Chapter 19

When Kestra entered the castle some time later, Noah was waiting at the door to greet her, a warmed blanket in his hands. He wrapped her up like a human burrito, drawing her in tight, adding his body temperature to aid against her violent shivering as he herded her directly toward the fireplace. He sat down, dragging her down ungently into his lap, a silent scowl on his face as he rubbed her arms and legs to encourage circulation.

His silence was a little unnerving, but she just sighed and snuggled into his warmth, her head on his shoulder and her cold nose pressed to his heated neck. She didn't have to read his mind to know he was probably pretty pissed off at her. She did give him credit for not scolding her like a child, though. Frankly, in spite of her effort to freeze out all of her troubling thoughts, she was still on overload and she just didn't know if she could've handled a scene at the moment. She felt as if she'd somehow failed him. After all, she'd promised him to be the steady one tonight, to help him through all the tumult of Samhain.

It was a hell of a way to pay him back after what he'd done to save her life.

Again.

She sighed. The heartfelt emotion behind it prompted him to cover her head with his hand, the heat and comfort of his palm bleeding into her. The added touches somehow ratcheted up the feeling of being protected and cared for. What she couldn't always understand was why it always felt so damned good. She closed her eyes and tried to fast-forward the moment, the entire relationship, five years into the future.

Where would this lead in five years?

Oh, hell. She was thinking in human terms still. She was immortal now.

Immortal.

That sort of gave her all the time in the world to screw up, fix it, and then try again. And she no longer had to worry about illness and being easily killed. Even in the face of a daunting enemy tonight, she had proven she was no easy target. With these Demon healers, the bounce-back rate was something else. Her senses were fired up to the max, and she was earning some wicked respect for the power she was developing as a Druid.

It was like being reborn. That, she realized, was how she'd been feeling these past few days. It was as if she'd been trapped for interminable ages in a chrysalis, and had just now figured out how to break free. She felt like a newborn butterfly. A kick-ass butterfly.

The fact that it all started and ended right here, in the arms of this man, was definitely in his favor. Noah made her feel beautiful and new, like she could risk shedding her protective shell. Not just physically. No. She'd been physically superior amongst humans for a very long time and she was used to that. Emotionally, she was navel lint. Or she had been.

That understanding made her heart pound, but this time she refused to push it away. Noah made her feel again. He made love to her and proved to her that she was capable of depths only he had imagined in her. He'd never once doubted it. Not even in dreams. He'd made it possible for her to accept easy touching and affection as if she'd been doing so all her life. The way they were sitting in cozy silence, for instance. She would never have accepted sitting in a man's lap. Enjoyed the stroke of sure fingers through her hair? The brief, brushing kisses across her forehead through her bangs? No. It was an act of submission and vulnerability to allow these things. This was how she had felt.

Before Noah.

And before Noah she'd been all alone. Strong, independent, powerful, and safe. But alone. Wrapped in sadness, heartache, and scars from the past. This man had stripped that all away, making it raw again, but only in order to repair it. Cosmetic surgery of the heart.

So that tonight she'd taken pleasure in the idea that they'd argued fruitfully.

It was such a normal thing to think about. A normal concern for a woman trying to have a relationship with a man. *Trying* to have one. Making the effort toward, and not against. And then to realize that she was happy to be shedding the Kevlar she had spent so much time strapping around herself.

She suspected she was setting herself up for a world of hurt.

Kestra laughed softly, and she could tell by a random muscular twitch that it had gotten his attention. Yet he still sat quietly. Was he listening to her thoughts? She didn't think so. She'd gotten the impression from his questions and honest perplexity earlier that he was trying to give her the privacy she was used to. She also knew he wouldn't always be able to do that. Even without trying, she could hear the hum of his presence in her mind. She suspected that as the ability progressed, it would be rather like having two people in her head.

Great. Now she would be a schizophrenic. She'd always figured she'd end up mentally unstable one day.

She sighed.

She supposed she would just have to stop resisting and learn to get used to it. In spite of having grown up with an empath in the house, Kestra suspected that this was going to be a huge adjustment for Noah, too. In fact, she realized that she hadn't given much thought at all to the changes and sacrifices he'd be making in order to accommodate her. All they'd spoken of was the benefits of her presence.

"You have been living the life of a bachelor for more than six centuries," she said suddenly.

Noah sat quietly for several heartbeats, each of which she could feel against the tip of her nose as it pressed to his pulse in his neck. She knew he'd heard her because his hands closed a little tighter against her.

"More or less," he said at last, releasing his hold so she could look at him. His expression was quizzical. "Why do you mention it?"

"Just that you're used to a certain lifestyle, and I'd say after that much time, they are easily what you could call habits of a lifetime."

"You . . ." His gaze narrowed until all she could see was slashes of smoke between the slits. "Are you saying that I'm incapable of changing my ways to accommodate you?"

"I'm asking why you would want to," she countered.

Noah relaxed beneath her, and she tried not to giggle when she realized it was so terribly easy to read him.

"I think you have the wrong impression of what my life has been like," he said dryly. "You must understand that Demons are very close to their families. We almost never choose to live alone if we have other single family members or parents still living. The holy moons play a part in that, but a minor one. Mostly it is about home and hearth.

"That does not mean I did not strike out on my own for travel, decadence, and overt troublemaking in my time," he pointed out. "But I was given responsibility as King at a very young age, so I sped through that period of my life fairly early on."

"That's good to know," she said firmly, a sparkle of humor in her eyes giving her away.

He smiled crookedly, looking far too charming and far too capable of all kinds of dissolute behaviors she dared not give too much thought to.

"The point is," he continued, "after my parents died and I moved my court to England, Hannah and Legna lived with me. Until Hannah married about thirty years ago. And then it was just Legna and me until two and a half years ago. In truth, I have only had my . . . bachelor pad . . . to myself for the sum of two years." He cast a wry look around the grandeur of the castle that looked far more like Grand Central Terminal than it did a lair for seduction.

"And how do you like living alone?" she asked.

"I hate it. With all my heart. I do not even have the number of guests I once did. Elijah and Jacob used to stay here constantly before they became wed. The children come often. A plethora of nieces and nephews," he explained quickly when she arched up a brow. Unable to resist, he pulled the pert eyebrow under the press of his lips as he chuckled.

"I was wondering how you have managed to maintain a child-free existence for over six centuries," Kestra remarked. "Because I know you didn't practice celibacy."

He gave her a dry look that made her laugh.

"Hardly," he said. "Demons are actually very funny about the nature of childbearing. Old-fashioned, you might say. We believe it takes a village to raise a child, but it must start with a marriage. We rarely give birth out of wedlock. Our healers have methods of seeing to that by request. It is not illegal to give birth out of wedlock, and there is no scourge against it, but it is understood that when it comes to a child of power, it is best to bring him or her into a complete family. It provides the best balance and control."

"So your healers have a way of keeping the women from getting pregnant?"

"Actually, they do, but it often is the male who takes responsibility for these things."

"Get out!"

"Seriously," he assured her. "Most Demon women do not need to practice birth control. Or they *did* not. There has been a change with cross-species relations now becoming acceptable. It is one thing to have fun with a Vampire or Lycanthrope, quite another to bear a child. Though I think everyone is still fairly prejudiced about these things. We were . . ." He frowned. "Well, I think racist is the best term for it. Elitist. And it holds over. A great many of the races are like that, and they would not sully themselves in an interspecies fling."

"But there are always the adventurous ones."

"Always," he assured her with a low chuckle. He looked into her eyes, brushing a finger through her bangs. "You are not going to ask me how many women I have been with, are you?"

Kestra burst out in a hard, shocked hoot. "Can you count that high?" she asked.

"Mmm . . ." He shook his head, the gleam in his eye nowhere near repentant.

"I didn't think so. Therefore, I won't be asking."

"Good." He gave a theatrical sigh of relief and she couldn't resist pulling his hair in punishment. "Ouch," he complained. She rolled her eyes.

"You have no shame," she accused.

"None whatsoever," he agreed. Then more seriously he added, "I have lived a long and full life, and I am not in the habit of looking back with regrets or second guesses about things I cannot change."

"I wouldn't expect you to. I'd rather focus on the here and now. I think I had a point to this conversation, but it got lost somewhere."

"I think you were disparaging my ability to give up my wicked ways."

"No. That wasn't it at all." She huffed out a sigh, sending her bangs fluttering. "I only meant to understand the changes you'd be forced to make now that . . . well . . . to accommodate . . ." She struggled to find a way of saying what she wanted to without attaching a presumptuous permanency to it.

"You," he said softly. "To accommodate you. To bring you into my life. To make you my mate."

Kestra's head dipped down and color flared over her cheeks until she was bright red. It was such an ingenuous reaction for such a jaded woman to have that Noah felt his heart swelling with his love for her. He wrapped his arms tightly around her and hugged her hard to his chest, almost as if he could make her feel it if he brought her close enough.

"It is okay to speak freely of my expectations, Kestra," he murmured gently to her, his lips against her blushing cheek as he did so. "I know what I want. I also know that speaking of the possibilities is not agreement or assent on your part. When you choose to stay with me, you will make yourself very clear."

"You're so arrogant." She laughed weakly.

"Hopeful. I am hopeful."

He lifted his head and then stood up with ease, keeping her in his arms the entire time. That was when she realized he hadn't ever really made a display of his strength, except in Sands's penthouse. The men she was used to took great pleasure in showing off. Living with Marines had been nothing but a constant exercise in testosterone. Noah kept his power understated. He knew he had nothing to prove. Just as she had nothing to prove to him.

She had thought he would never accept her as a woman of strength unless she proved it as she had been doing all her life. But she realized now that Noah had spent his entire existence around women of awesome power who were all treated as formidable equals. When he had tried to protect her, it was because he'd known she was out of her league.

Kes sighed as he walked away from the fireplace and began to climb the stairs with her. She was running out of arguments against him. She was running out of reasons why she shouldn't be with him. She couldn't conjure a single excuse for why this relationship couldn't work as it traveled into the future.

And that was perhaps the most frightening precipice she'd ever stood on.

Jasmine paced and cursed, cursed and paced, her temper having cleared out remaining partygoers long ago. The citadel echoed with her booted footsteps and her swearing fury. She was a raven-haired virago, her dark brown eyes flaming with red-limned rage.

She would never forgive herself for this.

Never.

She should never have allowed Noah to talk her into staying in Demon territory. Who besides Damien and herself would have been suited to fight these Vampire brigands? The Demons had done well enough, but at such a price! Too late. Too late to save him.

Stephan.

She heard a familiar footstep on the stone stairs and she raised distressed eyes to Damien. He held out an arm and beckoned her forward. Without thinking of the vulnerability it showed, she flung herself against him, allowing him to draw her into his embrace. He silently soothed her, as she would only ever have allowed *him* to do, sharing grief with her of his own. He had lost too much tonight, and he had felt it keenly. Felt it still. Would feel it far into the future.

Because tonight he had failed to protect his own, and come the morrow the entire Vampire society would be made aware of it. The weakness would shatter centuries of respect and properly discouraged ambition. The safety of his citadel would be in question for decades to come, if not forevermore. They would think him weak or infirm, consider him incapable of leading properly. They would see him as sharks would the scarlet cloud of blood upon the water. Those who would never have thought to challenge him before this now would.

For the throne of the Vampire monarchy was won by merit of combat alone. Only his death would force his abdication. And while he had always faced all comers and challengers in the past with easy success, there had never been any great number of them. Not since he had torn through a third of the Vampire population, all of whom were stupid enough to show up in high form on his doorstep during the first three centuries of his reign. After that, they had wisely given up and set about repopulating their ranks.

Now, between the issues with Syreena, the loss of control of the rogues, and the deaths of Stephan and three other highly valued and powerful members of the Vanguard, Damien wondered if they weren't right to doubt him. Feeling suddenly defeated, the Vampire Prince let his legs fold and he sat down hard upon the stairs, dragging Jasmine down to her knees between his legs as they held each other tightly.

He was the only one she would ever have allowed this close to her. They had loved one another since she'd been but a girl and he'd first taken her under his wing. Now she was the second most powerful Vampire in all the world, if not the second oldest, and the only one he would ever honestly fear losing to in a battle if it ever came to it. Simply because his heart could never sustain the level of betrayal it would take for her to ever challenge him.

No. Her loyalties were sound, for all her blustering and

bitching about Syreena. With her by his side, he need never worry about his throne. She and he could face anything thrown at them.

Had it been a year earlier.

Had he not had others to worry about now besides the two of them and all of Vampire society.

Damien glanced up at the stone ceiling, as if he could see all the way through it to his bedchamber and his bride within it. She was asleep now, healing quickly, settled under the care of the Monk Siena had sent to aid her. The Queen of the Lycanthropes and her Consort, the Demon Elijah, were also ensconced upstairs in a guest chamber, having come as soon as they'd heard of the attack upon their relation.

These were his family now. And they meant far more to him than a society of vagabond Nightwalkers who didn't have enough sense between themselves to be cautious and respectful of the opportunity he'd tried to give them by opening up the possibility of marriage, love, and true mates to them. They were so inured in their fickleness and debauchery that they couldn't see it all for the gift it was.

To be fair, though, neither could they really feel enough to care. As a whole, his society was pained and bored, jaded beyond words and hurting without understanding why. They didn't understand that they were lost, and that if only they would show patience and wisdom, he would try to help them find themselves again . . . as he had found himself. Even Jasmine, the stubborn daughter of his heart, if not his blood, had fought him tooth and nail all of this time even though she was loyal to him. In truth, she was afraid that his depth of love for Syreena would eventually preclude her from his life. She was afraid that if she listened to the lure of it too closely she would be charmed into thinking she had need of another herself. Jasmine was soft at heart, for all her quills. She, more than any of them, had been sensitive all of her years, falling into melancholy and torpor again and again because she couldn't bear the loneliness of the aboveground world.

But she had buried it all under anger, backbone, and an attitude tougher to scale than the Himalayas. Now one of her two best friends was gone, presumed dead judging by the amount of blood they had found with his scent on it. The psychic resonance of violence and death had reeked from the clearing Stephan had been destroyed in. Damien and Jasmine could still hear the warrior's death screams emanating from the earth and air, from his very blood. Vampires in a victorious bloodlust were capable of any number of depravities, so only the Goddess knew what the sick bastards who murdered him had done with the body.

Now all Damien and his loved ones could do was grieve together.

And wait to see what came with the new dusk.

Chapter 20

Kestra was filthy after her ordeals of the evening, having been a receptacle for blood, mud, and bark and who knew what else, so Noah didn't have to read her mind on the matter of a bath. He settled her on the edge of the tub while it filled with hot water. It was large and square and snuggled into a corner that included a bench in an alcove of stained glass and decorative stone and marble.

"This is the famed bathtub you've bragged about?" she teased him with her best bored tone and an exaggerated rolling of her eyes.

Noah turned from his task of adding a strongly scented oil mixture into the water. His eyes flashed with amusement and he raised a brow at her.

"It's not all that impressive. No Jacuzzi," she pointed out.

"No electricity. Nor will you find technology in a Demon household, as you discovered earlier. They do not agree with our biochemistry."

"Yes, well, they agree with mine." She pouted, pushing out her bottom lip and tempting him with its sexy fullness.

Noah moved to stand before her, then lowered into a crouch. He used a single fingertip on her knee for contact. "I am afraid this is something else that will change for you. Of course, there is electricity in the village, so if you miss anything too terribly you are welcome to seek it there. I could arrange for you to have a little cabin so you can hide from our primitive ways. You can have cable, hair dryers, and even high-speed computer connections."

"Is that so?" She looked duly surprised.

"Yes. Tech may not agree with us, but it is necessary in this day and age. I have human associates who are situated in the village who work for me in this fashion."

"Do they know who . . . what you are?"

"One or two. Longtime family friends. Heirs of longtime family friends. I need others to work full-time to manage my wealth as I have more pressing matters to attend to. Sometimes it is a matter of information I need. I would be a poor leader if I allowed myself to be ignorant of the times around me, even though those times do not always agree with parts of me."

"Yes. I can understand that. And no, I don't need electricity. I was a Marine, if you recall, and this"—she flipped a hand to indicate the luxury of the bathroom—"is hardly roughing it."

"Hardly," he agreed with a chuckle.

"And I am happy to know I can access the Net and online trading from the village. Or anything else like it. All in all, I'd say you have a pretty comfortable arrangement going on around here." She glanced away from him, fidgeting with a tatter on her dress a little. "I can't find too many complaints about the possibility of living here."

Noah felt his heart take a huge leap upward into his throat. It was the closest she'd come to telling him she wanted to stay. Oh, he was certain she already understood she *needed* to stay, but this was her way of making it her own choice. And she was choosing him. He could hardly breathe with the sudden surge of excitement that ran through him. He felt like a kid let loose in a candy shop. It took all of his effort and skill at moderating his expression so that when she looked up he wouldn't scare the hell out of her.

Her eyes met his, searching him for a response. He was far too happy to conceal everything he was feeling, so she could see the pleasure in his eyes and knew he understood the point of her comment. His hand closed warmly over her knee, his palm moving in a gentle stroke up her thigh, gingerly brushing over bruises and half-healed lacerations.

"We should get you in this bath," he said gently. "The oil is an herbal mixture Jacob made up for me. It is fairly strong, I warn you, but it will relieve your sore muscles and skin. It will also help you to sleep."

He reached for her torn dress, his fingers curling around what remained of the hem. Her hands immediately lowered to cover his, staying his actions.

"Noah," she said softly.

He smiled a little crookedly and looked into her troubled gaze. "Surely we have gotten over the shyness stage of our relationship," he admonished teasingly.

"No." She shook her head and smiled when he arched a brow. "I mean, yes. Yes, we're over the shyness stage. I only meant . . ." She released one of his hands so she could thread her fingers through a long, waving curl of his hair, sliding them down the soft length of it. Her voice was hoarse as she boldly explained her meaning. "I don't want to sleep, Noah. It's Samhain, and I don't want to sleep."

Noah dropped forward onto his knees, his balance completely lost as his head swam with heat and meaning. He couldn't speak, could barely swallow, as the sensation spread throughout his body. He shook his head, trying to refocus himself, the effort tremendous because she so easily aroused him. He reached up to push back her tangled hair, little bits of dead leaves fluttering free of it as he did so.

"Kes . . . no," he said quietly, pulling her to him so he

could press a fervent kiss to her temple. "You have been through enough. It is time for you to rest now."

She smiled, the expression whimsical. Kestra turned her face against him, taking a deep breath as she nuzzled first his neck, then his coarse cheek, letting the shadow of his jaw scrape over her face. She ended the caress with the brush of her lips over his ear, and she felt him shudder.

"Noble as that sentiment may be," she whispered, then, deliberately and slowly, "Baby," she continued, feeling his sharp intake of breath right to her satisfied soul, "I need you. I need you to make love to me tonight."

Noah made a low sound in his throat, a noise of masculine agony that only a severe battle of conscience could create. But Kestra felt his hand flatten out against her thigh, curving almost helplessly over her hip as he pulled her down onto his thighs. She pushed off with her feet, hitching herself higher than he intended, clutching his hips with her thighs, snuggling herself flush to his belly and chest. She wound her arms around his neck and hugged him warmly. His arms, tense and powerful, banded around her and dragged her more tightly into the embrace.

Kestra then framed his face with her hands and pulled him to her mouth. She had barely parted her lips against his when his hand cradled her head and he cast their weight to the side, rolling over until she was beneath his heated body and accepting the sudden and thorough aggression of his kiss. His tongue sought hers in an explosion of deep, velvety strokes, his need voluble in a chained groan. His hold kept her head and shoulders off the cold marble of the hard floor, but it allowed for a brace behind her hips that settled him perfectly against her. Her heat bled through his clothing quickly, and he was instantly reminded of his earlier intentions on his desk, and the fact that she wore nothing but the threads of the dress.

Kestra felt his reaction. She felt him hardening and swelling against her, the rampant burn of heat flaring in answer to his uncontrollable need for her. She liked knowing he couldn't control his need for her.

No sooner was the thought in her mind than he was launching himself back away from her, gasping deeply for a much-needed breath as he rose on his knees, half dragging her with him because she clung so tightly to him.

"No! Kes, no . . ." He groaned when she followed him, covering his mouth again for a brief instant before he cradled her face with his hands and pulled her away. "Please," he begged hoarsely, "please do not make me choose between honor and need, baby. Please . . ."

The request was so pained that it bought him her complete attention, as well as a respite from her aggression. He closed his eyes for a moment in a bid for inner and outer control. Then he forced himself to look at her, taking in her bruises and wounds and her soiled body. It gave him the anchoring he sought, as he knew it would. He stood abruptly, grabbing her hands and pulling her to her feet. He stepped to turn off the bathwater, then straightened to run both hands through his hair before turning back to look at her with a long exhalation.

"Bathe," he commanded her, trying not to sound short but failing.

She merely laughed at his back as he walked sharply away from her.

"We'll continue this discussion when I'm through," she called before he could shut the door.

"No, we will not," he called back, slamming the door shut.

Noah paced three brisk circuits down the length of his room before stopping to tunnel his fingers through his hair once again.

When exactly had he been delegated to a defensive position in these matters? Every time he turned around, she was wreaking havoc with his equilibrium. As long as he could remember, he'd been a very assertive personality when it came to dealing with women.

But she wasn't like any other woman in the world. He cared little for any of those in his history. Kestra held his heart. Because of this, he wanted to treat her like the treasure she was. He couldn't bear the idea of hurting her or being thoughtless with her. Perhaps he was being overcautious, but he would rather that than callous. No. He was in the right here and he was certain of it. She never seemed to recognize her own limitations. He didn't care if it was Samhain and Beltane all wrapped into one. None of that mattered when he knew she was hurting and exhausted.

But damn him to hell if she wasn't the most enticing creature on the planet. If she was determined, he knew she would push his buttons, just as she knew she could. She was already a proficient. Hell, she had been an adept before they'd even met. He supposed he could hope for the best, that Jacob's herb oil would do the trick and straighten out her priorities a little. Sometimes it was as if she had no sense of self-preservation.

"Noah!"

Noah's head jerked up when he heard the cry, his heart instantly leaping into overdrive. He hurried to the door, and then hesitated. He was instantly suspicious. He had avoided mind contact with her to afford her privacy, but he couldn't withstand any more of her tricky teasing, so he sought to touch her thoughts for the reason to her call.

Noah!

That level of horrified fear screaming through his mind was no trick. Noah crashed into the bathroom, fire instantly bursting from his fingers, immolating them to the ready. The only thing he saw, however, was Kestra seated and submerged in the bath. Then, after a beat, he saw she was shaking.

And that the water was glowing a phosphorescent green.

He hurried over to her, hearing her panicked breathing

and his name in a succession of cries that pitched higher with every iteration. His hands plunged into the water, dragging her slick body against his own.

The glow came with her. It clung to her skin like an aura. Noah could see auras just as she could, but he had never seen one with this uniformity of color. Nor this level of brightness. The glow was also increasing in field and ferocity.

"Easy, baby," he soothed her quickly, reaching to jerk a towel around her body.

He swung her up into his arms and carried her into the bedroom. He carefully set her onto the floor just beyond the foot of the bed, right in the center of a rug. He kneeled behind her, his knees bracketing her hips as he tucked her head under his chin and wrapped secure arms around her. He wasn't afraid. He could feel the energy emanating from her, growing stronger and stronger, seemingly with every second he spent notched up against her.

"Listen, Kes," he said in a softly modulated tone meant to bring her calm. "This is energy, and it is originating from within you, not an outside source. Do you understand?" She nodded and he heard her swallow hard. "You can control this. Do not let it control you. This is your power, whatever it becomes. It is no different than any other ability we are born with. It is innate, but it is also up to us to truly find the way to master it. Understand?"

"Yes," she said on a gasp, but he could hear her getting her breathing under control. He didn't blame her for her fear. The first time fire had blossomed from his body he'd been terrified. Especially because the incident had been triggered by anger and had been uncontrollable.

"Good," he praised her gently as she controlled herself to a more reasonable level. "Hold out your hands, sweetheart. Look. See how the power is strongest there?" Her wet hair brushed his chin when she nodded. "This usually means that your hands will be the best point of focus. You can channel this through your hands."

"Is it . . . is it an expulsion or an absorption?" she asked tremulously.

Clever girl, he thought, his delight in her mind making him hug her tightly in spite of the fact that she could present a danger to him so long as her power was unknown and uncontrolled.

"This I do not know," he told her. "But if I were to judge by the amount of energy you are burning, I would say expulsion."

"But I don't feel tired. I should feel tired."

Logic did dictate that had she been burning her own energy, she would be exhausting herself. And she was nothing if not logical. He sighed softly against the shell of her ear.

"Because it is my energy you are burning, *Kikilia*," he told her gently.

She gasped, instantly trying to pull away from him. He felt her trepidation. She was afraid of draining him. Of hurting him.

"No," he said, holding her firmly. "You cannot hurt me. You are a novice and I am an Elder Demon. The drain on my resources, even with my lack of sleep and the battles of the night, is negligible. Trust me, baby."

"Okay," she breathed, nodding readily. It pleased him that she did trust him and that she didn't even search his eyes or his thoughts before agreeing with him.

"We are symbiotic," he said. "We are one, inasmuch as we are two. I am the left hand. You are the right. What you take in, you must expel, or you will burn yourself out like a lightbulb faced with a power surge. First, feel the place within that draws power from me. Feel out and familiarize yourself with that connection."

"I can't. I don't know what you mean!"

"Shh."

Noah took her chin in hand and tilted her face up to him. He looked down into her wide eyes and smiled gently, every movement and every thought slow and easy so he wouldn't lead her to panic.

"I think I know what triggered this," he said, his lips twitching with amusement. "Your hormones were in an uproar."

She laughed incredulously at him, her mouth opened in shock.

He couldn't help but take advantage of the opportunity to prove himself. He caught her mouth up with his and kissed her with an intensity and fervor that left her winded by the time he came away for breath. Sure enough, she glowed like a lightning bug, the entire room now lighted from it.

"Extreme emotion is often a trigger for new power. Ask Bella to tell you about it sometime. She is a classic example." Noah omitted mentioning the fact that Isabella had almost killed him and Legna during that incident. "That place inside you, where you feel the center of your feelings when we kiss. Spiritual, not physical," he corrected dryly when she giggled. He didn't mind her humor. It told him she was becoming calmer and more rational. "This is the same place from which your power will branch to me. Think of it as a kiss, but in energy form."

"I understand. I feel it now," she said with no little awe. "It's just like touching minds, only from my heart rather than my head."

"Good. You have it." He knew she did because he felt the draw centralized around his heart, though it was only a physical manifestation of the connection. "Now, I cannot explain this as well for you, only because it is different for each of us. But to expel energy—in fireballs, for example—I draw from the 'well' of energy inside me. In your case, the glow indicates an overspill through all of your tissues. Your 'well' is your entire body. Be careful only to tap into the glow, and not your personal energy. This will keep you from being drained. Now"—Noah moved his hands in front of her, touching his fingertips together until the joined fingers formed a spherical shape—"to begin with, use two hands. Single-hand spheres are a skill left to later. Shape your hands in a ball, then simply channel the energy into the shape. I am not certain you can form cohesive shapes with whatever type of energy you are generating, but it is worth a shot. Hopefully it will be controlled this way."

"As opposed to . . . ?"

"Blowing up the bedroom."

"I had to ask," she muttered. She inhaled, exhaled hard, then matched the shape of his hands with her own. She imagined the green energy skimming off her skin and limbs to fill the space formed between her fingertips. At the same time, Noah drew together a fireball, showing her at a slow pace what it should look like.

Almost immediately a ball of green swirling energy began to form in the cage of her hands. She was breathing quick and soft, but it was controlled as she concentrated. Noah murmured soft encouragements and guidance against her ear until they each had a sphere of energy slightly larger than a softball within their grasp.

"Okay," he said easily. "Now be brave, baby. We are going to see what tricks this thing can do." She nodded trustingly and he took a deep breath. "It feels like a ball to you, with mass and form, so now you can wield it with one hand. It remains connected to your energy source until you throw it, so it cannot be dropped. Transfer it to a single hand . . . there. Good. Any good at pitching?"

"I throw like a girl," she said regretfully.

"That does not matter," he chuckled. "Just aim for the wall across from us. If you blow it up, at least it will only open to the hallway."

"Did I mention your teaching methods kind of suck?" she asked.

"No." He laughed. "Do it. No one is around but us. It is safe."

"Famous last words."

Instead of pitching the ball forward, underhand or overhand, she sidearmed it, flinging it free of her hand as if she were releasing a Frisbee. It was ingenious, a choice she felt gave her the best control and comfort, and she hit the mark on the money.

The ball struck the wall dead center.

And bounced off it in an arcing return toward them. Instantly they were both in motion, springing away from the unknown threat. Kes rolled over the bed and dropped off the far side, and Noah landed like a cat behind her. They both leaned around to see what the ominous little green ball would do next.

"Odds are, you are immune to your own power," he whispered, automatically lowering his voice in the face of a threat. "And since this is a form of energy, I am likely able to absorb it."

"Best to be safe than sorry," she finished for him. "I know."

Noah narrowed his gaze on the ball. It had changed. It still was aglow, but it seemed to have distinct mass at its core. It had also begun to pulse, a slow, steady strobe that seemed to have rhythm.

"Odd," he mused, moving to stand.

But Kestra grabbed his sleeve and jerked him back down beside her, probably not even realizing the impressive strength she'd used to do so.

"Stay," she commanded him, eliminating any impression of request so he would obey her. She felt him bristle, knowing it rubbed him the wrong way to be on the receiving end of a command. He wasn't used to it. She would've smiled if she weren't dedicating all of her attention to the sphere sitting in the center of the rug strobing out its strange green light. She was glad that he settled back, though, heeding her demand.

Noah waited while Kes's eyes narrowed on the orb.

Kestra watched, counting the beat of the swelling and receding light. Noting the speed. Sensing more than seeing that it was picking up in tempo, the time between the bursts of light shortening.

"Oh, shit!"

Kestra hurled herself out of Noah's reach with lightning

speed, twisting into a roll that avoided his grasp and brought her right on top of the ball of energy.

"Kes!"

She reacquired the ball, the green energy instantly blending in with the lighter glow that still clung to her skin. Kestra gained her full height and ran to the nearest window. Noah had barely made it halfway into her wake before she punched her fist and forearm into the thick glass, sending it shattering down around her. Then, this time in a full overhand arc, she hurled the ball out over the crenellations and into the air above the gardens. It was just about to reach tree level when it exploded with violent fury.

By then Noah had hold of Kestra, and he whirled her into the shield of his body as he turned his back to the force of the blast. The energy of it struck them, and he automatically absorbed it. But while he was able to prevent them from being thrown across the room, he wasn't able to keep the windows in their casements. Glass burst around them, the colored fragments showering them from all sides. He protected Kestra completely, unconcerned about anything else.

When everything had passed over them, they straightened, and now that the danger was passed, both were eager as they hurried to lean out of the empty window frames to see the damage she had wrought.

"Jeepers."

The softly spoken word of awe was the last thing Noah had expected, and he suddenly found himself laughing.

"I should think so," he chuckled as he surveyed the small brown crater that had once been a wisteria and willow grove. Now all that was left of the arbors and trees were the burnt stumps of wood and a still-falling shower of debris. "Remind me that all further practice and lessons of your power are to take place out of doors."

"Mmm," she agreed with a nod. "Sorry about the windows."

"Windows can be replaced," he pointed out with a shrug.

Then he pulled back into the room to look at her. "How did you know?"

She laughed and cast him a sidelong look. "Honey, if there is one thing I know, it's bombs."

"Of course." He crossed to her, his boots crunching over metal and glass. Then he scooped her up to protect her bare feet and marched them away from the debris field. His bedroom, and likely every room on that side of the castle, was a disaster. Yet he was grinning like an idiot for some reason. He was ridiculously proud of her, on so many levels. He had known she would be powerful, but he had never suspected anything like this. A manifestation of her best skills, magnified. It would make her training go fast and easy, and he could feel her excitement over all the possibilities. "You realize, of course, that you are officially out of business as a mercenary?"

"Of course," she agreed, unable to repress a forlorn little sigh. "But—"

"No." His tone was firm and brooked no arguments. He gained the hallway and crossed the landing, heading for the opposite side of the castle.

"I was only saying—"

"No."

She sighed with heavy resignation.

"Fine. If you're going to be all uptight and moral about it."

"Not to worry," he placated her with a chuckle. "You will have plenty of things to blow up in our world. Believe me."

"Promise?" she demanded.

"My word as your King."

"Ha!" Then, at his look of disdain, she eased his ruffled honor. "You aren't my King," she reminded him gently.

"Nevertheless, it does not change the value of my word."

"No, but you should watch how you put things."

"Funny," he mused as he kicked open the door of the bedroom Elijah used to inhabit when he'd spent great amounts of time as Noah's guest, "but I did not think I had to consider whether or not I was yours, King, man, or otherwise."

He settled her onto the bed and pulled away to give her a meaningful look. She was already mulling it over.

"I see your point," she said softly, reaching up to place a warm hand on his stomach as he stood over her.

"Conceding a point? To me? Seems you have just blown me away once again."

"Ha. Ha. Ha," she said dryly as he covered her hand with his own.

Kestra felt him stiffen suddenly and he tore his gaze away from her face. She followed his wide stare to the hand she pressed to his belly. For the first time she realized a red stain was spreading across his shirt. She sat up suddenly, trying to jerk her hand free to see his wound.

"Not mine," he corrected her softly.

Finally, she noticed the red streaks of blood crisscrossing her palm, forearm, and biceps, sliced from her hasty crash through the stained glass window.

"Wow. I never felt a thing," she said as he nudged her over and sat beside her so he could better inspect the damage she had done to herself.

"This is my fault," he muttered, clearly feeling it. "I should never have messed with a new power indoors. I know better than this."

"You were trying to calm me down," she reminded him. "I thought I was turning into an alien, for goodness' sake."

"Nearly seven centuries of living dictates I should have used my head," he argued, wincing when he saw there was glass embedded in her skin. "Sit still. I am sure Elijah has first aid equipment in the bathroom."

She watched as he disappeared into the bathroom, breaking her gaze away only briefly to seek strength from the heavens.

"You had to give me a control freak," she said with mild disgust. "I would have settled for 'a little bossy,' or even 'slightly stubborn,' but no . . ." She sighed, sounding very put upon. Then she addressed the man in the next room. "They're only superficial cuts," she called out.

"Not the one on your palm," he argued.

"Regardless, Gideon said I'd heal rapidly on my own. I don't see why you're getting your knickers in a twist."

"Because," he said heatedly as he approached the bed with a first aid kit in hand, "I damn well hate to see you hurt."

That was clearly the final word on the matter, mainly because Kestra was busy dealing with the warm and fuzzy feelings his remark had caused to well up inside her. Damn him anyway for turning her into a woman made of marshmallows.

He lifted his head from his inspection of her injured arm long enough to give her a look that told her that her thoughts hadn't gone unmonitored.

"Well, you are," she groused good-naturedly.

"Fair return for what you have done to me," he retorted, a sparkle in his smoky eyes.

She impatiently threw her legs over the side of the bed, fidgeting as he cleaned and dressed the gash in her palm.

"Oh, quit babying it," she complained when he was taking too long for her satisfaction.

With an exasperated sigh he grabbed her by the chin and forced her to look at him. "Are you in some kind of hurry I should know about?"

"Well, I was thinking I'd go outside. You know, take these babies out for a spin, see what they can do!" She waggled her fingers in his face even as a stern scowl radiated over his expression. "Oh, come on! It's like when you get a brand-new gun. A laser-sighted fine-lined semiautomatic with its first full clip. The first thing you need to do is shoot the damn thing! Get the feel. Ride the rush until your arms ache from the recoil. You know?"

Noah had to resist the urge to laugh and get caught up in

her enthusiasm. The parallel wasn't all that far off, actually. In that moment she practically reeked of her military training, and it fascinated him. And yes, she should get familiar with this new power as soon as possible.

"But not tonight," he said in a concise, no-nonsense tone. "Let us save it for the morrow, Kestra. You need rest, and frankly, I need at least an hour where you are not in danger of losing a limb . . . or even a healthy strand of hair, for that matter. Now settle down."

Damn it. She was pulling the pouting thing on him. Did she really think that was going to work on any intelligent man? Women had been pouting at him for six centuries. It didn't affect him in the least.

Except perhaps to make her look extremely kissable. Her lips had such a sweet pink blush to them, and it darkened considerably when she pushed them out in expression of her consternation. And why in hell was an ex-militia cum mercenary using a feminine wile like pouting, anyway? Women's activists had to be rolling in their graves.

Noah forced himself to look down at her arm and finish the task of binding her wounds. When she was wrapped in gauze from palm to shoulder, he finally gathered the fortitude to look at her face again. The pout had disappeared, replaced by an expression of abject disappointment and resignation.

"What?" He covered his disturbance with impatience.

"Well, you won't let me play with this power. You won't let me play with you. You won't let me do anything, and I don't think I like you very much right now."

"Play with you." Did she actually just say that? Noah swallowed hard as that lightning-quick awareness she so easily triggered in him leapt to attention. He was trying to remember why he wouldn't let her play with him, the issue lost in a jumble of erotic thoughts and confused priorities.

"I am . . ." He cleared his throat when his voice sounded a little too rough and aroused for his liking. "It is not my wish to deny you anything," he explained reasonably. "You are free to do whatever you like. I know you are an independent person. But," he hurried along when a wicked smile curled the corner of her delicious-looking lips, "but I am older and wiser when it comes to the world you have entered, and you have to understand that my advice has reason behind it. Good reason. And a desire to keep you safe."

"Hmm." She seemed to contemplate that for a second. Then she stood up and turned toward him as she pulled at her towel. The cotton cloth fell away from her body, leaving him with a breast-level view of her sleek body. "I have a desire to keep you safe as well," she told him softly. "Safe here, in my arms."

She slid her arms around his neck, stepping around his leg so she could get even closer. This brought the hard peak of her nipple to brush boldly over his lips. He made a repressed sound of need as she so easily mastered and called forth the fire from within him. It flowed over his skin and bones, melting through both until he was little more than hard, tensed muscle and an aching heaviness of arousal. All of which he knew she was counting on, shameless and relentless siren that she was.

"Noah," she whispered against his hair. "I want you. And I know you want me."

"Wanting you is not in question," he murmured, his mouth brushing over her warm skin as he spoke. He let the tip of his tongue touch the surface of her breast, and she caught a breath and shuddered. "I will always want you."

Noah gave in to her temptations, drawing her rigid nipple into the warm cavern of his mouth, flicking his tongue over her with expert speed and pressure until her knees went a little weak and she clung to him with a soft moan of delight. He left her with a teasing scrape of his teeth. If she wanted to play at seduction, he was more than happy to oblige.

"Oh, that feels so good," she breathed into his ear as she

rubbed her face against his hair. "I don't know how or why, but it makes me so . . . so . . ."

"Hot," he supplied for her roughly. "Hot enough that I can feel it radiating off your skin."

He reached out to caress the globe of her breast with a long, graceful stroke meant to tease ever so lightly. His fingers then drifted down along the curve of her side as he reached to suck on her dark, tempting nipple once again. This time his draw on her was tighter, rougher. He was more insistent on hearing her cry out, which she did readily. Her head bowed to touch his, her damp hair hanging against his face and neck a chill contrast to the increasing warmth emanating from him.

Noah moved to gently run his tongue over a fading welt traveling diagonally over the rise of her breast. She eagerly sank her fingers into his dark hair, holding his head to herself with a shuddering sigh. Her nails rubbed against his scalp as he moved to attend the opposite breast, the sensation sending a shiver down his spine.

"I feel as though I've waited all day for you to touch me. It's weighed in the back of my mind, rushing forward any chance it got, even with everything that's happened tonight," she told him.

The late night shadow of his whiskers burned over her skin; his tongue and lips scorched. Kestra felt his hands gliding into the bend of her waist and she sighed with contentment now that she was secure in the understanding that whatever his wishes a minute ago, he was now fully engaged in the moment. Noah broke away, pressing his lips to her breastbone as he chuckled against her.

"So sure of yourself, are you?" he asked as his heated hands skimmed down her hips.

She smiled into his silky hair.

"All evidence seems to point in my favor," she agreed, her sly tone daring him to refute her.

"And if I were to stop, just to teach you a lesson, my brat?" He asked this as his fingers slid to the V of her hips, brushing with teasing touches through trim white curls. She felt so soft and damp, her heat an exciting balm against the pads of his fingertips. Her sweet, sexy scent washed over him, as did a surge of craving for her that struck him low. He could never leave her.

Never. For the rest of his life.

Kestra gasped as he discarded his noncommittal teasing and slid his fingers into her welcoming flesh. Just as quickly they were gone and he was making a sound of deep frustration over their awkward positions. He practically gave her whiplash as he swung her down onto the bed with a bounce. He pushed her knees apart, his gaze hot and intent as she opened to his viewing and anything else he wanted to do to her. She was breathing hard enough to fill the room with sound, and he smiled at how eager she was to feel what he had taught her to feel. What they had learned to feel together.

Noah bent to kiss her knee, his mixed-colored eyes flicking upward to meet hers, making certain he kept her fully engaged. He brushed a seeking palm along the inside of her smooth inner thigh. His mouth quickly fell into its path, making a sound of anticipation hiss from her lips. Kestra's eyes closed in reflex, but the sharp squeeze of his fingers demanded she rethink breaking off eye contact with him.

"You wanted to play," he scolded thickly. "Let us play."

He pushed off with a knee on the edge of the bed and he landed over her entire body, braced on his hands, a palm on either side of her head and on his knees between her thighs. Kestra inhaled, taking in his aggression and his scent all at once. He pressed the front of his thighs to the backs of hers, pushing her farther open, leaving her exposed and vulnerable and making her heart pound when she realized he was still fully clothed and she was completely served up to his every whim.

"Ahh," he growled softly in her ear, his lips playing over

her sensitive lobe. "Finally she understands that two can play this game."

"May the best one win?"

"May we both win," he corrected, punctuating the sentiment with an erotic sweep of his tongue down the length of her neck. He shifted his weight to a single hand, resting his freed palm and widely splayed fingers against her collarbone. He swiftly skimmed downward over her breast, on to her belly, which dipped in an anticipatory tremble as he brushed her with a painter's creativity for a long minute, exploring all curves and sensitivities.

Kestra sighed with obvious relief when his fingertips finally returned to their hastily abandoned exploration of the ready folds of her feminine body. He exhaled hotly against her mouth a moment before catching her up in a kiss that plumbed the depths of his passion for her. She felt his wild thoughts bursting across her mind, taking her breath away.

So wet. So hot. For me. I could spend a lifetime learning how to be inside you.

Kestra clung to his shoulders as tense pleasure sprang through her body from all the attention he was paying her. But at those thoughts, she was suddenly galvanized into action, her fingers falling to his shirt, dragging it from the waistband of his pants. He groaned deeply when her touch slid up over the bare skin of his back, but he refused to remove his hands from her to allow her to strip him of it. She cried out when two long fingers slid into her ready opening, the nectar of her aroused body hot to his touch as it bathed him. He felt the surge of answering longing thickening in his groin, his erection straining for its favorite haven.

But he'd longed for her all night, on one level or another, having been twisted through a wringer of every emotion ever created, and he wouldn't give in too quickly now. For her, however, he had completely opposite plans.

He sought that special point of stimulation that so enjoyed the skillful sweep of his thumb. He combined this with the plunge of his fingers deep into her body and the sucking of his mouth upon her breast. He felt the sudden bite of her nails into his back and he shuddered in unison with her. Her hips lunged up off the bed to meet the rhythm of his fingers, just as he transferred his mouth to her belly and the sensitive line down the center of it. His progress below her navel deprived her of her grasp on him beneath his shirt, so she was forced to satisfy herself with a clutch of deep fingers in his hair, holding him to her—or perhaps pulling him away, he couldn't tell which from one second to the next.

When Noah's tongue replaced the work of his thumb against her, Kestra cried out with pleasure. At first it was a sound of denial, begging him not to push her to that level of hypersensitivity. Then it changed to acceptance, and finally encouragement. He felt the press of her knees against his shoulders, tasted the delightful ambrosia of her need as it built and flowed over his tongue. Her inner muscles clutched at his fingers, seeking blindly for release. A release he pushed her toward the next moment with an artful combination of strokes, both of taste and touch.

He loved the abandon of her orgasms, the vocal cries bordering on and sometimes surpassing screams. Still he pressed her, teased her, dragged out every last gasp and hitching whimper he possibly could before her strong legs practically kicked him away from her oversensitive body. Then, at last, he rose to his knees and stripped off his shirt. She lay spread out before him, flushed and ready still, gasping to catch her breath, all of it painting a picture of beautiful arousal that spurred him to strip faster.

When he was nude at last, he drifted up the length of her body using the brush of his mouth to herald his approach. He felt the trembling of her legs, the soft, gasping shudders of her breath, and it humbled him that she allowed him the trust and openness necessary for her to reach such a point of helplessness in pleasure. When she wound her arms around his neck and drew him down to her mouth, his heart pounded with the intimacy and emotion she was using to speak to him through them. Still she guarded her thoughts about the matter, and it stung him painfully, but he was willing to accept what she offered. It was more than she had been willing to give mere days ago.

For the moment, he allowed himself to be lost in the sensation of her silken legs wrapping around his, the press of her calves against his buttocks drawing him down to her, bathing his hardened shaft with welcoming liquid as he settled against her.

Kestra slid her hand between their bodies, seeking him, pressing him against her wet folds until he and her fingers were saturated, the head of his engorged penis rubbing her so intimately that they were both groaning with the eroticism. She had needed him forever, it seemed. While he had taken his time pulling pleasure from her body, she had writhed with the want of him. His manipulations had left her soaring, yet bereft, because she hadn't had him deep within the heart of her, hadn't clutched him to her very core where she so ached to hold him.

"Come inside me, Noah," she begged him on a gasp. "Please . . . please . . ." That word became a litany as she whispered the plea over and over, sometimes strangling it in her throat as he bided his time sliding against her. But she felt the rivulets of sweat skimming off his body to drop onto hers, saw the dampening of his hair that put increasing curl into the dark locks. She knew, though, what he was seeking. Knew he would find it if he kept teasing her a few moments longer.

She burst into release, colors exploding brightly behind her eyelids as they clamped down tight in reflex. Finally, as she was quaking and pulsing still, he found her threshold and began to ease into her.

Noah pushed against the rhythmic squeezing of inner muscles as he entered her. She was slick, but tight, trying to finish her spasms of pleasure and adjust to his girth at the same time. It was a breathtaking and unbelievable sensation, and his pulse pounded under the onslaught.

"Kes . . . ah, baby . . ." He could barely speak as he slid farther into her, her hands sliding down to clutch at his hips in guidance, goading, and desperation.

Kestra felt him shift, brace a knee, grab her hip for leverage, and then he sank to the hilt within her. How was it possible? How could he make every time feel like the first? As if it were something new and wonderful they were only just discovering? As they went, they became less wild, but more intense. Was that even a differentiation? Yes, yes, she thought, it was.

Because she was beginning to care for him, and beginning to allow herself to accept that he truly cared for her. As a person. For who she was. Not because of genetic predisposition.

And that changed everything.

He suddenly covered her mouth with his, his hands sinking into her hair and cradling her head with tenderness and warmth.

"Shh," he whispered against her kiss-swollen lips. "Time enough for thinking come the dawn. Just feel me, baby," he coaxed her gently. "For now, just feel me."

She nodded, allowing the sudden surge of panic to ease back into the racing pulses of passion. She did as he directed, focusing completely on the feel of his hard invasion into the very core of her. Noah began to move very slowly, drawing out each withdrawal and incursion back into her with blinding control. Kestra understood that all he wanted in the world was her pleasure, and he was going to go to hell and back to see she had it. She realized that he felt it was the only way he could express himself to her, the only way she would allow him to.

So he did so with the utmost of eloquence.

She pulled him back to her mouth and kissed him, her heart wrenching into a back flip as she put more feeling into it than she'd ever done before in her life. If he could use body language to fulfill the needs of expression, then she could, too. The kiss and the emotion she put behind it seemed to stir him as nothing else could. She felt it in the sudden slam of his body into hers, the impact as his breath shot out of him, and the pulsing spear of fiery heat that burned her suddenly from the inside out. Speed suddenly became all important. He pushed up the tempo until she couldn't see or think straight, never mind catch her breath. His mouth worked against hers between gasps for breath and pauses to take her a little bit harder and a little bit deeper.

"Sweet Destiny," he gasped hoarsely. "How you feel!"

Like heaven. Like hell. Everything . . . everything.

He resorted to the touch of their minds when he was too breathless to finish his decree. It was all the more intimate, so much more stirring, as if he were stroking her soul.

Noah felt the tumult of her mind when he touched it, the blur of thought and emotion too much to sort through, but he knew it was all focused directly on him, and that was all that mattered. He fought for control when that thought sent tension gripping readily through him, warning him that all it took was an emotionally intimate idea to bring him to the brink inside her. He forgot, however, that the door swung both ways. He left himself open to her divination and she snagged the realization of his avalanching need for release. Instantly she strove to thwart all attempt at control, stealing him blind and breathless as she flexed around him, coaxing with the rippling work of sleek muscles and artful hips. Her nails punctured the skin on his backside, and he realized he was lost.

He gripped the sheet so violently as he plunged into her that it tore, even as his fingertips bit right back at her where they grasped her hip. Coming inside her was like the crash of thunder, his entire body locking. He couldn't even make a sound, his jaw clenched as his breath froze and his orgasm robbed him of sense and strength. All he could do was jerk into her with each violent pulse, the roaring in his ears blotting out even her strangled cries of delight.

Noah was so profoundly shaken he could only brace himself over her as he trembled from head to toe. He felt her arms tighten around him, drawing his forehead down to hers, simply holding him while he tried to catch his breath and recover. After a beat he felt the urge to scream, so bad was his need to tell her how he felt, to not be afraid of scaring her away and just tell her. He hadn't felt such frustration in all his life, and that was saying something after nearly seven hundred years. He couldn't even guard his thoughts, so weak was his patience, and it only added to his dissatisfaction. If she were to reach for his mind just then, it would be there, a raw emotional display that could cost him everything.

He shouldn't do it, he knew, but he couldn't help himself. He rolled away from her and sat up on the edge of the bed, raking both hands through his hair. He was reaching for his clothes, jerking them on before she was even half aware he was doing so.

"Noah?"

He kept his back to her, knowing that his every emotion was written across his face, knowing that if he saw the bewilderment on her face he would do something rash and impassioned that he would come to regret.

She simply wasn't ready.

"Do not ask me questions," he said, knowing he sounded harsh, that leaving like this bordered on being cruel. "And . . ." He swallowed hard. "And do not try and take your answers, for you will not want what you find."

Kestra watched in shock as he stormed out of the room, the slam of the door reverberating until it echoed endlessly in her mind. *What in hell just happened?* She reached to pull her towel from the floor, feeling vulnerable and somehow rejected in her naked state. The liquid evidence of his explosive release into her body slid from her as she moved, reminding her of the appalling speed with which his mood had changed. And had he just demanded privacy of his mind from her? Yes. That was absolutely what he had meant. Her knee-jerk reaction of infuriation dismayed her in its hypocrisy. How often had she asked for that very thing and been willingly granted it? He had no less a right to it.

It only disturbed her because it wasn't in Noah to even desire such a thing. At least, she hadn't thought so. She stared at the door without blinking, even though she sensed he'd already left the castle. The sensation of bereavement that washed over her took her breath away. Tears stung her eyes as sharply as his abandonment had stung her feminine pride.

What had happened? What had she done to drive him away?

She was terrified that she might never get the chance to find out.

Isabella sat up with a gasp of shock.

She reached out blindly for Jacob, but his side of the bed was empty.

Samhain, she recalled. He was out hunting. She'd been left to recover from her earlier ordeal, lying down after she'd put Leah to bed shortly before three a.m. Dawn had broken in the meantime. She listened for the baby, certain that she'd made some noise to wake her. But silence greeted her, and she sensed her daughter slept on blissfully.

She was certain something wasn't right. She tried to recall if she'd experienced a vision in her sleep, that being the only thing other than Jacob or Leah that could wake her out of a dead slumber. That or a call to hunt. She touched on Jacob briefly and unobtrusively, checking his status while keeping far enough in the background so as not to disturb his concentration. He was in complete control of his quarry, and there was no pressure in his mind that there was more than a single transgression going on, one that she would be needed for.

Damn it all, she hated it when she got the willies like this and they went unexplained.

She got out of bed, tugging down the long slit skirt of her peignoir so it swirled into proper place against her ankles. Then she pushed away the heavy black mass of her hair as she strode barefoot to the baby's room just to double-check.

She had barely rounded the doorway when she crashed into a solid body.

She felt strong, heated hands curl around her upper arms, helping her right her balance even as her heart leapt into her throat. It took a panicked second for her to recognize the stormy gray and green of Noah's eyes.

"Jeez! Noah! You scared the crap out of me!" she exclaimed, jerking away from his grasp in her irritation. "Damn it!" She backhanded him across the shoulder for good measure. "You big jerk!"

"Bella . . ."

His tone tossed a bucket of ice on her bluster, and she drew in a breath of soft shock when she caught the full impact of his ravaged features.

"Bella . . ."

Noah fell to his knees before her, and to her continued shock and alarm, he caught her around the waist and buried his face against her stomach.

And wept.

Chapter 21

Bella was speechless and stunned, but above everything else, she was a woman of intense heart and empathy. Her hands instantly dove into his hair, holding him to her in comfort as his powerful frame was racked with his pain. She said nothing, didn't try to hush him, merely let him spend himself as he so clearly needed to do. She'd never thought to see him in such a way. Oh, she knew he was capable of great depth of emotion. It was the nature of his people, and it was what made him such a fine monarch. But he was also a controlled and private person when it came to showing those outside of his family anything that could be construed as insecurity. Projecting an image of an even keel was imperative to Noah. Others might be ruffled, but he must always appear calm and tranquil. In this way, he kept order and maintained respect.

Why he had come to her was the mystifying part. A week earlier . . . yes, perhaps . . . but as things stood?

None of it mattered, she realized suddenly. It no longer mattered to her, and, clearly, it didn't matter to him. He was in pain, and he'd come to her for comfort. Not his beloved sisters, not Jacob . . . *her*.

Touched, she had to swallow past her own sudden rise of tears.

Softly she began to stroke his hair, reminding her of the way she mothered Leah when she was distressed. It made her smile slightly. Noah and Leah were two peas in a pod. She'd always thought so. Jacob had often joked that he was suffering from "displaced father syndrome." He'd made the term up, of course, as a way of expressing his amusement over Leah and Noah's affinity for each other. It had been that way since her birth, and would always be that way, angry mothers notwithstanding. She knew she'd torn out his heart the day she had ripped Leah away from him as punishment for something she'd always known he'd been helpless to control. She, of all people, showing intolerance for one of the Enforced. Showing intolerance for her King, whom, as Jacob had so painfully pointed out, she loved very deeply.

Forgotten now. By them both.

She didn't kid herself into thinking his current agony was an attack of conscience over that matter, either. No. Noah had borne his pain in silence, accepting her cruelty as his due, and would never have imposed himself on her. He would have waited until she could find it within herself to forgive him. He wouldn't have caused her the heartache of begging for her forgiveness if she wasn't ready to hear it. It would have gone against Noah's powerful sense of honor.

After a few moments, Noah quieted. Bella bracketed his face with her hands and tilted his face up to hers, using her fingertips to sweep away the tracks of his tears. He showed no shame for his emotion, even when she pressed a sympathetic kiss to his cheek.

"Come with me," she urged, taking his hands and guiding him to his feet. She led him down to the first floor and they settled on the couch, next to each other so she could clasp one of his hands between her small palms.

"Are you well?" he asked, his rough voice so subdued

that she felt a fresh pang of empathetic pain blossoming in her chest.

"Yes. I am well," she assured him.

"I did not have the chance to thank you for coming to Kestra's aid."

The way he spoke her name was like a hammer to the back of her head. *Here,* she thought, *is the reason for his pain*. Kestra. His mate.

"I would've done as much for any of us. But I was grateful to be of service to you, Noah."

Her sincerity, coupled with the squeeze of her hands, made him swallow hard as he met her violet gaze and the open forgiveness that radiated from her. "Bella," he began hoarsely, "I never meant . . . I never wanted to . . ."

"Shh. I know. We don't need to speak of it, Noah. I, of all people, understand the duress you were under. I, of all people, appreciate the impetus of the Imprinting and the things we will do to see it through. I've come to realize that Leah was able to do what she did, young as she is, because she loves you so much she wanted to give you what you so strongly desired. How could I deny my daughter's right to give you such a gift?"

"Gift." His world of anguish was wrapped up in the word. "A gift I feel compelled to squander at every turn. I will destroy this. I will lose this precious moment because I cannot bear to be patient." He clenched his jaw tightly shut, dragging his hand from her grasp so he could comb the fingers of both hands through his hair. "I waited patiently for three hundred years for the end to the Lycanthrope war. A century for the Vampires to come to their senses before that. I have lived to the tempo of a methodical drum of peace as Shadowdwellers, Mistrals, and all Nightwalkers slowly came to the table. Ages of diplomacy and understanding, and yet I cannot bear out a week for the woman who will bring meaning to the rest of my existence.

"Bella, she is so afraid of getting close to anyone that

even a hint of emotion on her part or mine sends her into a tailspin. Logically, knowing how she was damaged into being this way, I comprehend why this is an obstacle for her and why I must proceed with care. But—"

"But your heart wants to shout from the rooftops? Logic be damned?"

He sighed heavily, not at all surprised that the insightful Enforcer already grasped his situation.

"I left her. I . . . I could not bear to stay, but leaving her was so wrong. So very wrong. I have never treated a woman in such a manner in all my life. I cannot think straight when I am with her!" His hands opened and closed into convulsive fists. "I am unused to holding back my emotions, Isabella. I come to you because you are my only bridge between the Demon and human cultures. The only one I truly trust to understand how important this is to me. Legna advises, but I am not certain she sees the truth because she loves me and is biased. At least you love me less more recently," he said wryly. "Perhaps enough to be practical and honest. Hopefully wise enough to guide me."

"Gee whiz, you sure don't ask much of a girl, do you?" she said with dry wit. He actually laughed softly at that. She reached to cover one of his fisted hands. "Noah, I've only one piece of advice for you. It's the only one anyone with sense should be giving you."

He looked up, taking a deep breath in preparation.

"I know very little about Kestra, and only spoke to her briefly today, but she is a reasonable and intelligent woman. When dealing with reasonable and intelligent women, there is only one thing you need to do." She smiled softly. "Be who you are. Be you, Noah. Stop hesitating, hemming, and hedging. That isn't who you are. You thrive in your confidence, just as you flourish when you share your emotions freely with those who matter most to you. She will never know who you are if you keep drawing up, reining in. She is afraid? She fears? And you fear she will run?" He nodded, eyes wide and expression intent. "Let her. The world is only so big, and she is only so strong. No one faced with your love can help but return it. She will come around. But she must come around to you, as you are. For who you are. Every stitch and every flaw."

"I feel as though I am being told the same thing from different quarters, but I am not getting the message," he said with a wry shake of his head.

"Because you're letting your fears rule you. And I understand that. Love is a frightening thing. Facing losing the object you love is damned terrifying. But . . . nothing ventured, nothing gained. Noah," she said, leaning in, "you're a beautiful man who has had to face a very difficult chain of events all at once. You aren't the first to quail under such circumstances, and you will not be the last. Samhain is passing, the worst part over. You will begin to feel more grounded soon. However, if she can bear up when you're at your worst, imagine how easy it will be from here on out. Stop coddling her. She's made of some pretty stern stuff, from what I saw. Be what you are meant to be, forthright and Demon and King, and then sit back and breathe."

"Breathe?"

"Just breathe."

Noah sat back and took a deep breath.

He exhaled.

Exhaustion got the better of Kestra and she'd fallen into a deeply troubled sleep by the time Noah returned to the castle. He found her in the Great Hall, curled up in front of the fire in his favorite chair, her face looking tight with confusion and hurt even in sleep. He cursed himself for that, disgusted with his lack of emotional control and how it had allowed him to injure her. It wasn't right to punish her for her shortcomings. She'd suffered enough punishment at the hands of men. More than enough.

Yet Isabella was right. He couldn't tiptoe around her anymore. She would panic, she would be terrified, and he had to expect it, but he could no longer allow her to think he was anything other than himself. It was like a lie, and he despised artifice. That was probably why this had rubbed him so wrong for so long. He had tried to be patient, but he'd been doing so in the wrong manner. He'd tried to hold back expressing his emotions when his patience would be better and more honestly spent in dealing with the fallout of his honesty, rather than avoiding it.

As he observed her sleep, he understood that she hadn't come here because she'd wanted to wait for him. She'd come here to avoid the bed he'd abandoned her in. Pain of his infliction. More mistakes. Well, it would end here and now, he thought with determination. He'd sworn never to hurt her intentionally, and he had just broken that promise. He had known it as he had walked away from her, and yet hadn't had the strength of honor to stop himself and control his inner turmoil. What did his pain matter in the face of hers? Had he always been this selfish? His mother would have been horrified by his behavior.

Or perhaps Sarah would have been far more understanding of his and Kestra's dilemma than anyone. The confusion and suddenness, the reluctance and independence his father had had to battle. And Ariel had been just as sure of his path and his love as Noah was, even in the face of Sarah's resistance. The sudden understanding of the parallels between Kestra and himself and his parents' initial relationship made him laugh with surprised understanding. How many times had he read his mother's handwritten fairy tale to Legna and Hannah after their parents had died? How many times to nieces and nephews? And again to Leah?

And only now was he understanding that there was a lesson in it that applied to his current situation. His father had approached Sarah's fears and rejection with nothing but confidence and the assuredness of the Imprinting at his back. He had been himself, beginning to end, exhibiting patience only to a point, and then laying out all his cards. And Sarah had run. Run like mad.

And he had chased. Caught. Coaxed. As Noah himself had done initially with Kestra, only he had forgotten to maintain the truth. To be blunt. To be who and what he was no matter what. His father had made only a single compromise, and that was his profession. What Ariel had never compromised were his feelings for Sarah and his knowledge that they would be together from that day forward. That he would love her and be loved in return. He had never doubted it.

"Oh, what a fool I have been," Noah murmured.

Kes opened her eyes at the sound of his soft, familiar voice. She sat up quickly, drawing his gaze with the movement. Their eyes met and matched, each looking turbulently at the other. They moved together, instinctively, though neither had intended to do so. She launched herself from the chair, and his stride ate up the distance between them. She threw her weight into his embrace just as he pulled her against himself.

"I am so sorry," he said, whispering the apology in her ear. "I have no excuse. Please forgive me."

"No. You do have an excuse, don't you?" she said softly in return. "But you won't use it because you're afraid it will disturb me."

"Nothing excuses leaving you in such a way. Nothing." He turned his head to kiss her soft cheek. "I felt your pain. I felt it with every step I took, and yet I could not get control of myself."

"And I felt yours," she countered, her hands framing his face and her head pulling back so she could study the emerald and smoke of his eyes. "Did you think I have to make an effort to touch your mind? Your feelings? When they are as powerful as that, they swim into me like a flood." Kestra felt him stiffen against her body, but a moment later he exhaled and relaxed.

"You knew?"

"That you love me?" she asked quietly, her gaze on him tender and sweet. "Yes. I've known it for some time now, Noah. It wasn't until you left me that I suddenly realized why you weren't telling me. That you were keeping it bottled up because you were protecting me. As always." She laughed softly. "Will you always treat me with kid gloves?"

Noah brushed the flat of his palm back over her tousled hair. He was momentarily speechless, and he was also amused. All his drama, and she had already known. More importantly, she was still there. That realization sent his heartbeat soaring with hope and delight.

"I am beginning to understand what a mistake that is. I will endeavor to do better in the future," he told her seriously.

"You do that." She smiled, a gentle tilt of her lips. "Your feelings for me aren't what causes me fear, you know," she said, an edge of sadness creeping into her voice. "Not anymore. I know that this isn't fanaticism for you. If it were, you wouldn't care enough to shield me from it like you've been trying so faithfully to do. I feel the honesty and the truth in your emotions, Noah. I am breathless with it. You're so sure, so unafraid of what you feel. In fact, I believe I envy you that."

"I love you, Kestra," he said, relief rushing through him at finally being able to speak the words aloud. "What about that could I possibly find daunting? You are beautiful, strong, and an enigma that I believe will always keep me fascinated, no matter how many lifetimes we live together."

"And you feel this way, even though you know I'm not sure if I can ever say the same?"

He didn't bother to hide the slice of pain that caused him.

"I do. But that does not mean I do not want reciprocation, Kes. Because I want it more than anything else. I need it. My soul needs your love. But," he said softly, leaning to kiss her lips to distract her from the anxiety he saw shimmering through her eyes, "I am going to find the strength to be patient for you. I am going to make you trust me enough to let go of that fear. I want to show you how beautiful sharing love with me will be."

Kestra swallowed hard, turning her face away as tears leapt into her eyes. He was so certain. So fearless. How did he find the courage? After losing his parents the way he had? After the friends and loved ones who had been torn away from him, how did he find the nerve to love so wholeheartedly? So easily? She realized then that she hoped she could learn from his example. That she could move beyond those memories of her parents' tragic end and the guilt she still felt about it. She knew she shouldn't blame herself for the actions of a madman, but she couldn't shake the idea that she'd been the catalyst for the loss of those she had loved so very much. But even that guilt was nothing compared to the gashes in her soul caused when they had been torn away from her heart.

"How do you do it?" she asked him suddenly. "How do you live through the ages like you do, watching everyone you love die? I don't understand you," she said in frustration, grasping at him as if she would shake him. "I don't understand how you can risk loving me! I can still be killed. I can still die. Only now it will likely be a violent occurrence because I don't imagine you have many natural deaths among your people. Explain it to me, Noah, please," she begged, leaning all of her weight against him. "Please."

"It's so simple a philosophy, baby," he murmured softly against her hair, pausing to kiss her ear through the soft strands. "Live in the moment. Especially when you live so long a life, you need to know that you cannot put off anything. Too often regret comes in the blink of an eye, as you yourself have seen and pointed out. I would rather live with loving you for a heartbeat of time than having never known the gloriousness of the feeling. How long do we have to cherish one another? I do not know. I will not waste a single precious moment thinking about it when I could be spending that moment making love to you."

To stress his point he caught her head between his hands and held her steady for his kiss. He covered her mouth, his hunger raw and unaffected. He kissed her as if it was, indeed, the last moment he would ever spend with her. Kestra realized he'd always done so, or desired to do so. Now that he no longer feared her learning about his powerful feelings for her, his kiss was flooded with an intensity she hadn't felt before. It dragged heat and unsteady heartbeats up from the center of her body. His hand lowered to her waist, catching the warmth of the bared curve against his palm. He suddenly broke away from her.

"Sweet Destiny, Kes, what the hell are you wearing?"

She shrugged. It was her standard nightwear. The white stretchy shirt hugged the wealth of her breasts, but ended an inch or two farther down her ribs than a bra would, leaving her midriff bare. The men's boxers were rolled over a couple of times at the elastic waistband to help them fit, and they were settled low on her hips.

"Pajamas," she said, as if he were a little dense. "It's daybreak, as you see."

"Pajamas? You call these pajamas?"

She settled her hands on her hips, just below the low line of the boxers.

"Do you have a problem with my choice in nightwear? Er . . . daywear . . . uh . . . sleepwear. Whatever!"

"No."

"No? Then why—"

He snatched her up off her feet and into his body, clutching her by the bared curves of her waist.

"I was admiring your wise choice," he growled with sexy intent just before he crushed her mouth beneath a hot kiss. He rapidly worshipped her wisdom by example, his hands skimming easily up under the shirt and cupping the bare weight of her breasts. He caught her nipples between his fingers, toying with the pressure he had learned she was responsive to. She bent backward, moaning into his mouth as she curved deeper into the hard press of his body. "I admire wisdom in a woman," he informed her heatedly, just as he abandoned her breasts and shot both hands down through the loose waist of the boxers so he could curve them over her hips and then her bare bottom. He used the grasp to drag her hips into connection with his, rubbing himself wickedly against her to show her the effect she had on him, the evidence jutting from beneath his clothes and into her soft flesh.

"Noah," she groaned, wishing she could tell him a thousand ways how much she loved his aggression. How hot and how wild it made her to feel so desperately wanted, as she was so clearly wanted by him.

"Yes, baby, I know," he panted softly against her lips. "Would you trade this moment away? Would you rather live in fear than feel this?"

He hauled her off her feet, giving her no opportunity to answer and no choice but to wrap her long legs around his hips and put her arms around his shoulders. He was across the room in an instant, it seemed, and she found herself once again sitting on top of his desk. She was no longer in a dress, but that did not faze the Demon King in the least. He sought for, and easily found, the valley of hot, wet flesh her position opened up to him. She leaned away from the savagery of his mouth at the first sure stroke of his fingers. He had unerring knowledge of her and he used it shamelessly. Kestra gasped, her back arched, thrusting her breasts upward for the catch of his mouth.

The combined sensation was maddening. She burned, laser bursts of pleasure zipping through her, traveling to a center point so near the sure slide of his fingers. Oh, how he touched her!

"No!" she answered him at last, even though he was pushing her to climax with skilled speed and she could barely breathe.

"I know," he breathed softly, clearly affected by her response. "Tell me what you want, Kes." She moaned with pleasure, her hips wriggling against his touch. "So many choices for living in the moment, baby love. Do you want my touch?" He stroked deep into her body with a slick finger. "Or can I taste you as you come? Or . . ." Noah dragged her close to the edge of the desk and removed his touch so she could feel the grind of his arousal against her heated sex.

Kestra was nearly blinded by all the sensations, not to mention the eroticism of his words and taunting actions. In a heartbeat he had dragged her to the border of bliss. She hadn't expected it, but that didn't mean she wasn't crazy for it. This was definitely living in the moment, she realized, and that was exactly the point he was making.

Her head jerked up, her vivid eyes faceted with desire and sexual fury. Her hands grasped his shirt and she dragged it open, heedless of the buttons ripping off and hitting the floor. She ran famished hands over his skin. He made a deep sound of pleasure when her nails scraped up his back and clung to his shoulders.

"Inside me," she uttered hotly as she licked over the dark pebble of his nipple, relishing the jerk that shot through his frame, and the shudder that followed. "I want you inside me. Deep. Connected to me as if we can stay that way forever."

Clearly he thought it was an excellent choice. The temperature of his body soared. Obvious pain flickered through his eyes, leading her into his thoughts where she came to understand it was because his clothing was lashing down the rampant need of an aroused body that had responded prettily to her words. They both moved their hands to rectify the situation. He rethought his assistance, closing his eyes as he reveled in the nimble swiftness of her hands and the loving way she surrounded him with her touch the instant she had freed him from his clothing. He had taken the opportunity to divert his hands to her flimsy boxers, shucking them off her just as easily.

Preliminaries were over. Kestra stroked him with a firm, knowledgeable touch, even as she used her legs around his waist to draw him to her. Noah could hardly breathe to make the sounds of ecstatic delight he wanted to as she guided him into her ready body. He made a single thrust, sheating himself inside her in a movement that expressed his desperate need to do exactly as she had asked. Once he was seated deep within her, the heat and honey of her wrapped tightly around him like a fist, he drew her mouth to his.

"I live to serve," he told her, teasing her lips with a nibbling kiss.

"If only that were always the truth," she sighed.

"Shut up," he said smartly, dragging a hand over her fresh mouth and pushing her back until she was sprawled over the desk, her laughter muffled by the seal of his palm. He used his free hand to grasp her hip so he could anchor her.

The laughter strangled into an exclamation of enjoyment as he very slowly drew out of her, then just as slowly returned. Her entire spine squirmed and she shuddered.

"Hmm," he said. "Liked that, did we?"

She nodded vigorously under the press of his palm.

"What about this?"

Kestra couldn't understand why all her sophistication and control always got shot to hell by him, but she responded to the clever undulation of his hips with a squeal she couldn't contain. He had a way doing things to her body that she was sure she'd never comprehend. He toyed with her methodically for several minutes, until in his concentration and distraction his hand fell from her mouth to grasp her other hip. Then she was left vulnerable to the echoes of her own cries bouncing off the high ceilings of the Great Hall.

He reached to press her thighs farther open, leaned over her, and used the hardwood of the desk as a counterpoint to add fantastic depth to his thrusts into her. He growled, seared by the sensation of achieving his goal, fulfilling her request to the best of his ability. He lost himself inside her, enveloped by her again and again, a paradise on earth, and a connection as purely elemental as he was. *Here*, he thought, *is true fire*. And she was its mistress.

In all honesty, there was little finesse to the joining. It didn't take long before they were both just reaching for the crash of their pelvises. Noah's exclamations of rising enjoyment quickly joined hers, ricocheting off the arches of the hall. She helplessly clutched his biceps, shoulders, and the edge of the desk, each in their turn as he strove to shatter her.

"Kes!"

It was a warning, and she knew it. She felt the gathering storm within him, knew she robbed him of all control so easily. She smiled, so content with the idea that she let herself fall away from the moment. She felt and heard the crash of his fist on the desk near her head and she had no cause to flinch. She knew he was frustrated because he couldn't bear the idea of possibly leaving her behind, leaving her unfulfilled. She suspected he knew she didn't even care.

"Kes!"

This time the cry was more than a warning. It was an exultation. She was so settled inside, so quiet, that she felt every surge, every hot pulsation as he slammed their hips together one last time and jetted into her. The sensation was indescribable, unequivocal, and it was all she needed. Her body flew apart on a primal level, bursting into an ecstasy only his pleasure in her could have ever triggered.

Noah was shocked by the force of her release, her back arching until he thought her spine would snap in two, her clutch on him violent, a powerful embrace that milked him to exhaustion. When they both fell over the desk, he found himself completely bemused. He could barely stand, for starters. But for a span of time there he had thought he had lost her, that he would end up being selfish in his release. Of course, he would have gladly resorted to one of the other methods he had described to her earlier, but he did not like the idea of not being able to bring her to orgasm first, if not simultaneously.

"You worry too much," she sighed softly, ruffling her fingers through his hair until the light caught the reddish highlights. She smiled when he turned his head and kissed her between her breasts. Then he braced his hands and pulled himself to his feet.

"What you do to me," he said with a grave shake of his head. He carefully pulled her shirt back to its proper place, making her giggle because she thought it a silly gesture of modesty considering they were still coupled together.

"You just had to get me back on this desk," she teased him. She took the hand he offered her, sitting up and wrapping her arms around his ribs. She pressed her cheek to his heart as she hugged him.

"Actually, I thought I was making a point." He paused a purposeful beat. "But now that you mention it . . . I am going to have a hard time studying at this desk from now on."

Kestra's response was to wriggle free of him and leap to her feet. She retrieved her boxers and shimmied into them with easy speed.

"I have no sympathy for you. Frankly, I like the idea of you sitting down here thinking about me, helpless to resist the memory of my delectable body." She gave her hair an impressive toss and added an equally impressive flirtatious look at him from over a shoulder. It was enough to still him from the action of straightening his own clothing. She laughed when she caught the telltale darkening of his eyes. "You can't possibly want me again already," she said with a careless flip of her hand as she walked away from him toward the stairs, her hips swinging in a fetching movement.

"I would not place any bets on that," he muttered darkly as he straightened his shirt.

She stopped to give him an exaggerated yawn, her humor over teasing him radiating into him like a tide. "But it's full daylight, baby . . ." She glanced at him from under her eyelashes when she whipped him with the nickname that she well knew squeezed the breath from his body. "Time to go to bed."

"Kestra . . ." Her name was a rumbling growl of warning.

She stretched, giving him a fine view of the line of her back and backside, then began to climb the stairs.

"What are you going to do?" she countered the unspoken threat carelessly. "Spank me?"

"Now, there is an excellent idea."

Kestra didn't even need to see him move. She knew his intention the minute it leapt into his thoughts. With a squeak of humor and excitement, she took off up the stairs at lightning speed while he was still gathering momentum with his dash across the Hall.

Chapter 22

Kestra glanced over the rim of her fluted glass, letting the champagne bubbles burst beneath her nose for a minute as she took the opportunity to run her eyes over the sight of Noah in formalwear. It wasn't the only dramatic change she had marveled over these past two weeks. As Samhain faded into the past, she began to see more and more what he had meant when he'd tried to explain the difference in his personality. In essentials, he was as he ever was: honorable, honest, sensitive, and intelligent. His sense of humor had surfaced with a vengeance, though, as well as the patience and diplomacy everyone else had come to know him for. To be honest, she almost missed the more hotheaded side of him. His well-paced and thought-out communication skills could get on her nerves sometimes, especially when she was itching for an argument. However, she'd also learned that it wasn't that his temper had decreased, so much as he had better tools and control over submerging it. That meant that if she tried hard enough, she could still ruffle him.

Kes smiled against her glass as she took a sip of the sweet, dry champagne. She'd seen the telltale straightening of his shoulders, a sign that he'd sensed her attention was on him. She could easily touch his mind now, and the reverse was also true, but they'd managed the skill in such a way that they tuned out one another's thoughts until they found a reason to pay specific attention. It turned out that this was actually a necessity. When Noah was working throughout the night, his mind worked at lightning speed. It gave her a massive migraine trying to keep up with him without having context for more than half of the issues he was dealing with. She would learn, of course, just as she was learning her new powers. For the time being there was far too much to handle. Besides, he had just as hard a time concentrating on all of his business if he allowed her rather militaristic thoughts about her training to disrupt his focus.

She had been training with Gideon when not with Noah, one reason being that in astral form Gideon could avoid blast damage, just as she could with her anticipated immunity to her own power. The catch was that she was immune to the energy blast, not the fallout. Debris and projectiles could harm her just as they would anyone else. So she had to either stand at ground zero, or get the heck out of Dodge, a skill that her speed and agility lent her great aid in.

In return, Gideon let her practice her power appraisal on him. The benefit to him? She had unlocked another mystery for him to pursue in his powers: the key to the ability for a Demon to heal a Lycanthrope. It was another power he had been experimenting with for some time, without any real success. It seemed that she was able to find these paths only because he was already close to the revelations. But he had told her that it might have taken decades or longer without her assistance.

She was tired, a little sore, and she hadn't had a moment alone with Noah for at least thirty-two hours. Not until tonight. Tonight she was showing off her socialite abilities. They were at a small, private dinner party at the Vampire Prince's citadel. The guests consisted of all those who had

had a hand in saving the life of his bride, including her sister, the Queen of the Lycanthropes, and Elijah. Damien and Syreena had concocted the idea as a gesture of thanks.

So Kes toyed with the rope of pearls that Noah had saved along with her life what seemed like a lifetime ago. She wore a breathtaking evening gown she had spent hours shopping for, finding a kindred shopping spirit in the sprightly female Enforcer. Held by the slimmest of straps, the simple dress fell in a sheer silk of dark wine, only an equally sheer but iridescent underdress of the same color making a somewhat subtle mystery of the bare skin beneath it. Even so, the slightly flared skirt was slit to her upper thigh, showing off a very long leg and a pretty pair of sparkling couture sandals in silver.

She held an image in her mind of Noah's expression as she had come down the stairs to meet him. She'd wondered if her expression had been quite so ravenous as his had been. He was gorgeous in black formal, the stun of his tight, energized body in tailored silk having dazzled her eyes and burned her body. His desire and appreciation had been just as obvious as he'd taken her hand to guide her down the last few steps. He had asked her if she had any modesty at all, the question posed dryly in spite of the burn of his eyes over the easily seen shadows of her body. She had told him she'd been born without it. That had made him laugh.

She smiled at the memory.

Suddenly he turned to face her, giving a backhanded excuse to his host and hostess as he left them and crossed the room toward her. Damien and Syreena exchanged amused glances behind his back, and Kes couldn't hide the laughter sparkling in her eyes as she took another sip of champagne. Kes had noted early on that there was no sign at all of Syreena's terrible wounds. She couldn't help but wonder, though, what was lingering behind the otherwise merry charcoal eyes.

When Noah reached Kestra, he grasped her by the arm and turned her back to the rest of the room, placing himself in front of her so he could watch everyone over her shoulder. "Are you having fun?" he asked, taking his gaze from the other guests long enough to rake smoky eyes down the teasing length of her dress.

"Why, yes," she said easily. "Your friends are always delightful."

"That is not what I mean, and you know it." He leaned close to her ear as he accused her. "You are projecting. It is driving me crazy."

"Is it my fault you're a sexual fiend?"

"I?" He chuckled drolly. "That makes you the pot and me the kettle."

"True," she agreed breezily, waving the argument off with an elegant hand. "But I can hardly be held accountable for every random thought. Males think about sex an average of once every ten seconds, I have heard. I should remind you, you are above average in all things."

The little factoid made him chuckle, his heated breath cascading down the back of her neck, bared by her upswept coiffure. She shivered and he noticed. She heard him take in a long, slow breath. He was drawing in her scent, she had learned. He did it often and with relish, and she'd learned to respond to it as the eroticism it was.

"So sweet," he murmured in her ear, his lips brushing the outer rim of it as he spoke. She made a little sound of feminine pleasure, and it sang through him like a low, throbbing note. "I have missed you," he said in earnest as he bent to press a kiss to the line of her pulse. He felt it pick up in tempo and he closed his eyes in an attempt to bear her responsiveness.

"You've been busy. I've been training."

"We should never be that busy," he scolded them both. "Now I am near you and I cannot touch you." In spite of that claim, his hands slid forward to lock around her slender waist.

"I thought Vampires and Lycanthropes didn't care about modesty," she countered.

"I care, *Kikilia,*" he retorted. "With the exception of your provocative wardrobe, there is only one man in this room who will see the intimacies of your body, Kestra. Only one who will know them inside and out."

"That was never in question, baby," she parried soothingly, kissing him just behind his jaw.

He snagged her chin in his hand before she could pull fully away, holding her for a quick, deep kiss, a reminder of how he was affected by her use of his nickname for her. He drew her close to his body, probably out of pure habit. She knew he hadn't intended it, but soon she was pressed tightly to him, his hand possessive on the small of her back as he kissed her again, his fingertips splayed toward the outward curve of her bottom.

"Ahem."

Kestra snickered into Noah's mouth when Isabella exaggeratedly cleared her throat very nearby. They broke the kiss, but Noah didn't relinquish the warmth of her against himself as they turned their heads to look down at the petite woman.

"I was wondering," she began thoughtfully once she saw she had their attention.

Kestra watched Noah's eyes sparkle as he allowed himself to walk into the baited trap.

"Wondering what?" he asked her.

"Well, I was talking to Syreena about her plans for the citadel's gardens come the new spring. See, she wasn't able to do much but instruct in a cursory cleanup for this year, having had so much to do with moving in and getting settled. So we were discussing possible growth for the sandy, rocky soil of the area, though beneath that is a deeply rich and fertile earth, she says."

"That is lucky," Noah said helpfully.

"Yes, well, it just reminded me of something I needed to ask you."

"Yes?"

"What the hell happened to your willow grove?"

Kestra burst into laughter, completely ignoring the abrupt pinch of Noah's fingers at her waist.

"Willow grove," he repeated. He didn't pretend to question it, just parroted her as his eyes shifted up to see Jacob and Elijah listening in with clearly planned attentiveness.

"Yes. Willow. Wisteria? Arbors? Pretty oyster-shell paths? What, you decided a big brown hole in the ground suddenly looked better?"

"As a matter of fact," Noah said with a handsome smile, "I rather like it. I think I will keep it that way. A reminder of a very good lesson learned."

"And the lesson being?" Jacob asked dutifully.

"Never underestimate the power of a woman," he said simply, adding a casual shrug. "Come, sweet, I believe you are out of champagne."

He swept Kestra away, leaving her breathless laughter in their wake.

When Kestra met Damien he'd been extremely polite, gracious, and grateful, practically overflowing with pleasure when welcoming Noah. Now, some time later, with his wife firmly secured to his hip, the Vampire was giving her a different depth as she watched him with more efficient perception.

Kestra had recently noticed that her ability to evaluate and map power had also left her with a heightened sense of awareness when it came to reading others. She had always been perceptive in taking another's measure, but now it was as close to telepathy as one could get, without the actual awareness of thoughts.

As she and Noah conversed with the Prince, this awareness kicked into overdrive. There was strain around his edges, ever so faint, and something she suspected only his loved ones would notice. He was tired, physically, his energy depleted in what she suspected would be life-threatening ways should he encounter trouble on a hunt. He was flush and warm, clearly having hunted earlier, so it was not a nutritional deprivation. Emotional? Perhaps, she thought, considering how close he had come to losing his wife.

That sobered her greatly. She did not know if the mating between them was as physically interdependent as the Imprinting was for Demons, but Jasmine had claimed he would never survive the loss of Syreena. She supposed she meant his devastation would have been impossible to endure. Had she been literal, too?

Kestra glanced at Noah from under her frosted lashes, her heartbeat picking up with sudden anxiety. For her and for Noah, it was indeed literal. If anything ever happened to him, she would have little more than two weeks to live. A death sentence she didn't deserve, nor did she appreciate the lack of control over her own life that it implied. Her existence hinged on his safety.

Kes hid the sudden rigidity of her body and the smarting behind her eyes under the guise of a delicate cough. Her ears were roaring and she tried to breathe and refocus on what Damien was saying to Noah. How had she even gotten off on this morbid tangent? Noah had lived nearly seven centuries. Did she think he would suddenly forget how to survive?

"Without Stephan, I am afraid the network we have been trying to put into place over the world has begun to unravel. Not so much the European sectors," Damien explained as Kestra's hearing slowly returned to normal. "They will always be easy to manage with Jasmine and me in such close company. It is the other continents I am concerned with. There were far more than two Vampires acting against us that night. I am afraid the reason we cannot find them, or Ruth and Nico for that matter, is because there is too much room out there for hiding."

"I agree. They will avoid the Nightwalker regions: Russia, England, France, New Zealand, Alaska, Romania, and, as you said, most of the European continent. At least until things are not so hot for them. But that leaves North and South America, Asia, and Africa open to becoming hideaways. There are less hospitable choices as well, of course, but they will want to lose themselves in a heavy human population."

"Also, they will want a playground," Damien added grimly. "Vampires can never go long without games to play. For games to be fun for Vampires of this lawless ilk, I would say screwing around with the lives of humans will be a high priority."

"On a mildly better side," Syreena put in, "I believe we can now expect that a slaughter with speed and viciousness through the Nightwalker species will not be easy to accomplish again. The Mistrals and the Shadowdwellers were given an unfortunate clarion call. They will be more on guard, more organized."

"As will we," Noah said soberly. "We have been too complacent. Our young will need a new set of rules now. They are the most vulnerable."

"We should think about it. All of us," Kestra pointed out firmly, not able to soften it because she felt so passionately on the topic. "Biologically speaking, most females aren't equipped to attain the strength and power levels that males can achieve. Protecting them will need more than just a strong consideration."

Damien didn't even blink. "Female Vampires are as powerful as the males, or can be if they desire it. There are many on the network."

"Female Vampires aren't in threat by Vampire rogues, though," she countered sharply.

"Kestra is right, you know." Syreena's hand went absently to her healed throat. "Powerful or not, women are at risk."

"Who are you charging with the supervision of the network?" Kestra asked.

"I had not . . ." Damien hesitated, then looked away briefly as he made a soft sound of frustration. "I was caught up in other things and have not designated Stephan's replacement."

Grief. Guilt. Pain. Worry. Love. Kestra saw it all swirling

around the Prince in a flash. He had indeed been caught up. Now she understood the exhaustion and strain. This had taken a toll in a way Damien was obviously not experienced with. She found it hard to believe he had never suffered great loss before, not after a millennium of life, and Noah had told her that Vampires tended to be emotionally callous. Obviously Damien had changed when he'd fallen in love with Syreena, leaving him more vulnerable than before.

"I would recommend a continental and global hierarchy of command," Kes offered. "It's too much for a single leader to manage. Seven commanders, one per continent, to whom hunters can report progress and occurrences. Then a single general or marshal to whom those commanders report. I think that'd speed up the warning process. Having Jasmine run between the courts is inefficient." She smiled to soften the remark. "The one who marshals the other leaders can be situated in Europe. I know you believe they'll avoid Europe now that we're on guard, but we are also the ultimate quarries. No point to being a rogue if you can't go hunting for power. Best to maximize coverage where the most game hangs out."

Kes felt Noah's arm slide warmly around her waist and she easily hooked her hand onto his shoulder as he drew her to his side with an appreciative little squeeze. She could feel his pride and delight easily; it was radiating off him like sunlight. She had the sudden urge to blush and fought it off with impressive aptitude.

"Kestra!"

"Hmm?" she asked when Syreena exploded out her name.

"Sweetheart," Syreena said with excitement, patting Damien's arm hard in her effervescence. "Why not have Kestra take Stephan's place controlling the network? She has military experience, she is obviously soldier enough to hunt and fight, and she has the ear of the Demon King. Sometimes right between her teeth." Syreena laughed teasingly at her own joke. "She's in Europe. And I hear she has some kick-ass power."

"She has the perfect power to fulfill that kind of role," Kestra was surprised to hear Noah say, "as well as the perfect command and organizational skills."

"But," Kestra said for him politely, arching a knowing brow at the other couple, making them chuckle.

"But," he agreed with a light laugh, "her ability to handle her own power is new yet. If she decides to do this, I would recommend you let Jasmine fill the position temporarily, giving Kestra several months to learn the ins and outs of her power and how to apply it to the military skills she already possesses. She learns damn fast, so I would say by Beltane."

"Five months. Hmm," Damien said speculatively. "Jas can still live in the citadel, an important detail, I assure you. With Stephan gone, her presence here is essential."

"I gather," Noah agreed with grim understanding. "If you do not wish to split her attention, I could—"

"No." Damien held up a hand. "Jasmine will be an excellent choice. We are secure here so long as we keep loyal Vampires heavily staffed, which I am already doing. If she works her command from here, it will be no different than what she does now. I think a project like this will be good for her. Kestra, if you accept the role as marshal over the net, when you are not training your power, you can be choosing your new soldiers. Familiarize yourself with the Vampires already cast out in the net. Choose your commanders from the hunters you meet. That would mean spending time in foreign courts like Siena's and Tristan and Malaya's as you gather the hunters they will offer."

"Better they come to my court, where she is protected and secure."

Kestra barely had time to bristle before his hand slid up to massage the nape of her neck. It made her second-guess her ire, as he knew it would. She realized this was a gentle reminder that, while her power was still young, she would be restricted in how far and how long she could travel from him.

"If she accepts," Syreena noted.

She felt their eyes turn to her, all but Noah's because he would always know before anyone else what her decisions would be.

"I am curious why you would choose someone so green and so landlocked. You should at least choose someone who can fly or travel with speed."

Syreena laughed as if Kestra had made a joke.

"Travel from the Demon court? With all those Mind Demons at your fingertips? Or you can choose an assistant of any element who can travel with speed."

"As for green," Noah spoke up with a sidelong look at her, "Druids power up really fast. They master their broader skills with incredible speed. Your secondary skills—militia, command, battle strategy, and evaluation of power and ability—you have been practicing those for a great deal of your life already. You will simply be building as you go. I would pit your mercenary tactics against a hyped-up Vampire any day. And I have."

Noah looked directly at her as he reminded her they had been together the moment she had bested a supernatural creature so much more powerful than she had been. Together in her thoughts. She gave him a slow, cocky smile before turning to Damien.

"Well, when he puts it that way, how can a girl refuse?" She laughed when they did. "Baby, you are such a romantic," she purred teasingly.

"Ah yes, they are so sexy when they appreciate our power," Syreena said loftily.

"I make it a point to never underestimate your power, love," Damien said, his grin easing the tension bracketing his features. Kestra could feel him relaxing at last.

"Mmm, well, I'm still pretty pissed that bastard got the drop on me," Syreena muttered, sighing her consternation.

"Sweet, you were understandably exhausted," Damien reminded her, placing a soothing kiss against her brow.

"That's no excuse," she said.

"All that matters," Noah interjected, "is that you are well and he is dead." He lowered his voice so only the four of them would be privy to his next remarks. "Besides, if I am not mistaken, the energy burn left behind in that room was indicative of one hell of a heat cycle, Syreena." The Demon King's eyes flashed with emerald amusement. "Damien is right, you were understandably exhausted."

Kestra snickered midsip of her champagne, sending bubbles up into her sinuses. Her coughing laughter eased their hostess's blush and they all joined her.

"Why do you think we had to wait two weeks to throw this party?" Damien said dryly. He had thoughtfully reached out to prevent Kestra from taking another sip of her champagne until after his remark.

It turned out to be a huge consideration. Kestra lost all composure, her laughter turning heads and sprouting grins among their friends.

"A toast," Noah said, raising his glass suddenly to the hosting couple. "To . . . to the fruits of our labors."

"Hear! Hear!" the entire room chorused, though their interpretation of Noah's implication was far different.

"I will definitely drink to that," Syreena said passionately.

Damien just grinned and touched his glass to the Demon King's.

Kestra needed to get used to a great many things as she adapted to Demon culture, but nothing was as much fun as mode of travel. Though they had used the aid of a Mind Demon to teleport to Damien's holdings, they did not leave by the same method. The longer foray home would take place in the form of smoke, a form utilized and guided by Noah. But to Kestra's ongoing delight, that form meant nothing to her senses. She was able to see, feel, hear, and experience everything as if she were flying like a fictional superhero. And because Noah was directing their travel, she didn't have to think about where she was going or how to get there. It was glorious, and a perfect thrill for her daredevil tendencies.

Noah, of course, could feel every moment of her delight, and it was as if he were seeing the experience afresh for himself. He wouldn't have thought such a thing possible for someone who had been traveling in such ways for centuries, but her enthusiasm drew him in. He found it a strange bittersweet experience, the way she so easily embraced the experiences of her new life. Yes, he wanted her to enjoy and even revel in his world; it would make everything so much easier for her.

But the more she rejoiced in everything else, the longer a shadow it cast on the one thing she held in reserve.

Him.

Not in their lovemaking. No, he had no complaints about that. And in her way he supposed she used that physical connection as a method of reassurance, expressing what she refused to acknowledge even to herself. She used it to coddle him so he didn't feel upset because he loved her so very deeply, and yet she turned away from all self-examination of her feelings. Never mind an honest verbalization. It stood to reason that he resented this at times. He would rather she just be natural and not try to effect what she thought he expected. If not for their connection of thought, he might have misread her confusion of signals long ago.

It was something he needed to discuss with her. He had allowed it to go on for too long. It was frankly uncomfortable for them both when she wasn't acting out of honest compulsion. He didn't want that. She didn't want that. Noah had no idea why she'd gotten the idea in her head in the first place. Although, if he had to make a strong guess, he would say it had come from spending a great deal of time with so many Imprinted couples of late. This party at the citadel had been only the latest gathering.

Politics and mending relationships and training schedules had made the castle a tizzy of Imprinted traffic. Gideon and Legna, Jacob and Isabella, Corrine and Kane—even Elijah and Siena had shown up regularly as Elijah was forced to pay greater attention to Demon matters than to his wife's abroad. Noah was coming to realize that Elijah would be forced to resign soon. He had been hanging on valiantly in the face of so many new foreign threats, as it was his forte and he knew Noah needed him badly, but the King and the Warrior Captain had both come to the grim conclusion that had Elijah been there, the guard would never have failed to protect Kestra from the Vampire attack.

But Elijah's interests were split now, and it was showing. Not that Noah begrudged him his happiness in the least. But the business of protecting his people must take precedence. He needed a suitable solution, because Elijah would not be an easy man to replace. They would be putting their heads together a great deal over the next few months, Noah thought. Meanwhile, until Elijah helped him choose his successor, things would be status quo. Noah's only regret, his only concern, actually, was that Elijah would come to visit even less than he already did when this came to pass. He sorely missed the Captain's irreverence, which kept them all from taking things too seriously.

Then again, Kestra was a pretty little replacement package. She reminded him of Elijah. The wit, the deadly turn her mood could take, her skills, and her outright enthusiasm for destruction. For battle. Yet their peaceful ways settled well on her. She would just rather be out on the front lines fighting to preserve that peace than letting others do it for her. He respected that. It would make for a sound monarchy, he realized, as he thought about Damien's proposal and her role in it. Like a chessboard. The King settled back and protected, bearing the political brunt and the regular office work required of him, while the aggressive Queen directed the methods of protection and faced down threats.

He rather liked the idea.

He didn't have egomaniacal ideals. He was powerful and could fight, but that wasn't the kind of King he wished to be. He only interceded, as he did in the instance of the threat to

Syreena, when the political ramifications called for it. He had always been satisfied to surround himself with advisers who were one hundred percent focused on their roles and tasks when it came to altercations. Elijah. Jacob. Bella. And now Kestra. He only grew richer for it. In so many ways.

They were about to exit the borders of Romania when a shimmer of sensation echoed over Kestra and Noah. Fear of inexplicable origins struck them. Not expecting this, Kestra panicked. Noah's experience served him a little bit better.

Easy. It is just a trick, Kes. He spoke softly in her racing mind. *Someone is trying to draw us out.*

The single sentence made all the difference in the world. Noah hesitated for a moment because she was with him. Would it be better to hit the ground and face the enemy? They would only chase after them if they tried to run. Was the area below them a geographical advantage for the enemy? Or was it merely opportunity?

Opportunity. They must have followed us. They had no way of knowing we would pass this way.

Bless her little strategic heart, Noah thought with delight. She was right.

Okay, baby. Get ready. As soon as I land and solidify us, you need to power up.

I'm already there, Kikilio.

A heartbeat later they landed square on their feet on the ground. As directed, Noah shuddered with immolation as it covered his arms. With her back so close to him that their hips were touching, Kestra's body flared with luminescent green. She committed herself, however, instantly forming a grenade-sized bomb in her hand. Both turned their full attention to the forest around them, seeking their threat.

"*Kikilio?*" he questioned in an amused whisper. "You have been spending time with Bella."

"You didn't think I was going to live in an environment where others could talk over my head in a language I don't understand, did you?"

"I see."

"So I finally know what *Kikilia* means," she added.

"I did not realize it was an issue," he mused, his sharp eyes watching shadows.

Before she could respond, the first attack exploded around them.

Or rather beneath them.

The ground suddenly gave way under their feet, collapsing even as water sprang up in a geyser between them, forcing them apart, severing their protective stance. Before they could draw breath they were plunged into a rapidly growing hot spring.

Kes didn't waste a single second. She surfaced and kept her eyes on the tree line as she swam furiously for the still-expanding shore. She didn't have to look behind her to see Noah was doing the same in the opposite direction.

She was relieved that one of the lessons she'd already mastered was the reabsorption of the energy she used to make her bombs. She was grateful Noah had insisted on it. Otherwise the energy grenade would've been abandoned in the water so she could swim and they would have been racing the explosion as well as the imminent danger around them. They'd learned that her bombs didn't start to count down until she actually let go of them, separating them from the energy aura she built them from. Rather like pulling a pin or lighting a fuse.

Kes, it is Vampires. The remaining rogues, no doubt. Be prepared for anything and everything. There is a pack of them.

They're going after you. They don't know who I am, so you must be the target. Kestra's heart was pounding so hard she could hear it in her ears as she surged out of the water.

The first thing she did was reach for the delicate silk of her gown. It was in her way and she had to shed it and her sandals ASAP. She tore the skirt clean away up to her thighs as she crouched low to the ground. In that flash of time, a shadow leapt out at her. It was the long shape of a sturdy pine one second; the next, it was surging up over her skin and plowing her down to the ground. She rolled with it, instantly realizing that there was a solid form to this supposed shadow, and that meant infliction of pain was highly possible.

On the opposite side of the water, Noah was in a similar predicament, only this shadow struck before he even had proper footing on the shore, split into three, and overwhelmed him within a matter of seconds. Noah's head crashed into the ground, stars bursting brilliantly inside his eyelids. He felt his assaulters getting a fast grip on him. They were choreographed as to timing and placement as they pinned him to the ground by his hands, waist, and legs, indicating that this was far better planned than a random assault.

Still, planning would do them little good. The Demon King tried not to laugh as he sent a sheet of immolating fire down the entire length of his body. As flame rippled down over his skin, popping and hissing as water evaporated, his assailants scrabbled for distance, crying out. And then Noah felt the crash of a wave of water.

The damn spring.

Steam exploded violently around him when the water doused his body. The wave continued, following him as he tried to roll free. He could not catch his breath, and no matter which way he struggled to move, the water followed. He realized he was in real danger of drowning under the onslaught if he did not focus. He rolled onto his hands and knees, tucking his head down as the crashing force of the water intensified. He sought outside himself for energy, and a half dozen sources flared into his awareness. He knew one of them was Kestra. He even had a fair idea which one it was because she resonated so differently from the others. If he cast a wide net and sucked in energy without discretion, Kestra would fall into the zone. She was still too young to bear the brunt of a full power drain, especially the one he would have to use to overcome such powerful adversaries. Also, if there were others lying in wait at a distance, he would be leaving her totally defenseless and himself to face further threats alone. Instinct told him that the forethought behind this attack would make that an unwise course of action.

Noah staggered, falling face-first into the drowned forest floor that was fast becoming a swamp. He needed to breathe. He needed oxygen. He felt something strike his back, and his face crashed into the deep water as his head was forced under. The fall of the water continued as his hands were stepped on to hold them in place. Again, waist and legs followed. Now he was at a distinct disadvantage. Vampires didn't need to breathe. He, unfortunately, very much needed oxygen. The Vampires were wickedly strong, and four against one were impossible odds without the use of his element. Well, part of his element. But he didn't need fire to gain advantage. Noah went for the nearest and most critical target. He focused on the Vampire holding his head beneath the water.

Kestra whipped her legs around her attacker, ignoring which end was up and settling for winding up on top by the time they finished skidding across the forest floor. The Vampire was slim and slippery as hell. He was also extremely strong. She barely had time to savor her dominant position before she was hurled off and away. She landed in the underbrush with a curse. Then he was on her again, his hand going for her throat and his knees crashing down painfully on her thighs. His other hand was only able to catch one of hers, but still he now effectively pinned her to the forest floor. He flashed a vicious pair of fangs and began to crush her throat beneath the clutch of a single formidable hand.

Kestra flashed phosphorescent green. Surprised, the Vampire blinked against the sudden flare of energy. It seemed almost as if he was fascinated for a moment. A moment that gave her an advantage. Her free hand curled into a circle and a small sphere the size of a Ping-Pong ball gained shape in her palm. Meanwhile, the Vampire realized he was about to face an unknown power and he took steps. His force against on her neck increased and he freed his hand from hers. She only had a second to think when he yanked his arm back and she saw gleaming in the moonlight. It was the worst thing to do when being choked, but she yanked her chin all the way up as those gleaming fingertips whipped across her shoulder, neck, and face, sharp razorlike nails scoring deep into her skin. Kestra's head jerked to the side with the force of the slices. She initially felt nothing save the nick of one against her cheekbone because the nails were so sharp. Pain would come later. But she had protected herself using the method she had described to Noah when he had teased her for her morbid choices on conversational topics.

While her pain was delayed, however, there would be no such luck for her attacker. Turning her face back up as his strangling hand forced blood to well swiftly out of her new injuries and tucking her chin back down to open a small portion of her airway, Kestra met the avaricious eyes of her assailant. He was leaning closer, clearly looking to taste her blood. Hands still free, Kestra reached out and jerked the Vampire by his belt.

He reared up, perplexed when he felt her thrust her hand down the front of his pants. His grip on her throat loosened with his shock and he looked down into the icy glitter of her eyes as she smiled at him.

Then she mouthed a word to him since she couldn't speak.

Boom.

The little ball had left her hand several seconds before that, of course, so by the time comprehension dawned, it was far too late for the Vampire. Still, he reacted as expected. He surged off her with a shriek of terror, grasping at his endangered crotch. Kestra was only aware of one thing. The Vampire was about to become debris and she needed to get the heck out of Dodge.

She took a hoarse, scraping breath and rolled back int the hot spring.

The Vampire exploded. His ribs became projectiles tha tore through the forest until they embedded into tree trunk with hearty thunks. The rest of him rained back down in a wide circumference. As far as debris went, it was mostly an issue of grossness as opposed to danger. Kestra surfaced relatively blood and guts free for her trouble, gasping madly for breath.

Kestra had barely begun to breathe for herself when sh felt Noah's distress. Her body and brain were pounding with the screaming need to breathe, even though she was sucking in oxygen by the ton. She fought to drag herself out of th water, still coughing and gagging as her swollen throa swelled shut. She swept back her wet hair, which had com undone, trying to free her field of vision so she could fin Noah. How could he be in danger? Her mind could not conceive of it. He was too strong and far too clever.

As she swept back her hair, the motion drew apart th edges of the deep furrows the Vampire had sliced into he skin and blood streamed out, a reflection of the horrific pai that finally struck. The agony didn't even wait until he adrenaline high wore off. It burned like a vicious, raking brand. Blood blinded her in one eye and she tried to wipe i away as she trudged around the edge of the pool to fin Noah.

Noah had to push aside the alarm bell of Kestra's sudde pain as it rang through his brain. Darkness was encroaching and if he lost consciousness he would leave her to the mercy of these monsters. He would leave all Nightwalkers to th mercy of Vampires who would have drunk the blood of a male Fire Demon.

None of those options were acceptable, and Noah fel rage and indignation flare to violent life. He reached for hi first target, using all of his focus to show him what real vampirism was all about. He sucked the energy out of the Vam pire sitting on his head with such savagery that the creature hardly had the strength to blink in reflex as it took a header into the flooded forest floor. Noah tried to break the water's surface, but lying on his face with his hands and waist still secured made it impossible in the time it took for a knee in his back and a hand on his head to replace the fallen Vampire's.

Turn to smoke! He heard Kestra's frantic cry, felt her rushing to help him. He feared for her safety, knowing she wouldn't think about herself.

I cannot. The water . . .

Kestra hadn't known this about him. She had never scanned him for power and weaknesses. Somehow they had never gotten around to it. But now she knew that he couldn't turn to smoke or flame under a deluge of water. It went against the laws of the elements. She should've known that and kicked herself for not thinking logically about it sooner.

She came around the curve, splashing through the flood rushing down the small slope as the water overflowed the rim of the hollow Noah was pinned down in. She saw them, four Vampires. One was facedown in the water, clearly a casualty of their fight to control the Demon King. One was literally sitting on him at legs and waist, another standing on his hands, the third had a knee on his spine and a hand on his head holding him away from desperately needed air. A spout of water was bursting out of the hot spring and arcing to crash down on their prisoner.

Kestra's spirit screamed as she felt the darkness overcoming Noah, felt his fear of leaving her behind to deal with these creatures on her own. Her frantic eyes shifted to a fifth Vampire. Clearly the leader, he was set apart from the danger of dealing directly with the Fire Demon they had captured. He stood on a boulder a short distance away, watching the entire incident.

No. There was more. Kestra's eyes narrowed as she used every new sense she owned to understand how to act. Here was the source of the water. That Vampire, she realized, was controlling it while the others worked. Kestra felt infused with fury all of a sudden, caging her hands together to form a ball the size of a grapefruit as she let the feeling overwhelm her. She knew the frustration and impotence backing the power of her anger was partly Noah's, but she used it all the same, and she packed it into the orb.

Just as the Vampire looked over and saw her, Kestra pitched the ball to him. Then she ran through the shin-deep water toward Noah. Aiming for the lightest-built Vampire, a female standing on her mate's hands, she plowed into her, flinging her off with the power of her momentum. They landed with a splash. Kes grabbed her, and taking another breath, she rolled the Vampire on top of herself.

The orb exploded.

Half submerged, Kestra felt a series of jarring thunks striking the body of the Vampire she held over herself like a shield. When the splashes around her stopped, she shoved the body off. The Vampire had taken a tree branch right through her head, so she was satisfactorily dead. She knew the same was true for the Vampire on the boulder because he had been at ground zero.

Her only concerns now were Noah and the other two Vampires. She had left Noah unprotected from the blast, but she'd had very little choice. She had been forced to use a wide-range blast in the hopes it would even the odds. Shaking water and blood out of her eyes, she sat up and looked for the Vampires.

She saw three more bodies floating in the suddenly still water.

"Noah!"

She ignored everything except the body floating facedown in his fine formalwear. She scrabbled over to him, grabbing him and calling to him as she turned his heavy weight over and onto her kneeling thighs to keep his head abovewater. His complexion was gray, his natural tan lost under the water and mud streaked over his face and surrounding his nose and mouth where his body had finally forced him to breathe in the silt.

Kestra shuddered in horror, feeling the suddenly cold absence of his presence in her body and mind. His thoughts had gone utterly silent.

Her spirit had been left hollow and alone.

She acted with the speed of desperation, falling back on her rather ancient first aid skills, trying to clear mud and filth out of his mouth to free his airway. The results were pitifully inadequate and she knew she had no choice but to keep trying. There was no way she was going to allow a pack of greedy bloodsuckers to deprive a grand race of their beautiful leader. She screeched in a breath past her partially closed-off throat, placed her mouth on his, and exhaled to fill his lungs, praying she was doing it right, that her breaths were full and deep enough.

She couldn't lose him. Not when she was just getting to know him. He was the first person to love her since her parents. She'd accepted that. She'd delighted in it. He knew how exceptional it was for him to make her comfortable with his extraordinary love. As Kestra breathed for him again, she knew she'd held back from him for just this reason. She couldn't bear to love someone and lose them. To be the reason they died.

Kestra began to cry, tears only because she had no breath to spare on sobs. She was surrounded by water, propping him on her knees. She should have him on flat ground, but she dared not waste time trying to haul him over to it. She breathed for him again, cursing Vampires and Nightwalkers and greed and everything else she could think of. He had cheated death for her; why couldn't she do the same for him? She had to. There was no choice. She must make him breathe and live. There were so many who needed him. The Enforcers, their little one, and so many others. *Sisters. Oh God, his sisters.*

Me.

Yes, she thought with a ripping pain through her soul. She needed him. She needed to tell him how much he had changed her. Changed her life. And how much she actually appreciated it. She needed to tell him how much joy he had given to her in just these short weeks. He couldn't leave not knowing that. She'd been so guarded, trying to protect herself, selfishly nursing old fears and wounds when he had needed to hear how she felt!

With the next breath, water spewed from Noah's mouth, but he still didn't breathe on his own. What she wouldn't give to be able to call for help like a telepath! Surely the others would be close enough to hear. Even Damien! Anybody who could get a medic for him.

"Baby," she prayed against his lips as she drew breath for him. "Please."

She pushed in a deep breath, and more water and silt came up. She cleared his mouth and pressed on.

Please, she implored in her thoughts as she repeated the cycle again, *please don't leave me. I couldn't bear it. I know I'm selfish as hell, but I need you to stay with me for a few more centuries. Please . . .*

Oh God, he won't breathe! Kestra shook him in her frustration, shivering as she felt his warmth ebbing away second by second.

"Stop it!" she yelled, though it came out as a croak. "You can't leave me! You bastard! You can't make me love you and then just leave!"

Kestra sobbed hard but refused to give up, fury fueling her determination. She dragged them both upward, her arms circling his chest under his arms, and she hauled him away from the water, searching for flat ground.

As soon as she found it, she threw him back on it and wasted no time in straddling his waist so she could lean in to listen for his heartbeat. She then added chest compressions to her first aid, putting her full concentration on them as she counted and traded off with pushing breath into his stubborn lungs. She cursed him, her face heating up as she put everything she had into her actions and thoughts. Kestra was frantic, scanning her brain, trying to figure out what else she could possibly do.

Suddenly she stopped.

A wild thought occurred to her. What could it hurt? she reasoned. He was dead if she didn't try something.

"Okay, *Kikilio*, let's make history," she murmured to him.

She closed her eyes and concentrated. She prayed she could do this. Much of her energy had always come from him. She had only just begun to learn how to draw energy from outside sources under his guidance, and she had sucked at it so far. But she couldn't afford to screw it up. Not now.

She began to glow a healthy green, pulling in from the creatures huddled in the forest, the motions of the wind, and the energy of life itself. Her hands flared bright, but she did not shape her energy.

"Remember what you said?" she asked him roughly. "You said we are symbiotic. We are one, inasmuch as we are two. I am the right hand. You are the left. What I take in from you, I must expel. You made me feel the place within that connected to you. It will work in reverse, my love," she insisted softly. "What I take from that path, I can give on that path. Take what you need and come back to me."

She laid her hands on his chest and continued her compressions, at the same time sending a sizzling conduit of energy into him. She focused through her mouth, through the kiss of her lips, the place where they had first birthed her ability to connect with him. So her mouth glowed and sparkled when she breathed into him slow and deep. She pushed on and on, until the glow around her began to fade.

Noah suddenly sucked in a harsh, gagging breath.

He threw her off him, rolling over onto his hands and knees and expelling mud and water with violent retching.

His black hair hung around his face lank with water and mud, and his body shuddered as he tried to take in an uncontaminated breath.

That was when Jacob and Isabella finally showed up.

They burst from dust to flesh in a heartbeat, scaring ten years off Kestra when they spoke up behind her.

"What the hell!"

Jacob rushed to the King, looking askance at Kestra.

"Vampires attacked us. He drowned. We need a medic," she croaked in short bursts.

"We know about the Vampires. Bella saw it in a premonition," Jacob said. "It took us a bit to track you."

"Here, sit," Bella urged Kestra while Jacob murmured something to Noah, who was still struggling to clear his lungs.

"Oh God, he's going to suffocate," Kestra said, tears stinging as they rolled over the slashes in her face.

"Jacob can help," Isabella soothed her. "Just give him a minute."

Kestra watched with wide eyes as Jacob leaned over his monarch, speaking softly to him. Suddenly, Noah was retching again, purging pure dirt and silt.

Then he took the first clear breath he'd taken in over fifteen minutes.

"Jacob is of the earth, remember," Bella explained. "He cannot heal, but he can draw out the silt and soil from Noah's lungs. No different than making dirt leave a hole."

All Kestra could do was nod vigorously in comprehension and sudden relief. Jacob helped Noah sit up and Kestra crawled over to him in a flash.

Baby. Are . . . you . . . okay?

His thoughts were as stilted as his gasping breaths, but at least they were there, back where they belonged, warm in her mind.

"Yes! Yes, I'm fine. You scared the hell out of me!" She switched to thoughts herself when her voice finally gave out.

You should have warned me about the water! Why didn't you ever let me scan you? You almost died!

You are not going to hit me . . . are you?

Don't you dare joke at a time like this! She glared at him, daggers of ice in her faceted eyes. *I will beat the crap out of you if you crack wise about this!*

Finally, Noah recovered enough to drag her into his embrace. He was racked with coughing, covered in muck, but he knew she wouldn't care about any of that. He knew she needed to feel him alive and breathing . . . such as it was.

I am sorry you were scared. We are okay now. Try and calm down.

She couldn't calm down. She burst into hysterics.

"Post-adrenaline crash," Jacob murmured helpfully, trying to explain her uncharacteristic unraveling. "I am leaving Bella here and I am going to get help. Do not move and do not attract trouble," he dictated sternly.

The male Enforcer left and his mate rolled her eyes at his ridiculous commands.

Noah was fully focused on Kestra. She was tearing his heart out with her sobs, and his heart already felt as if it had been through a building collapse. He cradled her head to his chest, resting his chin atop it between coughing fits.

Hush, baby. All is well.

I thought I lost you! I was lost. I fell! Noah felt the disjointed swirl of confusion and hysteria running through her. *I thought you were . . . I thought you were on the bathroom floor . . . in the garage . . . all alone . . . dying all alone!*

Noah suddenly understood. She had relived the horror of losing a loved one all over again. Her worst nightmare coming true.

Noah stiffened abruptly.

A loved one.

Noah closed his eyes as a tidal wave of emotion cascaded over him, drowning him, only this time in a little death that thrilled him.

Yes! Oh God, yes. I love you, and I'm so sorry I was too stubborn to tell you. Too cowardly. I love you, Noah. She began to press flighty little kisses all over his face, heightening the suddenly disconnected and heavenly feeling the Demon King was floating on.

You were never a coward, baby love, he told her, squeezing her tightly to himself. *No one can ever call someone a coward if they are brave enough to survive and love again. Never.*

I love you. You're my soul and my heart. I feel it every time I breathe. I knew. I knew when every day went by and just got better and better. I knew when Samhain passed and you became more and more beautiful. Painfully so, Noah. I met you when you were at your worst, and I love you so much that I actually miss your worst! But I bless your best. You've changed me and my world, and everything is so different now. Just because you were brave enough to face down a royal bitch and give her a good wake-up call.

Noah chuckled roughly, setting off another coughing fit that jiggled her against his chest.

Ah yes, that was brave of me, was it not? More than you will ever know, he added more seriously. *I think you will always confuse the hell out of me, baby. I fear I will never figure you out and I will be tripping over my feet and my tongue and my impulses for quite some time.*

You know what, I can handle that. But only if you promise me one thing.

What is that, Kikilia?

Stay the hell away from water!

Chapter 23

Damien crouched in the thick mud, rolling over the last Vampire's body as he inspected it with a grim expression.

"That is the last of the lot," he affirmed, standing up and swiping his hands against each other, more to remove the taint of evil than the mud. "At least this time."

"You sound sure that your people won't get the message," Elijah remarked, his humor somewhere far from the site that had almost seen the death of his King. "I think there is something to be said for a well-publicized ass-kicking."

"Mmm," was Damien's only agreement. After a moment he spoke, his tone dark and heavy with bitterness. "I have learned much in this past year, Elijah. I have learned how to love and how to fear, both with a depth I never knew. I have learned I have not done as good a job ruling my people as I once thought. I am certain, in fact, that ruling is a loose term. I presided over them. There is a difference."

"Damien . . ." Elijah protested, but the Prince held up a staying hand to cut him off.

"It is like running an orphanage of young children," he explained quietly. "You can manage the aesthetics, the accounts and feeding times, but if you do not control the children, even the best management is doomed to fail. They will have a limited environment, but they will run around like wild animals within that environment from the moment they wake until they collapse with exhaustion." Damien flicked a damaged gaze of midnight blue over his shoulder at the warrior. "I suddenly tried to impose rules on a madhouse full of wild children, and I am surprised they rebelled? It was a poor example of my supposed great wisdom."

"We have made worse mistakes," Elijah said cautiously, very aware that the Vampire was not in the mood for appeasement. "The wisdom comes in the rectification."

That got Damien's full attention, a brow arched in surprise.

"You are sounding suspiciously like a leader, Captain," Damien remarked, a twitch at the corner of his lips.

"I am one. Have been for some time," Elijah said with a dismissive shrug. "Managing unruly warriors with an itch for battle is no easy trick. Standing next to my wife as she presides over a people who hate the very sight of me has its moments, too," he added wryly. "But they are grudgingly forcing themselves to accept there is nothing they can do about it. One day, I am determined they will accept my command with the same ease of respect as they accept Siena's. But that day is long in the future. You, however, have the benefit of the majority. Your people love you, and they have been used to loving you for more centuries than I have even been alive. Those who don't love you will be forced to respect you. I do not doubt this. If I did, I could never reassure my wife that her sister is safe in your keeping. And if I couldn't reassure my wife, you would have a hell of a time on your hands." Elijah's look was pointed.

"I thank you for your confidence," Damien said graciously and without humor. "I think it is time for me to take some pages out of the Demon political handbook. Your system has worked, more or less, for some time, and I need to delegate in order to restructure such a structureless society."

"Keep in mind," Elijah warned, "the Council can be a damned nuisance as well as a help. Don't elevate anyone you can't trust, and don't give too much power away."

"Not to worry. I am Prince and will always be so. My wife has been itching for involvement and I see possibilities now that I am not going to fear the displeasure of my 'children.' And I must replace Stephan." Heavy sadness settled suddenly over him at the remark. "Jasmine will round out the beginnings of a new political structure. She will be pleased to be entitled. It may even keep her out of trouble for a while."

Elijah snorted with disbelief, making Damien chuckle.

"Look at it this way," the Prince said. "If I can reform her, I can reform anyone."

Damien found himself hosting the Demon King and his mate that night. Since the citadel was closest, the medic recommended it would be best for them to rest there and travel home the next day. Syreena and Damien did not mind, of course. They welcomed the company. As did Elijah and Siena, who had decided to spend the night as well. Noah and Kestra were tucked into a bed in guest quarters, healed to a point of comfort, their bodies left to do the rest over the next twenty-four hours.

Kestra was exhausted, both mentally and physically, but though her equally wiped-out counterpart fell asleep immediately, she couldn't rest so easily. She stopped her silent pacing of the room, donned a borrowed robe, and walked the halls of the citadel. She was wary, not liking the idea of being surrounded by Vampires. It was an understandable sensation, considering. But she tried to take Damien's assurances of safety to heart.

It was just about dawn, so the traffic in the castle had wound down to silence. Kes didn't encounter anyone else until she ran into Elijah in an alcove that doubled as a sitting area.

"Kes!" He greeted her cheerily, waving her over to a seat next to him. "How are you feeling?" he asked as she sat, curling her legs up beneath her.

"Alive," was all she had to say to that.

"I think that is a fair feeling," Elijah agreed. "I bet Noah seconds it."

"Yes." She paused several beats, but Elijah sensed she was gathering her thoughts and he let her do so. "I can't have children," she blurted out suddenly. "I love him and he loves me, but he deserves children! Elijah, he's a King. He needs heirs. Doesn't he? He's so wonderful with Leah and he loves kids. I see it. I feel it. He would be a magnificent father. What am I supposed to feel about this? How—" She choked on her own pent-up emotions. "How can Destiny pick someone like me for someone like him when I can't give him something he so clearly deserves?"

Elijah exhaled in a soft, introspective sigh.

"It's funny," he said gently, "how hard you are on yourselves when it comes to this. Women, I mean," he clarified at her sidelong look. "Syreena is a perfect example. She is frantic to give Damien an heir, and when she doesn't conceive, she destroys herself over it. Siena is no better. She is watching her sister play the baby game and I hear her thoughts and fears. She is afraid she will fail me. If anyone should fear failure to provide a child, it should be me. She is the one who needs the heir. It's my job to be a worthy stud."

His irreverent expression made her laugh in spite of her shaky emotions. Elijah realized she had been through an emotional wringer that day and she should not be tackling this topic just then, but clearly it was heavy on her mind. He suspected that she was sharing with him because he was pretty much a stranger and she was afraid to talk to someone she knew better. Yet he was close enough to understand the necessary particulars. He sighed, wondering when the hell he'd gotten so mature and wise.

"But they fear success and odds and possibilities," Kestra whispered softly. "I already know it is impossible for me to get pregnant."

"Does Noah?"

"Y-yes, but—"

"Ah. Always a 'but.' Kes, there is no 'but' here. You and Noah are Imprinted. This is as good as it gets. It is a magnificent blessing. Anything beyond that is icing." He sighed with regret. "And I don't think I need to remind you that there is a war around us. You know what war means, Kes. We're going to lose friends and loved ones, and they're going to leave children behind. Who better to take them in than their King and Queen? There are always children in the world in need of parents. Even in the Demon world."

"Adoption?"

"Adoption, fostering, hell—babysitting, if you dig that sort of thing. Kes, Noah loves you. He will never want for anything more ever again. The day he knew you were going to be his, he became rich and content. Anything else is . . ."

"Icing?" She laughed, her heart easing with something that felt a lot like contentment.

"Yeah," he chuckled. "And maybe the occasional candy flower."

Noah turned over in the bed, the remnants of pain creeping into his waking mind. He opened his eyes and groaned softly at the ache wrapped around his chest. His frantic mate had broken several of his ribs in her enthusiasm to revive him. Not that he was complaining, but there was no Demon medic at the citadel. They had been forced to settle for the skills of the Lycanthrope Monk whom Damien had decided to keep permanently on staff for his wife. It was all they had needed, really; their advanced self-healing skills were more than able to do the rest within a day or two.

Recalling how deeply wounded Kestra had been as well he suddenly came to full wakefulness and rolled over to find her on the other side of the bed. He gasped when he moved too fast, and his hand snatched up to his left side beneath his arm. He wasn't awake enough yet to steel himself against broken ribs, a bruised chest and heart, and lungs badly abused by water and dirt he could still taste in the back of his throat. Still, he felt a hell of a lot better than he had the night before.

He recalled his search for his mate and looked down at the bed.

Empty.

His brows knit in consternation and he instantly searched his mind for her.

Kes?

Yes?

He felt a new pain in his chest when the sadness he heard in her voice kicked him hard in the heart.

Where are you?

The east tower.

Well, at least she wasn't trying to hide from him, he thought with a frown as he tossed back the sheet and other bedding. He realized then that he had no clothing, his having been ruined the night before.

There's a robe in the closet, baby.

The simple domestic courtesy of her thoughts made him feel marginally better. She knew he was coming to her and her assistance told him she did not mind. The nickname, as always, soothed almost all ills. He found the robe and, not able to change form with so much damaged tissue in his body, he set about trekking to the east tower.

He was a little winded when he reached the top of the tower stairs, but the freezing-cold wind whipping over the turret was what truly took his breath away. Kestra was dressed the same way he was, in a simple terry robe, and had evidently been standing up here for quite some time. When he reached to touch her, she was nearly frozen.

"Merciful Destiny, Kes! You feel like ice!"

"Do I?"

Noah stepped up to her, pressing his front to her back, shivering at the difference in their body temperatures in the instant before he began to warm them with his power. He was afraid he would never understand why she did this. Did she not feel the cold, or did she do it on purpose as some kind of mental test or punishment? He could not tell.

"What is it, baby?" he asked, pressing a kiss on her ear near the stitches necessary to close the deep slashes she'd endured.

"It's so stark here," she said, drawing his attention to the mountain landscape that cradled the citadel. It was bleak with coming winter, the area gray with shale and a flat, calmed lake in the distance. Jagged black and gray rocks lined the bottom of the castle. It looked every inch the forbidding Vampire stronghold.

"Do not forget that beyond the ridges lie very lush forests. This spot is chosen for defensibility and its power to evoke superstitious thoughts in the local human populace. It keeps them away."

"This barrenness keeps them away," she reiterated quietly.

"Yes. That and the dominance of the citadel. It is a bit daunting."

"Noah." She turned in his arms, her chilled front coming into contact with his heated one. He kept his hands on her throughout the entire rotation, ending with them resting on the small of her back. She drew a quick breath, abruptly overwhelmed with how beautiful he was. She took a moment to see the life burning brightly in his eyes, cherishing its return to its proper place.

Then she forgot everything she was going to say, trading it for his embrace, her arms snaking around his ribs as she

reached for his mouth. He welcomed her readily, eagerly i
fact, drawing her mouth deeply under his. Her hair whippe
around them in the wind, her chapped cheek cold against th
brush of his nose.

Noah watched as Kestra pulled away, her full mouth glis
tening from his kiss as her troubled eyes flicked over hi
face. She brushed her fingers through his thick hair, playin
with it softly a long minute. Then her hands were on his face
touching his forehead and cheeks, absorbing every angle o
his jaw and chin, finally resting her thumbs against his mout
and rubbing them over his lips with precision and care. The
she brushed her fingertips over his lashes and waited for
minute until he looked at her so she could study his eyes.

"You're so beautiful," she whispered, her voice catchin
in a way that stabbed clean through his heart. Tears welled i
her crystalline blue eyes and the situation just about brough
him to his knees.

"Kes, tell me what is wrong," he demanded, unable t
bear her pain a moment longer.

"It isn't fair," she said hoarsely. "You're so beautiful. S
good. Such a wonderful man. You have so much love to giv
and so much wisdom to share. Everything about you de
serves to go on forever. If anyone in all this world deserves
child, Noah, it's you."

"Kes . . . damn it, Kes, do not do this," he growle
fiercely, jerking her hard into his embrace, ignoring the flas
of pain it caused as he squeezed the breath from them both
"Do not use any more excuses for pushing away from me.
cannot take it anymore. I will not live without you, do yo
understand me? I *cannot* live without you. Can you compre
hend that? How that feels? Can you feel how much it rips m
heart out every time I hear you threatening our future to
gether?"

"No! I mean . . . yes . . . Noah, that isn't what I meant,
she stuttered in shock. "I love you!" she insisted, pulling
away with a wriggle so he could see that truth in her eyes

"And I'm not going anywhere, even if I could. I don't want to leave you! That's my point. I feel . . . I can't make myself be unselfish. I know you said—oh, hell, I'm screwing this up!"

Noah smiled when she pressed a flustered hand to her forehead.

"I am sorry," he apologized gently. "I am listening. Make your point."

"I only meant to say . . ." She swallowed hard. "I'm sorry I can't give you that," she said, tears springing to her eyes. "I love you and you mean the world to me. I know we will always be together. I want to marry you and be with you as your mate forever. I want it so badly it closes up my throat and hurts my heart with more joy than I can possibly manage in a single lifetime. But you deserve a child of your blood, and I can't give you one, and I feel so much grief when I think of it. Oh, Noah," she sobbed, "you haven't grieved that loss yet, and I know you will one day, and it kills me to think that I'll cause you that kind of pain."

"Kes," he said softly, closing his eyes as her grief washed over him. "Hush, baby," he soothed, adding a soft, sibilant sound to the command. "You are right, and I will not insult you by denying it. I have not grieved that loss yet. I may never, or I may do so with as much pain as you are feeling now. I cannot foretell how I will come to feel about it. I can only tell you I will not love you any less for it. I need to know you know that." He released a breath when she nodded, feeling relief. "As long as you believe that, it will be borne and it will pass, and we will both survive to love each other as long as we may.

"I am sorry, too, that you will never have a child of your own blood. That you will never pass on this beautiful hair and these stunning eyes is a tragedy, and I feel the pain of that. I do grieve that your strength of character and your cunning will end with you. The world will be deprived of an incredible treasure. But"—he paused to kiss away the tears beneath her eyes, pulling her back so he could catch her gaze—"maybe Destiny is compensating for that by giving immortality to the original model, baby. She has that way about her, you know."

She gave him a watery laugh when he smiled gently at her. "How do you always know the right thing to say?" she demanded, giving him a shove against his ribs.

Noah flinched and grunted.

"Oh!" she gasped. "Oh, I forgot! Noah, I am so sorry!"

"Now I know how I got this way in the first place," he groaned exaggeratedly. "You have no idea of your own strength."

"Well, I've only had it for a few weeks. Cut me some slack!" She protested with all sass, but her expression was wide-eyed with concern and her hands brushed tenderly over his rib cage.

"Stop that." He chuckled, catching her hands when they went to untie his robe to better inspect the damage she had done. "I will start getting ideas with my unbruised body parts that do not go well with my bruised body parts."

Kestra clicked her tongue. "You're terrible."

"Rotten to the core," he agreed. "Now come downstairs with me out of this cold. We will eat and talk and . . ." He trailed off, a crooked smile playing over his lips.

"If you think I'm going to ask you to finish that sentence, you're out of your mind," she laughed, letting him lead her away.

"What?" he asked innocently, "I was going to say 'and plan the wedding.' "

"Mmm-hmm," she agreed without conviction. "And I'm the fainting type," she tacked on dryly.

"You are not the fainting type?" he asked with feigned shock as they started down the stairs.

"Nope."

"Well, how about a slight swoon?"

"Swoon!"

"Old-fashioned term?"

"Try *antiquated*."

"Are you casting aspersions on my age, young lady?"

"No. Just a little payback for *Kikilia*," she said smartly.

"That happens to be a beloved nickname handed down from generation to generation," he retorted.

"Oh? And you don't find 'sweet little girl' to be at all politically incorrect? Not to mention totally unsuited to me?"

"Not in the least," he laughed.

"Oh! Remind me to hit you when you heal," she growled.

"Only if you promise to remind me to do something to you when I heal."

She giggled at that.

"You need a reminder for *that*?"

"I anticipate needing *several* reminders for that."

Try the NIGHTWALKERS series from the beginning!
Start the journey with JACOB . . .

It was daylight once more when Jacob floated down through Noah's manor until he was in the vault, one moment dust dancing through the incandescent light, the next coming to rest lightly on his feet. He looked around the well-lit catacomb, seeking his prey. He heard a rustling sound from the nearest stacks and moved toward it.

There was a soft curse, a grunt, and the sudden slam of something hitting the floor. Jacob came around just in time to find Isabella dangling from one of the many shelves, her feet swaying about ten feet above the floor as she searched with her toes for a foothold. On the floor below her was a rather ancient looking tome, the splattered pattern of the dust that had shaken off it indicating it had been the object he had heard fall. Far to her left was the ladder she had apparently been using.

With a low sigh of exasperation, Jacob altered gravity for himself and floated himself up behind her. "You are going to break your neck."

Isabella was not expecting a voice at her ear, considering her peculiar circumstances, and she started with a little scream.

One hand lost hold and she swung right into the hard wall of his chest. He gathered her up against himself, his arm slipping beneath her knees so she was safely cradled, his warmth infusing her with a sense of safety and comfort as he brought her down to the floor effortlessly. In spite of herself, she pressed her cheek to his chest.

"Must you sneak up on me in midair like that? It's very unnerving."

She had meant to sound angry, but the soft, breathless accusation was anything but. Anyway, how angry would he think her to be if she was snuggling up to him like a kitten? Damn it, Demon or not, he was still a sinfully good-looking man. Jacob was elegant to a fault, his movements and manner centered on an efficiency of actions that drew the eye. He was dressed again in well-tailored black slacks, and this time a midnight blue dress shirt with his cuffs turned back. She could feel the rich quality of the silk beneath her cheek, and when she breathed in, Jacob smelled like the rich, heady earth he claimed his abilities from.

Besides all the outwardly alluring physicality, Isabella knew that he was extremely sensitive about all his interactions with others. She could feel his moral imperatives tingling through her mind whenever he was near. His heart, she knew, was made of incredibly honorable stuff. How could she find it in herself to be afraid of that? Especially when he had never once hurt her, even though there had been plenty of influences compelling him to.

"Shall I put you back and let you plummet to your death?" he asked, releasing her legs and letting her body slide slowly down his until her feet touched the floor.

The whisper of the friction of their clothes hummed across Jacob's skin, and he felt his senses focusing in on every nuance of sensation she provided for him. The swishing silk of her hair even in its present tangled state, the sweet warmth of her breath and body, the ivory perfection of her skin. He reached to wipe a smudge of dust from her delectable little nose. She was a mess. There was no arguing that. Head to toe covered in dust and grime and she smelled like an old book, but those earthy scents would never be something unappealing to one of his kind. Jacob breathed deeply as the usual heat she inspired stirred in his cool blood. It was stronger with each passing moment, with each progressive day, and he never once became unaware of that fact. He tried to tell himself it was merely the effects of the growing moon, but that reasoning did not satisfy him. Hallowed madness would not allow for the unexpected compulsion toward tenderness he kept experiencing whenever he looked down into her angelic face. It would never allow him to enjoy these simple yet significant stirrings of his awareness without forcing him into overdrive. True, he was holding on to his control with a powerful leash of determination. He was tamping down the surges of want and lust that gripped him so hard sometimes it was nearly crippling, but somehow it was still different.

Then he had to also acknowledge the melding of their thoughts as something truly unique. Perhaps a human could initiate such a contact if he or she were a medium or psychic of noteworthy ability, but she made no claims to such special talents. Every day the images of her mind became clearer to him. She had even taken to consciously sending him picturesque impressions in response to some discussion they were having with Noah, Elijah, and Legna. He believed that, if things continued to progress in this manner, he and Bella would soon be engaging in actual discussions with each other without ever opening their mouths. He didn't have fact to base that assumption on, but it seemed the natural evolution to the growing silent communication between them.

He had seen Legna staring at them curiously on several occasions. Luckily, because she was a female Mind Demon, she was not a full telepath. If she had been a male she would have been privy to some pretty private exchanges between him and Isabella. Nothing racy, actually, but he found Isabella had such an irreverent sense of humor that he wasn't sure others would understand it as he seemed to.

It was a privacy of exchange he found himself coveting. It was the one way they could be together without Legna or Noah interfering. It was bad enough that the empath was constantly sniffing at his emotions, making sure he kept in careful control of his baser side. Since the King was not able to subject him the usual punishment that was meted out for those who had crossed the line as he had with Isabella, his monarch had been forced to be a little more creative. Setting Legna the empathic bloodhound on him had done the trick. It was also seriously pissing him off. He knew she was always there, and it burned his pride like nuclear fire.

What was more, he couldn't keep his mind away from Isabella. And since even the smallest thought of her had a way of sparking an onslaught of fantasies that brought his body to physical readiness . . . well, it was the very last thing he wanted an audience for.

It had taken quite a bit of planning, and the deceptive use of herbal tea mixtures, in order to slip out from under Legna's observation so he could sneak away to the vault. The empath slept as soundly as the dead, and she would stay that way until this evening.

"I wouldn't have fallen to my death," Bella was arguing, her stubborn streak prickling. "At the most, I would have fallen to my 'broken leg' or my 'concussion' or something. Boy, you Demons have this way of making everything seem so intense and pivotal."

"We are a very intense people, Bella."

"Tell me about it." She wriggled out of his embrace, putting distance between them with a single step back. Jacob was well aware of it being a very purposeful act. "I've been reading books and scrolls as far back as seven hundred years ago. You were just a gleam in your daddy's eye then, I imagine."

"Demons may have long gestation periods for their young, but not seventy-eight years' worth."

"Yes. I read about that. Is it true it takes thirteen months for a female to carry and give birth?"

"Minimum." He said it with such casual dismissal that Bella laughed.

"That's easy for you to say. You don't have to lug the kid around inside you all that time. You, just like your human counterparts, have the fun part over with like that." She snapped her fingers in front of his face.

His dark eyes narrowed and he reached to enclose her hand in his, pulling her wrist up to the slow, purposeful brush of his lips even as he maintained a sensual eye contact that was far too full of promises. Isabella caught her breath as an insidious sensation of heated pins and needles stitched their way up her arm.

"I promise you, Bella, a male Demon's part in a mating is never over like this." He mimicked her snap, making her jump in time to her kick-starting heartbeat.

"Well"—she cleared her throat—"I guess I'll have to take your word on that." Jacob did not respond in agreement, and that unnerved her even further. Instinctively, she changed tack. "So, what brings you down into the dusty atmosphere of the great Demon library?" she asked, knowing she sounded like a brightly animated cartoon.

"You."

Oh, how that singular word was pregnant with meaning, intent and devastatingly blatant honesty. Isabella was forced to remind herself of the whole Demon-human mating taboo as the forbidden response of heat continued to writhe around beneath her skin, growing exponentially in intensity every moment he hovered close. She tried to picture all kinds of scary things that could happen if she did not quit egging him on like she was. How she was, she didn't know, but she was always certain she was egging him on.

"Why did you want to see me?" she asked, breaking away

from him and bending to retrieve the book she had dropped. It was huge and heavy and she grunted softly under the weight of it. It landed with a slam and another puff of dust on the table she had made into her own private study station.

"Because, I cannot seem to help myself, lovely little Bella."

Can't get enough Jacquelyn Frank?
Don't miss GIDEON,
in stores now from Zebra . . .

Gideon wore the habits of his lifetime like an unapologetic statement, and he wore them very well. He blended the male fashions of the millennium in a way that was nothing less than a perfect reflection of who he was and how he had lived. This only served to beautify his distinctive and powerful presence with his incidental confidence.

"Gideon," she said evenly, inclining her head in sparse respect. "What brings you to my chambers, so close to dawn?"

The riveting male before her remained silent, his silver eyes flicking over her slowly. Her heart nearly stopped with her sudden fear, and immediately she threw up every mental and physical barrier she could to prevent an unwelcome scan and analysis of her health.

"I would not scan you without your permission, Magdelegna. Body Demons who become healers have codes of ethics as well as any others."

"Funny," she remarked, "I would have thought you to believe yourself above such a trivial matter as permission."

His mercury gaze narrowed slightly, making Legna wish that she had the courage to dare a piratical scan of her own.

She was quite talented at masking her travels through the emotions and psyches of others, but Gideon was like no other. She was barely a fledgling to one such as he.

Gideon had noted her more recent acerbic tendencies aloud once before, irritating the young female even more than usual, so he resisted the urge in that moment to scold her again and let her attitude pass.

"I have come to check on your well-being, Magdelegna. I am concerned."

Legna cocked a brow, twisting her lips into a cold, mocking little smile, hiding the sudden, anxious beating of her heart.

"And what would give you the impression that you need be concerned for me?" she asked haughtily.

Gideon once more took his time before responding, giving her one more of those implacable perusals in the interim. Legna exhaled with annoyance, crossing her arms beneath her breasts and coming just shy of tapping her foot in irritation.

"You are not at peace, young one," Gideon explained softly, the deep timbre of his voice resonating through her, once again giving her the feeling that she was but fragile crystal, awaiting the moment when he would strike the note of discord that would shatter her. Legna's breathing altered, quickening in spite of her effort to maintain an even keel. She did not want to give him the satisfaction of being right.

"You presume too much, Gideon. I have no need for your concern, nor have I ever solicited it. Now, if you do not mind, I should like to go to bed."

"For what purpose?"

Legna laughed, short and harsh.

"To sleep, why else?"

"You have not slept for many days together, Legna. Why do you assume you might have success today?"

Legna turned around sharply, driving her gaze and attention back out of the window, trying to use the sprawling lawn as a slate to fill her mind with. Mind Demon he was not, but she knew he was capable of seeing far enough into her emotional state by just monitoring her physiological reactions to his observations. Legna bit her lip hard, furious that she should feel like the child he always referred to her as in their conversations. Young one, indeed. How would he like it if she referred to him as a decrepit old buzzard?

The thought gave her a small, petty satisfaction. It did not matter that Gideon looked as vital and vibrant as any Demon male from thirty years to a thousand would look. Nor did it matter that his stunning coloring gave him a unique attractiveness and aura of power that no one else could equal. All that mattered was that he would never view her as an equal, and therefore, in her perspective, she had no responsibility to do so for him.

Gideon watched the young woman across from him closely, trying to make sense of the physiological changes that flashed through her rapidly, each as puzzling as the one before it. What was it about her, he wondered, that always kept him off his mark? She never reacted the way he logically expected her to, yet he knew her to be extraordinarily intelligent. She always treated him with a barely repressed contempt, though she never had a harsh word for anyone else. He had almost gotten used to that since their original falling-out, but this was different, far more complex than hard feelings. Gideon had not encountered a puzzle in a great many centuries, and perhaps that was why he was continually fascinated by her in spite of her marked disdain.

"It is not unusual," she said at last, "to have periods of insomnia in one's life. Surely that is not what has you rushing into my boudoir, oozing your high-handed version of concern."

"Magdelegna, I am continually puzzled by your insistence in treating me with hostility. Did Lucas teach you nothing about respecting your elders?"

Legna whirled around suddenly, outrage flaring off her so

violently that Gideon felt the eddy of it push at him through the still air.

"Do not ever mention Lucas in such a disrespectful manner ever again! Do you understand me, Gideon? I will not tolerate it!" She moved to stand toe to toe with the medic, her emotions practically beating him back in their intensity. "You say respect my elders, but what you mean is respecting my betters, is that not right? Are you so full of your own arrogance that you need me to bow and kowtow to you like some throwback fledgling? Or perhaps we should reinstate the role of concubines in our society. Then you may have the pleasure of claiming me and forcing me to fall to my knees, bowing low in respect of your masculine eminence!"

Gideon watched as she did just that, her gown billowing around her as she gracefully kneeled before him, so close to him that her knees touched the tips of his boots. She swept her hands to her sides, bowing her head until her forehead brushed the leather, her hair spilling like reams of heavy silk around his ankles.

The Ancient found himself unusually speechless, the strangest sensation creeping through him as he looked down at the exposed nape of her neck, the elegant line of her back. Unable to curb the impulse, Gideon lowered himself into a crouch, reaching beneath the cloak of coffee-colored hair to touch her flushed cheek. The heat of her anger radiated against his touch and he recognized it long before she turned her face up to him.

"Does this satisfy you, my lord Gideon?" she whispered fiercely, her eyes flashing like flinted steel and hard jade.

Gideon found himself searching her face intently, his eyes roaming over the high, aristocratic curves of her cheekbones, the amazingly full sculpture of her lips, the wide, accusing eyes that lay behind extraordinarily thick lashes. He cupped her chin between the thumb and forefinger of his left hand, his fingertips fanning softly over her angrily flushed cheek.

"You do enjoy mocking me," he murmured softly to her, the breath of his words close enough to skim across her face.

"No more than you seem to enjoy condescending to me," she replied, her clipped words coming out on quick, heated breaths.

Gideon absorbed the latest venom directed toward him with a blink of lengthy black lashes. They kept their gazes locked, each seemingly waiting for the other to look away.

"You have never forgiven me," he said suddenly, softly.

"Forgiven you?" She laughed bitterly. "Gideon, you are not important enough to earn my forgiveness."

"Is your ego so fragile, Legna, that a small slight to it is irreparable?"

"Stop talking to me as if I were a temperamental child!" Legna hissed, moving to jerk her head back, but finding his grip quite secure. "There was nothing slight about the way you treated me. I will never forget it, and I most certainly will never forgive it!"

And keep the magic going with ELIJAH,
the sexy warrior captain . . .

The cold of another breeze rushed up from behind her, blowing at the brief skirt of her dress and whipping through her hair. It surrounded her, engulfed her, forcing her to come to a halt just as muscled arms appeared around her waist.

Siena sucked in a startled breath as the cold vanished, replaced by the warmth, the heat, of a familiar male body. She was drawn back against his chest, his hands splaying out over her flat belly and pushing her deeper into the planes of his hard body.

"Elijah," she whispered, her eyes closing as a sensation of remarkable relief flooded through her entire body. Every nerve and hormone in her body surged to life just to be held in his embrace, and she was light-headed with the power of it all.

He put hands on her hips, using them to spin her full around to face him. The warrior dragged her back to his body, seizing her mouth with savage hunger just as she was reaching for his kiss. She could not have helped herself. Not after the deprivation of all these days. But still, the weakness stung her painfully, leaving frustrated tears in her eyes.

It was all just as she remembered it. The vividness of the memories of their touches and kisses had never once faded to less than what it truly was. It was all heat and musk and the delicious flavor of his bold, demanding mouth. His hands were on her backside, drawing her up into his body with a movement she could only label as desperation.

Elijah had not meant to attack her in this manner, but the moment he had sensed her nearness, smelled the perfume of her skin and hair, he could not do anything else. He devoured the cinnamon taste of her mouth relentlessly, groaning with relief and pleasure as her hands curled around the fabric of his shirt and her incredible body molded to his with perfection. He pulled her hips directly to his own, leaving no question about how hard and fast her effect on him was. He felt her swinging perfectly with the onslaught of his pressing body and adamant kisses.

Everything was perfection. Top to bottom, beginning to end, and he had been starving without her. He also knew she had been just as famished without him.

She was the first to put any distance between them, by breaking away from his mouth, letting her head fall back as far as it could as she drew for breath hard and quick.

"Oh no," she groaned huskily, shaking her head so her hair brushed over the arms around her waist.

Even those strands betrayed her, reaching eagerly to coil around his wrists and forearms, trapping him around her effectively, just in case of the outrageous scenario that he might want to move away from her. She lifted her head and opened her eyes, their golden depths full of her desire, and her anguish.

"I did not want this," she whispered to him, her forehead dropping onto his chest when the heat in his eyes proved too intense for her to bear. "Why will you not let me go?"

"Because I can't," he said, disentangling one hand from her hair so he could take her chin in hand and force her to look at him. "No more than you can."

"I hate this," she said painfully, her eyes blinking rapidly as they smarted with tears of frustration. "I hate not being able to control my own body. My own will. If this is what it means to be Imprinted, it is a weakness I will abhor with my last breath."

Then she pushed away, defying every nerve in her body that screamed at her to step back into his embrace. She could only backtrack a couple of steps, however, because her hair remained locked tight around his upraised wrist, pulling him along with her . . . as if he wouldn't have followed her anyway.

When she realized her back was to a window, she felt a moment of panic. However, she realized no one was likely to see them, because they were over three stories up from the houses and people below.

"You call it weakness, and yet as affected as I am by it myself, I choose to call it strength."

His rich baritone voice echoed around her, making her heart leap in alarm. She grabbed his wrist and pulled him farther down the hallway, the dark shadows enclosing them as they reduced the potential for echoes.

"Why are you here? And do not blame it on a holy day that will not arrive for two days."

"I do not intend to 'blame' anything. I don't believe I need an excuse to see you, Siena." He reached for her face, but she jerked back and dodged him. "And it is because of that holy day two nights from now that I am here. We need a little bit of resolution between us before that night comes, Siena."

"I am not in need of resolution. If you are, you must come to it on your own."

She turned to walk away from him, but she forgot he was just as quick as she was. No one could outrun the wind. His hand closed easily around her forearm, pulling her back . . . and snapping the temper and pain she had been holding in tenuous control for days.

She released the cry of a wounded animal and flew at him. He saw the flash of claws and felt the sharp sting of their cut as they scored his face. Shocked by the attack for all of a second, Elijah reacted on instinct. He had her by her hair in a heartbeat, wrapping it around his fist in a single motion, turning her around so her back was to him and her claws pointed in a safer direction. She grunted softly and then screamed in frustration as she found herself trapped face first against the stonecutter's art.

His enormous body was immediately flush against her back, securing her to the unforgiving stone as he caught one hand and pushed it against the stone as well.

"Let go of me!" She struggled in vain, unable to move a micron in any direction. "You'll have hands full of a spitting-mad cougar if you do not release me this instant!"

"I highly doubt that," he purred easily into her ear, his mouth brushing over the lobe of it in a way that made her shiver involuntarily.

The story continues with DAMIEN,
available now from Zebra . . .

"You risked your life for mine as if you had no responsibility to an entire race of people! It was a foolish and ridiculous thing to do!"

"It would have been my mistake to make," he countered sharply. "I am not used to people criticizing my actions, Syreena."

"Well, perhaps they should! I would never have allowed Siena to do such a foolish thing!"

"Oh, really? Just as you prevented her from almost dying for the sake of her husband?"

It was a twisting knife in a very tender spot for her, and he knew it instantly by the expression in her eyes. It was only then that he realized she did indeed blame herself for her sister's near encounter with death that recent October.

"Was I supposed to let you bleed to death, Syreena?" he asked quietly, trying to take back the pain he had caused her with the balm of his words. "Why are you so eager to value my life above your own?"

"Because I am not so special that an entire people should be deprived of their monarch for my sake!"

"Lucky for you, I disagree with that assessment."

Damien understood, however, that there was baggage beyond her statement other than the immediate disagreement. Still, it did not measure up for him. She had never struck him as the type who devalued herself.

She looked at him as if he were completely insane for a long moment, her confused eyes searching over him for an answer and a logic that just was not within grasp. Then, without knowing why, she leaned in and kissed him.

Damien was shocked for a moment at the forward and illogical act, his hands reflexively circling her arms as her warm mouth pressed gently to his. Her unbandaged hand came up to lie against the side of his face, her contrary eyes sliding closed for a long, painful moment.

He felt, and then tasted, the salt of her tears.

She pulled away, only a couple of inches, her body trembling beneath his hands as he looked into her eyes with a confusion of emotions and sensations struggling through him.

"Why did you—?"

"Because," she interrupted with a sob catching at her words. "Because it is a fairy tale, Damien. And in a fairy tale, the Princess always kisses the Prince who rescues her."

It was an enchanting and ingenuous thing for her to say. She was a woman of great learning, amazing strength, and a sense of logic that negated any illusion of naïveté, yet she was willing to expose herself as a hopeful idealist in order to express her gratitude. He realized that it was a preciously protected streak in her makeup that very few people were allowed access to. It subsequently meant more to Damien than the most profuse and eloquent words of any language.

"Syreena . . ." He paused to clear the coarseness in his throat. "I am no hero," he told her with rough quietness. "You should not make me into one."

She defied the statement by forcing it into silence with the cover of her mouth.

This time Damien saw it coming, but it made him no better prepared. This time it was not a quick and simple expression of impulsive gratitude she was reaching to express. This was a little different, and on an instinctive level he knew it.

Completely in spite of the soundness of reason that rang stridently in his head, Damien allowed himself the luxury of the feel of her lips. Caught less off his mark and having had a moment to think about it, he returned the intimacy with equal warmth and measure. From one heartbeat to the next, his hands found their way into the hair at the back of her head, his fingertips sliding with careful languor, mindful of all she had suffered and been through and in no way wanting to cause her even a moment of additional pain.

Syreena was also sliding her fingers into a position that held his head to her, just in case he thought to argue with her any further about her desires in this matter. His darkening eyes were looking directly into hers, seeking for things beyond both their comprehension. She met his searching gaze with eyes full of surety and strength. She knew what she wanted, amazingly enough without a single doubt or second thought. This moment, those fascinating eyes messaged to him, was to be precious for them both. The next moment would come soon enough. But this moment . . .

This moment was for thanking, for gentleness, and, most of all, for feeling something that had no pain, struggle, or immediate ramifications to it.

It simply would be what it was.

And get excited about Jacquelyn's newest book,
the first in the SHADOWDWELLERS series,
coming in January 2009.
Turn the page for a sneak peek!

She had been the lonely, isolated sort even when there had been other people milling all around her, so she knew the meaning of desperation quite well. When that kind of solitude became too much to bear, that was when she would cut herself away from her normal routines and take a wild chance on something, like going to a New Year's party even if it meant driving on the most frightening night of the year.

Like a subconscious trigger, a wild rush of sudden illness overran her body the moment the thought entered her head. Chills and queasiness overwhelmed her and she had to stop and brace a hand against the wall for balance as her head spun nauseatingly. Her knees seemed to disappear and in an instant she was sinking toward the ground.

She nearly screamed when strong hands abruptly halted her collapse, their warm power drawing her back against a muscular and sturdy body. Even though she was dizzy and sick, she looked up over her shoulder and into curious dark eyes. His brow creased with clear concern as he jogged her a bit more firmly into his hold, a solid arm crossing her ribs to pin her tightly to his frame.

"I've got you," he assured her in a richly rumbling murmur that seemed to vibrate against her ear and all down her neck. She couldn't seem to help the little shiver the sensation provoked, her fingers reaching to grasp his forearm instinctively. The crisp feel of male body hair at his wrist tickled her fingertips, and Ashla was suddenly overwhelmed with a strange sense of intimacy. Discomforted, she tried to squirm loose even as she snatched her hands off him and made fists of resistance out of them.

"Be easy!"

It was a command, plain and simple. The sharp jerking of her body in his grasp made that quite clear to her. And that was to say nothing of the dark heaviness of his voice and the way it seemed so obvious that he was used to having his commands obeyed at every turn. Considering his talents with a sword, Ashla could see why no one would be compelled to argue with him.

And there it was, beneath the long black coat he wore, the thick buckle of the belt that held its sheath impressing itself into her backside from where it was slung at a low angle across his hips. This was what made her realize her feet weren't touching the ground. There was no way otherwise, with their disparate heights, that she should be finding herself within such intimate fitting with him. Ashla's face was washed with an upward wall of heat and embarrassment, her complexion burning as she gasped in a breath.

Coincidentally, as her thoughts were occupied by all this input that pushed aside her slightest memories of New Year's Eve, her feelings of illness were quickly brought to heel. She took a deep breath, wanting so badly to demand he put her down, to get furious with him, to just explode with all the stormy emotions she'd been besieged with ever since she had encountered him.

But she didn't do any of it. Ashla simply turned her face away from him, her hard, stressed breathing the only thing being freely expressed as she said softly, "Please, let me go."

"Really?" he asked, his richly resonant voice a prelude to his breath washing warmly over her face. "Because a moment ago I would have sworn you couldn't wait to get your hands on me."

Ashla gasped in a soft breath, trying to twist around in his hold so she could see his face. The way he said that . . . it was almost as if he were suggesting . . .

She squirmed angrily. "Let go!"

"I would," he mused, "if I wasn't worried you'd collapse to the ground. Also, I think I rather like you this way. It keeps you in one place long enough for me to get some questions answered."

The truth of the matter was that Trace was enjoying the way her temper seemed to swell and grow with every wiggle of her body and every denial he handed her. Not that he was being mean or anything, but it was intriguing to see the streak of fury that ran through his frightened little mouse. It fascinated him that, as angry as she clearly was, she refused to unleash herself on him, as he no doubt deserved.

"Please," she begged him, suddenly relaxing into a limp little creature of defeat. "Please don't."

"Don't?" he questioned. "Don't what?" Trace reached up to cup her small chin in his palm, his fingers sinking into the softness of her cheek with such ease that, for a moment, he feared he would bruise her unintentionally. He tilted her chin up, her head falling back against his chest until her pale blue eyes were blinking up at him. The shine in her overbright gaze warned him she was near to tears, so he was infinitely gentle as he looked down on her. "I'll not hurt you, *jei li*," he promised her. "What makes you think I would repay my debt to you in such unfriendly ways?"

Ashla laughed at that, fully aware of the edge of hysteria in the sound just by seeing him frown darkly at it. "Because I saw you use *that* sword to kill someone," she countered with a shudder as her eyes flicked down to the location of the weapon on his hip.

"Is that what worries you, *jei li*? That I am armed?"

Trace reached down immediately for the buckle of his weapons' belt. He slid his hand between their pressed bodies, and he found himself by incident gliding his knuckles along the curve of her backside.

She was wearing another dress, but this one was light and thin, some sort of calico or gauze cotton that barely provided a barrier to his touch. The impression was validated when he realized he could feel every stitch of the fabric of her panties. Trace unbuckled his belt and let it, the sheathed katana and the slightly smaller wakizashi sword fall with a careless clatter to the pavement. Had Magnus seen him treat his weapons in such a disrespectful manner, Trace would have gotten an earful and, potentially, a hard refresher on the subject. The priest had forged the weapons himself, signed his name to them, and honored Trace with the gifts. Magnus very rarely bestowed his masterful weaponry on others. This one had even been specially designed for Trace's unique left-handed style.

But all of that importance faded away with surprising speed as the vizier's full attention became quite riveted on the sweet warmth and shape of her provocatively nestled rear. The charge of sexual awareness that crashed through him so suddenly simply took his breath away. He was no stranger to sexual magnetism and all of its energizing benefits, but to find it so unexpectedly in so muted a package completely amazed him.

She was Lost, he tried to remind himself. By all rights, he shouldn't even be able to feel her in any depth of dimension. Anomalies notwithstanding, she *was* a ghost; merely the apparition of a woman who most likely lay in a human hospital somewhere connected to those brutally cruel machines that kept bodies alive well beyond sense and grace. Far beyond all dignity.

But it was so hard to reconcile all of that with the lushly

heated woman he held against himself; the one that squirmed provocatively whether she knew it or not; the one whose scent changed abruptly under the attentiveness of his keen senses, telling him he wasn't the only one affected by all this.